The Other Sister

a novel by

Pat Valdata

Plain View Press
P. O. 42255
Austin, TX 78704

plainviewpress.net
sb@plainviewpress.net
1-512-441-2452

Cover Art: The cover photo of Hungarian peasants in their Easter finery is from Stephen Spinder's book *Ten Years in Transylvania (Tiz estendo Erdelyben)*: Traditions of Hungarian Folk Culture: bilingual. Now in its second edition, the book's photos highlight the still vibrant folk culture of ethnic Hungarians in Transylvania. To order a copy, contact: Stephen Spinder Fine Art Photography; http://www.spinderartphoto.com. Budapest Tel.: 361-331-2601. Email stephen@spinderartphoto.com or stephenspinder@gmail.com.

Acknowledgements

I am very grateful to the American Hungarian Foundation, Hungarian Heritage Center in New Brunswick, New Jersey, for the use of their library during my research. The following publications were especially helpful: *Hungarian Heritage in New Jersey*, The Bicentennial Hungarian Heritage Committee of New Jersey (New Brunswick: Standard Press, 1975); *Children of Ellis Island: This Side of the Rainbow*, Yolan Varga in collaboration with Emil Varga (New Brunswick, I.H. Printing Co. Inc, 1988); and *A Catholic Hungarian Community in America: Saint Ladislaus Parish*, a booklet published in 1980 to celebrate the diamond jubilee of the church.

The following on-line publication was also very helpful: *The Hungarian Revolt: October 23-November 4, 1956*, by Richard Lettis (www.hungary.com/corvinus/revolt) originally published in 1961 by Charles Scribner's Sons, New York.

I am also grateful to Peter I. Hidas, August J. Molnar, and Margaret Papai for assisting me with my inquiries; to the two writers' groups who provided such good comments on the early drafts; to my dear friend, the late Catharine Cookson, for reading the first complete draft.

Finally, I thank the Viginia Center for the Creative Arts for granting me the time and place to complete the final revision of the manscript, and I give special thanks to my patient husband, Robert W. Schreiber, for his support all these years.

*To my mother, my sister, my aunt, my grandmother,
and to all the Hungarian women in the neighborhood
where we grew up*

Köszönöm

Margit

Chapter One
Hungary, May 1904

"You should have been there," said Mrs. Szabo as she walked into the front room. "Family is family, and you should have been there out of respect for your sister and your niece."

Margit removed her new handkerchief from the embroidery hoop and smoothed the linen flat in her lap before looking up to reply. Mrs. Szabo shivered involuntarily as Margit's eyes—cold and expressionless as a cat's—looked into hers.

"I'll not attend the blessing of any bastard brat," she said in a quiet voice so her father, in the next room, would not hear her.

"Ah, Margit, if the Good Lord can forgive, why can't you?"

"The Good Lord is not an older sister who was jilted, a spinster instead of a wife, a maiden aunt instead of a mother."

Mrs. Szabo shook her head, walked over to Margit, and kissed her on the forehead. She smoothed back the dark brown hair, piled in a wavy mass atop Margit's head, the one still beautiful thing left about her. Never quite as pretty as her younger sister, Margit was still handsome, but now her gray-blue eyes were like steel, and her thin mouth was pressed into an unremitting line.

Mrs. Szabo picked up the embroidered handkerchief. "This is lovely work, Margitka, the best you've ever done."

"It's all that's left to me now, Mama," Margit said bitterly. "Why shouldn't I be good at it?"

Her mother sighed. She almost wished Margit would scream and cry the way she had last summer. Was this quiet control holding back a storm of feeling, or had Margit ceased to feel anything at all? Why had it happened? Laci had been close to proposing, she was sure of that; he'd been courting Margit since midwinter. She was so joyful then, embroidering pillowcases and tablecloths for her future home. Then Laci came to Piros' birthday dinner. How animated Piros was that evening, full of stories about school life, with such happiness lighting up her face it seemed she'd turned into a grown woman almost overnight. While Piros talked, Margit sat quietly listening. Laci laughed and talked with Piros, like a big brother at first, but when Margit turned to talk to her father, Piros handed Laci a piece of cake, and their fingers touched. Mrs. Szabo had seen the impact of that brief touch in their faces. She knew what that touch had felt like: an electric current that sped from the fingertips up the arm straight to the heart and down into the loins. She had felt something like it herself the first time her husband-to-be had taken her arm, exhilarated and frightened at the same time, like the haybarn struck by lightning she had seen when she was a little girl. How quickly the bales had ignited; how quickly the barn had been consumed. Piros grew quiet, hardly able to eat her cake. And poor Margit, who had been the tolerant older sister while Piros chattered on about school, seemed to think her sister had finally talked herself out of stories, and happily filled the gap in conversation.

That night Mrs. Szabo prayed for Piros to let loyalty overcome love; and for Margit, that she could bear the coming sorrow, for in her heart Mrs. Szabo knew that Margit had already lost.

She looked at her daughter now with affection and sadness. "Go on with your own life now, Margitka. You're still young and pretty. There will be another man for you."

"Not like Laci," she whispered fiercely. "Never like Laci! I will never love anyone but him!"

She looked down at her lap as her father walked into the room, still dressed in his Sunday best black trousers and white shirt, with a black vest embroidered in red and yellow, though he had replaced his stiff black boots with comfortable slippers. He took a match from the box on the shelf next to the beehive-shaped oven and lit his pipe, puffing out smoke the color of his mustache. He pulled his watch from his vest pocket and compared it with the clock on the shelf, nodded once to himself, and replaced the watch in his pocket.

Margit sat quietly through this Sunday afternoon ritual while her mother watched her husband with rueful affection. How quickly he became predictable after their marriage, she thought. Would Laci fall into the same pattern? With Margit he would have, she suspected, but with Piros, no. Somehow, she knew that it would take more than marriage and children to cool that fire.

"Almost time for Emil," said her husband.

"Then I'd better make sure we have something for him to eat," said Mrs. Szabo. "Come, Margit, you can help me in the kitchen."

"As soon as I put these things away, Mama," she said, gathering up her embroidery and placing it in the wooden basket at her feet. Then she followed her mother.

Mr. Szabo also left the front room, but instead of turning toward the kitchen he opened the side door and leaned against the jamb, a small pleasure that he savored all the more because it was denied him through the winter. Because their house was set a little ways from their nearest neighbor he could look out over the village of Barackfalu, named for the ranks of apricot orchards that covered the hills around the town. To his left, up the street, was the school at which he was the master. To his right, downhill and toward the village center, he saw a man in the local costume walking steadily up Egri Street. Mr. Szabo had grown so used to seeing Emil Molnar in a suit that at first he failed to recognize his young friend, a neighbor's son whom he had taught at the village school, and who had grown up to attend college in Budapest. Now a journalist in his late twenties, working in the city of Eger, Emil stopped by weekly to visit with his former teacher.

"Good day, Vendel," said Emil as he approached the Szabo house.

"Good day to you, Emil," replied Mr. Szabo. "I didn't recognize you at first in those clothes."

"Well, it's been a year since poor Mama died, and this vest is the last thing she ever made for me. I wanted to wear something that reminded me of her. Besides, it makes a nice change from my city clothes."

The two men shook hands and stepped into the front room of the house, where they settled themselves into the corner benches. In this place of honor, between the room's two windows, Vendel Szabo conducted all his social business. Today the open windows let in fresh air, but in winter the room would be cozy from the warmth of the big oven. The only other furniture, besides the table on which the men leaned their elbows, was the large bed piled high in the traditional way with feather comforters and Mrs. Szabo's best dowry linens. At night the embroidered linens were carefully put away, replaced by more prosaic quilts.

Mrs. Szabo came into the room with a tray full of homemade bread, a wedge of cheese, and a plate of nut pastries. Emil stood up quickly to take the tray from her and set it down on the corner table. Then he turned to give her a hug. "How are you today, Szabo-neni?" he asked.

"I am fine, Emil, and you? You look so handsome today, like a real Barackfalu man."

"Thank you very much. And how is your new granddaughter?"

"Zsuzsi is a lovely, healthy baby, blessed today, thank the Lord."

"How happy you all must be," he said as Margit entered the room with cups and a coffeepot. "Hello, Margit," he said with a slight bow.

"Hello, Emil," Margit replied. She placed the coffee things on the table. "Excuse me, everyone, will you? I have a headache, and need to lie down for a bit." Without waiting for a reply she walked out of the room toward the loft stairs. Like most houses in Barackfalu, the Szabo home was constructed as one story with only a loft above, but instead of using the loft for storage Mrs. Szabo had furnished it as a bedroom for her daughters. She did not approve of the village custom that had the whole family sleeping in one room. Thus, as befit their station, second only to the mayor and his family, the Szabos had a two-story home. They also had enough land for Piros and Laci to build their own home next door, but in deference to Margit the couple remained in Laci's village. We do a great deal in deference to Margit, Mrs. Szabo thought.

"Well, Emil, let me pour you a cup of coffee," she said brightly to make up for Margit's rudeness. After settling the two men she excused herself as well. "I'll leave you to your conversation, then. Time to check on my weeds."

"Now, now, Örzsi," said Mr. Szabo. "You know very well that you keep the loveliest rose garden in all Barackfalu."

"If not the entire county," added Emil politely. Mrs. Szabo smiled and left the room.

After they had eaten, and Emil had lit his own pipe, the two men discussed politics, as they did every Sunday, both local issues and the latest news from Eger and Budapest. From politics the conversation moved to literature, and from literature to the newspaper business. When they finished that discussion they needed more coffee, and then a few more pastries. Emil wiped crumbs out of his thick brown mustache with an embroidered napkin. He cleared his throat.

"Margit has quite a way with a needle, hasn't she?"

Her father nodded. He had little interest in such things.

"Did she go with you today?"

"No," said Mr. Szabo with disgust. "She is as stubborn as ever. Pigheaded, in fact. I feel sorry for whoever ends up with her. Maybe Laci had a lucky break, eh?"

Emil's face reddened. He began to fuss with his pipe, shaking out the old tobacco and refilling it, tamping it very thoroughly.

"I think," Emil began, "that Margit has had a great disappointment. I had hoped she would be over it by now."

"So did we all. It's time she snapped out of this mood of hers. She has to go on with the business of living."

Emil cleared his throat again. "That's exactly what I was thinking. Do you think she would consider such a thing?"

Mr. Szabo puffed his pipe absently. "Such a thing?"

"As you said, going on with her life. You meant seeing someone else, didn't you?"

"You have someone in mind? A young friend of yours?"

Emil stopped tamping his pipe and lit it before answering. "Actually, I do have someone in mind. Me."

With his right hand Mr. Szabo caught his pipe as it sagged from his open mouth. "You, Emil?"

"I know I'm older than she is by ten years, but I have long admired her and have the utmost respect for her. I—I have felt this way for a long time, but then Mama died, and of course there was Laci. Do you think, that is, would you have any objection, sir, if I myself courted Margit?"

"Good God, my boy, certainly not, but you know what she's like. Are you sure you're up to it?"

"It may be just what she needs. If she'll have me." His face looked bleak and he lowered his voice. "Do you think I have a chance?"

"I'll never make guesses when it comes to women, Emil. She's a tough one—takes after her mother—but who knows? My boy, you have my blessing." He stood up. "Let's go in the garden and tell Örzsi."

Mrs. Szabo's eyes lit up like candles when Emil explained how he felt. She took his face in her hands and kissed him on both cheeks. "Ah, Emil, how I've been hoping for something like this. She feels so unwanted right now, it will do her good to have your attention. And who knows? In time, if you're patient, perhaps the lord will grant your prayers. Ah—listen! She's come downstairs. Go inside, Emil, go on."

Emil looked both pleased and alarmed as he walked back into the house. As he entered, he tapped lightly on the door, but Margit was so startled by his shadow that she nearly dropped the tray she was carrying into the kitchen. In her surprise she forgot to look miserable and for a moment her face was the pretty face of the old Margit.

"Here, let me take that from you," Emil said. "I didn't mean to startle you. I apologize."

By the time he put the tray on the table Margit had recovered her composure and her stiffness.

"It's nothing, Emil. I thought you had left and I was starting to clean up. What were you doing in the garden?"

"Just admiring your Mama's work. Margit—" He stopped.

She stood looking at him with her hands folded.

"Margit," he began again, "is my presence here so distasteful to you that you will only come downstairs if you think I am gone?"

"No, Emil, I didn't mean that. It's just that I've had a bad day today."

"But you never stay downstairs. Are all your Sundays bad now?"

"Yes."

"Margit, may I try to make them a bit less so?"

"What do you mean?"

"May I spend some time with you? Talking? Perhaps a walk now and then?"

"Why?"

"Margit, I know I am not handsome and I know I am older than you, but do you think if you got to know me better that you might, someday, perhaps, grow fond of me?"

"Emil Molnar, are you trying to ask me to marry you?"

He blushed at her directness. "Not yet," he said, and silently cursed his clumsiness.

Margit looked at him steadily. "I don't love you, Emil."

"I know. Perhaps, though, someday—"

"Most likely not. I gave my heart once, and it has been broken. I don't think it will ever be repaired."

"I see."

"Are you a gambling man, Emil?"

"Certainly not!"

"I mean, are you willing to take the chance that I may never love you?"

"Are you saying I may call on you?"

"I am saying that I will marry you, Emil. On one condition."

Emil was astonished. With unbelievable bluntness she was accepting a proposal he hadn't had a chance to make before he'd even had the chance to court her.

"What condition?"

"That you take me away from Barackfalu. Take me away from the memories, away from this house and this county, to a place where there's no chance of seeing my sister or her child—or her husband. Take me away, Emil, as far as we can go, and I will marry you. And I'll be as good a wife to you as I can be. I can promise no more."

Emil was so stunned—both by Margit's acceptance of marriage and her strange conditions—that he left the house without saying goodbye to her parents, and so it was Margit who broke the news of her betrothal to them. Thus began a flurry of planning and preparation for the second Szabo wedding in less than a year. Within a few weeks the banns had been posted in church and the whole district knew of the wedding. To Mrs. Szabo's surprise, Margit chose to be married in a European-style dress instead of the traditional Hungarian costume. The dress was nearly finished, and the wedding only weeks away, before Margit announced where she and Emil would live.

"Mm-HMM-hm?" Mrs. Szabo muttered because her mouth was full of straight pins. She spit them into the palm of her hand and looked up at Margit in amazement. "America?" she repeated.

Margit looked down at her mother, who was kneeling at the half-pinned hem of her wedding dress. Margit looked regal in its swirl of ecru silk, with matching lace at the throat. Lace trimmed the yoke of the dress and edged the cuffs, following the button-line halfway to the elbow. No less than ten tiny mother-of-pearl buttons closed each sleeve, and another fifty fastened the dress at Margit's back. She looked calmly at her mother and nodded.

"But Margit!" her mother wailed. "So far away! Is it not enough that you are leaving your home and this region? Isn't Eger far enough for you?"

"No, Mama."

Mrs. Szabo was stunned. First Piros married Laci in his town instead of theirs, to keep the gossip down, but at least it was nearby, and Piros wore the local costume, with its embroidery and ribbons and ten white skirts. Such a wedding was not good enough for Margit, who if she could not have the man of her choice was making up for it with her fancy silk gown and a ceremony at the biggest church in Eger. And who would be there? Herself, and her husband, an acquaintance of Emil's—five people in a church that held five hundred. And then? Not the usual walk from village church to the bride's home, followed by a lovely reception with violin music and dancing and fine homemade food, but a wedding lunch in a restaurant, among strangers, and then farewell.

Mrs. Szabo had thought Margit and Emil would take rooms in Eger, to be close to Emil's work, and then come home to his house in Barackfalu every weekend. Who would ever imagine they were moving to America, to the land of cowboys and red Indians!

"Where, where in that huge country are you going to live?"

"The town is called Hardenbergh."

"Har-den-bur-rug," Mrs. Szabo repeated. Such a funny word. "It sounds German."

"It's not German, Mama, it's American. Hardenbergh, New Jersey. Men from all over Hungary have been moving there to work for the Van Dyke Company. Practically half the city is Hungarian, Emil says, and everyone speaks Magyar. It will be like living in Eger."

"For you, maybe, but not for your Papa and me! Oh, Margitka, Margitka, I am old, and you are going so far away—I know in my heart I will never see you again!"

"Oh, Mama, don't say that, and don't cry, please don't cry!" Margit knelt down and took her mother's hands. "Please, Mama, it's for the best, don't you see? How can I live here? The only reason Piros doesn't visit is because I'm here. I've come between you. When I'm gone they will be able to move here. Laci will be a big help to Papa, and you will have Piros and your granddaughter back and be comforted. Be happy for us, Mama. It's such an opportunity for Emil. He's been a journalist for years but what has the newspaper done for him? Now he has the chance to start his own paper, to be the publisher and editor, and we'll make money and send it to you so you and Papa can come visit. Who knows, maybe you'll like it so much you'll want to move there, too."

Mrs. Szabo wiped her eyes. "Get up, Margit, you'll wrinkle your dress."

"Mama look at me. It's the only way I can be happy, Mama, the only way. A new start in a new country where no one knows the gossip about how my sister stole my husband-to-be. It will be a fresh start for me and a wonderful opportunity for Emil."

"And will you grow to love him, all the way in America?"

Margit stood up and smoothed her skirt. "He's a good man, Mama, and I will be a good wife to him."

Mrs. Szabo picked up the straight pins she had dropped and sighed as she finished pinning up the hem of Margit's dress. "A good wife is one thing, a loving wife is another. Margit, how does he make you feel?"

"Feel, Mama? What do you mean?"

"Well, for example, how do you feel when he takes your hand? When he kisses you?"

Margit was silent.

"How do you think you will feel on your wedding night?" said her mother without looking up.

"How am I supposed to feel?"

Mrs. Szabo stopped pinning and sat back. She looked out the window at the bees buzzing over the geraniums in the windowbox.

"Whole, Margit. You should feel whole for the first time in your life. Like a part of you that was missing had been found. That's how it feels with love, and a good thing, too, because even with love it—well, it can sometimes be—well, uncomfortable the first time. You should be prepared for that. I'm sure Emil will be gentle but even so, you may not like it at first."

Margit looked down at the yards of silk draped over her slim body. Beneath the skirt were layers of petticoats, and under that her chemise and her stockings and drawers, the soft armor that so far had prevented Emil from touching anything but her hands. How strange to think of standing before him in a thin nightgown, and then nothing at all, with his hands everywhere—her breasts, her buttocks, between her legs. How would it feel? Would it have felt any different with Laci? Margit took a deep breath, and told herself sternly not to think of it, but with the wedding only a few weeks away, she knew she would be able to think of little else.

"I'm sure everything will be fine, Mama," she said, but the tremor in her voice told her mother that Margit was not nearly so self-assured as she pretended.

She would see little of Emil before the wedding. He was busy settling their affairs so they could leave Hungary. His savings had been enough to buy them second-class passage on a ship from Hamburg to New York, and the train fare from Budapest to the port city, plus a little "persuasion money" to ensure their passage from Hamburg instead of the official exit port of Fiume, where exorbitant exit taxes and long delays were the norm. The proceeds from the sale of his house in Barackfalu were the nest egg that would start his newspaper once they reached America. Emil, once he got over the shock of Margit's request to live farther away from home than Eger, or even Budapest, was excited to think of moving. He loved his home, but since his mother's death there was little to tie him to the village. His only real friend there was her father, and the loss of their weekly talks was his one regret. Otherwise, America for him was the land of opportunity everyone said it would be, the chance to establish a Hungarian-language newspaper in a small city with a rapidly growing Hungarian population. Since 1900 the Van Dyke Company, a cosmetics firm, had actively recruited Hungarian men, so pleased were they with the first hard-working Hungarian immigrants they hired to do manual labor. Emil had spoken with one or two men who had returned from America despite the wages offered by Van Dyke. Their stories of homesickness, of feeling alienated among the American workers, made Emil realize that he had a skill that could bring a bit of Hungary to the immigrants. Like most Hungarians they were avid readers, who would no doubt welcome a newspaper in their own language. And, while providing a service to his countrymen, Emil would advance himself by becoming both editor and publisher of the *Hardenbergh Hirlap*.

To be honest, Emil also welcomed the opportunity to be far away from Laci and Piros. He knew his future wife was still deeply in love with the boy, and her estrangement from Piros was hurting the whole family. It would be better for everyone, he often thought, when he and Margit were gone. Perhaps, too, when he and Margit were together in a strange land, she might grow closer to him more quickly than if they had remained in Hungary.

Not more than three weeks after Margit's mother had pinned up the hem of her dress, Margit stood at the rail of the *Graf Waldersen* and watched the crowd below as they waved and called to relatives and friends who crowded the ship's rails around her. Some people wept openly as the ship began to move, others cheered; a few like Margit stood silent. She watched the crowd recede, the line of dirty harbor water grow wider as the ship began the ten-day voyage to New York. Emil had spent so much time in their tiny cabin, arranging things in his meticulous way, that he had missed the raising of the gangplank.

Margit didn't mind. She wanted time to collect her thoughts before joining Emil, for it seemed to her that this voyage separating them from home and family was more an acknowledgement of their marriage than anything that had happened in the past few days. Now she was irrevocably Mrs. Molnar, using her husband's name like any American woman, instead of retaining her own as she would have done in Barackfalu. She took on this new identity in the nearly empty church in Eger, when Emil slipped the plain gold band on her finger, with such a look of hope and love on his face that Margit had almost cried with shame. How unfair of her to accept his love when she could not return it! Yet there he was, marrying the woman who had asked him to give up everything for her, a woman who would be unable to love him back. She must never hurt him, she resolved; he was a good, kind, and loving man, and if all she could do was return the kindness then she would do so to the best of her ability. And yet she was relieved that they boarded the train immediately after the wedding luncheon, a pullman car whose single upper and lower berths—not to mention Margit's reserve in the proximity of the other passengers— prevented the consummation of their marriage until the train reached Hamburg yesterday.

In their hotel room last night Emil had been careful with her, almost shy at first, and even as his passion built he tempered it with restraint so that Margit set the pace of their lovemaking. Margit had been surprised at the firmness of his arm muscles, the softness of his skin. Although Emil was not a particularly handsome man, except for his deep brown eyes and long lashes any woman would envy, his body was athletic and lithe. Margit realized that under other circumstances she might well have been attracted to Emil Molnar. And yet, even when he entered her, with more pain than she thought possible, all she could think of was Laci. What did his arms feel like? What did his tongue taste like? Would it have hurt this much with him? When she clenched her teeth and moaned it was not because of passion or pain, but to keep herself from calling Laci's name out loud.

Now Margit watched the gulls that followed the ship as it turned out of the harbor, calling their own farewell messages as they zigzagged in the air. Mama was wrong, she thought. I don't feel whole. I feel split in two. Last night Margit Szabo ceased to be, and in her place was a stranger named Mrs. Emil Molnar. This morning, when Margit looked in the mirror to brush her hair, she was surprised to see her own familiar face there. She had half expected to see someone else's, or at least some visible sign of the change she had undergone. Her body was no longer her own; a man she had known for years, but really knew not at all, now had a claim on it, inside and out. Oh, Mama, thought Margit sadly, how can such a thing ever make a woman feel whole?

The deck began to rock as the ship reached open water, causing the remaining passengers at the rails to seek the shelter of their cabins and staterooms. Margit welcomed the motion and the resulting privacy. Swells rose up and sank down as far as see could see. But it's not too rough, she thought; if I took my shoes off I could jump in and swim back, back to Laci, back to where I could at least see him once in a while, for wouldn't seeing him at least bring some happiness? Wouldn't it be better than never seeing him again? She leaned forward, looking down at the white spray splashing up from the bow of the ship. No, I can never see him, because mere seeing would never bring happiness; it would only bring jealousy and sorrow and despair. And I could never reach shore from here—I'd be sucked under this ship in a moment. Would that be such a bad thing? If I just lean over a little more...

She felt a firm hand on her arm and looked up at a uniformed man, one of the ship's officers. "*Vorsicht!*" he said. "Be careful! We wouldn't want you to fall overboard, Frau..."

"Frau Molnar," Margit finished for him.

"Frau Molnar," he repeated, bowing and touching the brim of his hat. He smiled politely and waited while Margit turned from the mesmerizing water, nodded her thanks, and walked toward the stairs to join her husband.

Chapter Two
Hardenbergh, April 1911

Margit walked down Cherry Street one Wednesday morning too preoccupied with her shopping list to notice the petals that drifted like pink snowflakes onto her shoulders. Monsignor Andrassy was coming to dinner and she wanted to make her chicken *paprikas* for him. Margit knew pride was a sin but she could not help being proud of her cooking. Not many women in this town, she thought, spent as much time as they should on their own cooking. Margit was fortunate that she and Emil were unlike most of the immigrants arriving from Hungary by the boatload. With the money they had from the sale of his mother's house they had been able to make a down payment on a three-flat building in a modest part of town, equally far from the Van Dyke mansion and the tenements near the railroad station. The rent from the two upper apartments paid the monthly mortgage, and the small salary Emil paid himself took care of the rest. So far, thank St. Elizabeth, Margit had not been reduced to working in the dress factory like most Hungarian women her age.

She turned the corner at Hardenbergh Avenue and stopped at the butcher for a chunk of *szalonna* bacon, then continued on to the produce market where she chose fresh bunches of curly spinach and tender new peas. The milkman had left fresh sour cream that morning, so her only other stop was to get the chicken itself. Margit paused before the door of the poultry shop and took one last deep breath of fresh air before stepping inside. A small bell rang over her head as she opened the door, where she stood for a moment to let her eyes adjust to the dimness. Before her, on either side of a central aisle and as high as the top of her hat, were stacked rows of wooden cages. Each cage held three or four fowl: white spring chickens and brown ones, fat capons, a few ducks, and in one corner a solitary tom turkey who by himself filled one large cage. Feathers swirled around her feet as Margit walked slowly past the cages, peering in to find the birds with the brightest eyes and the cleanest feathers. Chickens clucked and squawked as she passed, holding her skirt so it wouldn't brush against the grubby cages.

At the end of the aisle was the store's counter, and beyond that the back room where the birds were decapitated, dipped in boiling water, and plucked. Jacob Weiss, the proprietor, stood behind the counter with a leather apron over his work clothes, wrapping a freshly killed bird for the only other customer in the store, Ilona Lukacs. The two women murmured "hello" politely, but without warmth, since Hungarian Protestants like Mrs. Lukacs and Catholics like Margit rarely communicated socially.

Holding Mrs. Lukacs' hand was a small boy wearing knee pants and a white shirt with a floppy bow tie.

"Say hello to Mrs. Molnar, Istvan," said Mrs. Lukacs.

"Hello," he said, then buried his face in his mother's skirt.

Margit turned her head. It was apparent that Mrs. Lukacs was expecting another child, and Margit experienced a brief pang of envy. Having even one child conferred a certain status on a woman. Imagine how fulfilled she would be if she had been able to have Laci's children! Yet, after nearly seven years of marriage, she received her period each month with a sense of relief, tinged with shame, and endured the smug look of matrons like Ilona Lukacs.

"Good morning, Mrs. Molnar," said Mr. Weiss as he rang up Mrs. Lukacs's purchase. "What can I do for you today?"

"Your best chicken," said Margit, causing Mrs. Lukacs to raise an eyebrow as she left the store.

"All my chickens are the best, Mrs. Molnar. You just show me the one you want."

"This one," she said, pointing to a cage one row down from the top.

Mr. Weiss opened the cage and thrust an arm inside. Despite the bird's pecking and flapping, Mr. Weiss caught it by the legs in a quick practiced movement. He held the bird head downward at arm's length so the flapping wings would not slap his thighs, and looked over his spectacles at Margit.

"Cleaned and plucked as usual, feet on?"

"Feet on," Margit affirmed. "And be sure to give me all the giblets."

"Would I not?" said Mr. Weiss as he walked toward the back room.

While Margit waited, she walked slowly up and down the aisle, looking into the chicken cages with mild interest but little sympathy. If the Lord sacrificed himself for Margit, these chickens could sacrifice themselves for Monsignor Andrassy. The Monsignor had been a great comfort to Margit since she and Emil had first moved to Hardenbergh. In the early days, before she'd learned enough English to get by, Monsignor Andrassy had made sure that a woman from the church accompanied Margit to the store. He helped Margit and Emil get settled in the strange new town, introducing them to his other parishioners, teaching them essential English words and phrases, recommending a doctor when Emil dropped a tray of type on his right foot and broke the big toe. Monsignor Andrassy was the first to subscribe to Emil's paper, and just last fall had asked Margit, out of all the women in the parish, to embroider a new altar cloth. He had become as much her friend as her spiritual counselor, and dined with the Molnars once a month if his parish duties allowed it.

"There you are, Mrs. Molnar," said Mr. Weiss as he laid the freshly plucked chicken on a square of brown paper. He wrapped and tied it into a neat bundle and wiped his hands before making change for Margit. "Enjoy," he said when Margit thanked him and left.

Margit inhaled deeply when she left the store and blinked her eyes in the bright sun. Now she could appreciate the fine spring day, the warmth of the breeze on her cheek and the fresh smell of the air. She hurried home with her purchases. She didn't want to be late with Emil's lunch.

She walked quickly through the alley between her house and the neighbors', grateful that Anna Puskasz did not waylay her once more to chide Margit for putting linoleum on her kitchen floor. "You're walking on all your money," Anna had said, shaking her head. "You're crazy to waste good money when you have a perfectly fine wood floor underneath." Since then Margit had managed always to be busy when Anna came to visit. Margit did not make friends easily, nor was she quick to forget an insult. She could not walk into her kitchen without thinking of Anna's criticism.

But her anger faded quickly when she stepped onto the gleaming yellow surface of the new linoleum. No more would she have to scrub the wooden boards that lay beneath it, or try to sweep without having crumbs fall between them. A spilled cup of tea was easy to clean up with a towel, and no longer left a stain and a damp spot for hours. Margit's eyes shone as bright as the waxed floor every time she looked at it. So modern! So American! Just like the icebox she placed the chicken in.

She stepped into the bedroom just long enough to hang up her hat and coat. She glanced in the mirror to make sure her hair was still neatly pinned on top of her head and hurried back to the kitchen. Once she had the fire going in the wood stove she was able to put the rest of the groceries away. She put the giblets and chicken feet into a pot of water with onions, carrots, and celery, to make a stock that would simmer while she and Emil had lunch. She set the bacon in the frying pan and cut two thick slices off the loaf of bread she'd made the day before. Then she watched the bacon carefully to render the fat without burning the meat. The meat she would serve to Emil for lunch, while reserving the fat to fry the chicken in later.

Like the other Hungarian men who lived in this part of town, Emil walked home for lunch every day. He left the newspaper office just before the twelve o'clock whistle blew at the Van Dyke plant, so he could arrive at the gate when the employees left the factory grounds. He enjoyed walking up the hill with the painters, machinists, and assembly-line workers whose subscriptions helped put food on his table. A few moments in their company on a fine day couldn't help but put Emil in a whistling mood.

Emil Molnar loved music. Each night, while Margit busied herself with needlework, Emil played the violin. He hummed while he washed up in the morning and whistled any time he walked. Margit could easily tell his mood by the tune, even though his taste ranged from Liszt to Hungarian folk tunes to Tin Pan Alley. His newspaper was the chief supporter of the Magyar Men's Marching Band, which paraded through the Hungarian section of Hardenbergh every third Sunday during fine weather, with Emil proudly holding one end of their banner.

Margit had grown so used to hearing his whistle as he walked up the alley at lunch time that she was surprised by the unaccompanied sound of his footsteps on the stairs. Emil walked in the door and kissed Margit on the cheek.

"Hello, Margit," he said.

Margit watched him as he walked to the sink to wash his hands. Seven years of marriage had put a few pounds around his middle, and seven years of a struggling newspaper had added gray hairs to his temples, but his back was as straight as a young man's, and his body as strong as it had ever been. Today, for the first time, Margit saw a hint of the old man to come. The absent whistle, the weary posture, the noncommittal greeting, so unlike his usual "Hello, my dear" or "Hello, my love,"—any one of those would be enough to concern her.

"Emil, what's the matter? Are you ill?"

"No, Margit, I'm perfectly fine."

"Then what's wrong?"

He sat down at the table with a sigh. "There's talk of a strike at the plant."

"A strike? Why?"

"One of the men was injured yesterday afternoon. He was repairing a piece of equipment and his sleeve got caught in it. His arm was crushed."

"How awful! But that's only one incident—surely not enough to strike over?"

"Not according to the men I talked to today. They told me there's a serious accident like that at least once a month, and numerous other incidents all the time. They say the plant's not safe. And on top of that, there's trouble brewing between our people and the Irish workers. The Irish want our people to stop working so hard. They say it makes the other workers look bad. They want a union, and say they'll strike to get one."

"Well, a worker should take a break now and then—a few extra pennies a day won't buy them land back home, and what good will land be if they work themselves to death?" Margit observed as she broke two eggs into the skillet. "But a union—that sounds like trouble, to me."

"I think there'll be trouble regardless. A prolonged strike won't do this town any good, and I can't imagine management accepting a union without a fight. What happens if it lasts all summer, or even longer? Next winter could see a lot of families go hungry. And starving families don't subscribe to newspapers, that's for sure."

Margit looked over her shoulder in alarm. "You don't think a strike could affect us, do you?"

"If it lasts long enough, it will affect us all. And if they bring in a union, where will that leave our people? All the big unions require U.S. citizenship. Even most of us who plan to stay haven't applied for citizenship, let alone the men who are here temporarily."

"Well, so far it's just talk, right? Maybe that's all it will be."

"Maybe," said Emil, but he didn't sound convinced.

After lunch, Emil usually sat and smoked his pipe while Margit cleared the table and did the dishes. She never let him help, although he would have been happy to do so. Today, though, Emil was anxious to leave early so he could catch up with the men on their way back to the plant, and perhaps learn more about the possibility of a strike. Margit, although she, too, found the prospect of a strike troubling, was more concerned with the present matter of readying her home for Monsignor Andrassy. After quickly washing the luncheon dishes she swept and washed the kitchen floor, then she proceeded to dust and sweep the entire flat while the floor dried. Their apartment, like the two above, had only three rooms, but those rooms were high-ceilinged and spacious. Crown molding decorated every room and a plaster medallion fanned out over the brass-plated ceiling lamps, which had a round, cut-glass bowl around each of the five electric bulbs.

Although Margit had finished spring cleaning only the week before, she opened the windows to air out the apartment. She put fresh crocheted doilies on the arms and back of their best chair and a fresh tablecloth on the kitchen table. She laid the table with good Budapest china and silver that had belonged to Emil's mother. Then she placed a vase of red tulips in the center of the table, tulips planted and tended with care by Emil, since she had not inherited her mother's skill with plants. All of Margit's artistry was with the needle. Plain sewing bored her, although she darned, hemmed, and mended without complaint because it had to get done. Her real satisfaction came from embellishment, like the pattern of roses and ivy embroidered on the tablecloth, and the green tatting on its hem that matched the tatting at the edge of each napkin. The doilies Margit had crocheted herself, in stars and flowers and spiraling geometric patterns. A line of embroidery edged Emil's vest and his initials were stitched onto his watch pocket. Margit's own petticoats and camisoles were bordered in cream, pink, or blue lace tatting, and all the house linens—pillow cases, sheets, table runners—were embroidered with silk thread.

Most afternoons, after her chores were done, Margit would sit in the front window with her needlework, or in summer on the front stoop, adding flowers and arabesques to curtains, antimacassars, and handkerchiefs. Today, however, she indulged in her other source of pride: cooking. From a towel-covered bowl near a sunny windowsill she pulled a lump of sweet, yeasty dough, kneading it on the floured board she laid across the sink. She divided the dough and rolled each piece flat, then spread over it a thick layer of poppy seeds cooked in milk and sugar. She rolled the filled dough like a jellyroll and placed it on a tin sheet while she prepared the next one. Each roll of *kalacs* was placed on the tin like a pale, plump sausage, the first already rising again by the time the last was made. While the kalacs was in the oven Margit browned her chicken with onion and paprika before stirring in the finished stock. While the chicken simmered she washed the spinach and shelled the peas. The peas she boiled with a little dried dill, while the spinach was dressed with crumbled bacon. Finally, she made dumplings from egg and flour, dropping them by spoonfuls into the chicken broth that would be thickened with sour cream just before serving.

When she had dinner under control, Margit cleared away the evidence of its preparation, swept the floor one more time, and removed her apron. She just had time to wash her face with a bit of rose water, change into her good silk dress, and re-pin her hair, when Monsignor Andrassy arrived. She knelt for his blessing, which he delivered in Hungarian, tracing the sign of the cross over her head with his small, chubby hand. The Monsignor was a diminutive man, shorter even than Margit's five feet four inches, with a spreading waistline thanks to the good cooking of his housekeeper, Mrs. Juhasz, and parishioners like Margit.

Margit led the old priest to his customary chair and handed him a glass of Tokay.

"You're looking well, Father."

"I am quite well, my child, quite well indeed. And you? On Sunday you seemed concerned about your dear father."

"Yes, I was. Mama had sent such a short letter, you see, and she was so upset it didn't make a lot of sense, but I received another letter yesterday that explained things much better. Papa's had a stroke, although according to Mama's second letter it was a very mild one. Apparently the doctor told them it was a warning that Papa should retire from teaching and lead the life of a patriarch, and let his children take care of him from now on."

"I am sorry to hear of his illness. I will pray for him, of course."

"Thank you, Father."

"Yet, although the letter you have had is reassuring, you wish you could be there to see him for yourself."

"Oh, yes, Father! It was always my desire that Papa and Mama should visit us here, and perhaps even move here, but we just never saved enough money to pay their passage."

The old priest raised an eyebrow and looked pointedly at the kitchen floor. Margit blushed.

"I know we didn't need a new floor, or the icebox, or new curtains, but it's Emil, Father, he keeps buying these things to please me. I know he wants an Edison phonograph, but he'll never buy one as long as he thinks there's something I want, or something that could make my life easier. He's a good man, Father; everything he does, he does for me."

"And have you thought of going back to visit your parents yourself? That would cost only half as much."

"How could I leave Emil?"

"How indeed? And why?" asked Emil as he stepped into the room. "Good evening, Monsignor Andrassy."

Emil knelt for the priest's blessing and then rose to kiss his wife's hand.

"So what is this talk of leaving?" He asked it lightly enough but Margit caught a flicker of uncertainty in his eyes.

"I told the Monsignor about poor Papa, and he suggested I go home to visit him."

"And do you want to go home, my Margitka?"

"Of course I would like to see Papa again, but as long as his condition is not serious I think my proper place is with you, Emil."

Emil nodded and squeezed her hand with relief. Seven years together did not change the fact that Margit still loved Laci, or at least the memory of him, and though she was genuinely fond of Emil he didn't fool himself that she loved him as much as he loved her. He didn't like to think what might happen if she were to return to Barackfalu and see the flesh-and-blood Laci again. He could only hope that, if she ever did go back, she would find the handsome Laci had grown fat and lazy.

In deference to their guest Emil firmly put aside his uncharitable thoughts, and dinner was as congenial as ever. Monsignor Andrassy always did justice to a good meal, and refrained from any serious talk until Margit had shooed the men into the parlor for a cigar and another glass of Tokay. He commiserated with Emil about the possible strike, and they talked of the consequences until Margit came in from the kitchen and picked up her crocheting.

"My word, Margit, you must have enough antimacassars to fill every house in Hardenbergh," Andrassy said.

"Not so many as that, Father, but when I finish this set you might find a family that could use it."

"Very gracious of you. I'm sure I can find a home for them. Thanks to you and the other fine ladies of the parish our poorest families will have doilies, even if they don't have indoor plumbing."

"Even we don't have indoor plumbing, Father," Emil reminded him. "You won't find many Hungarian families who do."

"Not yet, but I hear that Messrs. Boylan and Kelly have plans for new homes on vacant land just a few blocks from here, all two-family homes complete with bathtub and water closet."

"And the city will approve such homes, here in the Hungarian section?" Emil asked.

"The city will approve if Mr. Van Dyke wants his workers to live in better housing. With all this talk of a strike I wouldn't be surprised to find those plans approved and construction starting before summer."

"Van Dyke is a shrewd man."

"And a generous one. Guess what he has proposed?" asked Andrassy with such glee in his voice that Margit looked up from her handiwork.

"Next year," continued Andrassy, "will be the fifth anniversary of the completion of our church. To celebrate, Mr. Van Dyke has agreed to donate half the cost of an organ. Half!"

"Why, that's wonderful, Father!" said Margit.

He nodded happily. "We'll have to raise the other half, of course, but with a little work we can have an organ in our church by next Easter."

"How much do we need to raise, yet, Father?" asked Emil.

"Only $1500."

Emil whistled. "Only! It will take some doing to raise that much money in less than a year."

"It will be a challenge," agreed Andrassy. "And that's exactly why I'd like you, Emil, to head the fund-raising committee."

Emil and Margit looked at each other. To head the committee was an honor to them both, but they knew it would require that they give a substantial donation themselves. Although Emil and Margit were fairly prosperous compared with most of Andrassy's parishioners, they were by no means wealthy.

"Well," Emil said after Andrassy had bid them peace and left for the rectory with a roll of Margit's *kalacs* in his hands, "it looks as though I'll be trading a phonograph for an organ."

"At least we won't have to listen to that horrible church piano for too much longer. It never stays in tune from one Sunday to the next."

"Oh, it will be a fine thing for our church to have a real organ. The challenge will be to get our neighbors to help pay for it."

"If there's a challenge to be undertaken, you're the right man for it."

"Mm. I married you, after all."

Emil put his arm around Margit's waist and walked with her into the bedroom. He bent his head and rubbed his cheek against her hair. "You hair smells good. May I unpin it for you?"

"If you like."

Margit sat on the bed while Emil pulled the pins out, slowly, and combed it with his fingers until it lay loose over her shoulders. "Your hair is like silk tonight."

He pushed her hair to one side and kissed her neck, then her cheek, then turned her head and kissed her on the mouth. Margit kissed him back willingly. It hadn't taken her long, once she'd gotten over the loss of her virginity, to realize that if Emil could not satisfy her heart he could at least satisfy her body. She had no idea how many other women would be content with such an arrangement, but it suited her, and Emil would never know that when he lay sleeping afterward, it was still Laci whom Margit imagined lay next to her.

They awoke next morning full of plans for fundraising: bake sales, a summer carnival; Emil contributed a small portion of his advertising revenue, and for many months Margit had little time for needlework. Knowing how important the project was, she put aside her personal differences and exhibited a level of diplomacy that surprised everyone. When they were done, they'd raised the necessary cash well in time for installation of the organ by Easter, as Monsignor Andrassy had hoped.

Emil made sure that his paper carried full publicity for the project, prominently displaying the name of Van Dyke as the chief benefactor. He liked to think his paper played a small part in heading off the expected strike, although he knew that Van Dyke's new policy requiring all workers to take their allotted breaks, and the beginning of construction of the new housing project, had far more to do with it.

Their spirits were high when they walked into church on Easter morning to see the altar piled high with white lilies. They genuflected but, before stepping into the pew, turned around to admire the new organ in the choir loft above and behind them. The brass display pipes brightened the loft and the polished cherry console glowed warmly in the very center. When the organist played the opening bars of the processional the sound filled the church, echoing off the stone walls and pillars. Three altar boys led the procession, the lead boy holding a gold cross and the other two pure beeswax candles. Behind them walked Father Borsy, holding the censor that swayed with each step to send a cloud of incense toward the high ceiling. Last came Monsignor Andrassy, in white and gold vestments, blessing the parishioners with his right hand. In celebration of the new organ and Easter this was a High Mass, sung in Latin, but Andrassy's sermon was as always spoken in the language of his parishioners.

When it came time for the sermon, Emil tried to arrange himself against the hard pew as comfortably as possible. Andrassy was never a man of few words, and Emil knew the old man would not pass up this opportunity for a most lengthy sermon. He was right. It was nearly forty-five minutes before Andrassy began to wind up a speech that included every possible Easter topic, from death and resurrection and salvation to lambs and spring robins and birth and, of course, the new pipe organ, growth, and prosperity.

"My children, let me conclude by giving thanks to our dear Savior for His wisdom and guidance that has brought us all here to America. Where else could poor people of peasant stock not only meet the challenges of daily life, but also succeed to an extent undreamt of by their relatives abroad? Where else could we have worked together to build, with our own hands, our own sweat, this beautiful but humble temple to our Lord? Where else could we acquire, for the glory of Christ, such a musical instrument whose joyous song reaches the heavens for the first time today?

"How far have we come in a few short years, those of us who came here for a few dollars, eager to return home. For where is home now? Is it not right here in Hardenbergh? How many of you, looking only for work, came here and found a wife, a husband? Is not this edifice in which we sit a monument to the fact that we are indeed home? That we have built a new home, a new Hungary, right here in Hardenbergh? Look at the children sitting among you. You are rearing a new generation of Hungarians. American Hungarians. But how well do they know their heritage? Are they taught their language in American schools? Do they learn about Kossuth and Petofi and all their country's heroes? I submit to you a new challenge: I challenge you to put the same energy and the same resources that built this church and acquired that magnificent pipe organ in the choir loft—I challenge you to do the right thing for our children. I challenge you to build a Hungarian school, where our children will learn not only what they learn in the American schools, but also our language, our heritage, and our religion.

"My children, all of you, we live in a place and a time that are unparalleled in world history. We have prosperity. We have peace. We have a place in this society. Let us build, not just a school, but a future. May God bless you."

As they knelt for the offertory, Emil stole a look at Margit. He rolled his eyes, and Margit shook her head slightly. First the church, then the organ, now a school. They would have to raise far more than $1500 this time. It was going to take years, thought Emil—a lot of time, hard work, and prayers. He bowed his head. The prayers, at least, he could get started on today.

Emil

Chapter Three
September 1914

After the Magyar Men's Marching Band finished playing, with a great flourish of cymbals and drums, Monsignor Andrassy held up a pair of scissors in his right hand. The crowd of immigrants watching him applauded as he slowly lowered his hand and cut the red, white, and green ribbon draped across the doors of the new St. Elizabeth's School. Emil and Margit edged forward with the rest of the crowd to walk through the halls of Hardenbergh's only Hungarian grade school. Emil, like Margit and Monsignor Andrassy and all the members of their community, felt enormous pride in this new building. It was the culmination of years of progress, not only for this young immigrant community, but also for him personally. He had left Hungary as a struggling journalist, and now was publisher of Hardenbergh's only Hungarian-language weekly newspaper. He had worked hard to raise funds first for the church, then for the church organ, and now for this school. Best of all, he had Margit, whose loyalty and care had provided him with a measure of contentment he had not thought possible. All he lacked, he thought as they crossed the threshold into the lobby, was a child to attend this fine new school.

Emil looked at Margit as she admired the classrooms, the wide corridor, and the pride and joy of everyone—the assembly hall, with a hardwood floor large enough to serve as a gymnasium, and a raised stage on which pageants and plays would be performed. Her hair, under a flowered hat, was as dark as ever; her face, with its cool clear eyes and thin mouth, was almost as unlined as it had been ten years ago. Her figure, unlike those of the other young Hungarian matrons, was still slim; no childbearing had put weight on her stomach and her hips. As Margit smiled and pointed, did she notice the excitement in the eyes of the parents, and did she notice how lacking it was in herself and in Emil? Did she, he wondered, feel the lack as much as he did?

They moved toward the center of the hall, where a cloth-covered table held punch and homemade pastries. Emil poured Margit a glass of punch and then one for himself.

"Well, Margit, we've certainly done ourselves proud this time."

"Yes, everyone should be proud of this building. But what a lot of work, raising funds for it. It was bad enough when we built the church, let alone a whole school. Let's hope the Monsignor has no ideas for civic projects for quite a while."

"I don't think we'll be doing much of anything these days," said Laszlo Varga, the grocer, as he reached for a pastry.

"Why not?" asked Margit.

"The war, of course."

"Do you think a European war will affect us so much?"

"It's certain to," said Viola, the grocer's wife. "Already the price of flour has risen 50 cents a barrel."

"This is too happy an occasion for gloomy talk," said Margit. "Besides, it can't last long, can it?"

"I'm afraid it will," said Emil, "now that the Turks are involved. This war is no longer a border dispute between two countries. The whole of Europe is mobilized. Even our people will be fighting now."

"I heard," said Varga, "that some of the men from Van Dyke are planning to go home and fight."

"If they do," said Viola, "then surely the war will be over soon. Ah, there's Mrs. Horvath. She still owes us money. Excuse me, will you? I'm going to go over and make her feel uncomfortable!"

"I'm afraid your wife is as patriotic as she is frugal, Varga," said Emil. "But I think she's wrong. Shedding Hungarian blood won't bring this war to a timely end."

The grocer shrugged and picked up a slice of Margit's *kalacs*. "Let's hope it does. I have a younger brother there still, and three nephews, all of conscription age."

"Oh, Mr. Varga, you frighten me," said Margit. "Talking of your family makes it seem as though the war is right here."

"If it isn't, it soon will be," he said, shrugged once more, and walked off.

Margit put down her glass of punch. "Emil, it's so close in here. Let's step outside for air."

"You do look pale, my dear." Emil took her arm and led her to the wide doors at the back of the assembly hall. They opened into the schoolyard, a rectangular grassy area with two small trees flanking the steps. Emil had been there the day they were planted. Monsignor

Andrassy had blessed the trees, sprinkling them with holy water, and had prayed that someday they would tower over the two-story school building.

"I'm afraid our little sycamores can't provide any shade for you yet."

"I'll be all right, Emil. I just need some air."

"It is warm for early September," Emil said, but he knew it was worry more than heat that caused Margit's discomfort. She was thinking of Laci, wondering whether he would be conscripted into the army. Emil thought it unlikely, since Laci had a wife and family, and was Margit's age. He rubbed one finger between his neck and his starched collar. Laci was like a case of heat rash, he thought, just when you think you've gotten rid of it back it comes. That was Laci, still prickling, still enough of a presence to worry the woman he didn't marry, still Emil's competition, even after ten years.

Emil pulled his handkerchief out of his pocket and wiped off his face and hands. He folded the handkerchief up again, rubbing his thumb over the initials, in white silk thread, that Margit had embroidered there for him, and silently cursed himself for letting thoughts of Laci irritate him.

"Feeling better, my dear?"

"Much better. Shall we go back in?"

"To tell you the truth, I'd rather not. Would you mind very much if we walked home?"

Margit smiled. "To tell you the truth, I was hoping you'd say that."

Emil took her arm. "Let's walk down Kossuth Street."

Kossuth Street, named for the hero who had led a revolution against the Habsburgs more than half a century before, was only a few blocks from the school. It was a new street, one of a dozen carved out of an old farm on the south side of the city. Unlike the older section of town, which had streets barely wide enough for two motorcars to pass, this new section had streets wide enough to accommodate the cars with room for parking on either side of the street. The houses, built by Hardenbergh's most successful contractors, Boylan and Kelly, were all two-family structures, so close they might almost have been row houses. Each house had a small front yard, a narrow alley alongside it, and a narrow but deep back yard, large enough for a vegetable garden. Each apartment held not only a modern kitchen, living room, and bedroom, but a separate room for dining, a spare bedroom, and best of all, a bathroom, with a full-size tub, pedestal sink, and flush toilet. A full basement with a coal furnace and a full attic would be shared by both families.

The houses were identical on the outside, each a mirror image of the one next to it, but Emil thought that with a little paint and a few window boxes the street would be charming. Certainly, these homes were far superior to any home in Barackfalu, although no sight was prettier than Barackfalu in the spring, when it was surrounded by apricot trees in full bloom. But the loss of two weeks' beauty was a small price to pay, thought Emil, for the progress that these homes represented.

Emil stopped in front of one of the newest houses, still uninhabited. Newly sprouted grass was struggling against the late-summer heat, and the fresh white paint on the clapboards had yet to be dirtied by soot from the coal furnaces.

"What do you think of it, Margit?"

"What do I think, Emil? I think it's a house, like any other in this neighborhood."

"We could do it, you know."

"Do what?"

"This," Emil nodded. "It could be ours. I talked with Nagy at the Savings Bank, and we could do it. He'd take a partnership in the other house in place of a down payment on one of these."

"Emil! Are you serious?"

"Quite serious."

She turned from him to look again at the house and shook her head. "To have a modern house like this—so much room. What would we do with all the rooms?"

"Cook in one, eat in one, sleep in one, receive guests in one. Maybe crochet and embroider in the fifth."

Emil felt Margit shift position slightly, as though she were about to walk away, but she stood quietly. "The fifth room is supposed to be for a child."

Emil sighed and looked at the house. "Margit, I would give you that if I could."

"It's not your fault, Emil. It's God's will." She looked up the street at the new front porches. "Are you sorry you married me?"

He took her right hand in his, squeezed it hard, and whispered "Never!"

Margit's eyes met his for just a moment before she turned away again, and said in a shaky voice, "Let's go home."

Emil didn't want to walk home with Margit; he wanted to take her into one of these new houses and make love to her, and she knew it. He could feel her retreating from his passion, as she did any time his love for her overpowered him. Every time he thought the door to her heart stood open, she closed it suddenly, and the real Margit hid from him behind it. It happened any time he was generous, any time his gift showed her once again just how much he loved her.

They walked home silently. Emil opened the door for Margit, and followed her inside. She walked straight into the bedroom to remove her hat and her gloves. Emil watched her from the doorway as she put her things away. She came up to him without looking him in the eye, and took his hat from his hands.

"Emil," she said, and still holding the hat put her arms around him and kissed him hard. Emil had been expecting it, because every time she refused his love she offered her body instead. It was all she could give him, and Emil took it, because knowing she did it from guilt instead of love didn't make him want her any less. He led her to the bed, still kissing her, pushing up her skirt as she pulled down his suspenders.

Afterward, when they lay together, still only half undressed, Emil rubbed his cheek against Margit's hair and wondered how much more satisfying it would be if for once she gave him not just her body, but also her heart.

Only a month later Emil was almost as surprised as Margit to be the new owner of a two-family house on Kossuth Street. The banker, Georg Nagy, had indeed drawn up an agreement, taking a half-share in their old house in lieu of a down payment on the new one, and offering a 20-year mortgage at a fair rate. Now Emil was full owner of one house and half owner of another, with two existing tenants and two vacant flats to advertise in his paper. The war in Europe seemed very far away as he and Margit packed the few items of furniture they owned into a rented wagon. Although they were moving scarcely a half mile, she packed for a cross-country trip. Every precious piece of Budapest china was wrapped in newspaper and laid in a barrel. The embroidered linens were carefully packaged in bundles, with the framed portraits of Kossuth and Petofi, the poet, tucked inside for safekeeping.

When everything they owned was loaded in the wagon, Emil helped Margit onto the seat next to him and flicked the reins. As they drove away neither looked back at what had been their home for ten years. Margit had no regrets about leaving a tiny apartment with catty neighbors, and Emil, although he lived and worked in the Hungarian community, was Americanized enough to be a man of progress. Their situation was a symbol of the growth of their people in this town, where the Hungarian population had tripled in the past ten years. Hungarian workers, both the men at Van Dyke and the women in the dress factory, were valued by the factory owners for their hard work. They worked hard to earn money quickly. Some sent most of their wages home, but others saved their money for the day when they could return to Hungary wealthy enough to buy land for themselves.

Emil was as aware as any Hungarian man of how different his life would be in the old country. There, he would always be a man from Barackfalu. No matter that his father was a relatively prosperous landowner whose son had been to college, no matter that he had worked in the city instead of in the fields, he would always be a villager in the eyes of his countrymen. The determination that had gotten him as far as Eger would have taken him no further; he could never have risen above his station, no matter how hard he worked. It was worse for most of the immigrants, who would have been peasant farmers if they had not come to America seeking their fortune. Many went back to Hungary as they had planned, after four or five years in the factories, but many more stayed, lured by the possessions that were within their grasp in just a year or two. Emil knew of one man, a machinist at Van Dyke, who came home from work every day and counted all the light bulbs in his house, just because they were there and they were his.

Now more and more Magyars, almost all of them in their twenties and thirties, were settling in America permanently. The new school showed how many Hungarians were setting down roots in this New Jersey town. So were the new houses, like the one Emil and Margit pulled up to.

"Whoa," said Emil, and the team of draft horses stood still, one resting its hind foot, and the other dropping balls of fresh manure. Emil secured the reins and jumped down to help Margit off the high wagon seat. Gyula Farkas, Emil's typesetter, was already waiting there to help them unload. Farkas, a short but broad-shouldered young man, smiled and shook Emil's hand.

"Well, I was going to thank you for giving me the day off, but now that I see that wagon load I'm not sure I should!"

"Be glad the apartment was so small," said Emil. "Just imagine what we'll have after ten years in this big place!"

"Now, I've already washed and swept in there," said Margit, "so be sure to wipe your feet when you come inside, both of you."

The three of them unloaded the wagon, Emil and Gyula carrying the heavy furniture and Margit handling anything she deemed too fragile for male hands. There truly was little to unload. The Turkish carpet and the horsehair sofa with its matching chair went into the front parlor with the small mahogany table that would hold Emil's pipe stand and humidor. The iron bed frame and the unwieldy mattress were carried into the larger of the two bedrooms, followed by the bulky wardrobe, so heavy that even Margit had to help carry it inside. The kitchen table and its four chairs were placed in the center of the kitchen floor, which was covered with good quality linoleum. Emil's new Victrola and Margit's treadle-based sewing machine were the last pieces of furniture to be placed inside. They were followed by the crates and barrels that held china, glassware, and linens.

At Margit's insistence she personally unpacked everything, so Emil and Gyula went onto the front porch to smoke and talk. Emil's pipe was still packed away, so Gyula offered one of his cigars. Emil leaned against the porch rail and smiled as Gyula sat on the top step.

"Don't get too comfortable. She'll have us back in there to clean up the excelsior and remove the crates before you know it."

"Maybe we should go back in and help."

"No, no, no. A woman setting up her own kitchen is a formidable thing. Best to stay out of her way, believe me. Good cigar, by the way."

"Thank you. This is a nice looking street, Mr. Molnar," he said, nodding toward the slate sidewalk and the small maple trees that had been planted between the sidewalk and the dirt street.

"That it is, Gyula. But after all the hard work we did today, I think you should call me Emil. It's democratic. We're in America, after all."

"So we are." Gyula puffed on his cigar for a moment. "Do you ever get homesick, Emil?"

"Only in the springtime. I miss the apricot flowers, nothing else."

"Do you think you'll ever go back?"

"No." Now it was Emil's turn to be silent for a moment. "No, Gyula, there's nothing for me back there. Look how much I have now. Could I ever have had a home like this in Hungary?"

"None of us could. Are you planning on becoming a citizen, then?"

"What for?"

"I don't know. To vote, maybe."

"Again I ask, what for? What does it matter to me whether this Irishman or that Irishman runs the city?"

"Maybe a Hungarian will run the city some day."

"Not in my lifetime, Gyula. Maybe not in yours, either."

"Maybe in my son's lifetime, then."

"Your son? That's planning ahead, isn't it? You're not even married yet."

Gyula blushed. "I will be soon. The banns will be read for the first time tomorrow."

"My boy, congratulations. That's cause for pride, not for embarrassment."

Gyula blushed even more and looked down at his boots. "You see, Mr. M—Emil, we're going to have a baby."

"Ah."

"No one knows, of course, except you, now."

"No one shall hear from me, I promise you, not even Mrs. Molnar." Especially not Mrs. Molnar, he thought. Aloud, he said, "I'm glad you're doing the proper thing."

"Oh, but it's more than that, sir. I love her. She's a wonderful girl, and a good girl, it's just that, well, you know how it is, don't you?"

"Yes, I know how it is," Emil said gently.

"It was just the one time, I swear. And we'll be married just as soon as we can. No one will ever know, I hope."

"I'm curious why you have told me this, Gyula."

"Well, you see, I was hoping, if you don't have a tenant already, that you will consider renting your old apartment to us. Once we're married, of course."

"Ah yes, it wouldn't do to bring her to Kerekes-Neni's boarding house, would it?"

Gyula shook his head.

"But my old apartment doesn't even have indoor plumbing—yet. It would be much nicer to bring your bride to the upstairs apartment here."

"Oh, no, Mr. Molnar! I couldn't—this is much too fine. I couldn't afford such a place."

"Oho, so your boss is a skinflint who doesn't pay you enough to rent a decent apartment, is that it?"

"Certainly not, sir! I didn't mean—"

Emil laughed. "Gyula, Gyula, I was only teasing. Sit down, my boy. That's it. Tell me, who is your bride to be?"

Gyula took a deep breath. "Her name is Eva Kovacs and she works in the dress factory."

"All right. So you'll be married within the month, I take it?"

Gyula nodded.

"And you'll be a papa within a year. You're going to be a family man, Gyula, and a family man deserves a living wage and a good home for his family. So I tell you what. As a wedding present I'll raise your salary, and in exchange for a lower rent, you can be my maintenance man, both here and at the old place. I'm getting too old for carpentry, but you're young and strong and handy enough. What do you say?"

"You're very generous, sir."

"Then call me Emil and shake my hand on it. It's done, then. Good! Let's go tell Mrs. Molnar the upstairs is already rented."

Margit received the good news in the kitchen amid mounds of excelsior, with her arms full of platters and china. Glassware and linens were stacked all over the kitchen table and counter top.

"I just unpacked the last of it," she said after congratulating Gyula, "and as soon as you carry these empty crates out I can wash everything and put it all away."

"But you washed everything before you packed it," said Emil.

"And it's been inside of a dirty barrel. I'll not put dirty china in a clean cupboard."

Emil looked over at Gyula, whose expression clearly showed he was reevaluating the concept of domestic bliss. Grinning, Emil clapped Gyula on the back. "Come, Gyula, let's clear all this out and give Mrs. Molnar room to work. I'll give you a ride home."

"Come for dinner tomorrow, after church," said Margit. "Bring your young lady so we can meet her."

It was only a few minutes work to remove the empty crates and barrels and sweep stray bits of excelsior off the kitchen floor. Emil drove the wagon first to Gyula's boarding house, and then back to the livery stable. On the way home he stopped at Somogyi's tavern for a glass of beer and a plate of sausages cooked with sauerkraut and potatoes. He asked Somogyi to wrap up an extra serving so he could bring it home to Margit. When he got there she was nearly finished with the washing up, but he persuaded her to have some dinner first. He waited until she was finished to smoke his pipe, which Margit had located while he was gone, and over coffee she told him about the new neighbors who had visited. Margit was determined to be settled in before bedtime, so Emil helped her by drying dishes and putting them in the cupboards where she directed. One row of cupboards had glass doors, and in these Margit placed their fine china and few pieces of Austrian crystal. The cabinet frames were painted lemon yellow to match the kitchen walls, and smelled of fresh paint. Emil could understand why Margit wanted to wash everything before putting it away in these clean new cabinets. He had never lived in a brand new home before. Even the apartment they just left had been built more than fifty years before. He wondered how long it would take for the new house to feel like a home to them.

The next morning Emil found it strange to wake up in a familiar bed but in an unfamiliar setting. Sunlight streamed through the sheer curtains Margit had hung on the windows, lighting up the bare white walls. Soon, he knew, Margit would cover their plainness with wallpaper, and Emil hoped she would choose a flowered pattern, like the one in their old apartment. After ten years he had grown accustomed to seeing roses on the walls. Turning over, he found he had to reach out and touch the wall to bring it into focus.

He tried to get up without waking Margit, in hopes of letting her sleep late after all the work of moving, but the bells of St. Elizabeth's church woke her instead.

"What time is it?" she asked.

"Eight o'clock."

"Oh, goodness!" She threw the covers back and reached for her robe. "I must get up and get dinner ready so it can simmer while we are at church."

"Why not relax this morning? The next service isn't until ten."

"Have you forgotten that Gyula is coming? If I wait until after church we won't eat until supper time."

"Can I help?"

"Yes, by staying out of the way."

Emil did just that by filling the tub with hot water and settling in for a long soak. What a luxury to have a tub ready and waiting every day—no need to drag a washtub into the middle of the kitchen floor and fill it bucket by bucket from the kitchen sink. And what a perfect place to be while Margit flew about the kitchen, boiling cabbage and then stripping the cabbage leaves off the head to fill each one with meat and rice, rolling it into a neat bundle to be placed in a pot of sauerkraut and tomato broth. Emil slouched down until the water touched his chin and tried to ignore his growling stomach, which would not be filled until after Communion.

Even with Margit's cooking spree they managed to be on time for Mass, thanks to the conveniences of indoor plumbing and their new home's proximity to the church. After the service they met Gyula and his bride-to-be. She was a tiny woman, thought Emil, with sallow skin like many of the girls who worked in the factory, but her pallor made striking the darkness of her hair and eyes. Emil was pleased to see the pride in Gyula's face as he introduced her, and the tenderness with which he took her arm as they walked home. He was again pleased by her reaction to the new house, and by the way her eyes filled with tears when Gyula explained that the upstairs was to be theirs. The four of them walked up to see it. The high-ceilinged rooms looked large and empty. The end rooms would be full of sun in the morning and evening, but at midday the apartment was dim because of the closeness of its neighbors on either side. It would take a family to brighten it, thought Emil, and he envied them as they looked into the second bedroom, picturing a child's room in their minds.

Once downstairs Emil and Gyula retired to the parlor to smoke while Eva helped Margit in the kitchen. Suddenly they heard the sounds of someone being sick in the bathroom. Gyula stood up in alarm, but Margit came out and said, "Sit down, Gyula, your young lady has an upset stomach, that's all. She can lie down on our bed until dinner is ready."

When the kitchen table was set, Eva came in and sat down, looking paler than ever.

"Next time you come," said Emil, "we can eat in the dining room. Our new furniture won't arrive until later in the week."

"A dining room seems so fancy," she said in a quiet voice. "A kitchen feels more like home, don't you think?"

"Actually, I do," said Emil. "Maybe we'll save the dining room for Christmas and Easter, eh, Margit?"

"Sunday dinner, too, if we have guests," she said. "Company always makes dinner a special occasion."

Emil said grace with the fervor of a man with an empty stomach, and they began to eat, but Eva turned paler than ever and managed to eat only a slice of bread dipped in some broth. Emil was grateful that Margit seemed not to notice, especially when Gyula ate second and then third helpings. But right after they left Margit turned to Emil with her arms folded across her chest and said, "She's pregnant!"

Emil feigned surprise. "How can you say such a thing?"

"The smell of cooked cabbage doesn't make a healthy woman sick. She couldn't stand to be near food. You must have seen how little she ate."

"Maybe she did have an upset stomach."

"And the way Gyula treated her—as though she would break at the slightest touch. I tell you, she's pregnant. Why else would they be marrying so soon?"

"Well, you know how impatient young people are."

"Nonsense. When she has that baby, I won't be the only one in this neighborhood who knows about it. Everyone here can count, Emil."

"Well, and what if she is?"

"Living upstairs from us! I thought we left that sort of thing behind us in Hungary."

"Young people are young people regardless of what country they live in. And they're doing the honorable thing by getting married. What does it really matter if their firstborn arrives a few weeks early? Don't judge them too harshly, my dear. They're good people, and one mistake shouldn't change your opinion of them."

It was Eva herself who persuaded Margit to accept them, not by her words but by her manner. She asked Emil to give her away at the wedding, because she had no family in this country. Her father had died in the Hungarian coalmines two years before, and Eva had traveled to America alone as a steerage passenger. Even Margit was impressed by her courage in making the trip. Eva also asked Margit to bake the cake for their wedding reception, knowing instinctively that the surest way to loosen Margit's heart was to praise her cooking. But finally, her generous offer to help with the wallpapering turned Margit around. By the time of the wedding Eva's morning sickness had ended, leaving her with the seemingly boundless energy of the second trimester of pregnancy. Together, she and Margit papered both apartments. At Eva's insistence they did Margit and Emil's apartment first, and at Margit's insistence Eva did none of the ladder work. They found a pattern of yellow climbing roses for the two bedrooms, just as Emil had hoped, and one with peonies against a background of green latticework for the parlor. For the dining room Margit chose a plain paper in dark green to suit the formality of the room. Upstairs, Eva put a pattern of tan stripes and coral flowers in both the parlor and dining room, and a pale green paper patterned with ivy leaves in the bedroom. In the baby's room they put up yellow paper with tulips and cornflowers. They were done in time for the Christmas holidays.

Since they had no families in America, like most of the young Hungarian immigrants, both couples spent Christmas day together in Emil and Margit's apartment. Margit served goose and roasted potatoes, homemade noodles mixed with fried cabbage, and onions cooked with paprika and sour cream. Emil looked on this dinner with pride, and wondered how life could get any better.

Chapter Four
May 1915

Emil came home for lunch to find Margit sitting at the kitchen table in tears.

"My dearest, what has happened?" asked Emil.

"Papa—it's Papa!"

She handed him the letter, dated April 4. "My darling Margitka," Emil read. "May the blessings of our Lord be with you on this, the anniversary of His resurrection. I am so sorry to cast a shadow on your happiness in America, in your new home that sounds so lovely, but I must tell you the sad, sad news that my beloved Vendel, your Papa, had another stroke two days ago. This time, my sweet Margitka, it was our Lord calling him home, on the very same day that He Himself died for us. I try not to cry for your Papa, because he is at peace now, in heaven with God I am certain, but it is so hard to be without him! Laci has gone off to the war, and your sister and I are home with her girls and baby boy. It is a house full of women, now, with no man left to smoke a pipe in it.

"I want you to know, my dearest older child, that not a day went by without your Papa's kind words of you. You were in his thoughts and in his heart until the end.

"I know it will take a long time for this to reach you. I am glad of that, so this sad news cannot spoil your happy Easter. Give my love to the good man you married, and know that I am always, your loving Mama."

"Oh, my dear!" Emil said as he knelt next to Margit and took her in his arms. She sobbed against his shoulder so hard that his own eyes filled with tears. He thought bitterly of his complacency these last few months and realized how much he, too, would miss Margit's father now that he was forever out of reach. It had been difficult to say goodbye to Vendel, but Emil had always thought he'd see the old man one more time.

Emil lifted Margit gently off his shoulder and wiped her face with his own handkerchief.

"Oh, Emil! Never to see him again."

"I'm sorry we never brought them here."

"So am I. Emil, I should go to her."

"I know you should. I'll start making the arrangements this afternoon."

"Come with me?"

"You know I can't leave the paper. We'll talk to Monsignor Andrassy, and see if someone from the parish is going back for you to travel with. It's all right, Margit, we'll get you home to see your Mama."

"Let me get you some lunch, then. I'm sorry I don't have it ready. I haven't even cleared the breakfast dishes."

"Don't think of it, Margit. I don't expect you to clean house after getting news like that. I can get my own lunch, you know. I did it all the time before I married you."

Margit almost smiled. "No, let me get it. I need to have something to do."

"All right."

After lunch Emil made Margit lie down. "I'll get Eva. You shouldn't be alone right now."

"No, Emil, she's as big as a house. Let her rest upstairs."

"It won't hurt to ask. I'll just be a moment."

Emil bounded up the stairs and knocked on the door. Eva's footsteps were heavy but her smile was radiant.

"Mr. Molnar! How nice to see you at this time of day. Come in."

"No thank you, Eva. I just came to ask if you would be able to come downstairs until I get back home. Margit has just received word that her father has passed away, and I must get back to the office for a short while."

"Oh, Mr. Molnar, what sad news. Of course I'll come down."

He held her arm as they went down the stairs. Her gait was awkward with the child sticking out in front of her like the prow of a ship, but they made it down safely. When he left Eva was sitting on the bed with Margit, holding her hand.

Emil stopped by the office only long enough to tell Gyula what had happened. Gyula, who always ate his lunch at the office in case important news broke, shook his head when Emil explained that he had to book passage for Margit to return home.

"Emil, you know how difficult it is to travel abroad these days. It could be weeks before Margit can leave the country, and months before she can come back."

"I know, but it means so much to her I have to try. I'll be at Fehervar's Travel Agency, and then at home with Margit if you need me."

Gabor Fehervar was equally pessimistic when Emil explained what he needed.

"Well, Molnar, I'll see what we can do, but it's not a good time to be traveling, especially to a country that's at war. The British are blockading the Germans, as you know, and no German passenger liners have been to the port of New York since last August."

"I know, I know, just do your best, my friend. That's all I can ask."

"Hmm. The best we can do may be to get Mrs. Molnar on a neutral ship to a neutral port. We could try the Norwegian American line to Bergen, though it's risky with the North Atlantic full of U-boats."

"You don't think a U-boat would attack a Norwegian passenger ship, do you? Norway is a neutral country."

"It's unthinkable, of course, but still, wasn't an American merchant ship torpedoed just the other day? And America is a neutral country."

"A merchantman is far different from a passenger liner."

"True, but I wouldn't want my wife to be traveling to northern Europe right now. Perhaps we should consider a Greek port of arrival. Either way, Mrs. Molnar will have to travel a good distance over land, and that has its own hazards. Her journey could take months to complete."

"And what about her return?"

"Realistically? She could be stuck over there for the duration."

Emil sighed, then he stood up. "Well, Fehervar, do what you can."

"What I can or what I should? If I were you I'd talk Mrs. Molnar out of this trip altogether. Oh, well. Stop by in a day or two and I'll let you know what progress I've made."

The next morning Emil left for work early, without waiting for Gyula, hoping to gather the morning's war news quickly enough to stop at the travel agency on the way home. The *Hirlap* office was in a corner building in the Hungarian business section on Hardenbergh Avenue, next to the ice company. The front office was small, containing only Emil's desk, a coat rack, and three wooden chairs. Behind the front office was a larger room that held a table where the men could eat lunch, or Emil could spread out page proofs. Here, too, was Emil's pride and joy: the teletypewriter he had leased since the war broke out. With it Emil had access to the wire service reports cabled from Europe, just like the large New York dailies. Next to the teletypewriter a door led to a small washroom, and on the opposite wall another door led to the pressroom, with its Linotype machine and small press that produced 1,200 copies of Emil's weekly newspaper every Wednesday.

Emil hung his hat and jacket on the coat rack and headed straight for the teletypewriter to tear off the most important types of news: the latest dispatches about the European war and the baseball scores of the Giants, the Yankees, and the Dodgers. Normally, the paper hung halfway down the machine, with two or three terse reports; on a big news day, it reached the floor. This morning, Emil was amazed to see the paper not only on the floor, but doubled back and forth on top of itself like a ribbon of hard candy. He quickly tore off the sheet and began reading the last and latest dispatch.

" 'Official confirmation: less than 700 survivors of Lusitania'."

Emil pulled the paper through his hands to see the earlier dispatches.

" 'Agents of Cunard Line confirm Lusitania torpedoed by U-boat at 2:30 p.m. May 7 off Irish coast. Initial reports that all survived now known false. About 1200 passengers and crew went down with ship. Few first class passengers survive. Americans on board totaled 188. Vanderbilt missing'."

Emil was so engrossed in his reading that he didn't notice Gyula had entered until the young man called his name.

"Gyula! You're here—good. Didn't you see these dispatches yesterday?"

Gyula took a look at the earliest one. "Well, yes, we got the first one in just before we closed up for the day. But the dispatch said that everyone survived. That's not news, so I didn't think to get you."

"Take a look at the later ones."

Gyula whistled as he read the updated dispatches. "My God, how awful. But see, they didn't get here until after 10:00 p.m. We were all home and tucked in our beds by that time."

"Well, we're not in bed now. Get the others. We're going to print a special edition."

"You want me to get everyone?"

"No, no need—just get Bela. The three of us will be enough. Hurry!"

"Can you telephone the house to tell Eva and Mrs. Molnar we'll be late?"

"Good idea."

50

Emil thanked providence that he'd had a telephone installed here in the office and in their house. Although he rarely used it for business, preferring to meet with people face to face, Emil had subscribed to the telephone service for just such occasions. Once he was connected to Margit, he explained only that the ship had been sunk and he and Gyula would be delayed while they put together the special edition. Margit could hear in his voice that he was torn between his duty to his readers and his duty to her.

"Don't worry about me, Emil," she said. "I will be all right. Monsignor Andrassy will be coming over this afternoon. He telephoned just before you did."

Relieved, Emil sorted through the dispatches and began to compose the story. When Gyula came back with Bela he helped the older man get the press ready, then sat down at the Linotype machine. Soon the office was filled with the clatter of lead being transformed into lines of type. As Emil wrote each page of the story he handed it to Gyula. Gyula set the news into type, and Bela took the slugs of type and set them into a steel frame with metal blocks and wedges to hold them in place. Then Bela set the completed frame in the press and ran off a proof sheet for Emil to inspect. When Emil was satisfied with the quality, Bela printed the full run of pages.

Normally, Bela's assistant handled the cutting and bundling process, and another young man would take care of delivery. Today, Emil stood in as Bela's assistant as soon as he was finished writing. The three of them would hand deliver all the papers. By mid-afternoon they had produced 1,000 copies of the Lusitania story in a four-page special edition of the *Hirlap,* and hurried to get them delivered to their subscribers and the local stores before closing time.

Emil arrived home tired, with ink stains on his shirt.

"Emil, at last. I thought you'd be home before this. Did you manage all right?" asked Margit.

"Yes. Here's the special edition. I'm going to take a bath."

Wearily, Emil started the bath water running and took off his dirty clothes. He sank into the warm water with relief, but as the water reached his chin he thought of the cold waters of the north Atlantic and sat up again. Now that he was home, not a newspaperman anymore, just a man, he began to think of all the lives lost at sea barely one day before. What had he been doing for the past eight hours? He had been so concerned about getting the news out, about page proofs and deliveries, that he scarcely read the words he himself had written. Now he couldn't get them out of his mind. He thought of the passengers having lunch—such a simple thing, people do it every day—then two explosions, the great liner listing to starboard, lifeboats useless on the port side, and in less than half an hour, most of the passengers and crew were dead. What good were Vanderbilt's millions now? Yet how could Emil care about the fate of one man, when over twelve hundred men, women, and children were now drowned?

It could have been Margit, he thought as he scrubbed the ink off his hands and arms. It could have been Margit. He dropped the soap and washcloth and brought his fists up to his eyes to stop the tears. More than twelve hundred dead. And one of them could have been Margit.

He stood up and reached for his robe. Still dripping, he opened the bathroom door and walked into the parlor, where Margit stood next to the window, reading his words. She only had time to say "Oh, Emil, how horrible" before he wrapped his arms around her and clung to her. "Don't go, Margit, please don't go," he sobbed. "I am so sorry for your Papa, and for your Mama, and I know your heart must be breaking, but please don't go. Don't leave me. Don't leave me, Margit. Don't go."

"Emil—"

"No!" he interrupted. "It could have been you, don't you see that? First they strike at merchant ships, now the Lusitania, who knows what they will sink next? Innocent people are not safe from them, Margit. How can I see you off on a ship, when I might never see you again? I can't do it. I can't do it! Please don't make me say goodbye. Please wait. After the war we'll go together, I promise, but please, please don't leave me now. You may never come back!"

"Shh, Emil. Shh. I'll stay. I promise I'll stay." And she held him and comforted him, and he never knew that in her heart she cursed the day she had ever asked him to leave Hungary.

It was a solemn congregation that attended church the next morning. During his sermon Monsignor Andrassy railed against the German navy for attacking an unprotected passenger ship without warning, and against the Americans and British, for according to rumors the ship carried not only passengers but also munitions and gold for the British war effort. After his sermon, the priest announced Margit's loss to the parish and told them that he would say a Requiem Mass for her father the next morning. After church the parishioners stood in small groups, talking about the tragedies, but for them the sinking of the Lusitania was a faraway event. No relatives had been killed on the ship, but Margit's loss, underscored by her pallor and black dress, hit home. That afternoon a steady stream of visitors stopped by to pay their respects, even their old neighbor, Anna Puskasz, with whom Margit had quarreled for ten years. Emil wasn't sure whether Anna was being charitable or hypocritical, but he thanked her for coming anyway.

The next morning Margit, Emil, Gyula, Eva, and a number of their present and former neighbors attended the sorrowful Mass. Monsignor Andrassy wore the black chasuble of mourning and intoned the prayers for the dead first in Latin and then in Hungarian. Margit sat trembling next to Emil, who held her hand and wished the Mass would end. The church was warm and the air so thick with incense Emil was afraid Margit might faint, but she sat upright until the end. It seemed odd afterwards to have no casket to carry out of the church, no procession to the cemetery or graveside ceremony. There was nothing to do after the Mass but go home, and that seemed anticlimactic. The monsignor and Father Borsy accompanied the two couples back to their house, where they drank tea and ate slices of cake made by Eva that morning.

After the priests left, Margit turned to Emil and said, "Why don't you and Gyula go to work now? There's nothing for you to do here, and you have the next edition to get ready."

"Well, there's no reason for Gyula to stay," said Emil.

"Nonsense, there's no reason for you to stay either," said Margit. "What are you going to do all afternoon, sit here and watch me embroider? Eva and I can keep each other company. Go on."

The two men went to work with relief. It was good to have a routine to bury oneself in, and with the weekly deadline approaching Emil soon was engrossed in his work. With the hubbub of the past few days, his mail had piled up, and he sorted through the letters to see which required immediate response, which contained payments, and which contained new orders for advertisements. All those he stacked on top of his desk; the bills he put in the "to do" box, to be paid at the end of the month. He had been working for hours, although it seemed to Emil that he had just gotten started, when the telephone rang.

"Emil, it's me, Margit."

"Margit! What's wrong?"

"Nothing is wrong, exactly, but you'd better tell Gyula to get home right away. The baby is coming."

"The baby? Now?"

"Mother Nature follows her own schedule, Emil Molnar, not yours. Tell Gyula to stop by the midwife's house. Eva doesn't want me to leave her alone here."

"Of course not. Tell Eva that Gyula is on his way."

Emil had replaced the receiver almost before he said goodbye. "Gyula!" he shouted, before he realized that Gyula couldn't hear him over the clatter of the Linotype. He walked into the pressroom, put a hand on Gyula's shoulder, and smiled. "Gyula, you have an important errand to run. Go get Toth-neni and bring her to your house. You're about to become a papa."

Gyula's face turned pale. "Now?"

"Right now. Go, man. I'll take over here."

Gyula stood up, handed his apron to Emil, and hurried out the door. Emil watched him go, then rolled up his sleeves and sat down to work, trying hard to not feel envious of his young typesetter.

When Emil got home that evening Gyula was on the front porch, pacing.

"I thought you would be upstairs with Eva," said Emil with surprise.

"They threw me out."

"Whatever for?"

"God, Emil, it's awful. She's in such pain. It comes and goes, and while it's gone she's fine, but then the pain hits her and—I had no idea it was like that, Emil. They say it's going to be hours. How can she stand any more?"

"She can because she must."

"Never again! I swear, we'll never have another child. I won't do this to her again."

"Hush, Gyula, don't speak that way. You'll feel differently when this is over."

Gyula rubbed his hand across his eyes. "I'll be damned glad when this is over, I can tell you that."

"How long have you been out here?"

"I don't know. Over an hour, I suppose."

"Why don't I find out how things are going?"

"Yes, thanks. I—I can't go up there right now."

Emil patted Gyula on the shoulder and walked upstairs. Margit opened the door when he knocked. He was startled to see that she looked the same as she did every evening when he got home: neatly dressed in a clean shirtwaist and dark skirt, her face calm, not a hair out of place. Somehow he expected dishevelment, some hustle-and-bustle, if not outright chaos.

"Margit! Is everything all right?"

"Of course it is. I'll come downstairs and fix you dinner."

"No, no, you should stay here."

"Nothing's happening yet. All I'm doing is holding Eva's hand."

"Oh! Is that all?"

"What do you expect? She's still in the early stages. We've a long night ahead of us."

"Then I'd better see to Gyula. He's pacing back and forth like a caged animal."

Margit nodded. "We had to make him leave. He was making Eva nervous."

"Why don't I take him for a walk? We can get a bite to eat in town, and you can stay here with Eva."

"That sounds like a good idea, if you can get him to eat anything."

Emil heard a sharp cry coming from the bedroom.

"I'd better get back in there," said Margit.

Emil kissed her goodbye and went downstairs, where Gyula was still pacing. He stopped as Emil came out the door.

"Well?"

"Calm down, Gyula. Margit tells me there's a long way to go. Come on."

"Where?"

"For a walk."

"No, I need to stay here."

"There's nothing you can do here, Gyula, and if you keep pacing you'll wear the boards right off the porch. Come on. A walk will do us both good."

He walked down the steps and Gyula had no choice but to follow. It was a fine evening for a walk. The sky was still light and the air smelled like fresh-cut grass. On an evening like this Emil preferred to walk south, to the farmland that began at the edge of town. Not more than half a mile away Emil could find himself on a narrow dirt road, looking at a pasture full of dairy cows. He liked to lean on the fence until a curious one came over, and to scratch its head and fuzzy ears, but tonight he thought Gyula needed distraction, not contemplation, and so Emil turned north, toward the center of town.

They walked along the main street of Hardenbergh, where trolley tracks ran all the way down to the river. Before getting to the business district Emil turned west to walk past the Van Dyke building. He thought it strange that such a big factory could be built just to make perfumes and cold cream, powders and lotions. And yet Van Dyke was not the largest factory in town. The bronze works was bigger, as was the cigar factory, which employed half the young Hungarian women of the town. The other half worked, as Eva had, at the Hardenbergh Clothing Factory, which everyone called simply the dress factory, although they also made shirts, coats, and trousers that were sold in the big department stores in New York and Newark.

Emil led Gyula past the Van Dyke building to the river, where they turned east, past the steamboat dock, and then south until they came to the heart of downtown. Here, although the stores had closed for the night, couples strolled by window shopping, and the restaurants and bars did a brisk business. Emil suggested stopping once or twice, but this was not a part of town that Gyula came to often, and he preferred to go back to the Hungarian district. He did not speak English as well as Emil, and felt uncomfortable at the idea of dining among the Irish, Dutch, and Germans who had settled in Hardenbergh nearly two hundred years before the first Hungarians came here.

Emil admitted to himself that he, too, preferred the Hungarian district, where even at this time of the evening the scent of pork goulash lingered in the air, the sound of gypsy violin music sang out from a Victrola, and families sat on their front porches, conversing in Magyar and calling "Jó, Estét" to passersby. Emil had a writer's interest in language, and could find beauty even in the guttural sounds of German, or the high-speed American twang of a comedian on stage at the opera house, but he loved most the sounds of his own language, its trilled R and soft vowels, its familiar rhythms made for poetry and folk songs.

Their slow progress up the street, as they returned the greeting of their neighbors, made Gyula restive, so Emil turned into Somogyi's tavern at the corner. "Come in, Gyula, perhaps a glass of beer will calm your nerves."

Gyula grimaced but followed. Inside was no better than outside. Emil knew everyone in the Hungarian neighborhood, and between greetings and offers of beer he took half an hour just to make his way to an empty table. When he explained their situation, the married men clapped Gyula on the shoulder and bought him a pitcher of beer.

"Well, maybe just one glass," Gyula said, to the approval of the rest of them. Emil ordered a platter of sausages and ate well, although Gyula could swallow only one sausage. After he was finished with his dinner, Emil sat back and lit his pipe, intending to get Gyula home within the hour, but Gyula was toasted by one man and then another, and Emil to be polite had to drink as well. He had refilled his pipe twice before he thought to look at his watch. With horror, he saw that it was after midnight. Emil lifted his head to look for Gyula but moved too quickly, making the room spin. When the spinning slowed he saw Gyula slumped back in his chair, eyes open but not fully conscious.

"Gyula, Gyula, Gyula, we've got to get home."

"Mm?"

"Gyula, get up, man, we've got to get back to your pretty wife and your new baby."

"Mm? Baby? Mm."

Emil managed to stand up and motioned for Laszlo Varga to help him with Gyula. Together they lifted the young man and staggered toward the door. Once outside, the cool night air revived Emil somewhat and he waved Laszlo away. Slowly, with Gyula's limp arm around his shoulders, Emil steered an unsteady course for home.

Despite one wrong turn they arrived in a few minutes. Emil's apartment was dark but lights blazed upstairs. Emil left Gyula sitting on the top step of the porch and tiptoed up the stairs. He was halfway up when he heard a scream. He stumbled the rest of the way up as fast as he could and opened the door, leaning on the doorknob with one hand and grasping the doorjamb with the other. He saw Margit hurry past with an armful of towels. Her shirtwaist was half out of her waistband and her hair was falling around her neck and shoulders. She saw him out of the corner of her eye and hissed, "Not now, Emil. We'll let you know," as she passed by.

Emil stared at the empty kitchen for a moment before closing the door.

He hung on to the banister with both hands as he went down the stairs.

"They didn't even notice we were gone," he murmured to himself. "Didn't even notice." He began to giggle when he reached the front door.

"Gyula, wait till you hear this," he started to say, but Gyula was snoring, passed out against the porch railing with his head sagged to one side. Emil didn't think he looked very comfortable but knew he didn't have the strength to move him. Still giggling, he turned and walked into his own flat. It was all very well for a young man like Gyula to sleep on the porch steps; Emil intended to lose consciousness in his own bed, but when he saw the couch he realized he couldn't take another step, and on the cushions he fell.

Emil's sleep was deep and dreamless until the earthquake struck. The shaking of the couch must have knocked a lamp onto his head to make it hurt so much. The quake continued until he opened his eyes.

"At last," Margit said. Emil's eyes closed again and she gave his shoulder another hard shake.

"Emil Molnar, wake up this instant! Where is Gyula?"

"Mm? Gyula?" he asked. "Hello, my love." He reached a hand toward her breast.

Margit leaned back in disgust. "You're drunk! How much beer did you have last night? I asked you to take Gyula for a walk, not to bathe in beer. Where is he?"

Emil sat up, wincing, and rubbed his neck. "Um, last I saw he was on the porch."

"On the porch! Passed out like a common drunk, no doubt, for all the neighbors to see. Oh, Emil! How could you?"

Margit strode out to the porch. Gyula was still there, but during the night he had slid down to the bottom step, his left arm and leg sprawled on the sidewalk. Margit went back inside, and returned a moment later with a bucket of cold water. She carried it halfway down the stairs, and then dumped it on Gyula's head.

"Ow!" he bellowed. "What the—"

"Gyula Farkas, be quiet or all the neighbors will hear!" Margit whispered. "Get upstairs right this instant. Rinse your mouth and comb your hair. It's time you met your son."

That got through. Gyula stood up, groaning, and staggered up the steps. He almost bumped into Emil, who was finally awake enough to realize what must have happened upstairs.

"A son! A son!" Gyula said.

"Congratulations, Gyula. I'm very happy for you."

"A son," Gyula repeated, and walked upstairs.

Emil looked at Margit sheepishly. "Do you have a bucket of that ready for me?"

"No, I didn't want to get our couch wet. You look awful. And smell worse."

"You look exhausted."

She shrugged. "Eva did all the hard work."

"Last night, I heard her scream."

"It was a difficult birth. He's a big boy."

"A son."

He had tried to keep the longing out of his voice, but he was too tired and still half drunk. From the way Margit stiffened he knew he had not.

They stood awkwardly for a moment, then Emil said quietly, "I suppose I had better take a bath."

"Yes, you had. After all, you have a newspaper to give birth to."

"Oh, sweet mother of God, it's Tuesday." Emil turned toward the house with Margit's ironic words pounding in his head.

Chapter Five:
November 1916

Margit threaded another strand of red silk into her needle while Emil bounced little Ferenc on his leg. Ferenc giggled until he began to cough.

"Uh-oh," said Emil. He pulled the boy onto his lap and patted him on the back.

"I told you not to bounce him so high."

"Oh, he just swallowed wrong. He's all right. Aren't you, my boy? Give your Uncle Emil a big hug."

Ferenc wrapped his fat little arms around Emil's neck and settled against his chest.

"If you keep him quiet now he'll go to sleep at last," said Margit.

She and Emil were babysitting while Gyula and Eva went to the moving picture show at the Bijou. Since the baby came they rarely had the opportunity to go out, and Emil never turned down the chance to have Ferenc to himself for a few hours. Margit watched Emil as he held the baby, humming softly to put him to sleep. He would have made a wonderful father, she thought, and sighed. Although they had tried since they were first married, Margit appeared to be infertile, unlike her sister in Hungary, who at last count had had five children, one of which died in infancy, as well as two miscarriages. No doubt the war had prevented her family from being even larger. It seemed Piros had everything.

Margit knew that although Emil felt deep sorrow at being childless, he never once blamed her for it. How could he know that just seeing how happy he was with Ferenc was enough to make her feel like a failure?

Margit took a deep breath to quell the self-reproach she felt. If she was upset her stitches would be uneven, and she would have to rip them all out later. The vest she was working on was for Ferenc. Eva had sewn it and Margit was adding the embroidery. When it was done, Ferenc would have a miniature vest just like his Papa's. Margit planned to have it finished for Christmas.

The baby had been sleeping in Emil's arms for a few minutes when Eva and Gyula came back. They took their coats off and rubbed their hands before picking up the baby and kissing him.

"It must be getting cold out," said Emil.

"Frosty!" said Gyula. "The coldest day of the season, so far."

"How was the moving picture?" asked Margit.

"Wonderful!" said Eva. "Charlie Chaplin is so funny. You should see it."

She turned her attention to Ferenc. "How is Mama's little boy?" she asked as she took him from Emil.

"Mama-ma-ma-ma" he said, smiling. He wiggled and pulled at her shirt front.

"Hungry, are you? Well, let's go upstairs, okay?" She smiled at Emil and Margit. "Thanks for watching him. I'll see you later."

She walked upstairs to nurse the baby in privacy. Margit thought to herself that at eighteen months it was high time to wean the boy. Only peasants, in her opinion, nursed children beyond the first year. But Eva, although slight in build, had remarkably productive breasts, and seemed reluctant to stop feeding her son while the milk still flowed.

Emil offered Gyula a glass of Tokay, and the two men chatted quietly while Margit continued to embroider. When they heard Eva's footsteps upstairs, Gyula stood up to join her.

"Oh, I almost forgot," he said. "On the way home we ran into Janos Horvath. The postman had delivered a letter of yours to him by mistake. Janos was going to come over himself, but when he saw us he asked us to bring it for him. I don't think he's very fond of cold weather." He took the letter out of his coat pocket and handed it to Margit.

"Thank you, Gyula. Have a good night."

He said goodnight and went upstairs. Emil walked him to the door and then poked his head outside before locking up for the night.

"They're quite right," he said when he came back in. "This is the coldest night we've had all month. Is that from your mama?"

"Yes," said Margit, glancing at the return address. "Look at the post mark. This letter was written two months ago. That awful war gets in the way of everything. I write Mama every week, but she gets only a few of my letters. And her letters take so long to reach us. How long can it go on?"

Emil shook his head as he sat down. "Ow! What's that?" He reached under his leg and pulled up a wooden block with the letter C and a picture of a crow painted on it. "I'd forgotten about this. I'll take it upstairs."

Margit nodded as she opened the letter, eager for news from home. "My dearest Margitka," she read. "May the blessings of our Lord be with you and your dear husband. Every day I pray for you, that you will continue to prosper in America. How much I miss you, my child, but even so, I am glad that you are not here. Far away you may be, but at least I know for sure that you are safe, and that you have plenty to eat. A good harvest will help us here, thank the Lord, but I still dread the coming of winter. Everyone speaks of hard times to come—as if they are not hard enough already. Still, we must count our blessings while we can.

"Little Zsuzsi and Jolan are growing into real young ladies, and are a big help to their Mama and their old Grandmama. Little Deszo takes very seriously his role as the man of the house. He chops firewood and tends the cow and on fine days he leans against the doorjamb just as his Grandpapa once did. Your sister is well, now that she is fully recovered from having the baby, but he is colicky and keeps us all from getting as much sleep as we would like. It is the war, I am certain; the three older children were never so fussy.

"And so, that is the catalog of your family in Barackfalu, save one. I am reluctant to tell you this, but two weeks ago we received a letter from Laci's commanding officer, telling us that Laci was killed at Florina—"

Margit let the letter fall to her lap. She felt as though she were splitting in two. One of her floated somewhere behind her right shoulder, watching the other grip the arms of the chair as the room spun about her. Laci was dead!

Margit swallowed hard against a surge of nausea as her vision went gray. From far away she could hear Emil's concerned voice; her other self watched as he picked up the letter and skimmed through it. Her other self watched his face change and saw him reach for her but she couldn't feel the pressure of his hands on her arms. When he lifted her up she thought she would continue to rise, to float through the ceiling and the upstairs apartment, past the attic and through the roof into the cold, clear night, but Emil's strong arms guided her to their bed, sat her down, took off her shirt and skirt and shoes, and tucked her in. From far away she heard sobbing that continued even after the lights went out, but the darkness could not take away from her sight the words "Laci was killed...was killed...was killed."

Emil brought in a chair from the dining room and sat down heavily in it. He watched her by the light from the street lamps that filtered through the curtains. When, in the coldest, darkest hours of the night, he was sure that she had finally cried herself to sleep, he stood up, arched his aching back, and walked quietly out of the room.

The letter from Margit's mother was in Emil's vest pocket. He turned on the table lamp in the parlor, and sat down to read the whole thing again, slowly.

"...Laci was killed at Florina last month. His commander said that Laci didn't die in battle, but he was no less a hero of war. On the morning after the battle his horse stepped on a land mine. The explosion killed the poor horse, and Laci was thrown off and run over by a heavily loaded supply wagon. They say he died instantly. I know it was God's will for this to happen, but it is hard for me to understand why strong young men must die instead of useless old women like me.

"My dear, I know this news will sadden you; it has broken Piros's heart. It is my hope that now you will be able to send a word of comfort to your poor widowed sister, left alone to care for her aged mother and four children. Margit, it is time to forgive.

"Be well, my darling daughter. As always, to you and Emil, I remain, your loving Mama."

Emil leaned back in the chair and rubbed his eyes. So, that's over, he thought. His old rival was gone forever. Not that he wasn't sorry about Laci's death; any death was bad, especially such a senseless one as that. But now that Laci was finally, truly gone, Margit would be able to let him go. At least he hoped so. The depth of Margit's grief had stunned him. For hours she had sobbed. Any time Emil tried to comfort her, she pulled away from him, refusing to let him hold her, or even lay a comforting hand on her shoulder. Until she fell asleep, he sat with her, not five feet away, yet they could not have been further apart. Emil sighed and turned off the lamp. It will be better in the morning, he thought. Morning can lighten any sorrow and dispel any ghost, even Laci's.

When the bells of St. Elizabeth's pealed their call to morning Mass, Emil awoke, with a stiff neck, in the same chair. The only sound in the apartment was the comforting hiss of the radiators. Slowly, he stood and walked into the bedroom. Margit lay there, not moving, her eyes open but still red and puffy from the night's tears.

"Margit?" he asked. She didn't answer. "Margit? It's morning. Time to get ready for church."

She lay still.

"Aren't you going to church this morning?"

She closed her eyes. Someone knocked on the kitchen door.

Emil walked into the kitchen and opened the door. Gyula, Eva, and the baby were in the hall, their coats on, ready for church.

"Emil!" said Gyula. "Aren't you going to church this morning? Are you all right? You look as though you haven't slept all night."

"I haven't slept—not much, anyway. We received bad news in that letter you brought us. Margit's brother-in-law was killed in the war."

Eva shook her head and hugged little Ferenc closer to her.

"Tell the Monsignor we won't be coming today. Margit is too upset to leave the house, and I can't leave her alone when she's like this."

"But you can't miss Mass," said Eva. "Besides, she'll find more comfort in God's house than in her own."

"I know, but really, this morning it's impossible. Please go on without us."

He shut the door and put up a pot of coffee, then washed up while it percolated. If not for Margit, Emil would have been whistling in the comfort of the warm apartment, now filled with the aroma of fresh coffee. He made a pan of scrambled eggs and bacon, buttered fresh bread, and carried the works into the bedroom on a tray, but Margit would not be enticed to sit up. Reluctantly, Emil took the tray into the kitchen and ate some of the eggs and bread, but the food tasted flat to him and he put most of it in the icebox. He went into the parlor, lit his pipe, and sat down to wait.

Eventually, nature was able to do what Emil could not, and when Margit got up to use the toilet he went into the bedroom to make the bed. When Margit came out of the bathroom, Emil was holding a dress.

"Here, I'll help you put this on," he said. Margit's eyes brimmed over with tears.

"What for?" she asked.

"Because you can't stay in bed all day, and you can't walk around the house in your underwear."

"I'm not going to walk around the house."

"Then you'll sit in the parlor with me, but you'll be dressed."

"Not that one. I want the black one."

Emil looked at Margit for a long moment, then put down the dress he had been holding, opened the wardrobe, and pulled out the severe black dress Margit had worn after her father's death. She stood like a child as Emil draped the dress over her head. He put her arms through the sleeves and buttoned the back. He felt her shrink from his touch as he smoothed the material over her shoulders. He unpinned and brushed her hair, then clumsily put it back up again.

"I'm much better at taking it down," he tried to joke, but Margit didn't react. He led her to the parlor, and guided her into a chair. He placed her embroidery basket at her feet, and set a cup of coffee on the table next to her, but she didn't touch either. She simply sat.

Emil made a great show of reading a book and smoking his pipe as though it were a typical Sunday, but he couldn't concentrate on the words and clamped his pipe so hard in his teeth that his jaw began to ache. In a little while he heard Gyula and Eva return, and was relieved when they continued up the stairs without stopping. A short time later the front doorbell rang.

Emil was surprised to see Monsignor Andrassy standing on the porch.

"Monsignor! Come in. Let me take your coat and hat."

"Thank you, my son. I understand you and your wife have suffered a loss."

"Yes, Monsignor. My wife's brother-in-law."

"The loss of a relative is always sorrowful, but the knowledge that he is with God is comforting, as is celebrating His Mass."

"I know, Monsignor, but Margit was feeling quite ill this morning, and I felt compelled to stay with her."

"May I see her, or are we going to chat here in the front hall?"

"I'm sorry, Monsignor, please come in."

Emil held open the door for Andrassy to precede him. The old man entered the parlor with his usual imperious gait, but his manner softened as he saw the distress on Margit's face.

"My child, I bring you the blessings of our Lord Jesus Christ."

Margit looked up slowly. "I don't think our Lord has any blessings left for me, Father."

"You mustn't say that, child. Every death has a purpose; whether we know that purpose or not doesn't matter. And though sorrow is natural and understandable, we must also rejoice that another soul has gone to join the Lord."

"I cannot rejoice that the Lord has stolen Laci from me a second time."

Andrassy raised an eyebrow and looked quizzically at Emil. "Laci once courted my wife," he said in a matter-of-fact tone. "Before Margit and I were betrothed."

"Oh?" said Andrassy. He looked back at Margit but spoke to Emil.

"Perhaps, my son, you would give us a few moments alone?"

"Of course."

Emil picked up his pipe and walked into the kitchen. He refilled the pipe with tobacco from a jar on the kitchen counter and lit it before putting on his overcoat and stepping outside. The cool air was like a tonic on his face. The sun shone brightly but none of its warmth penetrated to heat the earth. Emil walked out into the garden, where the night's hard frost had blackened the last of his mums. Emil enjoyed gardening almost as much as Margit's mother did, but the newspaper left him little time to tend delicate flowers, so he set in the ground only hardy plants that could withstand his erratic care. In the spring the yard was full of white and purple violets, daffodils, and lily-of-the-valley. A few lilacs and forsythia, just twigs at this time of year, softened the border of their plot of land. In summer, what yard wasn't taken up by pepper and tomato plants was allowed to go half-wild with cosmos and nicotiana. Two rose bushes were the only truly fussy inhabitants, planted because Emil couldn't imagine a garden without at least a few roses. Today they slept under burlap covers.

Normally, Emil would have enjoyed the autumn browns and faded greens of his yard, but today it looked dreary and colorless, even in the sun. He knelt down and tore the dead mums from the frozen ground while he wondered what Margit was saying. If Andrassy could get Margit to talk to him, she would tell him things from the depth of her sorrow, things she would never say to Emil, and that Andrassy, as her confessor, could never reveal to him. How strange that Andrassy could have a piece of Margit's heart that he, her own husband, would never have. We should be each other's confessors, he thought, and not have to confide in that old man, even though he is our priest and our friend.

Emil took a deep breath and sighed a white cloud of vapor. Maybe I just don't like admitting that he can help her with this more than I can.

The back door opened and Andrassy strode out. Emil stood up and waited for him.

"Margit has made her confession," Andrassy said, "and she promises to be at Mass next Sunday."

"That's good," said Emil.

"And you, my son, is there anything you would like to talk about?"

"Tell me what to do, Father."

"Give her time."

"It's been twelve years."

"And have you known, these twelve years, how she felt about him?"

"Yes, but I thought—I hoped that after all this time she had let him go. I never thought she loved me, not the way I love her, but she promised to be a good wife, and she has never broken that promise, until now."

"Emil, she has kept his memory alive all these years. And what exactly she has felt for him is between her and God. Now, quite suddenly, she must let him go for good. It won't be easy for her, and you have a difficult time ahead of you. But I have no doubt, that with your love, she will once again be your good wife, and perhaps even more than in the past. But you must be patient, my son. She needs your help to get over this—infatuation."

"In twelve years I haven't been able to help her get over it, Monsignor. What makes you think I can help her now?"

"You must have faith, Emil, in God and in yourself."

"What if that's not enough?"

Andrassy smiled. "Faith is always enough, my son."

He clapped Emil on the shoulder and walked out of the garden. Emil stood there, watching him go, then he turned reluctantly for the house. In the parlor, Margit sat where he had left her, her hands clasped and trembling, her eyes staring blankly ahead of her. Emil leaned over and gave her a kiss on top of her head. She didn't look up. He sat down, and picked up his book again, but stared at the pages without seeing them.

All week Emil went to work with a heavy heart. He hated leaving Margit home alone. Eva had her hands full with Ferenc and could only sit with Margit while the baby napped. Emil came home for lunch each day to find Margit sitting in the parlor, if he had been able to coax her out of bed that morning, or still under the covers, if he had not. He made the two of them lunch but Margit ate little. He went back to work in the afternoon but came home early, leaving Gyula to finish up the day's work. And the weeks went by. Margit grew thin and pale. She slept much of the day and spent the night sitting in the parlor, or standing at the window, staring into the night. Emil, who had always been a heavy sleeper, found himself waking when she left the bed at night. When he fell back to sleep, he sometimes woke unexpectedly, and would lie in the dark, listening for Margit's movements.

Christmas was strained that year. Emil bought Margit a music box, but she had nothing to give him in return. He had shopped by himself for presents for Gyula, Eva, and Ferenc, whose little vest was finished by Eva, even though her embroidery wasn't as fine as Margit's. Eva cooked and the five of them had a quiet dinner. Ferenc made the dinner easier, distracting the others from Margit's disquieting passivity.

Andrassy took to visiting weekly. Margit kept her promise to him and went to Mass with Emil every Sunday, but she couldn't face the whole congregation and so they went to the dawn Mass attended only by the nuns. Aside from Sunday morning, the only time Margit showed any life at all was in the afternoon of Andrassy's visits. Emil had asked Andrassy to visit on Tuesdays, so he could stay at the office to wrap up the new edition of the paper.

On the Tuesday after Christmas Emil was reading over the page proofs when Gyula walked in with a cup of coffee.

"Here," he said. "You look like you could use this."

"Thanks, Gyula."

"Emil, why don't you go home? You look exhausted."

Emil looked at his watch. "Not while Andrassy is there. I wouldn't want to interrupt such an important conversation."

Gyula looked up at the sharpness of Emil's tone.

"Don't you think he's doing some good?"

Emil sighed. "I don't know, Gyula, I don't know anything anymore. It's been over a month. Nothing has changed. It's like living with one of the mannequins in Riley's store window."

"I guess we just have to be patient."

"Patient! I've been patient! How much longer do I have to be patient? How much longer will this go on? I'm no saint, Gyula. I want my wife back."

"I know."

"I'm sorry, my boy. I shouldn't have raised my voice to you."

Gyula smiled. "It's okay, Emil. Like you said, you're no saint. But I can't blame you. I don't know what I'd do in your place."

"That's the problem—I don't know what to do, either. Andrassy tells me to be patient, be kind, give her time, and I do, but my God, Gyula, how much time can it take?"

"Her brother-in-law must have been very special."

"He was a boy. What he had, I don't know; half the girls in the village were in love with him. Who knows what kind of man he became? I could understand having deep feelings for a grown man, but a wet-behind-the-ears boy, no. What Margit feels, or thinks she feels, isn't for a man, or even a boy, it's for a memory, a ghost, a will o' the wisp. How can I fight with that?"

"I wish I knew."

Later that night, Emil walked around the neighborhood before going home. Andrassy would have been long gone, but Emil was still reluctant to go back to the cheerless apartment. If Margit was still up she would be sitting, doing nothing, in the black dress she had worn since the day the letter came. She wouldn't let Emil or Eva wash it because she couldn't bear to be out of it for even one day. It made Emil wonder if she was beginning to go mad.

Maybe I'm the one who's mad, he thought. Standing here in the freezing cold in the middle of the night, not wanting to go home to see my wife dressed like a widow for another man. Oh, Margit, what have you done? Every time I see you in that dress I feel a knife go through my heart. It cuts away at my love for you and I'm afraid if this goes on much longer I won't have any left! And then what will I do? I need you, Margit, I need you to care for me, to worry about me when I don't come home on time, to cook for me and embroider for me and go to bed with me. That's love enough for me, Margit; if that's all you can give it's enough, and it always has been. Give it back to me, Margit, give back the little bit of love this monster in your heart has taken away.

Emil leaned against a tree and cried until a cold wind penetrated his sorrow and froze the tears on his face. He fumbled for his handkerchief with gloved fingers and blew his nose before turning for home. The apartment was dark when he entered, Margit already in bed. Emil undressed as quietly as he could and lay down. Within moments exhaustion and stress carried him into a dreamless sleep.

He awoke the next morning before Margit did. Although it was barely dawn he felt enormously refreshed. Sometime during the night he had made a decision, and now he got up quietly and dressed. He picked up Margit's black dress and tiptoed into the kitchen, where he took a stack of newspapers and a cup of congealed bacon fat that was sitting on the stove. He brought everything downstairs into the back yard. Next to the house lay the cylinder of chicken wire he used when he burned leaves and garden debris in the fall. He set it upright a safe distance from the house and crumbled newspaper into the bottom of it. Then he smeared the bacon grease on the black dress and stuffed it in the cylinder. He set more wads of newspaper on top of it. It took several matches on this cold morning, but he finally set the newspapers ablaze. He kept tossing in newspaper until the dress itself caught fire, and then he watched it burn. Well, he thought to himself, any neighbors up early enough to peek out their windows will get a good show this morning.

He stirred the burning dress with the handle of his rake and watched until the fabric was incinerated. Then he went upstairs and took a bath.

When he came out of the bathroom, Margit was awake and searching through the wardrobe.

"It's not there, Margit," said Emil.

She turned to him. "Where is it? I must wear it."

"It's gone."

She froze. "Gone? What do you mean, gone?"

"It stank, so I burned it."

She stared at him for a moment with her eyes opened wide, then ran to the back window. "Oh, no! Oh, no, no, no."

Emil stood behind her. "Margit, listen to me."

She put her hands over her ears.

"I said, listen to me!" he shouted. He grabbed her arm and turned her around, then pulled her hands away from her head and held them down.

"Your period of mourning is over, Margit. It's over, do you hear me? You're going to take a bath and wash your hair and put on a clean dress. Then you're going to come into the kitchen and sit down and have a nice breakfast, which this morning I will cook. But that's it, Margit. When I come home at noontime you'll make lunch, and we'll eat it together. When I come home from work tonight you'll make dinner, and we'll sit down like husband and wife and eat it together. And tomorrow morning, you'll get up and make us breakfast."

Margit squirmed and tried to free her hands but he held her fast.

"Don't worry, Margit. If my touch is that repulsive to you I won't ask you to make love to me and I won't force myself on you. But you promised to be a good wife to me, do you remember that? A good wife to me, Margit, and by God you're going to be that once again. You may no longer want to be and you may not feel it in your heart, but starting today you'll at least act like my wife again. I will not be the subject of our neighbor's gossip or their pity. It's over, Margit, do you hear me?"

Margit closed her eyes and said nothing. Emil squeezed her hands until she cried out. "You're hurting me!"

"And you're hurting me!" he shouted, but he released her. She rubbed her hands and looked at him with angry eyes.

"I'm sorry I hurt you, Margit. I'm sorry I let things go this far. But I'm not sorry I burned that horrible dress, and I'm not sorry for anything I've said. I'd rather have you hate me than have you feel nothing at all for me."

"I do hate you," she whispered.

"All right. I can live with that. Now go take your bath. The water's drawn."

Margit turned away from Emil and slowly walked out of the room. Emil stood, watching her, until she closed the bathroom door. Then he let out his breath in one great exhalation and looked down at his hands.

They were shaking.

Chapter Six
April 1917

Emil unbuttoned his jacket as he walked back to work after lunch, grateful that the long cold winter was at last replaced by the benevolence of spring. The unrelenting stress of the holidays was behind him, the long dark winter of despair was over, and he had begun to hope that Margit's heart would thaw with the coming of the sun. Not that their relationship was satisfactory. Emil had finally admitted to himself that it would never be as it once had been. That knowledge was like a weight carried in the pit of his stomach, making it hard to breathe. Some days Emil nearly cried for the simple lost pleasure in life he had once felt; then he cursed his naiveté. But on better days, on warm sunny days like this one, he could breathe deeply, almost pleased that his and Margit's life together had progressed from an armed conflict to a cease fire. They had breakfast, lunch, and dinner together, at first in silence, now with a little small talk on neutral topics. Margit had returned to keeping the apartment clean and had even begun to embroider again. When Emil kissed her goodbye in the morning and hello in the afternoon, as he always did, she no longer shrank away from him, though she had not yet softened to the point of returning his affections. Emil, who could not help being optimistic on such a fine afternoon, hoped they would soon return to normal relations as husband and wife.

Normal! Emil wondered if anything would ever be normal again. As his relationship with Margit stabilized, the rest of the world seemed to fall apart. Europe had become a slaughterhouse. For weeks the teletypewriter had printed disturbing news from Washington. Wilson, inaugurated only a month before, seemed closer and closer to declaring war on Germany. Each day Emil expected to see the report, but each day there was a new delay, culminating in a Senate filibuster to block the war declaration. He was beginning to hope that the talk of war was nothing but a rumor.

Shortly after one o'clock the teletypewriter's bell rang, announcing a piece of important news. Gyula, who was closest to the machine, lifted the paper to see what was being printed.

"Emil!" he called. "Emil! Here it comes!"

Not only Emil, but also Bela and the other employees came into the meeting room to see the news. Emil read the announcement over Gyula's shoulder.

" 'The President has signed an Act of Congress which declares that a state of war exists between the United States and Germany.' Well, gentlemen, there it is at last."

"What will happen now?" asked Gyula.

"To us?" said Emil. "Nothing. I expect the townsmen who have been practicing their marches and drills in the park will be sent off to the war."

"War. Hmph!" was Bela's only response. He turned back to the pressroom.

"Bela sets a good example for us," said Emil. "All right, everyone, let's get back to our work."

Business as usual seemed anticlimactic after the war declaration, but Emil was not going to relax his standards because of it. Since he had been in America, other publishers had established Hungarian newspapers in Hardenbergh, but most were short-lived and no real competition. Now there were two others, one so small it was more like a newsletter, the other more complete, but so poorly written and printed he had no doubt it would soon fail. Both competitors were weeklies; since January Emil had been publishing twice a week, on Saturday as well as Wednesday. The *Hirlap* was still the largest of the three Hungarian newspapers in Hardenbergh, the most successful and the longest established, and he intended to keep it that way.

As usual when there was important news, he became engrossed in his work, and did not see the policeman enter the office until the man was standing before his desk.

"May I help you, officer?" Emil asked in heavily-accented English.

"You Emil Molnar?" asked the policeman.

"Yes, I am."

The policeman tossed an envelope on the desk.

"See that this gets translated and printed." He nodded once and walked out.

Emil stared after him for a moment, then reached for the envelope and looked inside. He could read English better than he could speak it, and had no problem deciphering the contents.

"Gyula," he called. "Come listen to this."

74

Gyula came in, wiping his hands on a rag.

"By order of His Honor Mayor Francis X. O'Brien," Emil read, "in accordance with the President's War Proclamation dated April 6, 1917, all non-native inhabitants of the City of Hardenbergh who have not become naturalized citizens are to register as enemy aliens at the City Hall no later than Wednesday, April 11, 1917. All enemy aliens not registered by April 11 will be subject to arrest and confinement. Effective immediately, all enemy aliens seen loitering along the riverfront will be subject to arrest and confinement. Effective immediately all enemy aliens attempting to leave Hardenbergh without first obtaining a travel pass will be subject to arrest and confinement."

"But we're not Germans!" exclaimed Gyula.

"No, but our native country is allied with Germany. I can understand their reasoning, even though I do not like it."

"Emil, we've lived in this country for years! We work hard. We keep our homes in good repair. Our neighborhood is the cleanest in the whole city! Aren't we good citizens of Hardenbergh?"

"We're not citizens at all, most of us. That's the problem." Emil sighed. "We've no choice, Gyula. If we don't comply they'll arrest us."

Gyula shook his head. "What are you going to do?"

"We'll add it to today's edition. Here, they've given us a copy of the complete war proclamation. Paragraph after paragraph about enemy aliens. We'll have only three working days to get registered. Our people need to know immediately. We must put this on the front page, Gyula. Put it in a box under the war declaration story. I won't have time to translate the President's entire proclamation, but I'll do the important sections. In the Wednesday edition we'll include the whole text. In Magyar."

Gyula left Emil to his translating. Soon he had the complete text of the Mayor's order translated, and the major points of the President's proclamation. He'd have to do the rest of it on Monday. Grimly, he handed the copy to Gyula, and they began work.

Hours later, when the paper was on its way to every home in their community, Emil and Gyula closed up the *Hirlap* office and began the walk home. Shouts and the sound of breaking glass drew them away from their usual route. Around the corner and a block away, they saw a bonfire in the middle of the street. Above it, from a street lamp, hung an effigy of the Kaiser. Young men cheered and waved their fists as the effigy caught fire. Emil motioned for Gyula to leave and the two men slipped away unnoticed by the crowd.

"I've never seen anything like that," Gyula said in a quiet voice when they turned the corner.

"Nor I," said Emil. "They were young ruffians, no doubt full of whiskey. I shouldn't pay too much attention to them."

"There was a policeman on the opposite corner from us. Why wasn't he doing anything? Weren't they disturbing the peace? He should have arrested them."

"He was only one man. Against a drunken mob like that, an attempt to arrest any of them would result in more trouble, not less."

"That was an ugly crowd, Emil. What if their anger turns toward us?"

"The citizens of Hardenbergh are good people, Gyula. Why should they feel anger toward us? We mind our own business. We keep to ourselves. I shouldn't worry about it."

Emil gave Gyula a reassuring pat on the back and they continued home in silence. Emil didn't want to worry the younger man, but Gyula's question had occurred to him, too. He had never seen a mob like that, drunk and shouting, smashing bottles in the fire. What if their war fever became an epidemic? Would they bring their anger into his peaceful neighborhood?

To shake off his uneasy thoughts, Emil stopped to admire his garden before going inside. Coming home still did not bring the rush of pleasure it once had, and it had become habit for him to linger outside. Even in the coldest days of winter he would stop for a deep breath or two before opening the door. Now, though, he was genuinely pleased to stand outside and inhale the scent of the first daffodils to brighten the rear of the house. The light breeze rustled among the branches of his neighbor's cherry tree, whose buds were fat and ready to burst open in a cloud of pink blossoms. Emil felt a small pang of homesickness for the apricot trees of Barackfalu. Soon they would wrap the village in their soft flowers. For the first time, Emil found himself wondering if he would have been happier in Hungary.

When he walked into the apartment, Margit was sitting in the living room, fingering her rosary. She held the small crucifix in her right hand and touched it to her forehead, heart, and shoulders in the sign of the cross, then kissed the crucifix and put the white beads in her pocket.

Emil kissed her on the cheek. She looked at him, briefly, before moving past him to the kitchen.

"I wanted to say a rosary for the dead, all those who have died in the war, and all those who will die before it is over."

"That was very good of you," Emil said. He felt the weight return to the pit of his stomach. There was only one dead soldier she prayed for.

"I've already eaten, but I've kept your supper warm for you."

She took from the oven a platter of *retes*, squares of flaky strudel filled with sautéed cabbage. It was one of Emil's favorite dishes, but Margit had not made it in a long time. Emil knew it took hours to make, to stretch the dough so thin it became transparent, to cook the filling and spread it carefully on the dough, to roll up the strudel without tearing it. Margit usually made it during the winter, and the smell of its baking would fill the apartment, but this winter she'd had barely enough energy to cook the simplest foods. It was the first meal in a long time that she had cooked to please him.

Emil looked up at Margit. She poured herself a cup of coffee and sat down at the table, looking down at the cup she cradled in her hands. She was sleeping better these past few months, and the dark circles had almost faded from under her eyes. She was eating better, too, and had gained back some of the weight she'd lost. Her cheeks were pink again and her hair shone, although Emil could see the first splash of gray in it. Emil wanted to reach out and touch her hair, to pull out the pins that held it up and see it cascade below her shoulders. He wanted to get up from his chair and kiss her cheek, her lips, her neck, to pull off her shirtwaist and lift her breasts from the crocheted camisole, to reach under her skirt and petticoats and make love to her right there in the kitchen.

The clatter of his fork hitting the linoleum floor broke into his thoughts and he looked down in confusion.

"I'll get you another," said Margit. She stood up and took another fork out of the drawer while Emil breathed deeply to steady himself. She placed the clean fork next to his plate and bent down to pick up the one he had dropped. Emil looked at the back of her neck, smelled the scent of her lavender toilet water, and clenched his fist. Take it easy, he reminded himself. Just because she's made you strudel doesn't mean she's ready for anything else. Don't ruin it, Emil. Take it one step at a time.

"Thank you, Margit. I must be tired."

"Of course."

"The strudel is wonderful."

"I'm glad you like it."

Emil let the small talk and the routine motions of eating bring him back to a more stable frame of mind. He told Margit of the president's war proclamation, the mayor's order, and the bonfire.

"So," Margit said as she cleared the dishes. "We have to go to the City Hall next week."

"Yes."

"I've never been there."

"We'll go together. First thing Monday morning."

When Emil and Margit left their home at 8:00 Monday morning, accompanied by Gyula, Eva, and Ferenc, they thought they would be among the first on line, but when they got to the City Hall the line for registration was halfway down the block. Emil greeted the early arrivals, recognizing many of them from the Van Dyke factory. Almost everyone on line was Hungarian, plus a few Germans, Slavs, and Italians.

"Here so soon?" he asked one of them.

"So soon? I've been on line since 7:30. We're supposed to be at work by now. We'll all get docked for being here."

"That's not fair," Eva said to Margit. "They have to be here, just like us. We've been ordered to come."

"That won't make their foreman any happier," said Emil. "Almost all of the foremen are Irish."

They took their places at the end of the line, and waited with all the rest. The doors weren't unlocked until 8:30. The line moved slowly, and Ferenc grew restless.

"What's taking so long?" asked Eva. "It's hard to keep Ferenc still this long."

Gyula took the baby from her. Slowly the line moved forward. It was an hour before they stood at the foot of the imposing marble staircase, another half-hour before they arrived in the large foyer. A chandelier hung from the high ceiling, and the walls as well as the floor were of marble. Tall mahogany doors led from the foyer to the various departments of the city administration. A curved staircase led up one side to the second floor, where the mayor and city councilmen's offices were located. A large desk stood in the middle of the foyer. Normally a policeman sat there, directing visitors to the proper office. Today, this desk was used to register the illegal aliens. Not one, but a half-dozen policemen stood around the foyer, each holding a dark billy club. A harried looking clerk took down names and addresses and handed out the bright yellow registration cards. The clerk, it soon became clear, was the source of the delay, since he spoke no Magyar, and many of Emil's countrymen spoke little or no English.

The clerk was having difficulty with the couple immediately in front of Emil.

"How long have you lived in this country?" he asked for the second time.

"Nem értem," said the Hungarian man.

"He doesn't understand," said Emil. Emil turned to the man and asked the clerk's question in Magyar.

The man answered Emil with relief, and Emil helped him complete the registration process.

"I don't know why you people don't learn to speak English," said the clerk.

"Most of us know enough to get by," said Emil, "but this building—so big, so fancy—and the policemen, these things make people nervous, make them forget the words."

"If you're no friend of the Hun you have nothing to be nervous about. Your name?"

"Emil Molnar. And this is my wife, Margit, and our neighbor—"

"One family at a time. Your name Molnar, M-O-L-N-A-R?"

"Yes."

"Emil and Margaret."

"Margit."

"That's what I said, Margaret."

"No, it's Margit. M-A-R-G-I-T."

"In this country it's Margaret. Address?"

Emil opened his mouth to protest but Margit squeezed his hand and shook her head. He took a deep breath before answering, "118 Kossuth Street."

"Children?"

"None."

"How long have you lived in this country?"

"Since 1904."

The clerk looked up in surprise. "And you never became a citizen?"

"No."

"I don't understand you people. Have you always lived at this address?"

"No. We moved three years ago."

"Previous address?"

"12 Cherry Street."

The clerk stamped two yellow cards and handed them to Emil.

"Carry these at all times. If you are stopped you must show the card to the police. If you do not have it with you, you will be arrested. Next!"

Emil and Margit moved aside to allow Gyula's family to register. A policeman stepped forward and told them to move out of the building. They went outside and waited for Gyula and Eva at the top of the steps.

When the Farkases came outside they were followed by a policeman.

"You—Molnar," he said, pointing at Emil with his billy club.

"Yes, Officer?"

"Clerk needs you to translate. Come back in here."

Margit looked at Emil apprehensively and he squeezed her hand. "Go ahead, my dear, I'll be home as soon as I can. Go with Eva and Ferenc. Gyula, you'll have to open the office today."

Emil stood next to the clerk, helping him with the newer immigrants, all morning. His stomach began to rumble toward noon, and he was looking forward to going home for lunch, but another clerk came out to replace the one who had worked all morning. By one o'clock Emil badly needed to relieve himself, but it took him a quarter of an hour to work up the nerve to ask the clerk where he could do so. The clerk, annoyed at the interruption, motioned an officer to the table. "Escort this man to the washroom. And make it snappy."

The policeman took Emil through one of the large doors and down a flight of stairs. They returned as quickly as nature allowed and Emil took advantage of the break in duty to request a chair. Another officer was dispatched to get one, and Emil gratefully eased his weight onto the chair and off his aching feet. Promptly at 5:00 p.m. the City Hall doors were closed, despite the long line of immigrants still waiting outside.

"Tell them they have to come back tomorrow," said the clerk to Emil. "You come back tomorrow, too."

Emil started to protest, but thought about his countrymen waiting on line for hours, missing maybe a half-day's work, and then nodded his head.

For the next two days Emil helped the City Clerks. Any immigrants from a country allied with Germany received a bright yellow card; others were given a white card. All of the cards had "Registered Alien" printed on the top. Emil realized that they must have been printed and ready long before the Mayor's order.

By Wednesday it was apparent that not everyone could be registered by the normal end of the working day. Emil was not released from duty until eleven o'clock at night. All he'd had to eat was a sandwich that he'd kept in his pocket until the clerk allowed him to use the restroom at noon. As on the day before, while the officer waited outside, Emil hurriedly ate the ham and bread, drinking water from the tap to wash it down.

Emil walked home tiredly. The night before he had gone to the *Hirlap* office to work, where he stayed until midnight. Today was the first day his paper went to press without his direct supervision. He was eager to get home and see how it turned out.

Gyula was waiting on the porch when Emil arrived home.

"Emil! At last—we were worried about you. Did everyone get registered?"

"Never mind about that. Where's my newspaper?"

Gyula grinned. "Right inside."

Gyula led the way in. Margit, who had been pacing back and forth, pushed past him and put her arms around Emil. "You're home!"

Emil was taken aback; it was the first time Margit had touched him like this in months. As he put his arms around her she pulled away suddenly and rubbed her hands awkwardly on her skirt.

"I was worried," she said. "This awful business has everyone on edge."

Emil smiled at her. "Well, I'm home. Everything's going to be all right." To Gyula he added, "My newspaper?"

Gyula handed him the paper, then sat down next to Eva on the couch. She squeezed his hand. Margit went into the kitchen for coffee. She brought it out on a tray and poured four cups while Emil stood in the middle of the room, holding the paper up so no one could see his face. He read the whole issue, turning the pages quickly, without saying a word. When he was finished he folded the paper neatly and looked at Gyula.

"Well, I see I'm beginning to make a newspaperman out of you. Well done."

Gyula let out his breath and everyone smiled. Margit passed out the coffee while Emil told them of the day's events. He yawned and put down his cup.

"I'm afraid not even coffee can keep me up tonight. It's been a long, long day. Goodnight, everyone."

He was so tired he scarcely managed to undress and brush his teeth. He was half asleep while he wound his alarm clock, and nearly slept through its ringing the following morning. With a groan for his stiff back, Emil got up and got ready for work. He spent the rest of the week on the President's war proclamation, translating the full text of it for the *Hirlap.*

The town of Hardenbergh seemed gripped by war fever. After its front window was smashed, Zimmerman's Shoe Store was renamed Carpenter's Shoe Store. The German restaurant on Elm Street closed for lack of business. Recruitment posters sprang up in every storefront, and a bond drive was scheduled in the opera house. Young men began to appear in uniform, notably Claude Van Dyke, the eldest son of the manufacturer, whose picture in uniform was printed in every paper in town, even the *Hirlap.* The Van Dyke Company began to lose workers to the war, mostly office clerks and foremen, but their work force was largely made up of immigrant labor and was little changed, although a few Hungarians and Germans returned to Europe. The company announced a new line of cosmetics, the Red, White, and Blue label. In addition to making women's face powder, they began to make medicated foot powder for soldiers.

Emil and Gyula spent more time in the office as more war news came in, but Emil took a long lunch on Friday to go shopping. He went home that evening with his heart beating fast, and even whistled as he opened the door. Margit looked up from her embroidery in surprise.

"Hello, Emil. You seem to be in an especially fine mood tonight. Has something happened?"

Emil took a deep breath. "Not yet, but it will tomorrow."

"What happens tomorrow?"

He reached in his pocket and pulled out a small package. "Your birthday." Emil placed the package in Margit's hand and kissed her cheek. "Happy birthday, my dear."

Margit looked down at the package and swallowed hard. "But I didn't give you anything for your birthday last month."

"That doesn't matter. All that matters is that you open your present."

Margit slowly pulled apart the bow that held the package together and carefully unfolded the paper wrapping. The box was made of velvet, small enough to fit in the palm of her hand. When she opened it, Margit saw a gold chain with a small heart hanging from it.

"Oh, Emil!" She began to cry.

Emil knelt down beside her. "What's wrong? Don't you like it?"

She shook her head. "Of course I like it. It's beautiful."

"Then what?"

"After everything that's happened—still you give me your heart."

Emil took her hand and kissed it. "Always."

Margit pulled an embroidered handkerchief out of her pocket and wiped her eyes.

"I don't know what to say."

"Let me put it on you."

He unclasped the necklace and draped it around Margit's neck. She fingered the heart while he fastened it on.

"It's lovely, Emil. Thank you. I wish I had something to give you in return."

Emil moved his hands to Margit's shoulders. "You have." He kissed the back of her neck. "It would be the nicest birthday present you could give me."

Margit sat so still Emil was afraid he had made her angry, but in a moment she took a deep breath and began to unpin her hair. Emil gave her shoulders a squeeze and reached up to turn out the light.

"Emil! Not here!"

He bent down and rubbed his face in her hair. "Right here. Right now." Then he put his arms around her and pulled her onto the floor.

Afterwards, when Margit had gathered up her clothes and gone into the bathroom, Emil lay on the floor in the dark. His body felt the satisfaction it had craved for months, but his heart felt no joy. Although Margit had been stiff at first, almost virginal, her body soon responded to his touch, but where there once had been, if not real love, at least a friendly passion, now there was no emotion at all. He had made love to her body, but her soul might have been miles away. He'd won a victory of sorts tonight, but it was an empty victory. The old weight that had been oppressing him, the one with Laci's name on it, had been replaced; this new weight had no name, but was heavy with the knowledge that what little he'd had, he lost when Laci died, and now he knew he would never get it back.

Chapter Seven
December 1917

The church bell ringing.

Emil was walking down Hardenbergh Avenue to buy tobacco when he heard the church bell ringing. That's odd, he thought to himself, why would the church bell ring at this time of day? The bell rang on Sunday mornings, ten minutes before Mass; it rang joyously for weddings and solemnly for funerals; it rang at midnight on Christmas Eve, but it never rang to announce that Emil Molnar was about to purchase pipe tobacco. He felt Margit sit up in bed and he opened his eyes. Outside, the church bell continued to peal.

"Emil, do you hear that?" asked Margit.

"Mm—I was dreaming. I heard it in my dream."

"It's the middle of the night." She got up and turned on the light. Emil blinked in the sudden brightness and squinted to look at the alarm clock.

"It's two o'clock in the morning, Margit. Something's wrong. I'll get dressed."

"I'll come with you."

"No, Margit, why should you get dressed on such a cold night? Go back to bed and stay warm."

Instead Margit put on her robe. "I'll make a pot of coffee. You'll need something hot to drink when you get back."

Emil kissed her cheek. "Thank you, Margit. I hear Gyula stirring upstairs—I'll ask him to come with me."

Gyula was already on his way down when Emil opened the door. "Ah, good, you heard it, too," Gyula said. His broad shoulders, wrapped in a heavy woolen coat, seemed to fill the landing. Like Emil, he had dressed hurriedly, without washing his face or combing his hair, but when the two men stepped outside the cold air roused them fully awake. They could see other figures running toward the church, and they hurried toward the sound of the pealing bell.

The church was only two blocks away, but by the time they got there a small crowd of men had already gathered in front of it. In the white glow of the street light they could see Monsignor Andrassy handing something to the men, but it was the other glow—the yellow one—that drew their eyes. Through the open doors of the church they could see yellow flames. The nave of the church was on fire.

Emil pushed forward and touched Andrassy's arm. "Monsignor! Has anyone called the fire department?" he shouted over the sound of the bell.

"Yes, yes," Andrassy answered. "But they haven't come yet. Father Borsy has been ringing the bell for help. In the meantime, we must get out anything we can. I must save the consecrated host! Come!"

Emil didn't think it wise to try to save anything, but Andrassy ran back into the church before he could object. He and Gyula followed the old priest. The interior was lit by the flames rising past the altar. The curtain that formed a backdrop to the altar—a purple one for advent instead of the usual white—was burning up. Flames scorched the carved wooden frame around the curtain, and smoke billowed up toward the high ceiling. The marble altar glowed, backlit by the fire. In its center was the small niche, with a single door of gold, which held the consecrated host that remained inside at all times, except during Mass. Andrassy tried to open it, but the heat from the flames in front of him made him step back. Already the red carpet under the altar was beginning to smolder, ignited by flaming bits of cloth and wood that dropped from the burning curtain. On the right, in Andrassy's office, were the parish records. Andrassy sent Emil and Gyula to get them.

"Throw them out the window—get them out of the building!" he shouted.

To the other men who had followed them in he pointed to the statues, arranged along the walls of the church, each draped in somber purple. "Get the statues! Pull the stations of the cross off the walls! Save anything you can!" Andrassy himself hurried to the left, into the room where the priests put on their vestments for Mass, and where the gold chalices, patens, and other implements of Mass were stored. Even in his haste he genuflected before the altar.

Emil and Gyula had just entered the office when they heard the welcome clamor of the fire engines.

"Thank God," said Emil. "Now something can be done."

"The church bell has finally stopped ringing," Gyula said.

"Eh? I hadn't even noticed."

They looked around the office. It held simple furniture: a desk and two chairs, a bookcase filled with thick volumes, a small crucifix on one wall. A heavy door led directly to the churchyard. Emil tried the door but it was locked. The window, made of stained glass, with a picture of Saint Ladislaus on it, had a lower pane that swung down for ventilation. Emil opened that, and told Gyula to pass him the big ledgers that contained the parish records. He tossed them out to the pavement as smoke from the sanctuary began to enter the room.

"Hurry, Gyula! We can't get out through this door, and the window is too small to crawl through."

"That's it, Emil. Should we try to save anything else? Papers from the desk, maybe?"

"Forget it! The important records are safe. Let's get out of here!"

Emil took out his handkerchief and dipped it into the font of holy water before placing it over his mouth and nose. He led the way into the sanctuary. The fire had spread over the whole altar area and the large wooden crucifix over the altar was now in flames. Firemen had unrolled a long hose and trained water on the burning crucifix. Emil and Gyula squeezed past the vicious stream of water and ran down the side aisle.

Outside was a chaos of firemen and parishioners. Hoses snaked up the church steps. A group of firemen carrying another hose ran past Emil and Gyula, shouting "Get out of the way!"

"Where's Andrassy?" asked Emil.

"He's still inside!" called one of the men who had carried statues.

Emil grabbed the arm of Chief Haggerty, who was shouting orders through a megaphone.

"Monsignor Andrassy is still in there!"

"I can't spare any men right now," said the chief. "We're waiting for another company to get here."

"Let me go get him!" cried Gyula.

"No!" said Emil.

"Are you crazy?" said Haggerty. "Besides, he's probably passed out from the smoke by now."

"I'm strong—I can carry him."

The chief looked at Gyula for a moment, then nodded. "Okay, but be careful. Don't even try if it's too hot. And stay out of the way of my men!"

Gyula nodded and went inside. Emil waited tensely. Two minutes went by, three minutes, but Gyula did not come out. Emil ran around the side of church toward the rear of the building. On his left was the house that the parish used as a convent. The firemen had evacuated the nuns, who stood wrapped in blankets in a cluster outside their home, their hastily put on habits in disarray. A group of firemen aimed a hose at the wall and roof of the convent, to prevent its catching fire. The cold water rained down on Emil as he ran between the buildings. He heard a crash, and glass breaking, then a thud. A figure lay on the ground in front of him.

"Monsignor? Monsignor Andrassy!"

"Window," said the priest. "Get Gyula!"

Emil looked up at the window but saw nothing except black smoke pouring out. He stepped past Andrassy and tripped over a bulky form, but when he reached down he realized it was only the chalice and other valuables, wrapped in a vestment of some sort. He looked around the back of the church, but saw there was no door on this side. He came back to the window and called for Gyula. There was no answer. He grabbed the window frame and tried to pull himself through but had to fall back because of the smoke.

Andrassy coughed and tried to get up. "Gyula...broke...window... pushed...me...out," he said, then began coughing again.

"Are you hurt?" asked Emil.

Andrassy shook his head.

"Come, Monsignor. We have to tell the firemen that Gyula needs help."

Emil pulled him up and put the old man's arm around his waist. They walked as quickly as Andrassy could manage to the front of the church, under the spray of water. Emil delivered Andrassy to the nuns then went back to the fire chief, who was gesturing to a crowd of firemen from the second company, which had finally arrived.

"Gyula! Did he come out?" asked Emil.

"No. What about the priest?"

"Over there. Gyula pushed him out the window. You've got to get Gyula out!"

The Chief motioned to two of the firemen. "The room off the altar—someone's trapped."

The men nodded and went inside. Emil tried to follow them but the fire chief pulled him back.

"You can't go in there! I don't want any more civilians hurt."

"He's my friend!"

"I don't care if he's the Pope! Get back!"

Emil moved out of the way, shivering. His clothes were soaked. He hadn't noticed how cold it was until now. Icicles hung from the roof of the convent. I should be taking notes, he thought. I'm a newspaperman, I should be interviewing the fire chief, Andrassy, anyone. Please, Lord, please let Gyula be all right. Please.

Emil bowed his head and tried to pray. All he could say to himself was please, please, please. He hugged his arms to his chest and stamped his feet to the rhythm of the word in his head: please, please, please.

He looked up when someone behind him shouted, "Here they come!" The two firemen came out, carrying Gyula between them. They brought him down the stairs and laid him gently on the wet sidewalk. One of the firemen leaned on Gyula's chest and the other pulled Gyula's arms up over his head. They worked on him for several minutes, pressing his chest and pumping his arms, while Emil watched, please, please, please running through his head like a stuck record. Finally, the firemen stopped. They put Gyula's arms down and placed them across his chest. The one who had been kneeling over Gyula looked up at Emil and shook his head.

"I'm sorry, mister. We tried."

Emil looked down at Gyula. His face was grimed with smoke but otherwise he looked like he was sleeping. A young man, a strong man, a good friend.

Emil knelt down and put his hand on Gyula's chest. It neither rose nor fell. The firemen stepped back and cleared away the throng of parishioners who had gathered around them, but Emil didn't see them, or anything, for a long time.

He felt a hand on his shoulder and dried his eyes. It was Andrassy, standing next to him with a purple sash over his shoulders.

"I share your sorrow, my son. I will administer the sacrament of Extreme Unction now. I pray his soul is in heaven for what he has done."

Emil stood up when Andrassy knelt down to give Gyula the last rites. He clenched his fists as the priest began to murmur in Latin. God forgive me, he thought, but I wish Gyula had never gone back inside. I should never have let him go in. I should never have brought him here.

The nuns came over to Gyula's body and knelt around it while Andrassy performed the sacrament. Afterwards, one of the nuns came up to Emil.

"Mr. Molnar?"

"Yes, Sister?"

"We'll pray for the soul of your friend. He was very brave, and we're very grateful to him for saving Monsignor."

Emil wanted to say "Pray for me, too, Sister, because I wish he hadn't," but all he did was nod.

"Here's a blanket. You must be terribly cold."

Emil thanked the nun, but instead of wrapping the blanket around himself, he unfolded it and laid it over Gyula's body, covering his face.

Another nun walked up to Emil. "Mr. Molnar, I'm sorry to intrude on your grief, but could you speak to the fire chief? We can't find Father Borsy anywhere."

It took Emil a moment to remember that Borsy had been ringing the church bell. Gyula—his throat clenched thinking about it—Gyula had noticed that the bell stopped ringing. Emil, if he had even thought about it, assumed that Borsy had left the church when the firemen arrived.

"Of course, Sister." Emil told Haggerty about the missing priest.

"Damn!" said Haggerty. "How do you get into the bell tower?"

"There's a door inside the vestibule, on the right-hand side."

Haggerty went inside the church. Again Emil waited outside. The interior of the church was dark again; the firemen had put the fire out, but they were still inside, their hoses fanned out across the church steps. Many of the crowd who had been watching had already gone home, the interest of the fire unable to compete with the comforts of a warm home. The nuns stood vigil over Gyula's body. Emil felt a rush of gratitude toward them. He didn't know them very well, since he had no children in school, but he was glad they stood by his friend. Oh, God, he thought, how will I tell Eva?

Steps shuffled on the stone floor of the vestibule. Emil turned.

Chief Haggerty came out with Father Borsy slumped over his shoulder.

"Oh, no."

Haggerty squatted down to shift Borsy's weight onto the top step. "He's dead, but it can't have been from the fire or the smoke—all that was at the other end of the church," he said. "How long was he ringing the bell?"

"Ten or fifteen minutes, I think, maybe more."

"He was an old man, and bell ringing is hard work. Maybe his heart stopped." Haggerty took off his hat and rubbed his face. "Can you help me carry him down the stairs?"

"Of course."

Together they picked up Father Borsy and laid him next to Gyula. Once again Monsignor Andrassy performed the last rites, kneeling on the cold sidewalk, the nuns in attendance, weeping and praying. Emil stood off to one side until they were done.

Andrassy stood up slowly. "Let us not grieve, Sisters; tonight our Savior has called two of his souls home. We will pray for them every day. May they rest in peace, happy in the bosom of God."

He turned to Emil. "My son, you must be very cold. Come into the rectory to get warm and dry before you go home. I will ask the firemen to bring our friends."

Emil nodded. His teeth were chattering so hard that he could not talk. Monsignor Andrassy spoke to the fire chief, who dispatched four men to carry the bodies into the rectory. Andrassy led the way. The nuns followed the bodies into the building, and Emil walked behind them.

The rectory was a small building, much like the typical homes of the neighborhood, with a front hall opening into the parlor, sliding doors dividing the parlor from the dining room, and the kitchen in the rear. Andrassy and Borsy each had a bedroom upstairs.

There was no other place to put them, so the firemen placed the bodies side by side on the dining room table. A nun set two candles on the sideboard and lit them. When the dead were suitably arranged, the nuns turned their attention to Andrassy and Emil. One went into the kitchen to put up hot water, two others retrieved blankets from an upstairs cupboard, and one took off Emil's shoes and socks. In a few minutes he and Andrassy were wrapped in blankets and sitting with their feet in basins of hot water. A nun gave each of them a mug of tea.

When the living were taken care of, the nuns returned their attention to the dead. They returned to the dining room, knelt down, and began a rosary.

"How did the fire start, Monsignor?" asked Emil when he was able to talk.

"I do not know. I was awakened by the sound of a car, driving very fast. I got up to look outside, and saw a light in the church. I got Father Borsy and we went outside to take a look. Normally we would use the side door, but I misplaced the key, and so we went in the front. When we saw the fire, Father Borsy ran upstairs to ring the bell, while I returned here to call the fire department."

There was a knock on the door.

"Come in," called Andrassy.

Chief Haggerty stepped inside. He took off his hat and stood in the hall. "Please don't get up, Monsignor. I'll only be a minute. Don't want to come in and get soot on your floor."

"Please, will you have a cup of tea?"

"No, thank you. I have to get back to my men, wrap things up. I thought you'd want to know. We found a gasoline can in the church."

"A gasoline can?"

"Yes, Monsignor. It means the fire was set, deliberately. It was arson."

Andrassy grew pale. "But why would anyone set fire to a house of God?"

"Because we're at war," said Emil, bitterly. "Wilson finally declared war on our native country yesterday. It's them against us. It'll be open season on the dirty hunkies, now."

Haggerty shook his head. "Not everyone feels that way. But there's a bad element in every town, just looking for a way to make trouble."

"Are any of that bad element in the fire company, Chief? Is that why you took so long to get here?"

Haggerty took a step toward Emil. "Look, mister, I can understand you being angry with what happened tonight, but know this: we got here as fast as we could. We did the best job we could, the same we'd have done for St. Brendan's across town. We did a good job."

"Of course you did, Chief," said Andrassy. "And we thank you."

Haggerty nodded. "Me and the boys want you to know we're real sorry about your friends."

"Thank you, and God bless you all."

Haggerty nodded again, looked briefly at Emil, and walked out.

Emil pulled his socks and shoes off the radiator and put them on. He tugged so hard at his shoelaces that one of them broke.

"Emil, we must forgive our enemies."

Emil stood up. "You forgive them for me, Monsignor. I have to go home and tell a lovely young woman that tonight she became a widow."

He pulled on his damp coat and walked out the door. He was in no hurry to go home but the cold forced him to walk quickly. As he walked he tried to think of how he could tell Eva what happened to her husband, but his mind was blank. All he wanted to do was go back to sleep, and not have to face any more grief.

By the time he reached his front door, he was shivering so badly he could hardly use the key. Margit heard his fumbling and opened the door.

"Emil! You've been so long! You must be freezing." She held open the door and looked out as Emil walked by. "Where's Gyula?"

"At the rectory."

"What happened? Was it a fire? We heard the alarms."

"Yes. The church. It's been put out."

He handed Margit his coat. She wrinkled her nose.

"This smells awful—and it's damp. Here, give me all your clothes. I'll put them out in the hall until morning."

"Where's Eva?"

"Upstairs—we've been waiting up there. She didn't want to wake Ferenc by bringing him down here. Why don't you run a bath? I'll go up and tell her Gyula will be along later while you get cleaned up."

"No, Margit. I'll go upstairs myself."

"Emil? Is Gyula all right? He's not hurt, is he?"

"Come upstairs with me."

"Emil!"

"Hush, Margit." He climbed the stairs heavily and knocked on the door. Eva opened the door with a relieved smile.

"Emil, come in. I'm so glad you're back! I've had the strangest feeling tonight, ever since you left. Come in, Margit."

She held the door open a moment, looking into the empty hall, then turned to Emil. "Gyula didn't come back with you?"

Emil shook his head. Eva looked from him to Margit, and back to Emil.

"Is he hurt?"

Emil reached for her hand. "Eva, I'm so sorry." He swallowed hard. "He's gone."

"Gone? What do you mean, gone?"

"He died, Eva."

She snatched her hand away.

"No! No—you're wrong! There's been some mistake. Gyula's all right—he must be all right!"

"He saved Monsignor Andrassy's life, but was overcome by the smoke. The firemen did all they could."

"No! Oh, sweet mother of God, no!" She sank to her knees. "Gyula, Gyula, come home to me, come home!"

Margit knelt beside her and took Eva in her arms. From the back bedroom came a loud wail.

"Emil, the baby," said Margit.

He nodded at her and walked into the baby's room. Ferenc stood up in his crib, rubbing his eyes. "Mama!" he cried.

Emil walked over and picked him up. "Come to Uncle Emil," he said. "Your Mama's in the next room. We'll go see her in a minute."

"Mama!" he whimpered. Emil hugged him close and rocked him from side to side. "Hush, my little man. Mama needs you to be quiet."

But Ferenc could hear his mother's sobs and continued to cry. Emil rocked him until he cried himself to sleep, then kissed him and put him back in the crib. He stood there for a moment, looking down at the baby, then tiptoed out of the room. Margit had gotten Eva onto the couch, and sat with her arm around the younger woman with Eva's head resting on her shoulder. Emil wanted to say something, anything, to erase the look of pain from Eva's eyes, but Margit motioned him to go downstairs. He nodded tiredly and left.

Emil's hands felt heavy as lead when he undressed and drew a bath. At any other time he would doze off a few minutes after sinking into the hot water, but this dark morning he soaped and rinsed mechanically, scrubbing away the soot, the smell of burned cloth and wood. When he was finished he didn't have the strength to get up, so he lay back in the gray water, brought his fists up to his forehead, and cried.

The bath water grew tepid before Emil was able to get out of the tub.

He dried himself and put on clean pajamas and walked into the bedroom. Margit was still upstairs, and would most likely stay with Eva the rest of the night, what little was left of it. The bed was cold, and Emil had to curl up under the down comforter to stay warm. He hugged

Margit's pillow to his chest and burrowed under the covers to hide from the gray light of dawn.

When Margit came downstairs Emil was already up and dressed.

"Were you able to sleep?" she asked.

"A little. And you?"

She shook her head.

"How is Eva?"

"As you would expect. She finally fell asleep from exhaustion. I came downstairs to see if you needed anything, and to change."

"You haven't had any sleep. You should go to bed."

"Eva will need someone with her when she wakes. And Ferenc will be stirring soon. I'll be all right. Let me make you fresh coffee."

"Don't bother, this is fine. I've already heated it."

"But it's from last night."

"It's good enough."

"Some breakfast, then?"

"I'm not hungry."

Margit poured herself a cup of coffee while Emil sat down at the table with his cup. He looked up at the ceiling, as though listening for footsteps.

"Can you tell me what happened?"

He told her, everything he'd seen and done the night before.

"Father Borsy and Gyula died a hero's death," said Margit when he'd finished.

Emil slammed his cup on the table. "Gyula died a stupid death! Why should he give his life for that of a pompous old man?"

"Emil!"

"Well, he is."

"He's the heart and soul of our community, and one of God's ordained priests. Don't ever speak of him that way!"

"And how many years has he left? Five? Ten? Is that worth Gyula's whole life?"

"It was God's will."

"God's will! Does knowing that make it any easier to bear?"

"Yes."

"Well, I envy you, Margit. I'm not so pious. I'm too angry to appreciate God's will."

"He will forgive you for saying that."

"I hope so, because I can't forgive myself for letting Gyula go back in that church. We were safe, Margit, safe, and I didn't try hard enough to stop him."

Margit rubbed her eyes. "Emil, it wasn't your fault."

He clenched his fists. "It has to be someone's!" Suddenly he stood. "I have to go to work."

"Emil—"

"Don't expect me for lunch today."

His coat, still smelly and damp, lay on the hall floor with his other clothes, so he put on his old coat, the one he wore for gardening in the fall. Its shabbiness suited his mood. The sun was masked by a layer of clouds that seemed heavy with snow, and that suited Emil's mood as well.

He walked straight to the church, but had to step carefully when he got there because the sidewalk was full of ice. Icicles hung from the carved doorway, from every window and along the roof. They hung from the convent as well, from the rectory, and from the wrought iron gate between the buildings. Emil picked his way carefully up the icy steps and opened the church door. The draped statues stood in the vestibule in a forlorn group. No one had been here yet to replace them in their proper alcoves. Inside the unheated church were more icicles, hanging from the altar and the choir loft. The altar itself was blackened from the smoke and cracked across the middle. Above it, the rose window was open to the morning air, only a few shards remaining in their lead frames. A piece of the roof had caved in, showering debris on the scorched carpet in front of the altar. Everywhere he stepped he stirred up the acrid odor of the previous night.

If no one had been hurt Emil would have thought the parish extremely lucky. The fire did not extend past the altar rail, and the rest of the church, although damaged by smoke and water, was unburned. It was all repairable, all but the most important thing: Gyula.

Emil sighed and left the church. He walked next door to the rectory, and was just about to knock on the door when a large car pulled up to the curb. A uniformed chauffeur trotted around to open the door. Emil recognized the man who got out, but had never met him. It was Jan Van Dyke himself.

Van Dyke was dressed in an immaculate overcoat, with dove-gray gloves and a felt homburg. He carried a walking stick that he used to help ford the river of ice on the sidewalk. Emil suddenly wished he'd worn his other coat.

"Good morning," said Van Dyke, with a slight bow. "I am Jan Van Dyke. I am here to see the Monsignor."

"I am Emil Molnar, publisher of the Hardenbergh *Hirlap*."

They shook hands.

"Gathering details for your story?"

"Actually, I came to see how well Monsignor Andrassy had recovered from last night."

"Were you here, then?"

"Yes, I was."

"Perhaps you could show me the church before we go inside?"

"Certainly."

Emil led the way into the church, aware that he still smelled faintly of smoke. Van Dyke walked past him, silent except for an occasional "Hmm." He walked up to the altar rail and turned around slowly, then nodded once and walked out.

"Come with me," he said to Emil.

Van Dyke tapped on the rectory door with the handle of his walking stick. Mrs. Juhasz, the housekeeper, took their hats and let them into the parlor, then went upstairs for Monsignor Andrassy. Van Dyke strode into the parlor and stood in the middle of the room. He smoothed his white hair, just once, then stood perfectly still, seeming to admire the doors that now closed off the dining room. Emil could hear noises behind the doors, and wondered what was being done in that room.

Andrassy came slowly down the stairs, coughing slightly. "Mr. Van Dyke," he said, extending his hand. "May God bless you this morning. Hello, Emil. Mrs. Juhasz, some coffee if you please."

They sat down, Van Dyke on the sofa, Andrassy and Emil in the two chairs. Emil's chair faced the dining room, and he couldn't take his eyes off the door.

"Monsignor, what is happening in there?" he asked.

"The undertaker has just arrived."

Van Dyke frowned. "Undertaker?"

"Yes, Mr. Van Dyke. My assistant, Father Borsy, and a young man of the parish, Mr. Molnar's tenant, were killed last night."

Van Dyke looked from one to the other. "Please accept my deepest sympathy. I did not know. My chauffeur mentioned the fire—his brother is a fireman, you see—but he didn't tell me any details, except that it was arson."

Andrassy nodded. "And what may I do for you this morning, Mr. Van Dyke?"

"I want to offer my services. I'm prepared to have one of my men come by to assess the damages, and I will personally take care of the expenses of repair."

Emil and Andrassy looked at Van Dyke in surprise.

"You're very generous, Mr. Van Dyke," said Andrassy.

"Monsignor, your people are a very important part of my work force. The loss of their church will hurt their morale, and that will make their work suffer. I am merely being practical. I also want to assure you and your parishioners that the ill will demonstrated by this arson does not extend throughout the city of Hardenbergh. People of conscience—regardless of their heritage—are rightfully appalled by such an act."

"God will bless you for this, Mr. Van Dyke," said Andrassy.

Emil could see tears in his eyes.

Van Dyke stood up. "It's settled then. My man will be here later this morning. Please don't get up. I'll see myself out." He nodded to Emil and strode out.

Andrassy clasped his hands together. "That man has been very, very good to us. Such generosity! We are blessed to have him in this town."

"Too bad he's not the chief of police. He'd have our arsonist in jail by now. I don't suppose there's a suspect?"

"No. The police stopped by last night, rather this morning, after you left. You must be patient, my son, their investigation has just begun."

"Do you really think they're trying hard to find the culprit?"

"Justice will be done; whether it happens in this world or the next is not my affair. Nor is it yours."

"No. But somehow I think we'll end up settling for the next world's justice. Anyway, Margit wondered if you were feeling well enough to stop by our house to see Eva. She's very distraught."

"Of course, my son. I'll be there as soon as I can."

Emil left the rectory and took a last look at the ruined church before turning toward his office. For the first time in his life, he wasn't looking forward to going to work.

Chapter Eight
March 1918

The spade bit into the hard clay with a satisfying crunch. Emil liked the sound. He liked turning over the cold spring earth: the first spadeful of red dirt, moist from the spring thaw, scarcely dry enough to work. He liked the heft of it, the way it broke into clumps when he tipped the spade and sent the clod thumping against the ground. When he had dug out a long trench, he put down the spade and went at the clods of dirt with his fork, breaking the clay into smaller and smaller pieces.

He had worked this soil since before the war. Each fall he added the summer's compost into it, yet every winter's frost seemed to compact it to clay again. It was hard work to break it up, but Emil enjoyed hard work, and even though he'd spent all morning in the *Hirlap* office, the fresh air gave him his second wind. After a winter spent indoors it was good for a man to use his muscles again, to break into a sweat, to feel a satisfying soreness in the back of his legs at the end of the day. He stopped a moment to look at what he had accomplished so far, and felt again for the packet of seeds in his sweater pocket. In his mind he could picture the pea patch: vines filled with fat pods, the green peas bursting with sugar, so tasty he could eat them raw. It was an annual miracle, that such sweet goodness could come from this lifeless clay. Maybe that's why peas were his favorite vegetable, because they were the first to transform this ground into a garden each spring.

He looked up when he heard the back door swing shut, but instead of Margit calling him to supper, there stood Eva on the back porch. She came down the four steps carefully, sat down on the next to last step, and tucked the folds of her brown skirt behind her ankles.

"Hello, Emil," she said.

"Good afternoon, Eva. You're looking very well today."

"Thank you. I feel quite well. It's a nice change from the past few months."

"Where's Ferenc?"

"Helping Margit in the kitchen."

"He has the makings of a chef."

"I know." She smiled, and looked down at her thickening waistline. "I wonder what this one will be like. Strong like his Papa, I hope."

Emil winced. Her ability to speak so easily of Gyula still eluded him.

Eva looked up and down the row of neat back yards.

"You're the first to break ground this year."

"I decided to take advantage of the warm afternoon." He began digging another row.

"Emil, we have to talk."

Emil dug harder at the ground.

"Emil!"

He sighed, and straightened up, leaning on the spade handle.

"Eva, there's nothing to say."

"You know there is. You've both been so kind to me, through Christmas and the past few months when I've been so sick. I'm very grateful, as you well know. But my settlement from the Benefit Society won't last forever. I have to move."

"You can't move now, not with a child on the way."

"What else can I do? A rented room will be enough for me and Ferenc, and will make the settlement go further. Besides, you should rent a big apartment like this to a family."

"You and Ferenc are a family, and soon you'll be three. And what will you do when the settlement does run out? You can't go back to the factory, not with two little ones."

"No, but I have enough to get by until the baby is born, and then I can take in sewing."

"You can do that here."

"Emil—"

"I'm serious. And if the rent is too much I'll lower it to what you can afford."

"You can't sacrifice your own income."

Emil put down the spade and walked over to Eva.

"Is it too painful for you to stay?" he asked. "Are there too many memories?"

"There are many memories, Emil, but they are all good ones."

"And would Gyula want you to give them up?"

"Gyula would not want me to accept charity."

"Charity is what you give those you don't know. Friendship is what you offer those you love. I miss Gyula more than you can know. I don't want to lose you and Ferenc as well."

Eva's eyes filled with tears. "Emil, you are so kind—"

"It's not kindness," he said harshly. "I feel—responsible for your welfare."

"It wasn't your fault."

He leaned on the porch railing and picked at a fleck of paint. This will need painting soon, he thought automatically. Gyula would have done it.

"It wasn't your fault, Emil. Gyula went into that church of his own free will. And I will never let his son—his sons—forget that their Papa was a hero." She put her hand over Emil's, briefly. "We'll stay, Emil, as long as we can. Thank you."

Emil nodded once and walked back to the garden. He picked up the spade and resumed his attack on the hard ground before going inside. The spade bit deep into the ground with each stroke, as though he could dig out his emotions with the dirt.

An hour later it was Margit who came to the door to call him to supper. He stood up straight and arched his back. The rows were finished, dug and broken up, the rocks picked out, needing only to be raked smooth for planting. It was a perfect time to stop. He set down the fork and walked up the porch stairs, took off his shoes, and walked in the kitchen. Whatever chaos Ferenc had caused was largely cleaned up by then and the table was set for the evening meal. Emil washed his hands and face before scooping the small boy into his arms and giving him a kiss.

"And what did my little man help his Aunt Margit make today?"

"*Palacsinta!*"

"My favorite!" He gave Ferenc another kiss before setting him onto the chair. Propped up by the Sears and Roebuck catalogue, Ferenc was just able to reach his fork and plate. Margit pulled a platter from the oven and set it in the middle of the table. She said grace and then Eva cut her son's *palacsinta* into small pieces. A hint of cinnamon wafted up from the thin crepes, half of them rolled around pot cheese filling, the rest filled with Margit's apricot preserves. Main dish and dessert all at once, they were indeed one of Emil's favorite foods, and he ate heartily before taking Ferenc outside to help him plant. He showed Ferenc how to sprinkle the peas so they weren't too close, and how to push them under the dirt with one finger. Ferenc enjoyed poking them down.

"Will they grow today?" he asked.

"No, not today. Not until the air is warmer, and the sun is warmer, and you don't have to wear a sweater anymore."

"That long?"

"That long."

Ferenc suddenly lost interest in poking the peas down.

"Go help your Mama and Aunt Margit clean up, then," said Emil. He finished his planting and filled the watering can, then moistened the ground over the peas to set them firmly in the dirt. When he was done watering he lit his pipe and strolled past the front of the house.

Much of the neighborhood was doing as he did, taking advantage of the warm weather, relaxing on newly washed front porches, or hanging the last of the screens. Emil nodded and said hello as he passed. The neighborhood was growing rapidly, with several new streets, yet the town still ended abruptly, and in less than ten minutes' walk Emil was in the country. He turned into the woods to gather twigs for the peas to climb on, stepping carefully to avoid trampling the small white flowers that dotted the forest floor. Bloodroot they were called, because the sap from their tubers was red. Their petals fluttered in the smallest breeze, and in places they were so thick they looked like patches of snow. Now, with the evening shadows carpeting the forest, they stood with folded petals, ready for the night.

Emil listened to a woodpecker drumming on a tree, to the song of a robin. This time last year he'd been full of hope; the sounds and muddy smells of spring had filled him, if not with happiness, at least with pleasure. This year winter lingered inside his heart. How he wished he could turn the clock back, and hold Gyula's arm, and prevent him from going back into the church! God forgive him, but he wished with all his heart that Gyula were still alive, and that it was Andrassy who lay in the cemetery.

Emil had never much liked Andrassy, but now he hated the old man as a reminder of what he had lost. Even worse, from Margit's point of view, he had not been to Communion since Gyula died. And next Sunday was Easter. Margit would expect him to receive Communion with her, but how could he? He had not been to confession, for how could he confess to Andrassy that he wished him dead? Andrassy would absolve him, if Emil could truthfully confess to be sorry for his hatred of the priest, but he wasn't sorry, and saying so would just compound the sin. Emil sighed. If only life could be as simple as planting peas.

He walked home with his bundle of twigs and stuck them into the garden so the peas could twine around them when they sprouted. When he finished it looked as though a small November forest had sprung up in his garden. Soon he would be able to add spinach to the plot, and onions, and when the ground had warmed enough he would plant tomatoes and peppers. Around the vegetables, in the border of the yard, he could see daffodils poking up through the ground. If the warm weather held he would unwrap his beloved roses.

Emil gathered up his tools and brought them to the back porch. Standing under the porch light, he wiped them down and rubbed them with a thin coat of oil. He leaned the fork, the spade, and the rake against the back wall, next to the hoe. Maybe this spring he'd have time to build a cabinet for them, to keep the rain off and keep them handy during the spring and summer. It wouldn't be very nice looking, not like Gyula could have made for him, but it would have to do. Emil shook his head. Again and again his thoughts returned to Gyula.

He went into the kitchen and washed his hands. Margit called to him from the living room where she sat crocheting.

"Did you finish your planting? I saw you walk off before."

"I needed some brush for the peas to climb on. I just had time to finish before the light faded." He pulled on his slippers and relit his pipe. "I had a talk with Eva before supper."

"Oh?"

"She wanted to move out."

"Nonsense! Where would she go?"

"That's what I said. Anyway, I think I've convinced her to stay, but she can't afford to pay much rent. Our income will be a little tight until she can get established."

"Doing what?"

"She wants to take in sewing."

Margit frowned. "If all she does is take in sewing she won't make much. There are plenty of seamstresses in town."

"Maybe she'll get lucky, and make a dress for Mrs. Van Dyke. That'll give her money to live on for a year."

Margit stopped crocheting and looked up. "Emil, what a wonderful idea!"

"Margit, I was joking."

"But why not? You've seen Eva's work—her stitching is exquisite. She could become the dressmaker to all the rich women in Hardenbergh."

"And is she to knock on Mrs. Van Dyke's front door and invite herself in?"

"Of course not. But you told me that Mr. Van Dyke himself talked with Monsignor Andrassy after the fire. And Van Dyke himself paid for the church repairs. Perhaps Monsignor could call on Mr. Van Dyke and mention it."

"Are you serious?"

"Yes, I'm serious. I'll discuss it with Monsignor tomorrow, after Mass." She picked up her crocheting again. "I could have mentioned it this afternoon, if I'd known."

"This afternoon?"

"At confession."

"Oh."

"You haven't gone to confession in a long time."

"No."

"Don't you think you should?"

"That's between me and God."

"And what about next week?"

"What about it?"

"Emil, Easter! How can you not receive communion on Easter, of all Sundays! And this will be the first Mass in our church since the fire, a Mass of thanksgiving as well as resurrection."

"Margit, enough of this, please."

"You're a leader of the community. People will notice."

"Let them."

She put down her crocheting again. "Have you so much hate in your heart, Emil?"

Emil looked away from her. "Yes."

"Oh, Emil, did you really think the police would find the arsonist? Did you think they'd really care about our church? You must find it in your heart to forgive them, Emil."

"I can forgive them, Margit, but I cannot forgive myself."

"You did all you could."

"I don't want to talk about it anymore. I mean it."

Margit crocheted in silence for a few moments.

"Why don't you play some music?" she suggested. "You haven't played your violin in months."

"I haven't felt much like playing. I'll play a recording if you want to listen to something."

He lifted the lid of the Victrola. A record already lay on the turntable. He cranked the handle and placed the needle on the record, then stretched out on the sofa. For the rest of the evening he tried to let Mozart fill his empty heart.

The next morning Margit spoke to Monsignor Andrassy after church. He thought her idea a splendid one, and conveyed it to the pastor of the Dutch Reformed Church, who suggested it to Mrs. Van Dyke. And so, on a day when Emil's peas were beginning to twine around the brush he had provided for their tendrils, Mrs. Van Dyke sent her car for Eva. She returned several hours later to show Margit and Emil the bolt of cloth Mrs. Van Dyke had provided.

"It's the most beautiful silk I've ever seen! It's from China! Look at the design— you can only see it when the light shines just so." She held the fabric up so they could see the birds and bamboo that were woven into the white fabric. "She wants it a month from now, for a garden party she's giving. It will be the most beautiful dress there. And Margit, she's tall and slender, just like you, so I can try it on you for size. Isn't it marvelous!"

"I'm very happy for you."

Eva looked at Margit, and then at Emil.

"You did it, didn't you? I don't know how, but you arranged it."

"It was Emil's idea," said Margit.

"But it was Margit who mentioned it to Monsignor Andrassy, and so on," said Emil.

"I'm so grateful to you both. If she likes this dress, and tells her friends, well...."

"Then you'd better do a good job, hadn't you?" asked Emil.

Eva laughed. "Good? This dress will be perfect."

She kissed them both and went upstairs. Emil smiled.

"Personally, I think she liked the motorcar ride the best."

Margit said nothing. She'd said very little to Emil since Easter. Emil knew that she feared for his soul; he hadn't been to confession in months, and hate was a mortal sin. From her point of view if he died without confessing his sins he'd go straight to hell. Emil, however, was beginning to think that the only hell was here on earth. He had to wonder, too, about the compassion of a God who would kill a young man in a fire in His own house. Emil shook his head and almost laughed. Now he would have to add blasphemy to his list of sins.

He took comfort from his work, where the war news kept him busy. His new typesetter, Sandor Hegedus, was a young man, still a teenager, and his enthusiasm for the news and his new craft was infectious. He wanted to learn everything he could about the business, and Emil was glad to be his mentor.

At home Emil took comfort from his flourishing garden. Fertility was everywhere. His roses sent up new shoots from every pruned stalk, the spinach grew large whorls of leaves, onions fattened under ground, and where the peas, now composting in a corner of the garden, had once lavished Emil with pods, tomatoes and peppers hung heavy with their fruit. Eva grew as big as she had with Ferenc, and even the neighbor's cat had kittens. As Eva had hoped, Mrs. Van Dyke was most pleased with her dressmaking skills, and did recommend Eva to several of her friends. Eva turned her dining room into a sewing room, and had steady orders, enough to keep her busy until after the baby was born.

All in all, thought Emil as he picked ripe tomatoes in the back yard, it had been a fortunate summer. Although the fighting in Europe continued, the latest talk put the end of the war before the end of the year. Of course, the talk was always of the war's end, but now that the American army was over there it seemed to be a real possibility. There had been no further hostilities toward the Hungarian community, and if it were not for the never-ending lists of battle casualties and war reports, Emil could almost have forgotten that the war existed. What it was really like in Europe he couldn't imagine; here, all was peace: a garden full of ripe vegetables, and roses blooming.

The peace was shattered when the back door flew open and Margit ran down the back stairs. Emil stood up so suddenly he knocked over the tomato basket.

"Emil! Get Toth-neni!"

"The baby? Now? Isn't it too soon?"

"It may be a few weeks early, but she's been in labor for hours. She didn't say anything because she was trying to finish a dress. But her water just broke, so it's coming, and much faster than Ferenc did. Hurry!"

She ran back into the house while Emil wiped his soiled hands on his trousers. He wanted to pick up the spilled tomatoes but knew this was hardly the time to give in to neatness. Why one baby came so slowly while another seemed so eager to be born was beyond his comprehension. It would be so much simpler if it were a consistent process. When one tomato plant ripened, all the others of that variety ripened as well. It was easy to plan a harvest. Why were humans so unpredictable?

He ran to Toth-neni's home, a small apartment over a storefront on Cherry Street, annoyed that the old woman refused to install a telephone. Emil suspected that it made her feel important to be fetched in person. But what if she weren't there? He almost came to a standstill with the thought. Lots of babies were born in September. What would he do if she were not at home?

He reached her apartment in a few minutes and climbed the stairs two at a time, knocking on the door until it was opened by an old woman with a flowered kerchief on her head.

"Toth-neni! I am so glad you're home. It's Eva's time."

She nodded and smiled and reached for a cloth satchel that stood ready next to the door.

"Let us be off, then; the second child seldom waits as long as the first to greet us."

Emil had no idea how old Toth-neni was; she was one of those elderly women who never seem to age. Her hair was always wrapped in a kerchief, and her round face was as wrinkled as the day she delivered Ferenc. For an old lady she was surprisingly quick; Emil nearly had to trot to keep up with her.

"I was afraid you might be delivering elsewhere, and not be home," he said.

"Oh, that's not so likely these days as it was a few years ago. I don't deliver as many babies anymore. Most young girls want to go to the hospital. The hospital! What sort of place is that to be born in?"

She kept up a steady chatter all the way to Kossuth Street, then she held up her hand when Emil opened the door for her. "Thank you, I can find my way from here." Emil was left standing in the doorway. He closed the door and sat down on the front step, then stood up again and looked at the door. He patted his pockets for his pipe but they were empty. Frowning, he tried to think of where his pipe was but his mind was blank. He walked around the side of the house to the garden, and was startled by the overturned basket and spilled tomatoes. He took out his watch. Such a short time ago, yet he'd completely forgotten about it. He squatted down to set the basket upright, and absently piled the tomatoes in it, thinking all the while of the women upstairs.

Last time, when Ferenc was born, he'd taken Gyula for a walk. Last time, he'd hardly considered what was happening upstairs. This time, he fretted and wondered and fidgeted almost as much as an expectant father.

The screen door banged open and Margit came down the porch steps with Ferenc, crying and squirming in her arms.

"Take him," she said. "He's just awoken from his nap."

"How is it going?"

"It's nearly time." She hurried back to the stairs, leaving Emil with a handful of cranky toddler.

"Ferenc, would you like to help Uncle Emil pick tomatoes?"

"No."

"Would you like to go for a walk?"

"No."

"What would you like to do?"

"I want Mama."

"Mama can't see either of us, right now. Come, let's look for ladybugs."

Emil put Ferenc down and took his hand. "Come on, Ferenc."

They found a ladybug on a cabbage leaf. Emil took it off the leaf and put it into Ferenc's hand. The crawling insect distracted Ferenc enough for him to stop crying, and Emil sighed with relief. He looked down at Ferenc, whose stocky build and dark eyes were just like Gyula's. It's not right that a man should die before his child is born, thought Emil. Gyula hadn't even known about the baby.

Emil knelt down next to Ferenc.

"Ferenc, do you remember your Papa?"

Ferenc looked up into Emil's eyes. "My Papa died."

Emil wiped a dirt smudge off his cheek. "Do you miss him?"

"Mama says he lives in heaven now."

"Yes, he does."

"And she says he looks down on us every day and smiles." Ferenc transferred the ladybug to his other hand. "Why can't I see Mama?"

"Mama's busy, Ferenc. We'll see her soon. Tell me, would you like a baby sister? Or a baby brother?"

"I don't care. Mama says if I have a baby brother or a baby sister I'm going to be the man of the house, like Papa was."

"You're going to be a big, strong man, someday," Emil said, looking up toward the house. "Just like your Papa."

From the open window came the sound of an infant crying. Emil stood up.

"Come, Ferenc, let's see if we may visit your Mama now."

He took the little boy's hand and walked into the house. Ferenc hurried up the stairs and stretched his hand for the doorknob. He managed to get the door open and pushed his way inside, calling "Mama! Mama!"

Margit intercepted Ferenc and led him to Eva's side. He climbed onto the bed and curled against his mother's side. Emil came in slowly, almost shyly. He stopped in the doorway, but Margit motioned him in. "A boy," she said in a soft voice.

"So soon?"

"This was much easier on her." Margit smiled. "It's all right, Emil, you can come closer."

He stepped up to the bed, where Eva cradled her firstborn. She looked pale, with little beads of perspiration on her lip and forehead, but she smiled. "A boy, Emil, what did I tell you?"

"Congratulations, Eva."

Toth-neni stepped up to the bed with the new baby. "Here he is, all cleaned up for his Mama." She placed the baby in the crook of Eva's arm. "What are you going to name him?"

"Balint, after Gyula's father," she said. "Ferenc for my father, Balint for Gyula's." She kissed Ferenc on top of the head. "Now I have two fine sons. I have been blessed."

Emil placed his hand on Margit's shoulder and went back downstairs. Outside, the sun creased the garden with shadows. Emil stood on the porch and felt for his pipe, then remembered he'd misplaced it, probably in the house. He leaned against the porch rail, feeling suddenly light headed. He should do something, but what was there to do? There would be no real celebration this time. There was no father to get drunk with, no father to clap on the back, no father to talk with of his child's future, his dreams of success. When Ferenc had been born—Emil shook his head. What good was there in thinking of that happy time? Today was born a little boy who would never know his father. That was the situation now, and no amount of wishing would bring Gyula back to see his new son.

Emil stood up straight and stretched his back. The sun was going down, and he still had work to do. He walked past the cabbages and their ladybugs and knelt once more among the tomato plants. He picked one tomato, a second, a third. He held the ripe tomato in his hand and looked down at the smooth red skin that stretched over the plump fruit, trying to regain the satisfaction he'd felt that afternoon when he began his harvest. Then he turned the tomato over, and threw it down in disgust, for the bottom half was blackened and rotten.

Chapter Nine
October 1918

The sound of automobiles moving slowly down the road made Emil look up from his proofreading. He watched as the funeral procession moved by. Yet another influenza victim was being taken to the cemetery. From the number of cars and the expensive-looking casket the victim must have been wealthy. How democratic a disease, he thought, to spread its devastation to rich and poor alike.

When the cortege passed by the street was eerily quiet. Only two weeks ago it had bustled with automobiles and delivery trucks, horse-drawn wagons and bicycles. Last week the daily commotion of city life swelled to bursting with the Fourth Liberty Loan Drive parade. Most of the townspeople had attended the bond drive parade and the rally that followed it. Who noticed a few soldiers coughing or sneezing? It was common enough to catch cold in early fall, when the temperature was warm one day and cool the next. But this was no mere cold.

The illness had swept through the city so fiercely that funerals were a daily occurrence, and the obituary column in the *Hirlap* had grown from half a column to a full page. Schools, theaters, and churches were closed. The hospital was so full that beds lined the halls. In the Van Dyke Company, the work force, already depleted because of the war, was down by a third. Absenteeism was just as high in other factories. People stayed home because they were sick already, or because they were afraid of getting sick. Only doctors, nurses, and Red Cross workers hurried about.

Emil shook his head and returned to proofreading a special notice from the mayor's office he was putting on page one. The notice announced a new law—hastily passed the night before—requiring everyone to wear a gauze mask when outside. The new law also prohibited open sneezing, spitting, and coughing. Anyone doing so without using a handkerchief would be fined $10. Emil wondered if the new law would do any good. The disease was a killer. Not only were the very young and the very old especially susceptible, as with almost any disease, but this new influenza struck down the healthiest people of all: young men and women in their twenties. Soldiers in Camp Dix were dropping as fast as their comrades in the trenches of France. The eldest of the Van Dyke boys had survived a grenade explosion only to be killed by influenza on the ship that was bringing him home.

And the disease had invaded Emil's community. Bela called in sick this very morning. Toth-neni was already dead. How many more would the influenza take?

He rubbed his eyes. With Bela sick, Emil and Sandor had to do his work as well as their own. Emil had not even gone home for lunch, but ate a sandwich while he worked.

At 6:00 Emil called to Sandor, "Let's go home."

Sandor looked up from the Linotype machine. "I have only a little more to do to finish this page. Why don't you go ahead? I can close up as soon as I'm done here."

"Are you sure?"

"Positive."

"All right then, I'll see you in the morning. Thank you."

"Goodnight, Emil."

"Goodnight."

Emil was glad to have Sandor in the office, especially today with Bela sick. Sandor had worked at the *Hirlap* for nearly a year now. He was a quick study and an industrious worker; he had filled Gyula's shoes more easily than Emil could have hoped.

Emil put on the gauze mask a Red Cross worker had given him and walked home. The few people he saw about—the trolley conductor, a policeman, a doctor hurrying along with his black bag—all wore their masks. Emil didn't like the mask; his mustache caught in the gauze fibers, and he hated being unable to see a person's face.

He walked past the corner tavern and was surprised that it was closed. "By order of the Department of Public Health" said a sign on the door. "Closed to prevent spread of Spanish influenza." Somehow Emil didn't think closing a saloon would do much to prevent it. On every street he passed houses with a black ribbon on the door.

When he got home his own house was dark.

"Margit?" Emil walked into the living room and turned on the light. Margit's crocheting lay in a tidy pile in her basket, but she was not there. He walked through the dining room into the kitchen and turned on the light. Nothing was on the stove. The table was bare. He peered into the bedroom and the sewing room but Margit was not there. He began walking up the back steps. Margit opened Eva's door as Emil reached the landing halfway up the stairs.

"Don't come any closer, Emil. Stay there."

"Margit? What's wrong?"

"Oh, Emil! The doctor was here. It's Ferenc and Eva. They have it—the influenza."

"No!"

"I'm sorry, I had no time to call you; I've been upstairs with them all day. The doctor says I shouldn't come downstairs. I might infect you."

"But you're not ill."

"Not yet." She began to cry. "The doctor says we've all been exposed."

"Margit!" Emil put his foot on the step.

"No, don't come up! Please don't! It may be too late but don't take the chance."

Emil hesitated on the landing.

"How are they?"

"Too soon to tell," said Margit. She blew her nose and wiped her eyes. "Ferenc took sick after breakfast, and Eva shortly afterwards. Ferenc had been playing with the Horvath children last weekend, and their whole family is ill."

"Could it have come from me, because of Bela?"

"I mentioned Bela to the doctor, and he said no, you would have gotten sick first. But Ferenc played with those children, and we've both picked him up, so many times in the past few days." She shook her head. "We're in God's hands now."

"What can I do?"

"Nothing. Stay downstairs. Please, Emil. I'm frightened. Ferenc is very ill; it came on so quickly. One minute he was fine, and a little while later, he had a fever of 104. And Emil, Eva is nearly unconscious. She keeps asking for Gyula."

"Oh, no."

The baby began to cry. Margit blew her nose again and put her hand on the doorknob. "I must go in now. I'm sorry I can't get your supper."

Emil walked down the stairs slowly. Ferenc was a strong little boy. He would be all right. And Eva! How old was Eva now, only twenty? So many people that age were dying. Emil thought of all the obituaries he'd written in the past week: Erzebet Nagy, 20 years; Kalman Biro, 24 years; Istvan Hegedus, 31 years; the list went on and on, a catalog of young men and women, all dead from influenza.

He stood in the middle of the kitchen as if he did not know where he was. Supper was the last thing he wanted right now, but if the sickness was in this house he'd have to keep up his strength. He took leftover ham and potatoes out of the icebox and fried them. While they cooked he set the table and put up a pot of coffee. He ate mechanically, out of necessity, not desire, listening all the while to footsteps upstairs, and little Balint's cries.

He ate half of his light supper and pushed the rest away. The coffee had finished percolating, so he poured himself a cup and sat down to think. He and Margit, and Eva and the boys, acted more like an extended family than neighbors. They were always up and down, in each other's apartments. How many times had he picked Ferenc up since he had played with the Horvath children? How many times had Ferenc kissed his mother, his little brother, Margit? Would the influenza take them all?

Emil wished, like Margit, he could place his fate in God's hands.

Upstairs, the baby's cries continued. Emil scraped his uneaten dinner into the trash and washed the dishes. He stared into the sink as the water drained, leaving only a few soap bubbles. One by one they popped and were gone. And still the baby cried.

"Enough," said Emil. He took the ham out of the icebox and cut off a thick slice. He put it between two slices of bread and wrapped it in a napkin, then picked up the coffeepot and went upstairs.

Margit looked up in horror when he walked into Eva's kitchen. She was holding Balint and rocking him back and forth.

"Emil! What are you doing?"

"I can't sit downstairs while you're up here trying to nurse everyone. I was with Ferenc yesterday and today, so I've already been exposed, and if I'm going to get this influenza I'm going to get it whether I'm downstairs or up here." He poured a cup of coffee and set it on the table. "Here. Give me the baby, and drink your coffee. There's a sandwich for you as well."

Margit was too tired to protest. She gave up the baby and sat down heavily at the table.

"I'm too tired to eat, but thank you for the coffee."

"You have to eat to keep up your strength. Eat the sandwich, whether you want it or not."

Emil rocked Balint while Margit drank her coffee and ate a few bites of the sandwich. The baby cried no matter what position Emil put him in. Emil felt the baby's diaper but it was dry.

"He's hungry," Margit said. "Eva's too sick to nurse him, and he won't take cow's milk."

Emil put Balint's cheek up to his. "Shh-shh," he said, and then frowned. He felt Balint's cheek and forehead.

"Margit, he's burning up."

"Oh, no." She came over to them and put her hand on Balint's cheek. "Oh dear God, Emil—"

"What do we do?"

"Put him in the cradle, wash him down with a cool cloth. I don't know what else to do."

"We'll put him in Ferenc's room, and then I can look after the boys while you take care of Eva."

"Yes, that would be a help."

He gave Margit the baby and went into Eva's room to get the cradle. Only one small lamp was on, set on top of the chest of drawers, but even in the semi-darkness Emil could see how sick Eva was. She was the first victim of the illness he had really seen, and her appearance shocked him. Her face was gray and beaded with sweat. She moaned and coughed and when she moved her head Emil saw bloodstains on the pillow.

"Eva?" he said, but she either did not hear or could not answer. He picked up the cradle, which had been next to her bed, and took it quietly out of the room.

In Ferenc's room the scene was the same. One small lamp, and the little boy as ill as his mother. They placed the baby in the cradle and Margit wiped his face with a damp cloth.

"Margit, the blood I saw?"

"She has nosebleeds. There aren't any more clean pillowcases. Can you find another baby blanket? Look in the bottom drawer."

"I'll turn on the light."

"No, don't, it hurts their eyes."

Emil brought Margit the blanket and then put a cool cloth on Ferenc's forehead. Margit settled Balint in the cradle and stood up. "Try rocking it," she said. "I'll see to Eva."

Emil put a chair next to Ferenc's bed, and pulled the cradle nearby, so he could sit and minister to Ferenc and rock the cradle with his foot. After what seemed like years the baby finally stopped crying, whether because he slept or was exhausted—or was just too sick—Emil had no idea. He was too grateful for the quiet to think about it. Ferenc moaned and writhed and perspired no matter how much Emil wiped his little face. Once or twice the little boy opened his eyes but they were unfocused, and even when they looked directly at Emil they did not see him.

Emil dozed in the chair, waking when one little boy or the other cried, or coughed, or moaned. Once, Ferenc began talking about spiders and ladybugs, and Emil realized he was delirious with fever. Emil undressed Ferenc and bathed him all over with cool water. He changed the diaper that Margit had put on Ferenc when he became too ill to get up, and did everything he could think of to make the boy comfortable. It wasn't enough.

At dawn Margit came into the room, rubbing her back.

"How is Eva?" Emil asked.

"The same. And these two?"

"The same."

She nodded, and winced. "My head hurts."

"It's no wonder, with all you've been doing."

"I'll heat up the coffee."

Because both boys were sleeping, for the moment at least, Emil followed Margit to the kitchen. She fumbled with the matches, trying to light the stove.

"Why don't you let me do that? You're exhausted."

"I'm all right," she said, and then swayed so badly she gripped the edge of the stove to keep from falling. Emil caught her in his arms and led her to a chair.

"Margit, you must get some rest." He brushed her hair away from her face and tensed. Margit's cheeks were flushed and her eyes were glassy. Emil touched the back of his hand to her forehead and felt a jolt of fear pass like a wave through his body.

"Margit, can you walk to the couch? Come, I'll help you."

"No," she said, trying to brush his arm away. "I must go back to Eva."

"You can go to her in a little while. She's sleeping, Margit. You need to sleep, too. Just for a few minutes. Come on, come on now." She leaned against him as he put his arm around her waist. He half walked, half carried her to the couch. He took her shoes off and tucked a blanket around her legs, a crocheted blanket Margit herself had made. Emil could see her fingers holding the wool, looping it with the crochet hook into an intricate pattern of flowers. Now she pressed her fingers to her temples.

"How long have you had a headache?" he asked.

"I don't know—an hour, maybe."

"You should have told me right away. You need to rest." He undid the first two buttons of her blouse. "I'll be right back."

He hurried into the kitchen, filled a bowl with cold water, and grabbed a dishcloth. He returned to the parlor and dipped the cloth in the water, squeezed it out, and washed her face and neck. He dampened the cloth again and placed it on Margit's forehead.

"This will make it feel better."

"Mm." She closed her eyes. "It's so bright in here."

"I'll draw the blinds."

After he pulled the blinds shut Emil knelt down next to Margit and took her hand.

"How do you feel?"

"Terrible. Everything aches."

"I know. You just rest quietly. I'll check on the others."

"All right. Thank you, Emil."

He squeezed her hand and got up. Eva and the boys were asleep, or unconscious, he didn't know which. He went into the kitchen and tried to light the stove to heat the coffee, but his hands were shaking so badly he couldn't light the match. Emil gave in to the fear and sank into a kitchen chair, sobbing.

Oh, God, he thought, I don't even know if you exist, but if you do, help me, please. I don't know what to do. I don't know what to do.

When it was fully light Emil called Sandor.

"I can't come in, Sandor, they all have it. Margit got sick this morning. There's no one else to take care of them."

"I understand, Emil. What do you want me to do?"

"Only what you can. Set the obituaries—there will certainly be more of them today. Make sure the gauze law is on the front page."

"That reminds me—after you left, we got a flyer. The city and the Red Cross have set up an influenza center. There's an emergency number to call. Charter 1-2-3. Anyone who needs help should call that number."

"Put that on the front page, too. Move whatever you must."

"How long will you be out?"

"I don't know yet. I'll let you know as soon as I do. I haven't missed a day since we had to register at the City Hall. If anything comes up you can't handle, just call me."

"Don't worry, Emil. I'll take care of everything. And Emil, I'm sorry Mrs. Molnar is sick."

"Thank you, Sandor."

"My grandmother says a warm vinegar pack will cure anything."

"I'll keep that in mind."

Emil put the phone down and rubbed his face. Twenty-four hours worth of stubble scratched his hand but he had no time to shave. He had four patients to care for.

He spent the day in a waking nightmare. His patients were too sick to move, to talk, to eat the soup he'd found in the icebox and heated. Balint wouldn't drink milk, and was already too weak to suck from a bottle, so Emil dipped his finger in water to moisten the baby's tongue.

He changed diapers on the two boys and carried Margit to the bathroom, but Eva was too ill to tell Emil when she needed to relieve herself, and so she wet the bed. Emil stripped the sheets and cleaned her off, averting his eyes, putting a new nightgown on her before he stripped the old one off. Then he went down the basement to scrub the sheets and soiled nightgown in the washtub and hang them up to dry.

He moved in a circle from wife to neighbor to boy to infant, with cloths soaked in cold water for the forehead, and cloths soaked in warm vinegar for the chest. By midday he was exhausted, and sat down at the kitchen table, too tired to eat anything but a raw egg mixed with milk. The house stank of illness and he wanted to open the window, but he was afraid the cold breeze would give his patients a chill. He was afraid for Margit, who lay on the couch and moaned with pain; for Eva, who lay in her bedroom and wheezed with the effort to breathe; for Ferenc, who thrashed with fever in his small bed; and for Balint, who lay in a terrifying silence, too weak to cry.

Emil stood up and stretched his sore back. He was changing Margit's compresses when his head began to ache, and washing Balint's little face when he began to have trouble swallowing. When he stood up to wash Ferenc he became so dizzy he had to sit down again. He pulled out his handkerchief and wiped the perspiration off his brow, then blew his nose. His headache seemed to creep down his neck and across his shoulders. He shook with a chill as though someone had opened the window.

"Not me, too, not me," he whispered. "I have to take care of everyone else."

He walked slowly back to Margit. She had been dozing but now her eyes were open. She turned her head slowly to look at Emil and moistened her lips with her tongue.

"You look so tired," she whispered.

"Margit, I think I'm getting ill." He sat down on the edge of the couch.

Her eyes opened wider. "I must get up then," she said, and tried to lift herself up on one elbow, but could not, and fell back, breathing hard.

Emil reached for her hand. "I'll get help. I'll get someone to help us."

Charter 1-2-3. Sandor had told him about that number a few days ago—no, only that morning. It seemed like such a long time. Emil stood up slowly and walked downstairs, leaning against the wall the whole way. He sank into a chair and picked up the telephone that seemed almost too heavy to hold. He lifted the earpiece off the cradle.

"Number, please," said a woman's voice.

"Charter 1-2-3," Emil said, as distinctly as he could.

"One moment while I connect you."

Emil no longer had a sense of time. It might have been one moment or one hour before the calm voice answered, "Hardenbergh Influenza Center."

With a great sense of relief, Emil said, "I need help."

Something cool touched his forehead, something pungent hurt his nose—Emil opened his eyes. He saw a white ceiling, turned his head, saw the yellow roses of the bedroom wallpaper. He turned his head the other way, and looked at a figure dressed in blue.

"Margit?" The figure turned. "*Ki az?*" he asked. "Who is that?"

The woman walked toward him. She had red hair and green eyes, and wore a blue dress with a white collar and cuffs. She smiled.

"Welcome back, Mr. Molnar. We've been that worried about you."

Emil closed his eyes and frowned with the effort to speak English. "Who are you?"

"I'm Mary O'Donnell, a visiting nurse. I've been by every day since you called, don't you remember?"

"Called?"

"Charter 1-2-3. The influenza center. You called for help, three days ago."

"Three days?" Emil thought he remembered calling, but everything was a jumble in his mind—babies crying, women moaning, a voice asking how many ill in the house, arms carrying him to bed, a face that was Margit's one minute and Gyula's the next, a list of names, a long list, too many names....

"Mr. Molnar, can you hear me?"

Emil opened his eyes again. "What's that smell?"

"Camphor. Mr. Molnar, you've had the influenza, but you're getting better. Do you understand?"

He nodded. "Margit?"

"Margit? That's your wife, isn't it? She's doing fine—I'll get her on my way out. I was just leaving."

Emil looked at the nurse. At first he had thought she was young, but now he could see that her hair was streaked with gray, and there were laugh lines around her eyes. She was kind, he thought, though he didn't know how he knew. And she had gentle hands. He smiled. She smiled back.

"I'm glad to see you're coming back to us. Now I have to tend my other patients. I may not get back to you, now that you're better. But I'll pray that the good Lord restores you to health quickly."

"Thank you."

He heard her leave, and a murmured conversation, then Margit walked in. She looked tired, with dark circles under eyes, and thin and pale, but not as sick as she had when he laid her on the couch.

She smiled, and sat down on the bed. "How do you feel?"

"Like I've been run over by a milk wagon and two teams of horses."

"You'll feel better soon."

"And you?"

"I'm almost well again. The nurse says by tomorrow I'll feel good as new."

"I'm glad. How is Eva?"

Margit's eyes darkened. "She has pneumonia. She's in the hospital."

"How bad is it?"

"I don't know for sure. Today is the first day I've been up. She was taken to the hospital the day you called for help. The nurse says they may have caught it in time, thanks to you."

Emil closed his eyes, wishing he were still unconscious. When he opened them again, Margit was looking down, fidgeting with the belt of her robe. He was afraid to ask the next question.

"The children?"

"Ferenc is next door," she said, with a false brightness in her voice. "They've been taking care of him for two days."

She paused, and Emil knew what her words would be before she said them.

"Balint is dead." He made it a statement, not a question.

She nodded. "Also the day you called. There was nothing anyone could do."

Emil closed his eyes to fight the tears. "And where is he now?"

"In the basement of the church."

"What?" He opened his eyes in surprise.

Margit continued to look down at her lap. "There's no other place to put the bodies until they can be buried. There aren't enough coffins. They're doing it all over the city. Churches, schools, any large building."

"My God!" He reached for her hand, and when he grasped it she began to cry. She lay down next to him, and together they cried for Balint, and for all the dead lying in all the cold church basements in Hardenbergh.

Chapter Ten
November 1918

Eva was released from the hospital on the day the armistice was signed, and it seemed that all the church bells and factory whistles sang for her return home. She was one of the lucky ones, thanks to the patronage of Mrs. Jan Van Dyke, who worked in the Red Cross. She had been in the Influenza Center when Emil called, and when she learned that Balint was dead, she made sure that Eva received the best medical care available. Eva thus recovered from pneumonia, although she had nearly died, and on her release from the hospital was even thinner and paler than when she had worked in the dress factory.

Mrs. Van Dyke came in person to escort Eva home in her own chauffeured car, and graciously invited Emil and Margit to ride with them. Emil rode up front with the chauffeur, whom Mrs. Van Dyke addressed only as O'Brien, and the three women sat in the rear, Eva in the middle, all of them swaddled in rugs.

"Mrs. Van Dyke," Eva said. "I wonder if I might ask a favor."

"Of course, my dear."

"On the way home, could we stop by the cemetery? I haven't seen—the place, yet."

Emil grimaced as Mrs. Van Dyke instructed O'Brien to turn toward St. Brendan's, the Catholic cemetery. He hadn't wanted to go back there for a long time. He and Margit were the only people at little Balint's funeral three weeks before, when the grisly backlog in the church basements had finally been cleared up. To Emil's annoyance Monsignor Andrassy, untouched by the epidemic and in the peak of health, said the Requiem Mass and presided over the funeral. The three of them had stood in the cemetery on a warm Indian summer day, the kind of day that makes one think of anything but death, and watched as the unpainted pine casket was lowered into the tiny grave.

Now O'Brien turned into the cemetery gates and drove past the evidence of the disaster that struck Hardenbergh. On every side were new mounds, still unmarked with headstones, the reddish-brown clay unsoftened by grass at this time of year. Emil couldn't decide which were worse—the raw new graves, or the grassy old ones with their somber headstones. He was glad Balint was laid to rest next to his father, instead of alone. A child's grave looked too small in any cemetery.

While Mrs. Van Dyke walked over to her own son's grave—he had survived the trenches, but not the epidemic on the troop ship bringing him home—Emil and Margit led Eva to Balint. It was easy to find him; the ground in front of Gyula's headstone was raw earth. The stone, plain gray granite with a simple cross cut in the center, bore Gyula's name only; the stonecutter had told Emil he was many weeks behind on his orders, especially since one of his own apprentices had succumbed. The back orders of new headstones would have to be completed before he made additions to old ones.

Eva stood at the grave and bowed her head while Emil and Margit remained a few paces away. Margit took out her rosary and Emil removed his hat. He listened to the unceasing sound of bells, a wild paean instead of the mournful tolling of the weeks past. All over the city, people laughed and kissed and danced in celebration of the armistice, but Emil found it hard to rejoice in the midst of so much death.

Eva knelt down and fingered the fading yellow chrysanthemums nestled at the base of the headstone.

"You planted them, didn't you, Emil?"

"Yes."

"Come along, Eva," said Margit. "You mustn't stay out so long in this cool air. You mustn't catch a chill."

Eva nodded, placed her fingertips on her lips, and then touched Gyula's name. She stood up and walked back to the car. Emil thought she looked even paler than before, if that were possible.

They rejoined Mrs. Van Dyke and O'Brien and arranged themselves in the car once again. They rode home in silence.

"Mrs. Van Dyke," Eva said when O'Brien stopped the car in front of the house. "Would you like to come in?"

Mrs. Van Dyke leaned out of the car and took Eva's hand. "Thank you, my dear, but you need to rest, not entertain company. Perhaps another time."

"Of course. Thank you again for bringing me home."

"It was my pleasure. Goodbye, Eva, Mr. and Mrs. Molnar. Home, please, O'Brien."

As the car pulled smoothly away from the curb, Emil took Eva's arm and led her into the house. He had just closed the front door behind them when Ferenc tore down the steps. Eva knelt down and wrapped her arms around him. She covered his face with kisses while she rocked him back and forth, crooning, "My baby, my boy, my sweet boy," over and over.

Mrs. Horvath, the next door neighbor, came down the stairs at a more sedate pace, apologizing for losing hold of Ferenc.

"It's nothing at all, Mrs. Horvath, thank you for watching him," said Margit.

"Yes, thank you," said Emil as he held the door for her. With a smile and a nod she went outside.

Margit motioned to Emil to leave mother and son alone.

"I'm glad Mrs. Van Dyke did not come in," she said as they entered their own apartment.

"Why should that make you glad?" asked Emil with surprise.

"Think of us trying to entertain Mrs. Jan Van Dyke!"

"What's wrong with that?"

"Oh, Emil, imagine a rich lady like that in here! She's used to the finest linen, bone china, sterling silver, and a household staff to serve her. What do we have that can compare with what she is used to?"

"We have table linens that you embroidered, Budapest china, and silver plated coffee spoons. Are you ashamed of those things?"

"No, I am not, but she's from a different social circle—I can't imagine what Eva was thinking of to ask her in."

"She was merely repaying a kindness. Anything less would have been impolite."

"And she was politely refused."

"Now you sound offended. I thought you didn't want Mrs. Van Dyke to come in."

"I didn't—but she didn't have to refuse so quickly. It's as though she didn't want to come in."

Emil shook his head. "She was being very gracious—and you're being very contradictory."

"Let's not talk about it anymore. I'd rather forget the whole thing. Would you like a cup of coffee?"

"Frankly, I'd prefer a glass of brandy. It was cold, standing out there."

"Brandy at this time of day? Aren't you going to work?"

"Yes, I suppose you're right. Coffee, then."

But when Margit brought Emil his coffee he put a splash of brandy in it. "A compromise," he said.

Margit shook her head. "Do you want an early lunch?"

"No thank you. I do have to get to work, today of all days."

He drained his cup and took out his handkerchief to wipe his moustache and beard. Since he had been ill and too weak to shave he'd let his beard grow in. It was too flecked with gray for his liking but otherwise suited his face, or so Margit said, and he'd let it remain.

He kissed Margit goodbye and walked out the back door, as usual, to pause a moment in the garden before setting out to work. Only a few hardy mums remained in bloom. Much of the garden was overgrown with weeds, and Emil shook his head at the disorder. Even this had been disrupted by the epidemic. Maybe now that Eva was out of the hospital and the armistice was signed, he'd have time to restore neatness.

The neighborhood was quiet in comparison to the rest of the town, although small groups of women had gathered over back fences to talk of the news. While Emil, like everyone, was glad that the war was at last over, he wondered what would become of Hungary. Dissolved from the old empire, it was still on the losing side, and was sure to pay for its part in the war. Already, according to the news reports, Bolsheviks were agitating for Hungary to become Communist, like Russia. On the east, Romanian soldiers had crossed into Transylvania. Emil had a vision of his country being chopped into little bits, like garbage thrown to a pack of dogs.

As he walked closer to downtown the tumult grew louder, and he was glad to close the office door behind him and get to work. Work was always a solace; even when all the news had been bad, that there had been news at all meant work, and work had a way of driving his personal cares far away.

Emil was surprised at how quickly their lives resumed their normal pattern once Eva returned home. With the double horrors of war and disease gone for good, people could return to everyday activities once again, taking care of their own homes and families, tending to business, relishing the simple pleasures of daily life. Emil worked and gardened, Margit cooked and embroidered, and Eva resumed her dressmaking. Eva and Ferenc continued to eat Sunday dinner with Emil and Margit, who were glad to see Eva regain her strength and health. Ferenc had recovered more quickly than any of them, and seemed the only one who did not mourn the loss of Balint. Indeed, he seemed quite pleased to have his mother's full attention once more.

It had been so long since they had received any word from Hungary that Emil was startled to see a Hungarian postmark in the afternoon mail nearly a month after Eva's return. The war had made it almost impossible for Margit's mother to send letters, and since the United States entered the conflict they'd had no correspondence at all. Margit rarely spoke if it, but he knew the lack of news worried her. He would not be surprised if this letter renewed her desire to visit her mother, a trip long delayed by the war. Emil sighed. More disruption, just as life was getting back to normal. He glanced quickly through the rest of the mail, and then looked again at the foreign letter. The handwriting wasn't familiar, so he turned the envelope over to look at the return address. It was from Barackfalu, as always, but the name above the address was Piros'.

Emil frowned as he walked in the door. Why would Piros, of all people, write to Margit? He hoped Margit's mother was not ill. He put the letter at the bottom of the pile.

Margit started when Emil walked into the kitchen.

"Emil! Why did you come in through the front door?"

"I saw that the mailbox was full, so I picked up the mail and came in that way."

Now that he was inside he could see why Margit had not gotten the mail herself. She was making *retes* on the kitchen table, rolling the filled strudel dough into an oblong for baking. She would have spent all afternoon preparing the dough.

He kissed her and peeked in the oven. "Mmm-potato. And that's cabbage you're finishing? We'll eat well tonight."

"Close the oven door or you'll ruin it and have nothing at all to eat," she said. "Is there any important mail?"

Emil took off his coat before answering. "I'll wash up and then sort through it."

When he came out of the bathroom Margit was putting the strudel on the baking pan. He watched her remove the first pan from the oven and put the second one in. The smell made his mouth water. While she cleared the table he took a plate from the cupboard and a fork from the drawer.

"Emil!" Margit said with mock exasperation.

"Someone has to taste it," he said, lifting a piece of strudel from the pan onto his dish. He cut off a forkful, blew on it briefly, and put it in his mouth. "Oh—hot!"

"Of course it's hot. It just came out of the oven. You know it should cool to room temperature before you eat it."

He stepped quickly to the sink and cupped his hand under the faucet. He scooped cold water into his mouth, and turned to Margit with a grin. "It's delicious," he started to say, then he stopped. Margit stood at the kitchen counter, holding the letter from Hungary in her hand. Her face was blank, and her voice expressionless.

"It's from Piros," she said.

Emil said nothing.

"It will be bad news."

"Margit—"

"You read it. I don't want to." She put the letter on the kitchen table and sat down.

Emil put down his plate and sat down as well. Slowly, he reached for the letter and opened it. With a glance at Margit, who sat very still with her eyes focused on the wall and her chin jutting up at an angle he knew all too well, he began to read aloud.

"15 November.

"Dear Margit and Emil,

"Everywhere there is talk of armistice, so I write this letter hoping you will receive it soon. I know you don't expect and probably don't want to hear from me, but I have nowhere else to turn for help.

"The war has been a hard time for us. There is never enough food, even here in the villages, and the past few months a terrible plague has passed through the region. So many have died, it breaks my heart to tell of it. My two youngest are now with the angels, and our dear Mama as well—"

Emil put down the letter. "I'm so very sorry, Margit."

Margit put her head in her arms and sobbed. Emil had hoped that death was behind them, that they could get on with life and put aside mourning, but it was not to be. It was as though some wicked-humored god or demon was always there to mock their small happiness with more sorrow.

Poor Margit, he thought. First to lose her Papa, and be unable to go back home because of the war, and now to lose her Mama, just when overseas travel was possible again. He remembered how sad her mother had been the day they left on the train for the start of their journey to America; while everyone else fooled themselves with thoughts of returning, only her mother's face showed the truth.

Emil massaged the back of her neck, then he wiped his own eyes and picked up the letter.

"Shall I continue reading?"

Margit nodded.

"I am very sorry, my sister, to tell you this sad news. I am grateful, though, that you have your dearest Emil to comfort you, for I have no one but my sweet Dezso, who tries very hard to be a brave little man.

"You cannot imagine what it is like here. There have been riots, and soldiers everywhere—not our fine Magyars but uncouth Romanians, who have passed through the region like a scourge. The streets are not safe for good people anymore.

"The worst news I have yet to tell you. A few days ago, I sent Zsuzsi for bread. There's so little flour, we're not allowed to make our own; a village baker makes the bread, and doles it out a little at a time. So I sent Zsuzsi, may God forgive me, and she was on her way home, when one of the soldiers grabbed her and dragged her into an abandoned house."

Emil looked at Margit in horror, but her face did not change.

"The soldier, may he rot in hell forever, molested my sweet little girl, do you understand? Can you understand what it was like to have her come home after that? To look into her eyes, and see her tears, her terror—oh, Blessed Mother in heaven, why are such things allowed to be?

"Margit, I ask you, please, no matter what you may think of me, please let me send my little girls to you in America, where they will be safe from the filth that walks the streets of Barackfalu. They are not safe here. It breaks my heart in pieces to think of sending them away when they are so young, but I am so afraid it will happen again if they stay.

"Please, dearest Margit, send word as soon as you can. Please take my little girls and keep them safe for me.

"It may take a few days for me to get this letter out of the country—it cannot go through the normal post. I await your answer with hope. God bless and keep you both.

"Your loving sister, Piros."

Emil swallowed hard. That such a thing could happen in Barackfalu! He felt a rush of anger pass through him like a flame that left him hot and shaking. Zsuzsi couldn't be more than thirteen or fourteen. For a pig of a soldier to have his way with her was unthinkable. God, he thought, where were you when that little girl needed you? How could you let such a thing happen?

He took a deep breath and folded the letter carefully. If he could not find the soldier and kill him, then he would do what he could to help Zsuzsi and Piros. He looked at Margit. Her face was set like stone.

"Margit? What do you think?"

"Never."

Emil was shocked at her vehemence but not surprised at her reaction.

"We owe it to them."

"We owe them nothing."

"They are your family, whether you like to remember it or not."

"I will not have that child in my house."

"Margit!"

She slapped her hand on the table. "She's a bastard, and she takes after her mother. I won't have that little slut living here."

"She's only a child, and she was raped!"

"That doesn't happen to decent women. No! I won't discuss it. Mama is—Mama is dead, and it's because of Piros and her bastard I never saw her again. It's because of Piros I left home, because of Piros I left Papa and Mama, because of Piros I married you! She stole my life and now you want me to take in her children? Have you lost your mind? What do you think I am? They will never set foot in my house, never! Never!"

She swept the letter off the table and stalked into the bedroom, slamming the door behind her.

Because of Piros I married you.

The words echoed in Emil's mind. He wondered if Margit even heard herself say them. But they had been said, and once uttered, would not be taken back. Emil almost laughed, he felt so ridiculous. How completely he had fooled himself! Even in the worst days, after Laci had been killed, he had hoped Margit would come back to him, and at times it seemed she had, yet now he saw how absurd his hopes had been. Margit would never really come back to him, because she had never really been his. Not once in fourteen years. What he thought was a marriage was a different kind of partnership, merely a domestic arrangement of mutual convenience, a chimera, shimmering and lovely from a distance but evaporating into nothing when you looked at it closely.

Emil picked up the letter, folded it, and put it in his pocket, then sat, unmoving, until a persistent smell from the oven made him remember the *retes* baking there. He took a crocheted potholder from a hook next to the stove, pulled the pan from the oven, set it on top of the stove and turned the oven off. The *retes* hadn't quite burned. He supposed he should be glad that Margit's hard work was not ruined, but he found he no longer cared. He wasn't hungry, and whether she had made strudel that day or leftovers was of no importance anymore. He turned out the kitchen light and walked into the living room. In darkness he sat down to take off his shoes. In darkness he lay down on the couch and pulled a crocheted blanket around his shoulders. In darkness he lay for a long time, not thinking, not feeling, letting the melody of a Hungarian lullaby float over and over through his head.

How long he lay awake in the dark he had no idea, and whether he slept and whether he dreamed he could not recall, but when the morning light filled the room he rose to wash up. The bedroom door was still closed. When he had bathed he put on the same clothes and walked into the kitchen. Margit had not been up yet. Baking utensils still filled the sink and the pans of *retes* lay in the same place as the night before. Emil cut himself a slice of cabbage strudel and ate it cold as he walked out of the house.

It was so early only the milkman was about. Emil patted the horse's nose and fed it the last tidbit of strudel from his hand. He waved to the milkman and walked on, his breath forming small clouds. The ground was frosted over, and the air smelled like snow. He walked out of town, south into the countryside as he liked to do, but he didn't pause to watch the cows, or stop to admire the view. He just walked, until he was warm enough to open the buttons on his coat. He stood for a moment, breathing the fresh air, then reluctantly turned back to Hardenbergh. By the time he got back to town the Cherry Street coffee shop was open, so he went inside for a cup of coffee and a slice of honey cake. When he reached in his pocket to pay for his breakfast he pulled out the letter along with his cash. He stood for a moment, staring at the letter, turning it over and over in his hands, then put it back in his pocket, paid for his meal, and went to see Monsignor Andrassy.

Emil never thought he would see the day when he would seek out Andrassy's advice, but he knew the old man was the only one who could get through to Margit, if anyone could. He knocked on the rectory door without hesitation. Andrassy himself opened the door.

"Emil! What a surprise. Come in, my son, come in. I've just finished Mass, and was about to sit down to breakfast. Will you join me?"

"I've already eaten, Monsignor, but I wouldn't mind a cup of coffee."

"Indeed, it's a cool morning. Sit down, sit down. It's just as well you've eaten. Mrs. Juhasz has an attack of rheumatism, so I'm fending for myself today."

He poured the coffee and spread jam on his toast. "Well, Emil, suppose you tell me what is wrong."

"How do you know something is wrong, Monsignor?"

"You, of all people, do not come to me of your own accord. And, if I may say so, you do not look like a man who has had a good night's sleep. Now, I know you think me a foolish old man—no, don't try to protest, we are of different generations, and young people always think their elders are foolish. Something has been troubling you for a long time. You haven't been to confession in years. I fear for your soul, my son."

"I'm not here to talk about me, Monsignor. I'm here because of Margit."

"I see. What about Margit?"

"Her mother died."

Andrassy traced the sign of the cross in front of Emil. "May she rest in peace. I will of course stop by today to console her, and I assume you want a Requiem said?"

"Yes, but that's not all. I think you'd better read this letter. We just got it last night."

Andrassy took the letter from Emil and read it slowly, moving his lips as though he were reading his prayers. His face never altered from its usual look of composure, although he closed his eyes and shook his head after reading it.

"I shall pray for that poor child. Do you intend to send for her?"

"Unfortunately, Monsignor, my wife does not want the child."

"Ah."

"Please talk to her. She won't listen to anything I say."

"I will do what I can."

"Thank you, Monsignor."

"And is there nothing I can say to you, my son?"

Emil stood up.

"No, Monsignor. Nothing. I'll see myself out."

Emil had no idea what to expect when he got home that evening. He walked in the kitchen door warily, but the kitchen was spotless, everything from the night before put away, the floor scrubbed. A pot simmered on the stove. He walked into the living room, and saw Margit sitting in her chair, crocheting, as always. She did not look up when he came in.

"Margit."

"Yes?"

"Did Monsignor Andrassy come by today?"

"Yes. It was thoughtful of you to ask him. He'll say a Requiem Mass next Monday for Mama."

"Did he say anything else?"

"Nothing of importance."

"I see."

They ate dinner in silence. Emil ate mechanically, scarcely noticing what he ate. While Margit cleaned up he went upstairs to play with Ferenc and stayed till it was the little boy's bedtime. Eva looked at him curiously when he said goodnight.

"Emil, are you all right? Margit told me today about her mother. I'm very sorry."

He paused in the doorway.

"Thank you. I'm fine. I just didn't want to mention it in front of Ferenc."

"Of course. But I meant, well, I am surprised you aren't spending this time with Margit. She must be heartsick."

"Heartsick does not do justice to Margit's feelings, Eva. Good night."

When he went downstairs Margit was putting her crocheting away.

"Are you coming to bed?" she asked in a neutral voice.

"I think I'll stay up a while."

"As you wish."

When she had gone, Emil turned the light off, and lay down on the couch as he had the night before.

In the morning they rose in silence and dressed in silence and walked to church in silence. After his sermon Andrassy announced the death of Margit's mother. Margit sat dry-eyed, and after church received condolences with unaccustomed composure. Emil sought out the priest while she was occupied.

"Monsignor?"

"Yes, my son. I spoke to Margit yesterday about her nieces."

"And?"

"She's had quite a shock, the news about her mother's death. I think you should give her time."

"Those little girls don't have time, Monsignor."

"I understand, my son, and sympathize, but your responsibility is to your wife. Give her time, and then you can decide about it together. May God bless you, my child."

"Keep your blessing," Emil muttered after the priest had moved away. If Andrassy could not get through to Margit, it was hopeless. Emil could not face the long Sunday afternoon. After walking Margit home he left her at the door.

"Aren't you coming in?" she asked in surprise.

"No. There are some things at the office I want to catch up on."

"Can't it wait? Today is Sunday."

"No, it can't. Don't wait dinner for me."

He turned abruptly and walked down the stairs without giving her his usual kiss good by. He left so quickly he did not see Margit's face harden as she walked in the house. He did not know what his own face looked like until he passed a store window and was startled by the look of fury that stared back at him. He stopped, and took a deep breath, forcing his shoulders to relax, his fists to unclench. After a few minutes he walked on, but he passed his office and went into a part of town he rarely entered. It was an area of shops and small factories, and he stopped in front of a tavern with an auto mechanic shop on one side and a cheap rooming house on the other. He walked in, met the stares of the patrons with a brief nod, and ordered a bottle of cheap brandy and a glass. He took them to the far end of the tavern, sat at a dark table covered with dirty oilcloth, and opened the bottle.

He sat and drank all afternoon, talking to no one, eating only a cold beef sandwich. He left only when it grew dark, and then only because a woman approached him. He was so drunk that at first he asked her to sit down, but as his head and her meaning became clearer, he stood up suddenly and staggered out the door.

That was Zsuzsi's future, he thought as he stumbled home. In a village like Barakfalu, everyone would know what had happened to her. No village boy would think of marrying her. With no hope in Barackfalu, she'd end up in Eger, like the tawdry woman who'd approached him in the bar, and she'd die of consumption or worse by the time she was twenty-five.

Here, no one knew but Andrassy, and he reacted with compassion, as much as he could squeeze out of that ancient heart. Here, she could go to school and marry a nice boy and raise a family. Here, she could start over.

He fumbled with his key and opened the door. What else can I do, he thought. What else can I do? He slumped heavily on the couch and lay down in his shoes, coat, and hat.

In the morning Margit was furious.

"Did I marry a drunkard then? You woke the whole house when you stumbled in last night. I'm surprised you didn't wake the whole neighborhood. Don't you care what anyone thinks? You're a man of position in this community. How many people will buy your precious newspaper if you come home nights stinking of cheap whiskey and shouting on top of your lungs?"

Emil held his hands to his temples. He didn't remember anything of the night before. He'd had cheap brandy, and eaten a greasy sandwich, but after that everything was blank.

"Did I actually shout? Fancy that."

"Emil Molnar, don't you care what the neighbors will say about you?"

"No, Margit, I don't care a damn about the neighbors. What I do care about is that you don't care about why I got drunk in the first place."

"And am I supposed to ask why?"

"No, because you already know why." Emil sipped his coffee. That, at least, put a temporary halt to the tirade.

"I don't know what you're talking about," she said, finally.

"All you have to do is say yes, Margit, to an act of charity. Be the good Catholic in practice that you pretend to be every Sunday."

"I will not stand here and be insulted." She turned to leave the room.

"Just say yes, Margit."

Emil was not surprised when her only answer was the slamming of the bedroom door. He finished his coffee and put on his coat and hat. The cold air of outdoors helped him wake up even more than the coffee, and even though walking made his head hurt it was better than listening to Margit this morning. For once he did not pause in the garden, nor did he stop at his own office door, but he continued on to the telegraph office, where he paid for a wire to be delivered to Piros. It read, simply, "Send them at once. Emil."

For the first time in three days Emil smiled.

He worked cheerfully and hard all day. He whistled Beethoven's "Ode to Joy" on the way home and bounded up the stairs with energy. Margit looked up from her crocheting in surprise.

"Good evening, Margit."

"Emil. Shall I get dinner?"

"Dinner can wait a few moments. I have something to tell you." He rubbed his hands and rummaged through his record collection until he found the ninth symphony, and put it on the Victrola, while Margit looked at him quizzically.

He turned to her, smiling. "I've sent for them."

Margit's face registered puzzlement, then understanding, then anger.

Emil held up his hand as she opened her mouth.

"Before you say a word, let me speak. This morning I heard you ask over and over 'Don't you care?' about all sorts of things. Well, I do care. I care about family and I care about children and I care about obligations we take on in this world. I most assuredly do not care a whit about what the neighbors think, but you do. Now, I know you are opposed to having these children in our house, but you will get over it, Margit, I assure you that you will, because if you do not welcome these two girls into our house with an outward show of acceptance—not love, which you seem incapable of, merely acceptance—then my dear, I will see to it that every neighbor of ours knows about it in rich detail. I will print the story in the *Hirlap*, if I have to, but everyone whose miserable and worthless opinion you value so highly will know how uncharitable, self-centered, and unforgiving you are."

"Emil!"

He leaned over and put his hands on the arms of her chair, making her sit back.

"Mark my words, Margit. So far only you and I and Andrassy know how you really feel. You do not want that known throughout our community. I will make myself a laughingstock if I have to, but I will tell everyone what a bitch I have married if you do not adjust your thinking and behave like a good, Christian sister and aunt. Do I make myself clear?"

Margit sat with her mouth open. Emil watched fury and embarrassment and shock play over her features.

"Do I make myself clear?" he repeated.

"Yes," she hissed.

He smiled again. "Excellent. Shall we have dinner?"

He stood up, and Margit preceded him into the kitchen. She placed supper on the table and sat down, but ate nothing. Emil, on the other hand, ate heartily. That night he slept in his own bed, although both he and Margit turned their backs to each other, and slept as far apart as they could in a double bed.

The next day Emil gave Margit enough money to buy a bed for the girls.

"Get whatever you think they would like," he said. "I don't know anything about young girls, or their tastes. We'll have to get them clothes, too. I'm sure you'll do a superb job of that. You and Eva know what is fashionable these days."

He thought his spirits could get no higher, but ten days later, when he received a telegram from Piros confirming their arrival, he was filled with joy.

"Arriving New York February 17 on *Rotterdam*. God bless you." Emil kissed the telegram and put it in his pocket.

Then began the long wait for their arrival. Christmas was an uncomfortable and subdued day, although he and Margit both put on a good show of Christmas spirit for Ferenc. Each week of the brand new year he felt tension increase in their house. Margit bought the new furniture and helped put up fresh wallpaper, but largely in silence.

When the day finally approached, Emil knew better than to ask Margit if she wanted to accompany him to New York. He made a single reservation on the train and spent the trip imagining a house full of children. To his disappointment, he learned that the girls, as steerage passengers, had been detained at Ellis Island. They would be released at Jersey City, but possibly not for days. Emil went to Jersey City and booked a room at the cheapest hotel he could find. Every day, for three days, he waited and searched for them, wondering how he was to identify them among the crowds of people who had been released from Ellis Island. He knew they were accompanied by a married couple, but there would certainly be more than one family arriving with two young girls. How was he to find them?

In the end, it was easy. The younger of the two looked so much like Piros that Emil had no trouble picking them out. How Margit would deal with the resemblance he couldn't imagine, but he was grateful for it. He walked up to them, two thin girls with kerchiefs on their heads, and a young couple standing uncertainly behind them. He stopped a few feet away, removed his hat, and smiled.

"*Isten hozta Amerikába,*" he said. "Welcome to America."

Zsuzsi

Chapter Eleven
August 1921

As the crowd leaving the Majestic Theater strolled along Lincoln Street, two girls in white dresses turned south on Hardenbergh Avenue to window shop on the way home. Although almost all of their clothes were hand made, Zsuzsi and Jolan were eager to see the latest fall styles in the back-to-school displays of Pearlman's Department Store and B. J. Harding's. The two large stores, which had occupied diagonally opposite corners for the past forty years, dominated the downtown shopping district.

"Look at the new waistline, Zsuzsi," said Jolan. "Doesn't the dropped waist look comfortable?"

"It does, but think of wearing serge and gabardine again. I can't imagine it on such a hot day."

"I wish we were old enough to put our hair up," said Jolan, holding her thick, dark braid off her neck.

"I'd like to get my hair bobbed, like Theda Bara. Think how easy it must be to take care of—and so cool at this time of year." Zsuzsi held up her own braid and looked at her reflection in Pearlman's window.

"Your neck would get cold in the winter."

"Then I'd wear a scarf. I wear one anyway."

"Aunt Margit would have a fit."

Zsuzsi sighed, and let go of her braid. "You're right, she would have a fit. I bet Mama would let me do it, if she were here."

"I wish Mama would come here to stay with us."

Zsuzsi put her arm around Jolan and led her past Carpenter's shoe store. "I wish she would, too. Maybe someday there'll be enough money for that."

"Maybe someday we can go home to see her."

"Ugh, home! I miss Mama too, but I don't ever want to go back there. Horrible little village, horrible little houses. No moving pictures, no ice cream sodas. I'm glad to be here in America," Zsuzsi said with conviction.

"I'm glad, too, I suppose. Uncle Emil is a darling, even if Aunt Margit is a pill."

"Hush, Jolan, you shouldn't call her that."

"Well, she is."

Zsuzsi tried to look stern but in a moment began to giggle. She caught Jolan's eye and that set her sister to giggling, which soon escalated to outright laughter. They were laughing so hard they didn't even notice the young man loitering outside the tobacconist's shop. He took a cigarette out of his mouth and tossed it to the street before jogging a few steps to catch up.

"Hi, there, sweet pea," he said to Zsuzsi. "You sure seem happy today. How 'bout we go for a little walk and you can make me happy, too?"

Zsuzsi stiffened and moved closer to Jolan. She told herself that it was still daylight, that nothing could happen, especially with Jolan there. But Jolan was no match for this rough talking boy. Even though they were close to their own neighborhood, where the Hungarian-owned stores were located, there were few shoppers on the streets now that the stores had closed for the afternoon. Zsuzsi began to tremble.

"What do you say, sweet pea?"

"Just ignore him," said Jolan in Hungarian. She put her arm around Zsuzsi's waist.

"Couple of hunkies, eh? Tell you what, kid," he said to Jolan. "Why don't you get lost so I can talk to your pretty friend here?"

Zsuzsi's face reddened. Looking straight ahead, the two girls began to walk faster. The man matched their pace and grabbed Zsuzsi's arm.

"Now, sweet pea, don't run away. I just want to talk to you."

Jolan stopped and faced him. "No!" whispered Zsuzsi, but Jolan stepped between Zsuzsi and the stranger.

"You leave her alone."

He laughed. "Why don't you leave us alone, kiddo? Twenty-three skidoo."

"I said you leave her alone!" She kicked as hard as she could, cracking her heel against his left knee.

Taken by surprise, the man cried out and bent over to rub his knee.

"You little bitch!"

He straightened up and raised his arm to hit Jolan, but stopped when she stood her ground and put her fists up. He laughed again. "You want to fight me? Crazy bitch?"

"I said leave her alone and I meant it." She came at him but the man easily blocked her punch and shoved her so hard she fell down. He walked toward Zsuzsi, who stood with her back against a lamppost, but a passerby called out "Hey! What's going on?" The young man looked around, saw an older and larger man walking toward them, and hurried off.

The older man offered Jolan his hand. "Are you all right? Do you need help?"

Jolan rubbed her elbow and scowled up at him. "I'm fine and we don't need any help." She stood up by herself and wiped the back of her dress.

"Are you sure? Have you hurt your arm?"

"I said I'm fine! Just leave us alone."

"Well, okay, if you're sure."

"I'm sure," she said, and walked over to Zsuzsi.

Their would-be rescuer smiled and shook his head. "*Szivesen*—you're welcome!" he called before turning back.

Jolan blushed and walked over to Zsuzsi, who began to cry.

Jolan hugged her sister hard. "It's all right, Zsuzsi, it's all right. He's gone. I wouldn't have let him near you. I'd have gotten up and beaned him. It's all right, it's all right."

"He hurt you," Zsuzsi said when she could speak. "I'm so sorry."

"What are you sorry for? It's just a scraped elbow. I've gotten lots worse from climbing a tree. He was a hooligan—I wasn't going to stand there and let him bother you. Don't worry. I'm fine." She took a handkerchief out of her pocket and wiped Zsuzsi's face. "It's okay. Everything's okay, really. Let's go home, all right?"

Zsuzsi nodded. Jolan kissed her cheek and gave her a hug. "Come on, let's go."

When they got home, Margit was on the porch, fanning herself.

"Jolan," she said, "you've torn your dress."

"Yes, Aunt Margit. I tripped and fell down. I'll fix it tonight."

"That's one of your best dresses. You should be more careful. A young lady watches where she steps."

"Yes, Aunt Margit."

"And what's the matter with you, Zsuzsanna?"

"She has a headache," said Jolan hurriedly. "It's the heat. She just needs to lie down for a few minutes."

"If the heat bothers you, Zsuzsanna, you'd do better to sit out here on the porch with a cool drink."

"Yes, Aunt Margit," said Zsuzsi. "But I feel a bit light headed. I'll lie down for a little while and then come outside."

Jolan gave Zsuzsi's arm a tug and led her into the house. They took off their dresses and went into the bathroom to wash up. Zsuzsi sat on the edge of the tub while Jolan dabbed at her scraped elbow. Then she took a washcloth and, kneeling in front of Zsuzsi, gently wiped her sister's face.

"There, you look much better," she said. "Are you feeling all right, now?"

Zsuzsi nodded. "Thank you."

Jolan dampened the washcloth again and draped it across the back of Zsuzsi's neck. Zsuzsi smiled. "I do have a bit of a headache, so you didn't really lie to Aunt Margit."

"I never lie, especially to Aunt Margit."

Zsuzsi's smile deepened. "How badly is your dress torn?"

"It's nothing. I can take care of it later."

"I'll sew it for you. It was my fault it got torn."

"Zsuzsi, you know you're hopeless with a needle. I'll mend it myself. I don't mind."

"Thanks, Jolanka. Aunt Margit would just find fault if I did it."

Jolan sat down next to her. "She'll find fault with my stitches, too. You should be glad you're so good at drawing. I can't do anything well enough for her."

"Jolan, that's not true."

"You know it is. She doesn't like how I cook, how I sew, how I crochet or embroider. Nothing I do pleases her. She doesn't criticize you half so much. I think she likes you better."

"You shouldn't think that, Jolan. Besides, I don't think she really likes either of us, if you want to know the truth."

"At least she gives you half a chance. What have I done to make her dislike me so?"

Zsuzsi squeezed her sister's hand. "You haven't done anything, it's just her way. Look, we'd better get dressed and go outside. Aunt Margit probably wonders what we're doing in here."

They put on clean cotton skirts and blouses and walked onto the porch. "Where's Uncle Emil?" Jolan asked Margit.

"He went up the street for a walk. He should be on his way home by now."

"May we go meet him?" asked Zsuzsi.

"Are you feeling better so soon, Zsuzsanna?"

"Oh yes, Aunt Margit, much better. May we go?"

Margit nodded. The two girls hurried down the steps and up Kossuth Street. In a few blocks the sidewalk ended and the street narrowed to a country lane. On one side was a large pasture where a herd of Guernseys lay chewing their cuds. On the other was a long stretch of woods. The two girls walked in the shade of the trees, next to a tangled thicket of honeysuckle and brambles. Jolan absently plucked at the last of the wild blackberries.

"Be careful not to get berry juice on your clothes," Zsuzsi warned. "Think what Aunt Margit would say if you ruined two outfits in one day."

Jolan made a face and wiped her fingers on a spray of honeysuckle leaves. She took an exaggerated step over a pile of horse droppings and mimicked, "A young lady watches where she steps."

Zsuzsi giggled and pointed down the road. "Not so loud! There's Uncle Emil."

The two girls ran to meet him. Emil smiled and held his arms out to them. He hugged and kissed them in turn, and then walked on with an arm around each niece. He gave Zsuzsi an extra squeeze. It had not been so long ago that she would have shrunk away from his touch, but Emil's kindness and gentle manner had won her trust. Now he was a haven of warmth for her, unlike Margit. Zsuzsi couldn't understand how her aunt could be so different from her mother, who was always quick to hug and kiss her daughters. When the two girls first arrived in Hardenbergh Margit had been coldly polite; she stiffened when the girls kissed her goodnight and never kissed them back. Now she was somewhat more relaxed, but still aloof, and always formal in her manner. Aunt Margit never hugged anyone, not even Uncle Emil, unlike her mother and father, who always had laughed and touched and kissed.

"Is something the matter, Zsuzsi?" asked Emil.

"Not really, I was just thinking about Papa and Mama."

"Are you still homesick?"

"A little, I suppose. Not that I want to go back; I love living here, it's just that everything was so wonderful before the war, before Papa died. I wish it had never happened."

"We all wish it had never happened, Zsuzsi, but I mind it less than I used to because it brought you and Jolan here to us." He hugged them closer. "Nothing ever stays the same, Zsuzsi, as much as we would like it to. It's no good wishing for what used to be—none of us can have what is past. So the best thing is to look forward, toward the future; your life is ahead of you, not behind. Don't ever let your life be ruled by memories, good or bad. Happiness lies ahead, remember that."

"I will, Uncle Emil."

They stopped to look at the cows, which were still were lying in the grass, chewing, except for one who rubbed her hindquarters on a fence post. She turned around when she had taken care of her itch and allowed the girls to scratch her head.

"And now," said Emil, "tell me about school. Are you looking forward to it?"

"I suppose so," said Zsuzsi. "I wish summer didn't go by so quickly, though."

"And what about you, Jolan?"

Jolan grimaced. "I'd rather it be summer all year long."

"And have no Christmas?"

"Of course I want Christmas. I just wish I didn't have to sit in a boring classroom for months and months. It's not so bad for Zsuzsi; she graduates this spring, but I have another whole year after this one. It feels like forever."

"Well," said Emil, "if you really feel that way I suppose we could let you work in the cigar factory instead."

"I'd have to roll cigars? All day?" Jolan's look of horror made Emil and Zsuzsi laugh.

"I guess I can stand school for a while longer if that's my only choice," said Jolan.

"It's not really so bad, is it?" asked Emil.

"School is all right," answered Zsuzsi. "We just don't have many friends "

"Why is that?"

"I guess because we aren't Americans," said Zsuzsi.

"You already speak English better than I do. Shall I discuss it with your English teacher, perhaps?"

"No, Uncle Emil!" said Zsuzsi. "Please don't do that. It's not just our accents—it's lots of things."

"Such as?"

"Such as American girls don't wear earrings to school," said Jolan. "They don't get their ears pierced like we do."

"But your earrings look lovely," said Emil. "Don't you like them?"

"We like them, Uncle Emil," said Zsuzsi. "They just make it harder for us to fit in."

"Oh," said Jolan. "Let's not talk about school any more. It's weeks away yet."

But the last few weeks of summer slip by quickly, and it seemed as though only a few days had passed when Jolan and Zsuzsi dressed in their uniforms for the first day of school. In their gray wool jumpers, they looked almost like twins, although Zsuzsi was taller and more slender than her sister. Her eyes, the same clear gray-blue as Margit's, were accented by the gray cloth of her uniform, while Jolan had the deep blue eyes of their mother.

When they were ready to leave they met Eva on the porch. She stood proudly next to Ferenc, for whom this was the first day of school. He fidgeted and wiggled in the St. Elizabeth's boys' uniform, short pants of navy gabardine and a starched white shirt with a stiff collar above a navy blue bow.

"All ready," said Eva. She bent down to give Ferenc another goodbye kiss but he wiggled away.

"I want to go to school just like Zsuzsi and Jo-Jo," he said.

"We'll take good care of him, Eva," said Jolan. She held out her hand for Ferenc.

"Don't forget, Ferenc, I'll be waiting for you right in front of the school when it's time to come home."

"Yes, Mama."

"He's never been away from home before." Eva's eyes filled with tears. "He's growing up so quickly."

Ferenc tugged at Jolan's hand. Zsuzsi gave Eva a hug, and they walked down the steps.

"Be sure to hold his hand crossing the street," called Eva.

Ferenc pranced and skipped all the way to St. Elizabeth's, where Zsuzsi and Jolan delivered him to the nuns. But he pulled back when he saw the sister's flowing black habit.

"I want Mama."

"Don't you want to go to school anymore?" asked Jolan. Ferenc shook his head.

Zsuzsi knelt down in front of him. "Now Ferenc, you're a big boy now, and big boys go to school. You want to be a big boy, don't you?"

Ferenc nodded.

"Well, then, you have to go to school. All the other boys are going in. You don't want to be a little boy who runs back home to Mama, do you?"

Ferenc shrugged. Zsuzsi put her hand on his back and gently pushed him toward the nun, who smiled and held out her hand.

"Hello, young man. I am Sister Ursula."

"Go on," whispered Jolan.

Ferenc reluctantly stepped forward and took Sister Ursula's hand.

"Thank you for bringing him," she said. They walked into the school building together, past the sycamores that flanked the steps. Ferenc looked back at Zsuzsi and Jolan, who smiled and waved.

"Poor little thing. He looks terrified," said Jolan.

"He'll be all right, once he gets used to it. Besides, it's only a half-day for him today. He'll see his Mama soon enough. But we'd better go or we'll be late for Mass."

The two girls walked on to St. Brendan's. The imposing brick church stood next to the high school building, which all the Catholic students in Hardenbergh attended, regardless of their ethnic background. Inside the church, Zsuzsi and Jolan sat with their respective classes. Seniors like Zsuzsi sat in the front pews, right behind the nuns. Juniors sat behind the seniors, sophomores behind the juniors, and freshmen in the rear. Boys sat on the right-hand side of the church, and girls on the left. Mass on the first day of school was required at St. Brendan's, as was Mass on the first Friday of the month, and every Friday during Lent.

After Mass the students formed lines two by two to enter the high school assembly hall. Zsuzsi found herself standing next to a new girl. They weren't allowed to talk on line, so Zsuzsi couldn't say hello, but she would have smiled a welcome if the new girl had ever looked at her. Instead, the girl stood hunched over, looking down at her shoes. Wisps of brown hair hung in untidy strings along the side of her face, masking her expression, but Zsuzsi saw that the girl had plain features, except for a sprinkling of freckles across her nose and cheeks. She had no time for further observations because Sister Aloysius rang the brass bell to start the school day. The lines of students filed into the building. After assembly, Zsuzsi entered her classroom and took a seat next to the window, near the front of the room. The new girl sat down two aisles away. She tried to walk straight to the back of the classroom but was shoved aside by a group of senior boys, who filled all the seats in the back row of the classroom.

The students stood in unison as their teacher entered the room. "Good morning, class," said the nun, imposing and ageless in the severe black habit of a Sister of Charity. "I am Sister Patrick."

"Good Morning, Sister Patrick," said the class.

After Sister Patrick led the morning prayer, the class sat down while she called the roll. "Mary Alice Andrews."

"Here."

"Agatha Barry."

"Here."

"Edward Boylan."

"Present."

"Gertrude Bornheimer."

On hearing the unfamiliar name, everyone turned to look at the new girl, who blushed and said "Here" in a quiet voice.

One or two girls giggled. Edward Boylan muttered "A kraut." He smiled to his friends but his smile faded when he realized that Sister Patrick was staring at him.

"Gertrude is a new student this year," said Sister Patrick. "I am sure you will all make her feel welcome. Do I make myself clear, Mr. Boylan?"

"Yes, Sister," he said.

Zsuzsi shook her head slightly as the roll continued. Eddie Boylan was a popular boy, not used to being embarrassed in front of the entire class like that. Zsuzsi was glad she wasn't the new girl. It was hard for a new student to make friends, but easy enough to make an enemy of someone like Eddie.

The first day of school went by quickly, unlike the days to follow. Zsuzsi soon realized that English and algebra would be as difficult as ever, that civics would be easy and interesting, religion easy and boring, and chemistry challenging but fun. When the bell rang to signal the end of the class day, she met Jolan in front of the school, as she always did, to walk home together.

"We have a new girl in our class," said Zsuzsi, after they had compared notes on their classes and teachers. "Her name's Gertrude Bornheimer."

"What's she like?"

"I don't know, really. Terribly shy and quiet."

"Worse than you?"

"I'm not that bad! She stares down at her feet all day. She's as drab as a mouse."

"She doesn't sound too interesting, that's for sure," said Jolan.

"I wonder where she's from?" Zsuzsi said, thoughtfully.

She was able to find out two days later, when she and Gertrude were assigned as partners in Chemistry lab. Here they could speak to one another as they practiced weighing materials.

"So, Gertrude, how do you like St. Brendan's so far?" asked Zsuzsi as she tried to pour exactly one ounce of sodium chloride onto the scale.

"It's all right."

"Where did you go to school before?"

"In Pennsylvania. We just moved from there."

"Did your father get a job here? Is that why you moved?"

Gertrude nodded.

Zsuzsi frowned. Trying to talk to Gertrude seemed as easy as trying to balance the touchy scale. Gertrude seemed uncomfortable talking about herself—maybe Zsuzsi was asking too many questions.

"My father was killed in the War," she said. "I live with my aunt and uncle."

"You're lucky."

Zsuzsi thought that an odd response, although, if she were orphaned, and had no relatives, where would she be?

"I suppose you're right," she said. "By the way, only the nuns and my aunt call me Zsuzsanna. Everyone else calls me Zsuzsi."

Gertrude took her turn using the scale. She had trouble weighing a precise amount, because she tipped the bag of salt too far, spilling it all over the scale and onto the table just as Sister Joseph passed by.

"Sweep it up and start over, Gertrude," said Sister Joseph.

"Yes, Sister," said Gertrude, but her hands were trembling so badly she only spilled more.

"Relax, I'll take care of it," said Zsuzsi. She looked at Gertrude curiously. Gertrude stood hunched over, her face so pale the freckles stood out vividly. She looked about to burst into tears.

"Gertrude, it's only a little salt. Throw a pinch over your shoulder and everything will be fine."

"What?" asked Gertrude.

"My Aunt Margit says you should throw a pinch of salt over your shoulder any time you spill it, and then you won't have bad luck."

Slowly, Gertrude reached out and picked up a pinch of salt. She threw it over her shoulder and then wiped her hands on her skirt.

"See? Everything's fine. You don't have to worry about Sister Joseph, you know. She's a peach. There, all cleaned up."

"Thank you," whispered Gertrude, so quietly Zsuzsi could hardly hear her. She stepped up to the table and poured salt carefully onto the scale. Zsuzsi watched her, wondering what on earth could make a girl so frightened. Maybe she had never been to Catholic school before. Nuns certainly looked forbidding in their severe habits, and many of their teachers were strict, but usually only young children, like Ferenc, were actually afraid of them.

Sister Aloysius' brass bell signaled the end of class and put a stop to Zsuzsi's musing. As they gathered up their books and walked to the door, Gertrude turned and almost looked Zsuzsi in the eye.

"I like to be called Trudy," she said, and slipped through the door before Zsuzsi could reply.

On Monday Trudy was almost late for homeroom. She walked in just before the bell, holding her head down even more than usual. She brushed her hair with one hand as she walked to her seat, and sat down holding her hand up to her face as though she had a headache. When Sister Patrick called the roll, she answered in such a quiet voice that Sister Patrick looked up from her attendance book.

"Gertrude," she said, "Sit up straight and take your hand from your face. Young ladies sit erect with their hands folded."

Trudy complied slowly. When she held up her head the whole class could see a large bruise across her cheekbone. Her classmates murmured in surprise until Sister Patrick rapped her desk for silence.

"Gertrude, what happened to your face?" she asked.

Trudy blushed. "I—I walked into a door last night."

"I see," said Sister Patrick. "Have the school nurse look at it before first period class."

Trudy hesitated. "It's just a bruise, Sister. It doesn't hurt much at all."

"Gertrude, I said go to the nurse."

Trudy swallowed hard. "Yes, Sister." She stood up slowly and walked out of the room with tears in her eyes.

Zsuzsi frowned. How could anyone walk into a door that hard? It looked awful, and must hurt terribly, despite what Trudy had said.

Sister Patrick continued the roll. When the bell rang for first period class, Zsuzsi gathered her books and stood up. Behind her, Eddie Boylan whispered to his friends, "You don't get a shiner like that from walking into any door."

Chapter 12
November 1921

A few weeks before Thanksgiving, Trudy missed several days of school. On Wednesday Sister Patrick called Zsuzsi to her desk, just before the end of the last class.

"Gertrude Bornheimer has fallen and broken her arm," said Sister Patrick. "She will be out of school for several more days. You seem to be fairly close to her, Zsuzsanna, so I would like you to bring her the next few days' assignments. We don't want Gertrude to fall too far behind in her schoolwork."

"Yes, Sister," said Zsuzsi. "But I don't know where she lives."

"I've written her address for you." Sister Patrick handed the paper to Zsuzsi. "Do you know where that street is?"

"Yes, Sister."

"Good. Then you can take these assignments to Gertrude after school."

Zsuzsi took the envelope from Sister Patrick and returned to her desk. Since September she and Trudy had slowly become friends, beginning with their partnership in Chemistry lab, where Trudy's clumsiness was offset by her ability with figures. While Zsuzsi handled all the materials of their experiments, Trudy did the calculations. Soon they began to have lunch together, and over sandwiches Trudy slowly opened up: She was an only child. Her father had worked in the coalmines of Pennsylvania, but he had never stayed at any one mine for a long time, so they moved frequently. When her father developed a bad cough, the doctor had forbidden him to work in the mines any longer. He had tried his hand at farming for a short while, but was unable to do the work, and so they came to Hardenbergh, where Mr. Bornheimer got a job as a packer in the cigar factory.

Although Trudy never spoke of it, Zsuzsi guessed that her father wasn't making very much money packing cigars. Trudy's clothes were ill-fitting, and her luncheon sandwich was usually scanty, sometimes only buttered bread. Zsuzsi often shared her own lunch, and tried to include an extra apple, or a second piece of cake, especially for Trudy.

She had heard of Water Street, where the Bornheimers lived, but had never been there. Trudy always went straight home after school, and never invited Zsuzsi to accompany her. Zsuzsi invited Trudy home several times, but Trudy always had an excuse for declining.

Zsuzsi met Jolan after school and they walked to Water Street together. Zsuzsi was glad for Jolan's company. Water Street was in the oldest part of Hardenbergh, only a few blocks from the center of town, but in an area of factories and run-down rooming houses, with a tavern or small store on most corners. The streets were unpaved and bare of trees. They passed the cigar factory where Mr. Bornheimer worked, a large brick building with small windows, so dirty they couldn't see anything inside except for the yellow glow of overhead lights. Two blocks beyond they turned onto Water Street and began walking toward the river.

Zsuzsi looked again at the address. "Trudy's house is on the other side of the street."

"Let's walk all the way to the river, and then turn and come up the other side," suggested Jolan. "After all, it isn't more than a couple of blocks, and we've never been here."

They walked past the small, two-story houses. In style they weren't so different from the houses on Kossuth Street, but they were smaller, and shabby, with peeling paint and sagging roofs. There were no front yards, so the porches opened directly onto the street. Three little girls playing jump rope stopped and stared as Zsuzsi and Jolan passed by. Otherwise the street seemed deserted.

The two girls stopped when they reached the end of the street. They were standing on a small bluff overlooking the river, maybe fifteen feet below. The river flowed past sluggishly. A wagon wheel lay in the brown water next to a soggy newspaper. Several empty bottles lay scattered along the shore. A steep path, just a narrow, bare patch in the weeds, led down the bluff to the river's edge.

"The water looks so dirty up close," said Jolan. "It doesn't smell so good, either."

Zsuzsi frowned. "Come on, let's go."

She led the way to Trudy's house, the third house from the end. The porch steps creaked as they went up to the front door, which had been painted red once. The walls of the house had flecks of once-white paint on them but were mostly bare weathered boards. Zsuzsi noticed a coating of grime on the windowsill.

She knocked on the door. In a moment she heard slow footsteps. She expected to be greeted by Trudy's mother but instead Trudy herself answered the door. She looked even more disheveled than usual in a rumpled nightgown, and was so pale her freckles stood out sharply on her face. Her left arm was bent and lay in a sling with splints protruding toward her fingers, which were bruised and swollen.

"Zsuzsi! What are you doing here?"

"Sister Patrick asked me to bring you our assignments. This is my sister Jolan. May we come in?"

Trudy looked dismayed. "I guess so. The place is a mess, though. My mother works, and I can't clean house with this contraption on my arm."

"That's all right," Zsuzsi said. "We won't stay long."

Trudy stood aside so they could enter. They were standing in a dark, narrow hallway, facing a flight of stairs. When Trudy shut the door the sour smell in the hall made Zsuzsi want to hold her breath.

"We live downstairs," said Trudy. She led them down the hall into the kitchen. It was a small room, just large enough to hold an ancient wood stove, an icebox, a sink, and a small table. Dirty dishes covered the table and more were stacked in the sink. When Zsuzsi stepped into the kitchen something crunched under her feet.

"It doesn't usually look like this," Trudy said. "I haven't been able to take care of things since I broke my arm." She stood in the middle of the room awkwardly. "I've been in bed."

"Then you must go right back to bed," said Zsuzsi. She smiled. "We'll tuck you in."

Trudy led them into a room that held a single bed and two chairs whose frayed arms were not even covered by doilies. Beyond this room, through an archway partly covered by a threadbare curtain, Zsuzsi could see another unmade bed.

Trudy got into bed and Zsuzsi fluffed up her pillow, then helped her lean back. Jolan sat down on one of the chairs after first removing a shirt that smelled strongly of tobacco. Zsuzsi arranged the covers around Trudy and then sat carefully on the edge of the bed.

Trudy closed her eyes for a moment. "Sorry. It still hurts."

"I'm sorry we made you get out up," said Zsuzsi. "Can I get you anything? A glass of water or something?"

"No thanks. My mother will be home in an hour or so. She works at the cigar factory, too."

"I didn't know that," said Zsuzsi.

"How did you break your arm?" asked Jolan.

Trudy looked down at her fingers. In the dim light they looked like purple sausages. "I fell. Down the porch steps."

Zsuzsi shook her head slightly. Trudy was certainly clumsy, no doubt about that. She almost always had a bruise on an arm or a leg. But falling down a flight of stairs—even little Ferenc was more sure-footed than that.

"Well, we don't want to tire you out," she said. "Let me give you these assignments." She showed Trudy the papers from Sister Patrick. "I'm supposed to pick these up from you on Monday. Will you be able to do them by then?"

"I think so. At least it's my left arm that's broken. I can still write. I'll probably feel better by then, too."

Zsuzsi stood up. "Well, you take care, all right? And if you need help with anything, call me."

"We don't have a telephone," Trudy said in a quiet voice.

"Well, I guess I'll see you on Monday, then. Don't try to get up."

"Goodbye."

"It was nice meeting you, Trudy," said Jolan.

They left the apartment and stepped onto the porch. Zsuzsi took a deep breath, relieved to be out of that cramped and dirty little house. She looked down carefully as they walked down the steps. The handrail was a little wobbly and the stairs creaked but they were sound. There were no loose boards to trip on, no rough edges to catch a heel, nothing to make anyone fall.

They walked home silently. Zsuzsi had never seen anything like that house. Even in Hungary, during the worst of the war, when everyone was hungry, there had been water from the well to wash with, and brooms to sweep clean the packed dirt in front of the houses. Zsuzsi may have worn a patched dress but it had been a clean one.

It was a relief to get back to Kossuth Street, where the trees softened the view, even without their leaves, where the houses were clean and the yards well kept.

"I never noticed before how clean our street is," said Jolan.

"Neither did I."

"I saw a cockroach in their kitchen when we walked through it. I haven't seen one of those since we moved here."

"Well, don't tell Aunt Margit or she'll make us take all our clothes off before we come into the house," said Zsuzsi.

On Monday Jolan was waiting for Zsuzsi at the school steps.

"You don't have to come with me every time, you know," said Zsuzsi. "I'm sure you don't really want to."

"That's okay. Besides, would you rather go back alone?"

"Not really. Thanks."

Zsuzsi was, in fact, relieved that Jolan was there. The poverty of Trudy's neighborhood, and the squalor inside the house, made Zsuzsi so uncomfortable that she wished she'd never agreed to get Trudy's assignments. But this time the house was somewhat cleaner. Mrs. Bornheimer must have been able to clean over the weekend, for most of the dirty clothes were out of sight, and the floor had been swept. The table and sink still had dishes on them, but only one meal's worth. Trudy, too, looked stronger, though she was still pale and unable to stand for very long.

"Sorry about the mess again. I just can't do much around the house yet," Trudy said.

"Trudy, no one expects you to do anything with a broken arm. There's no need to apologize," said Zsuzsi.

"Why don't I do the dishes for you?" asked Jolan.

"No, please don't do that," Trudy said quickly. "It's very kind of you to offer, but there's no need."

"Trudy, your mother will be awfully tired when she gets home from work. It won't take me long at all, and she'll never have to know. You can tell her you managed it, somehow."

Over Trudy's protests, Jolan went into the kitchen. Trudy sank back against the pillow, her cheeks red under the pallor.

"We don't have any hot water in the house," she whispered to Zsuzsi.

"That's all right," Zsuzsi said. "We used to heat water all the time in Hungary. I'll light the stove."

Between them, Zsuzsi and Jolan managed to light the unfamiliar stove, and using cold water scrubbed out a pot until it was clean enough to hold wash water. While the water heated, Zsuzsi and Trudy went over the week's schoolwork. Then Zsuzsi dried the dishes as Jolan washed, with Trudy sitting at the kitchen table, directing Zsuzsi where to put the clean dishes and pots.

When they were done, Zsuzsi said, "We still have hot water. Would you like me to wash your hair for you?"

Trudy reached up and touched her hair, which lay in greasy strings, combed but by no means clean.

"Think how good it will feel," said Zsuzsi. "I know when I've been sick, one of the first things I do is wash my hair. It makes me feel so much better, and you certainly can't do it yourself with that sling."

"No," Trudy said hesitantly, "but it's getting late. It'll be dark soon, and you should get home before—before dark."

"We have plenty of time. Come on."

Jolan brought a chair over to the sink, and helped Trudy sit in it. She leaned back, and Zsuzsi poured water over her head, and then soaped her hair. Trudy closed her eyes and sighed.

"Doesn't that feel good?" said Zsuzsi.

"It feels wonderful."

Zsuzsi smiled. She remembered, when she was little, how much her mother enjoyed washing her hair, and Jolan's, on bath day. Now she knew why. It felt good to wash someone else's hair, to feel the suds squeezing through your fingers, and the silkiness of long hair as you rinsed it clean.

"There," she said, when Trudy was sitting upright again, with her hair still wet but clean and combed. "Much better."

Outside, a four o'clock whistle blew.

"Thanks so much, for everything," said Trudy. "But now you really had better go. It's getting late."

"All right. We'll see you in a few days."

The girls left the house and began walking home. Up ahead, a man turned the corner and began to walk unsteadily toward them. He was tall and thin, and stared down at the sidewalk in front of him. Zsuzsi reached for Jolan's hand. "Let's cross the street," she whispered. Jolan nodded.

As they stepped off the curb, the man tripped on the uneven slates, reaching for a porch rail to steady himself. He must have seen them walking, for he looked up and glared at them with bloodshot eyes. Zsuzsi and Jolan walked on, but Zsuzsi turned her head to watch the man's progress. He stumbled up the stairs of Trudy's house.

"That must be Trudy's father," said Zsuzsi.

"What was wrong with him?" asked Jolan.

"I think he's drunk."

"Drunk? What about prohibition."

"Don't be naive, Jolan, prohibition just means you can't buy it in stores. Even Uncle Emil manages somehow to get a bottle of brandy now and then."

"Poor Trudy," said Jolan.

"Poor Trudy," agreed Zsuzsi.

They walked past the cigar factory, and merged into the crowd of workers who were going home for the day.

The following week, Trudy was able to go back to school, much to Zsuzsi's relief, but shortly after Thanksgiving Trudy was absent again. After school, Zsuzsi told Jolan she was going to Trudy's house.

"But Zsuzsi, we promised Eva we would take care of Ferenc this afternoon. She has a fitting to do, remember? And Aunt Margit is waiting for us to watch him so she can go to the poultry store before it closes."

"Oh, darn. Jolan, would you mind watching Ferenc by yourself? I'm worried about Trudy. She's missed so much school already. She may have fallen, and hurt her arm again. I just have to make sure she's all right."

"I don't mind watching Ferenc, but do you mind going there alone?" asked Jolan.

"Not really," Zsuzsi lied. "I won't stay long, I promise. Tell Aunt Margit I'll be home as soon as I can."

"All right, if you're sure. I'll see you in a little while."

Zsuzsi walked as fast as she could to Trudy's house, telling herself the whole way that she was perfectly safe. It was still daylight, after all, and when she returned the street would be full of factory workers. But the walk seemed longer than when Jolan was with her, and a cool breeze blowing off the river made the air damp and chilly.

When she got to Trudy's house, Zsuzsi knocked on the door and waited. There was no answer. She knocked again, and a third time. Finally, she heard Trudy's voice.

"Who is it?"

"It's me, Trudy. Zsuzsi. May I come in?"

"No, go away, Zsuzsi. I'm—I'm all right. Please go away."

"Are you ill, Trudy? You were absent today."

"It's nothing. Please go now."

Zsuzsi hesitated. Trudy didn't sound like she was sick, but she also didn't sound like everything was all right.

"Trudy? Please, let me in for just a moment. Please, Trudy? It's getting cold out here."

In a moment she heard the sound of a key turning in a lock. The door opened a few inches.

"Trudy?" Zsuzsi pushed the door open gently and stepped inside the dark hallway. "I won't stay long, I promise. I just want to make sure you're okay."

"I'm fine," Trudy said, holding her head down.

"Then let's go in the kitchen for a few minutes." Zsuzsi began walking down the hall before Trudy could protest. The kitchen was even dirtier than the first time she visited. She cleared newspapers and an assortment of dirty clothing off the chairs and sat down. Trudy came into the kitchen slowly. Zsuzsi stood up as Trudy moved into the light.

"My God, Trudy, what happened to you?" Her friend's left cheek was bruised, and her lip was split and swollen.

"Nothing," Trudy said. She walked to the table with an odd, shuffling step, as though it hurt to walk. She sat down slowly, wincing with pain.

"Nothing? You're hurt! Do you want to lie down" asked Zsuzsi.

"No!" said Trudy. She cradled the sling in her left arm and shifted slightly to get more comfortable.

"Then let me at least get you a pillow," said Zsuzsi. She walked into the next room over Trudy's protests. The bed was in disarray, with a coverlet thrown over the bare mattress. Zsuzsi smoothed the covers and then picked up the pillow. Hidden beneath the pillow was a rolled-up cloth—a bed sheet. Why would Trudy have wadded up her sheet like that? Zsuzsi unrolled the sheet, and saw a reddish stain marring the cloth. Slowly, she pulled back the faded coverlet. The mattress, too, was stained, a dark rust color, the color of blood.

Zsuzsi felt sick. She backed up until she stumbled against a chair, and sat down heavily. She hadn't thought about it in such a long time, it had begun to seem almost unreal, like a dream. Now she remembered too clearly the rough wool of his uniform; the buttons sharp and cold against her skin; his hands lifting her dress, then covering her mouth; the sour smell of cheap wine on his breath; the pain. Pain and blood.

She got up slowly and replaced the sheet and pillow. It seemed to take a long time. Her heart was beating so hard she thought surely Trudy must hear it. She took a deep breath before walking back into the kitchen, where Trudy sat without moving, her head down, arms folded tight across her middle.

Zsuzsi sat down and swallowed hard before speaking. "Trudy, I know what happened to you."

Trudy looked up for the first time. "What do you mean?" she whispered.

Zsuzsi began to cry. "The way you're walking. The way it hurts you to sit. I saw the sheet, and the mattress. I know because it happened to me, once. A long time ago."

Trudy stared at Zsuzsi. "No!"

"Who did this to you, Trudy?"

Trudy shook her head.

"Do you know who he was? Did he follow you home from school yesterday?"

Trudy shook her head again and began to cry. Zsuzsi knelt in front of her and took Trudy in her arms. When they could speak again Zsuzsi said, "Please, tell me what happened, Trudy. Maybe I can help. You have to talk to someone, you'll go crazy if you don't."

"I can't! He'll kill me if I tell!"

"Who, Trudy? Who'll kill you?"

"I can't tell you."

"All right, then I promise I won't tell anyone. Not anyone! I mean it. I won't tell anyone, not even Jolan, I promise, Trudy. I promise."

Trudy took a deep breath. "Swear you won't. Swear it."

Zsuzsi took her rosary from her pocket. "I swear on my rosary, Trudy. I won't tell a soul."

Trudy wiped her eyes with the back of her hand. "It happened last night. Mama has been working at night, to earn extra money. We need more money. I told her I'd quit school and go to work in the factory, but she wants me to finish high school. She said she'd do anything to keep me in high school, to keep me out of the factory. So after she works all day, she comes home for a quick supper and then goes back to the factory, to clean. She started Monday. And she doesn't get home till almost midnight." She picked at a thread on the cuff of her nightgown. "My father drinks. Did you know that?"

"I guessed."

"Last night, he came home drunk. It happens all the time. Mostly he just falls asleep, but sometimes he acts crazy. He did this." She put her hand to her face. "And this." She held up her broken arm. "You see? I'm not as clumsy as I pretend to be." She tried to laugh, but began to cry again instead.

Zsuzsi held her right hand. "Go on."

"He—last night, he came home. He wanted to know where Mama was. He was so drunk, he'd forgotten that she was at work. When I told him, he got angry. He hates that he can't support us anymore, he hates that she's working two jobs. It's why he drinks. But he gets so angry. And then, last night, he started to cry, and he said"—her voice dropped to a whisper—"only one thing made him feel like a man anymore, and now even that was taken away, now that Mama worked nights. And then, he looked up at me."

Zsuzsi felt like she was going to be sick again. "Oh, my God, Trudy! Not your own father!"

Trudy nodded. "I tried to stop him but he hit me and then..."

Zsuzsi put her arms around Trudy again. Her mind flew from thought to thought, that it was monstrous, so much worse than what had happened to her, someone must be told, someone must stop it, Trudy couldn't spend another night in this house, she must get help, before her father came home.

Zsuzsi sat back on her heels, and held Trudy's hand. "Does your mother know?"

"No. She mustn't find out, ever. It would kill her. And—and he might hurt her."

"Trudy, you can't stay here."

"I have to."

"But tonight, what if—what if he..."

"It'll be okay. When he gets as drunk as he was last night, he feels guilty afterward, and he's nice to us for a few days. He won't do anything tonight."

"Even so, come stay at my house."

"No."

"Trudy, you can't stay. You have to get help, at least see a doctor—"

"No!"

"You can't pretend nothing's happened."

"Yes I can." Trudy nodded. "And I will. It's the only thing I can do."

"But what can I do?" asked Zsuzsi.

"Nothing! Nothing, don't you see? If you tell anyone, if you try to do anything, anything at all, it'll just make things worse. You don't know what it's like—not what happened last night, but what happens all the time. When he gets angry—you just don't know! You live in a nice clean house with nice clean people! You don't know anything about it!"

"I can't just walk away, Trudy, as though nothing's happened."

"You must. It's the only way you can really help me. And go now, please, before he comes home. If he sees you here, and sees your face, he'll know I told, and it'll be worse, much worse for me. Believe that, Zsuzsi, the worst thing you can do is try to do anything at all." She squeezed Zsuzsi's hand. "Go home now, please. Do it for me. And remember, you swore not to tell."

"But, Trudy!"

"You swore. Now go. Before the whistle blows."

Zsuzsi nodded. She walked slowly into the hall, out of the house, into the cold fresh air. The sun was hidden by a blanket of thick cloud and the light was already dim, as though someone had put a dark shade over a lamp. By the time Zsuzsi reached home it would be nearly dark. She turned up the collar of her coat and walked down the stairs. She hesitated, tempted to go back and bring Trudy home with her, but she knew it wasn't possible. Too many questions would be asked, and she had sworn to keep Trudy's secret. Already the secret pressed on her conscience like a great weight.

She began to walk home, toward light, toward warmth, where there was no secret so terrible it could not be borne.

Chapter 13
December 1921

Eva's dining room table was as usual covered with fabric and thread; the untidiness never changed, only the colors and textures differed from season to season. Today a bolt of burgundy velvet lay half unfolded across one side of the table; on the other, hastily shoved aside to make room for the fabric, was a jumble of spools and bobbins, pincushions, tape measure, and patterns. The table itself had been pushed close to the wall to make room for the dressmaker's dummy that stood in the middle of the floor, wearing only a skirt of the burgundy velvet. The sewing machine was next to the window, to catch the best light.

When Zsuzsi came upstairs, she saw Eva kneeling on the floor, picking up hundreds of tiny glass beads, the same rich wine color as the velvet. She knelt down and began picking up the beads that had rolled toward that end of the room.

"Let me guess," she said. "Ferenc came running by and knocked these off the table."

"Not this time," sighed Eva. "Ferenc is safely next door, playing with Istvan. This was my fault. I reached for the pincushion and knocked this over. Of all days! I have three gowns to finish before New Year's Eve, and I'm only half finished with the first. I shouldn't have taken on so many orders."

"Let me pick up the rest of these, so you can get back to work," suggested Zsuzsi. "Then I can help you."

"Thanks, Zsuzsi." Eva handed her the box of beads and stood up. "I was about to fit the bodice when I dropped the beads." She picked up a shapeless piece of velvet and began to pin it to the dummy. By the time Zsuzsi picked up the last of the beads, Eva had transformed the swatch of velvet into the bodice of an evening gown.

Zsuzsi looked at the gown. The low-cut bodice narrowed to a small waistline that met the skirt with a V-shaped seam. The skirt was simple in design, soft folds of velvet that would swirl beautifully in a waltz.

"How are you going to finish it?" asked Zsuzsi.

"With bead work, at the neckline and hem. A good three inches of beads, sewn on in little waves, up and down along the hem and here on the bodice."

"Oh, Eva, that alone will take weeks." Zsuzsi looked critically at the dress. "Who is it for?"

"Mrs. Cahill's daughter."

"She's quite thin, I suppose? It doesn't look as though she has much of a figure."

Eva smiled. "She's as flat as a thirteen year old. Why?"

"Well, I was thinking that if you draped lace along the neckline, so that it fell into a V that matched the one at the waist, it would make the proportions look better, don't you think?"

"It certainly would be flattering," said Eva. She took a piece of lace off the table and held it up to the dress.

"You see," said Zsuzsi. "If you make it a good, deep piece of lace, it will cover much of the bodice, and then you can leave off the beads."

Eva nodded. "It would take care of almost half the bead work. It would certainly save me time, but more than that, it would be a charming effect."

She looked at Zsuzsi and smiled. "You have a good eye. Maybe you should become a dressmaker, too."

Zsuzsi shook her head. "No, I can't even sew well enough for Aunt Margit's approval, let alone have your skill. You make dresses that look like they come from Paris!"

"And when have you ever seen a dress from Paris?" asked Eva. "I'll tell you what, since the lace was your idea, why don't you help me choose it? If we work together we can finish the gown today."

"I'd love to."

"Good. Then go into that cupboard. I have lots of lace left over from summer dresses. Pick the one you think will suit this gown."

While Zsuzsi looked in the cupboard drawers, Eva unpinned the bodice and brought it to the table. She swept a cluster of bobbins aside and began to lay out the pieces for basting.

"What is your Aunt Margit doing today?" she asked.

"Some sort of church committee meeting. Final planning of Christmas decorations, I think."

"And Jolan?"

"She left to go Christmas shopping."

"Why didn't you go with her?"

"I don't know. I suppose I'm just not in the Christmas mood, yet."

Eva looked up from her basting. "Less than two weeks before Christmas? Are you coming down with something, Zsuzsi?"

"No. I'm fine."

Eva watched her for a moment, then she stood up. "I'm going to make some coffee."

She walked into the kitchen and poured the morning's cold coffee into a small saucepan. She added sugar and milk, then lit the burner with a match and set the pan on the flame. While the coffee heated, she went back into the dining room, where Zsuzsi was holding two pieces of lace.

Eva looked at them critically. "The ivory, I think, don't you?"

Zsuzsi nodded. She put the other piece of lace away and then helped Eva pin the bodice pieces together. Eva threaded a bright yellow through the needle and basted the first pieces together.

"There," she said. "That's going well. Let's have our coffee. It should be hot enough by now."

Zsuzsi sat down at the kitchen table. Unlike the dining room, the kitchen was spotless, so clean even Aunt Margit would approve of it. The table topped with porcelain looked just like the one downstairs, but it was white with blue trim, instead of yellow and green. Otherwise the kitchens were identical, from cabinets to icebox to stove. Only the color differed upstairs, where bright white walls and cabinets trimmed in blue matched the table. White ruffled curtains embroidered with yellow and red tulips made the room look cheerful even on cloudy days like this one.

"Now tell me," said Eva when she had poured the coffee into mugs, "what's bothering you?"

"Nothing's bothering me," said Zsuzsi. The lie was so transparent, even to Zsuzsi, that she blushed.

"Then why have you been so quiet lately? Especially at Christmas, you should be excited and happy."

Zsuzsi longed to blurt out the whole story. The past few weeks she sometimes felt as though she would burst with sorrow and fear for Trudy, who was back at school now, but if possible, more subdued than ever. It wasn't right, but how could Zsuzsi break her word?

"Like I said before, I'm just not in the Christmas spirit yet."

"You miss your mother, don't you?" asked Eva.

Zsuzsi sighed. "Of course I do. I wish we could be together. But that's not—I mean—that's part of it, I guess."

Eva sipped her coffee and frowned. "Zsuzsi, you know I would never interfere with your family life, but if something's wrong, and you want to talk to someone, you can be sure I'd keep your confidence. If you want, anything you tell me would be just between us."

"That's just it," Zsuzsi said quietly.

"What do you mean?"

"I mean, is it always the right thing, not to tell a secret?"

"If you've given your word, you must honor it," said Eva.

"What if you shouldn't have given your word?"

"You should know better than to make a rash promise."

Zsuzsi nodded. "But what if I did?"

Eva thought for a moment. "Well, I suppose if no one is hurt by it..."

Zsuzsi grimaced.

"Oh, dear," said Eva. "If someone is being hurt—Zsuzsi, are you in some kind of trouble?"

She shook her head.

"Well, then," continued Eva, "I suppose it depends. If a sin is being committed, and you know about it, don't you have a moral obligation to stop its happening?"

"Even if it means breaking a promise, and being disloyal?"

"I don't know if I can answer that for you, Zsuzsi. Maybe I'm not the right person to ask. Have you talked to your aunt or uncle?"

"I can't."

"Then it sounds like a matter of conscience—something that's between you and God. Maybe you should take your problem to the confessional."

Zsuzsi looked at Eva in horror. "Oh no, I couldn't do that!"

Eva held Zsuzsi's hand. "Dearest, if someone you know is doing wrong—"

"No, no," Zsuzsi interrupted. "A wrong is being done to someone I know."

Eva frowned. "Is it a matter for the police, then?"

"I don't know. I'm not sure. It's, you see, it's a family matter."

"Then it must be resolved by the family. If I were having a family problem, I'd seek the help of my priest." Eva squeezed Zsuzsi's hand and carried the cups to the sink.

"Let me do that, Eva. You need to work on the gown." Zsuzsi turned on the tap and rinsed the cups. Eva made everything seem simple. If you have a problem, then go to the priest. Zsuzsi could imagine trying to explain Trudy's situation to Monsignor Andrassy! If there were another priest—after all, what is told in Confession is a secret that a priest could never reveal. It would be almost like telling no one at all. But not quite. Zsuzsi sighed. She had promised not to tell anyone. That included any priest, even if she went to St. Brendan's to avoid confronting Monsignor Andrassy.

Maybe Trudy was right to act as if nothing had happened. After all, it hadn't happened again, at least not to Zsuzsi's knowledge. But that didn't mean it would never happen again, someday. Zsuzsi was sure it would. He had done it once. Maybe the second time would be easier, and the next easier still. She shivered. She had to do something, and soon, but how could she without breaking her promise?

Eva looked up as Zsuzsi walked into the dining room. "I didn't think the cups were that dirty," she said drily.

"I'm sorry, I didn't realize how long I was taking. What can I do to help?"

"As preoccupied as you are, the biggest help you could be is to go outside and do some Christmas shopping. Get some fresh air, and come back to help when you can keep your mind on your work."

"But the gown! You do need help."

Eva smiled. "It's all right, Zsuzsi. This is going very quickly now. Go ahead, take your mind off your troubles for a few hours. Scoot!"

Reluctantly, Zsuzsi went downstairs, put on her coat, and stepped outside. It would be dark in half an hour—she didn't relish the idea of walking all the way downtown alone. Instead, she decided to stop by the *Hirlap* office, and walk home with Uncle Emil. If only she could tell him! Surely he would know what was best.

Emil was bent over his desk when Zsuzsi arrived, his unlit pipe dangling from his lips.

"Your pipe's gone out again, Uncle Emil," said Zsuzsi.

Emil stood up with a smile and let the pipe drop into his hand. He hugged Zsuzsi before laying the pipe in an ashtray.

"What brings you here? All done shopping?"

"I didn't go. I helped Eva for a little while, then thought I'd walk you home. Let me refill this for you."

Zsuzsi loved filling her uncle's pipe. She tapped out the ash and scraped the bowl clean, then opened the humidor and inhaled the sweet fragrance of the tobacco. She filled the bowl and tamped it down, as Emil had taught her, then handed him the pipe and matches.

Emil relit his pipe with pleasure. "Thank you, my dear. I have only a little more work to do, and then we can go home."

"Is there anything I can do?"

"You can look at these page proofs and tell me if my old eyes missed any errors."

"You're not old, Uncle Emil." Zsuzsi kissed him on the cheek as she took the page proofs from him. They were all advertisements. The Magyar Men's Marching Band was to play at the St. Elizabeth's Christmas Pageant. The Children's Choir was to present tableaux on the nativity. A speaker named Imre Fekete was to give a speech at the Athletic Club on New Year's Day, on the topic of Hungarian Communism since Trianon.

Zsuzsi looked up briefly as Sandor Hegedus walked in. "Hello, Sandy," she said.

Sandor fumbled with the strings of his apron and blushed. "Hello, Zsuzsanna." He cleared his throat. "I'm all finished, Mr. Molnar."

"That's fine, Sandor," said Emil. "I'll close up tonight. Have a good evening."

Sandor nodded. He hesitated in the doorway, watching Zsuzsi. Emil followed his eyes and suppressed a smile. "Is there anything else, Sandor?"

Sandor started, and blushed again. "No, Mr. Molnar. Good night." He nodded toward Zsuzsi. "Good night."

Zsuzsi said good night without looking up again. After Sandor left, she handed the proof sheets back to Emil. "They look fine, Uncle Emil."

"Good. Let's close up then."

They turned out the lights and Emil locked the door. Emil held out his arm to Zsuzsi; she slipped her arm into his and they began to walk.

"Shall we go straight home, or stop for a cup of coffee on the way?" asked Emil.

Zsuzsi considered the idea. "Aunt Margit wasn't home when I left, so I suppose we have time to stop."

They went into Woolworth's and sat down at the lunch counter. Emil ordered coffee for each of them and two slices of chocolate cake.

Zsuzsi giggled. "Uncle Emil, before dinner!"

He winked. "I won't tell if you don't."

They talked about the *Hirlap* and the coming holiday. Zsuzsi was glad for the easy conversation, for the crowds of holiday shoppers coming in and out of the store; the light and warmth and people made life seem safe and normal. Outside, in the cold darkness, she again took Emil's arm.

When they were halfway home Emil said, almost casually, "You seemed to have attracted Sandor's eye this evening."

"What do you mean?"

"I mean that he seems to fancy your company."

"Oh, Uncle Emil, you must be mistaken!"

"Maybe, maybe not. He's a fine young man, a hard worker, very good with his hands. Most competent. Until he sees you. Then he becomes a butterfingers, and turns beet red at your slightest look."

Zsuzsi said nothing.

"Have you given any thought," asked Emil, "to next summer?"

"Next summer?" Zsuzsi could see her breath as little puffs of fog in the streetlights. Who thinks of summer during winter's darkest days?

"Well, what do you plan to do when you graduate from high school?"

Zsuzsi was taken aback. "I—I don't know."

Emil smiled. "That's all right. You've plenty of time to think about it. To tell you the truth, sometimes I wish you could stay in high school forever. But you are growing up, and someday soon you'll want to begin a life of your own. It might not be such a bad idea to settle down with a nice young man like Sandor."

"Uncle Emil! Are you suggesting that I—"

Emil stopped walking and kissed her hand. "I'm not suggesting anything. You're still very young, with your whole life waiting for you, and the last thing I want is for you to make any decision about it hastily. No, I only want you to consider the options available to you, so that whatever you come to decide about your life, you do it with careful thought. Make decisions with your head, not with your heart, and you'll avoid making big mistakes."

"I think I've already learned that," Zsuzsi said. "I've made a promise I don't think I can keep."

"Do you want to tell me about it?"

"I can't. I promised I wouldn't. Oh, Uncle Emil, have you ever done anything like that? Made a promise, and then discovered it was a mistake to do so?"

Emil was silent. Zsuzsi looked at him. Under the street lights his face seemed lined and harsh, with a hard expression she had never seen on him before.

"I'm sorry, Uncle Emil. I shouldn't have asked."

Emil patted her hand. "If you have a problem, you have a right to ask for help. How else can you learn, but from your own mistakes, and maybe from the mistakes of others?"

Zsuzsi did not know what to say. She couldn't imagine Uncle Emil making any mistakes at all. He was so strong, so knowledgeable, and above all, so kind.

"I think you are old enough to hear about a promise I have been unable to keep," Emil said. "I promised I would love your Aunt Margit for the rest of my life."

Zsuzsi gasped. Whatever she had been expecting Uncle Emil to say—and she wasn't sure she expected anything at all—it certainly was nothing like this. "Uncle Emil, maybe you shouldn't tell me this."

"I think I should, my dearest, because it directly affects you."

"Me? How could it?"

Emil squeezed her hand. "You'll see." He sighed, a deep breath that sent a huge cloud of vapor swirling under the light. "A long time ago, when we still lived in Hungary, I was very much in love with your Aunt Margit. If you had seen her then, Zsuzsi! She was beautiful, with thick, dark hair, and a sweet smile. She doesn't smile much now. But then! I think I loved her from the moment I first saw her, after I'd graduated from the university and begun working. She was embroidering that day, as always, and her face had a rapt, almost prayerful expression. When she looked up from her embroidery, she still had that look in her eyes, and it went straight to my heart." He stopped to turn up the collar of his coat. "Unfortunately, she already loved someone else."

"Who?"

Emil turned toward Zsuzsi. "She loved your Papa."

Zsuzsi froze. Surely she heard wrong. "What did you say?"

Emil touched her cheek. "I said, Aunt Margit was in love with your Papa. And I think he may have been in love with her. This was a long time ago, Zsuzsi, before you were born."

"But what happened?"

He smiled, a smile that held more sadness than Zsuzsi could have imagined.

"Your Mama happened."

"I don't understand."

Emil nodded. "Who does? But when your Papa saw your Mama, whatever he had felt for Margit flew away. Most likely, he had been only fond of Margit, but he truly loved your Mama, with real passion, and she loved him, too, and so they were married. It was the right thing to do, I still believe that. They should have had a long and happy life together."

"They were happy. They did love each other," said Zsuzsi. She swallowed hard to avoid crying.

"Yes. And I thought, in time, that Margit would let your papa go. After you were born, I told her how I felt, and she agreed to marry me. We came here, and built a life, and were content. Or so I thought. I learned, too late, that Margit never stopped loving your Papa. I should never have married her, Zsuzsi. That was the mistake I made, because I no longer love Margit, I only pity her."

"Pity her? Why?"

"Because she can never be happy in this life. That is very sad."

"What about you?"

"Oh, I have the satisfaction of my work, and that is more than many men have. But best of all, I have you and Jolan in my life, and you girls have given me happiness beyond measure." He smiled again, a full smile with no sadness in it, and hugged Zsuzsi hard. "I wake every day and thank the good Lord for bringing you to me."

Zsuzsi leaned against the soft wool of Emil's overcoat. She loved the smell of pipe tobacco in the fibers, the way she felt warm and secure when he hugged her. How could Aunt Margit not love him?

She let go reluctantly. "You are so good to us, Uncle Emil, and I love you, and so does Jolan. But I think Aunt Margit must hate us both."

"No, you're wrong about that. I won't deny, it took some adjusting on her part to have you with us. But we never had children of our own, and your aunt was as sorrowful as I about that. I think she has come to want you here as much as I do, but her pride will not let her show it. I'm not sure she knows how, anymore, and maybe that is the saddest thing of all, to love but not be able to show it."

Zsuzsi nodded. "Does Jolan know any of this?"

Emil shook his head. "I feel that I've given you a great burden, Zsuzsi. You've helped take a great weight from me, and I'm not sure it was fair to you.

"I'm glad you told me. This is one secret I'm not troubled to keep. Jolan should know, some day, at least part of it. Not now."

"And what of your other secret? A promise you made but do not want to keep?"

"I'm still not sure, Uncle Emil. I think I have to wait and see."

Emil kissed her on the forehead. "You know best. You really are growing up. Let's go home."

They walked home in silence. Trying to imagine her mother, her father, and Aunt Margit crowded thoughts of Trudy from her mind. Part of her was thrilled at being treated like an adult, made party to such grown up feelings and knowledge, yet part of her longed for simpler times. Now she understood why Aunt Margit never spoke of Mama, and why Mama was so reluctant to come to the United States. Zsuzsi feared she'd never see her mother again. She felt a pang of homesickness stronger than she'd felt in a long time, and after dinner, wrote a long letter to Piros. It was a long time before she fell asleep.

Her emotions were in such a turmoil that Zsuzsi found it even more difficult to focus on the Christmas holiday as the days went by, but when Aunt Margit put away the scrub brush and began to devote her days to baking, Zsuzsi knew she had to take part. She finished her shopping in one expedition after school. She wrapped presents upstairs in Eva's apartment the next day, where they would stay hidden until Christmas Eve. On the last day of school before the holiday, she came home to an empty house. Jolan was in the chorus, practicing for the school Christmas pageant. Uncle Emil was at work, of course, and Aunt Margit at church, decorating. The apartment was fragrant with baking. Zsuzsi took a deep breath, savoring the rich smell of warm yeast dough. Trays of *kifli* lay cooling on the kitchen table. Zsuzsi popped one into her mouth. The dough crumbled into flakes as she chewed, releasing the sweet apricot and walnut filling. She moaned with pleasure and took another before walking upstairs. Eva's apartment, too, was empty. The burgundy gown was gone from the dressmaker's dummy, so Eva must have been delivering it, most likely with Ferenc to accompany her. Zsuzsi sighed. She had hoped for company this afternoon.

She went back downstairs and looked at the *kifli.* Aunt Margit had made hundreds of the small pastries. Surely she wouldn't mind if Zsuzsi gave some to Trudy? Certainly neither Trudy nor her mother would have time to bake anything for the holidays. She took a fresh napkin from the drawer and piled the *kifli* into it. She planned to give Trudy her Christmas present on Christmas Eve, but there was no reason not to run over right now with the *kifli.* It felt good to have something purposeful to do.

The cold afternoon air brought out the pink in Zsuzsi's cheeks as she walked past house after house decorated with evergreens and holly. She walked quickly past the drab cigar factory and turned onto Water Street. Here was little evidence of Christmas. The street was almost eerie in its emptiness. Practically everyone who lived here worked. Even children took odd jobs to help support their family. No one here had time to gather evergreen boughs. No one here could afford the sugar and nuts to make pastries. Zsuzsi wished she had brought enough *kifli* for every family here.

She knocked on Trudy's door and waited. There was no answer. She tried peeking through the front windows but the shabby curtains were drawn. She knocked again. No one seemed to be home. Zsuzsi didn't want to leave the pastries on the porch. She would have to carry them home again, and wait until Christmas Eve to give them to Trudy. Reluctantly she walked down the steps. She was two houses away when she heard a door open and a rough voice call "Who's there?"

She turned. Trudy's father stood in the doorway, holding the doorjamb with one hand, a half-filled bottle dangling from the other. He peered down the street toward the river, then he turned to look in Zsuzsi's direction. She ducked behind the porch steps of the nearest house. He was the last person she expected to find at home, and the last person she wanted to meet, alone on a deserted street. She carefully looked through the porch railing. Mr. Bornheimer stood on the porch, swayed, and took a drink from the bottle. "Who's there?" he asked again. "I heard you knock. Come out and show yourself."

Zsuzsi pressed against the steps, trying not to make a sound. She heard him lurch down his own porch steps, then she heard a thud and a curse. She eased herself up a little to see better. He had fallen, and was struggling to rise again. What if he began walking this way? Zsuzsi looked around. She could run down the alley between the houses, but there was a fence around the back yard of this house. What if she couldn't get over it quickly? He might catch up to her—how could she explain why she was hiding? And what might he do to her if he became angry?

She looked toward Trudy's house again, and began to tremble with relief. He was walking away from her, toward the river, zigzagging in a ragged path from side to side. She held her breath as he walked on. When he reached the river, she would turn and run for home. As drunk as he was, he could never catch her, even if he turned and saw her then. She watched him stop and sway. He had reached the small bluff over looking the river. She stood up, and took a step backwards.

Her foot hit a small rock, which crashed into the wooden step with a hollow sound. Bornheimer turned and looked right at her.

"Who are—" he started to say, but as he turned the motion threw him off balance. He waved his arms, trying to regain his footing, but he slipped and tumbled out of sight.

Zsuzsi wanted to run for home, but knew she had to see if he was hurt, and if so to get help. She walked to the bluff, her heart pounding, and cautiously looked down. Mr. Bornheimer lay on his side, nearly in the water. He moaned and pushed himself over with one arm, crying out as he did so. He rolled onto his back amid shards of glass from his whiskey bottle. Then Zsuzsi saw one large piece of jagged glass sticking out of his thigh. Bornheimer pulled at it, but his hands were covered with blood, and all he managed to do was twist it deeper into his leg. Zsuzsi gasped as blood began to squirt from his leg in an arc.

Bornheimer looked up at her, squinting his eyes as he tried to focus. "Help," he called. "Help me."

Zsuzsi looked around. There was no one on the street. She looked back down at Bornheimer. A large puddle of blood had already formed and began to congeal on the cold ground. It spurted out of the wound rhythmically, landing with an audible splash. He must have severed an artery. If she went for a doctor, he would bleed to death before she got back. Bornheimer looked up at her with wide, round eyes. The urgency of his situation came through to him, drunk as he was.

"Help me!" he shouted hoarsely. Zsuzsi remembered the *kifli*-filled napkin she still held in her hand and started toward the path down the bluff. She would have to make a tourniquet to stop the bleeding. If she didn't, he would surely die. She reached the bottom of the bluff and paused to untie the napkin. The puddle of blood had grown enormously, in just a few seconds. Bornheimer held both hands over the wound, but the blood still spurted through his fingers.

"Help me." He whispered this time. Zsuzsi looked at his bloodshot eyes and then his bloody hands. They had been bloody before, the times he'd hit Trudy, maybe the day he'd broken her arm. And there'd been a lot of blood the night he raped her. Zsuzsi stared at the blood pulsing through his hands. It didn't arc so high now. Bornheimer breathed in rapid, shallow breaths, and his face had become very pale. His eyes were open wide with fear, and she could see how gray the whites of his eyes had become. He looked at Zsuzsi, too weak now to ask for help, but she understood that he was pleading with her to help him.

His hands began to shake, and they slipped off the wound. The blood arced once more, then pulsed more slowly, no longer squirting into the air, just flowing, in small gushes, down his leg. Zsuzsi watched, perfectly still, as the trembling diffused over his whole body. His teeth chattered, as though with cold. He stared at Zsuzsi without understanding, and then with growing panic as he realized what she was doing. He struggled to get up, struggled to say, "help me," but he could only shudder and move his lips. His eyes rolled up, and the shuddering stopped. Only a last trickle of blood soaked into his pants leg. A dark stain showed at his crotch, and Zsuzsi smelled the acrid odor of human feces.

Slowly, she backed away from the river's edge. She felt a small sharp pain in her hand. She had been clutching the napkin full of *kifli* so hard that her fingernails had cut into her palm. Blood welled up in four small curves against her skin. She dumped the *kifli* into the dried weeds along the rive bank, wrapped the napkin around her hand, and turned to walk up the path to the still deserted street. She walked slowly, taking deep breaths. By the time she reached the corner, she no longer felt like vomiting. With her hands in her pockets, she walked past the cigar factory toward home. It was already dusk, and very cold, but she walked slowly.

For the first time in a long time, she wasn't afraid to walk home alone in the dark.

Chapter 14
April 1922

A large party gathered at the Molnar home on Easter Sunday. In addition to Emil, Margit, Zsuzsi, Jolan, Eva, and Ferenc, there were two guests, Trudy Bornheimer and her mother. Everyone wore their Easter best, and no one saw any need to mention that both Trudy and her mother wore dresses made over from two of Eva's. Trudy wore an apple green whose color set off her eyes and made her freckles look charming. Mrs. Bornheimer's pallor was so deep that even a lemon yellow frock could not brighten it, yet her smile when Zsuzsi brought her a cup of coffee was so full of genuine pleasure that for a moment she was almost pretty. Zsuzsi smiled back, happy to do anything to erase the frown of worry that was Mrs. Bornheimer's usual expression. The woman had seen so much of grief in her life that she seemed almost always on the verge of tears.

Lately, Zsuzsi noticed, even though she still worked two jobs at the cigar factory, Mrs. Bornheimer seemed less tired. She seemed like a woman who had a huge burden removed from her shoulders. Even at the funeral, just before Christmas, an undercurrent of relief lay below the grief and shock, although Zsuzsi was sure no one else was aware of it.

She went into the kitchen, where Margit orchestrated the final preparations for Easter dinner.

"How are our guests, Zsuzsanna?" asked Margit.

"To be honest, I think they're a little uncomfortable. They aren't used to being waited on. Mrs. Bornheimer keeps asking to help, but I think Uncle Emil has charmed her into sitting still."

"Poor woman," said Eva as she stirred the *turos teszta*, homemade buttered noodles tossed with cottage cheese. "She looks exhausted."

"She looks scandalous," said Margit. "She should still be wearing black. Her husband was buried less than six months ago."

"Oh, Margit, no one goes into such deep mourning anymore," said Eva. "Besides, black looks dreadful on a woman with her complexion. Let the poor thing have a little color in her life." Eva poured the noodles into a serving platter. "Here, Zsuzsi, you can set this on the table now."

In a matter of minutes the table was loaded with food. A smoked ham had the place of honor in front of Emil's seat, ready for slicing. The noodles had been placed at one corner of the table, a bowl of mashed turnips at another, a dish of beets at the third, and homemade bread at the fourth. In the center, on either side of a vase of lilies, were ranked dishes of Margit's preserves: pickled onions, green tomatoes, cauliflower, sweet gherkins, stewed ripe tomatoes. The table was set with Margit's best embroidered linen tablecloth and napkins. Mrs. Bornheimer picked up her napkin with such care that Zsuzsi suspected she had never touched such fine cloth before. As Emil said grace, Zsuzsi privately added her own thanks for all she had, and her wishes that Mrs. Bornheimer might someday have pretty things of her own.

It took all of dinner and a platter of *kalacs* before Mrs. Bornheimer and Trudy seemed really comfortable. It was good to see the two of them laughing and talking. After dinner, Zsuzsi, Jolan, and Trudy did the washing up while the grownups relaxed, and Ferenc played with his toy motorcar.

"Shall we go for a walk?" suggested Emil when the girls had finished. He took Ferenc by the hand and led the way. The three women came next, and behind them the three girls. They strolled around the neighborhood and through the town, as did many of their neighbors, exchanging greetings, noting everyone's Easter finery, comparing their own dresses and hats to everyone else's.

When Ferenc became tired the grownups turned for home. Jolan tactfully went with them, taking Ferenc's free hand, and leaving Zsuzsi alone to entertain her guest. They walked arm in arm down Kossuth Street until it became a country lane.

"This has been the nicest Easter Sunday I've ever known," said Trudy. "You don't know how wonderful it's been!"

"I'm so glad you came," said Zsuzsi.

"Do you know, when you asked, I don't think Mama thought you were serious. We've never had an Easter dinner like that. Does your aunt always cook so much food?"

Zsuzsi laughed. "Only when company comes. She likes to impress people, I think."

"Well, she impressed me all right. I don't think I've ever eaten so much. And the table was so pretty! I'm sure you're used to it, but I've never seen such needlework. Such soft napkins, such pretty dishes. And I don't think Mama's ever seen so many fine things, either, except maybe when she was a girl. It's been so long since she was waited on, and treated like a lady. I think your Uncle Emil is just wonderful, the way he spoke to her."

"What do you mean?"

"Oh, Zsuzsi, we're not the same class as you and your family, yet your Uncle treated Mama and me as though we were."

Zsuzsi looked at Trudy in surprise. "Trudy, my sister and I grew up in a little village, on a farm. We aren't rich! We didn't have anything at all until we came to America, not enough clothes, not enough to eat. You don't know what it was like during the war. And as for all the things we have now, why, it's just because that's all Aunt Margit does. She's always embroidering something."

"Maybe so, but she has the time to do it, because she doesn't have to work. Your uncle is such a good man, he takes care of you all. Poor Mama, she's still working two jobs. She's so tired all the time she doesn't even have the strength to do the mending." Trudy fingered the skirt of her dress. "I've never worn anything so pretty in my whole life."

"You look lovely in it."

Trudy blushed. "I know I should feel ashamed—Mama says it's wrong to accept charity—but people have been so nice to us since—since December. The way all those women from the factory came over after the funeral, and cleaned the house from top to bottom, and gave us things. It's nice to have things, and to be able to keep them neat and clean. We could never do that before because he always—oh, Zsuzsi, I know it's wrong and I'm going to burn in hell forever, but I'm glad he's dead! I'm so glad he's dead!"

Zsuzsi hugged her hard. "It's okay, Trudy, I understand. And I don't think it's wrong to be glad now. It was meant to be, after all, or God wouldn't have let it happen, so it must be God's will, and who are we to question God's will? So it's all right to feel happy, if things are better now, because God made it so. He wouldn't want you to be ungrateful, would He?"

Trudy shook her head. Zsuzsi could feel Trudy's tears soaking into her shoulder, and reached into her sleeve to pull out a handkerchief. "Here," she said, stepping back to wipe Trudy's face. "Don't cry anymore. It'll make your eyes all red, and you look so pretty today you don't want to spoil it."

Trudy blushed again. "Do you really think I look pretty? I almost feel pretty, in this dress. I just wish I had wavy hair, like you do."

"I think your hair looks lovely," said Zsuzsi. And it did, for Trudy was keeping it clean and shiny, and brushed neatly into a bow at the back of her neck. It was one more pleasant change in her life, another good thing to think about when memories of Mr. Bornheimer's pleading face and trembling hands made it difficult for Zsuzsi to sleep.

Zsuzsi closed her eyes and took a deep breath. Those memories belonged to the cold dark of winter, not the bright sunshine of Easter. She opened her eyes again and looked at Trudy. She did look pretty, still a bit too thin, but her eyes had lost their deep shadows. She no longer looked like a deer about to cross an open field; she had the first glimmerings of confidence, and walked with her head up, and met people's eyes. The change was more internal than external—it went beyond clean hair and a new dress, and Zsuzsi was glad.

Impulsively, she kissed Trudy on the cheek. "Better?" she asked.

Trudy nodded, and laughed. "Even your handkerchiefs are embroidered!"

Zsuzsi laughed, too, as they walked back home.

That night, when she had pulled the covers up to her chin and the images of a cold river bank and puddles of blood threatened, she closed her eyes tight and thought instead of Trudy's smile, of her clean hair and how good it smelled, and how good it felt to hold her close.

For the first time in many weeks Zsuzsi slept without nightmares, and woke refreshed to the warm light of morning. As the season progressed it seemed she had never seen a spring so beautiful. She and Trudy often walked down Kossuth Street after school, to talk and laugh, to pet the newborn calves and make nosegays of spring beauty and violets. Some days Trudy sat in the shade of an oak tree while Zsuzsi sketched in her note pad, trying to make her pencil capture a clump of wild daffodils in the new grass, not just the way they looked, but the way they smelled, and moved in the breeze, their softness when she and Trudy picked them and wove them through each other's hair.

Most of the time she put her pad down in frustration.

"Sister Thomas says you have a good eye for sketching," said Trudy on one of those days when the beauty around them was too much for Zsuzsi's pencil.

"I know. She tells me I should enroll in art school, but I don't want to think about that. It's weeks and weeks until graduation. I wish it would never come! I wish it could stay just as it is now, spring forever and ever."

She moved into the shade next to Trudy, and took her hand. "What could be more perfect than this?"

"Nothing," Trudy said with a yawn, and they dozed, still hand in hand, until they heard Jolan calling from the road.

"What is it?" asked Zsuzsi, sitting up.

"Time for supper," said Jolan, leaning against the fence.

"Oh! We fell asleep." She and Trudy stood up, brushing their skirts, and walked over to the fence. "Jolan, wait up," Zsuzsi called, but Jolan walked on ahead. She was waiting on the porch steps after Trudy said goodbye.

"What's wrong?" asked Zsuzsi, seeing the scowl on her sister's face.

"You never spend time with me anymore!" Jolan blurted.

"Jolan, that's not so."

"Yes it is! You're always with her. You're always talking about her, and visiting her, and going for walks after school with her. You always used to walk home from school with me. Now you walk home with her."

Zsuzsi walked up the steps and sat down next to Jolan. "I'm sorry, Jolan, I didn't realize."

"No, you didn't," Jolan interrupted. "You have such a crush on her you don't notice anyone else."

"I don't have a crush on her."

"Then she has one on you. Either way, it's the same thing. You're always together."

Zsuzsi put her arm around Jolan and gave her shoulders a squeeze. "Jolan, I'm sorry you feel left out. I didn't mean for that to happen. Look, you're welcome to come along, anywhere we go."

"They say if two's company, three's a crowd."

"Nonsense! That would never apply to you. You're my sister, and my best friend. You'll see!"

But the next afternoon, Jolan walked with them only a little way before turning for home.

"Jolan, what's the matter?" asked Zsuzsi.

Jolan shook her head. "It's no good. I just feel like going home. I'll see you later."

"Jolan," Zsuzsi called, but Jolan turned her back and walked home.

"What's wrong?" asked Trudy.

Zsuzsi sighed. "She's jealous of the time we spend after school. I asked her to walk with us today to show her she's welcome to come along. If she doesn't feel welcome, I can't help that."

"Do you want to go home with her?"

"No, I'll talk to her later. Let's go on."

Trudy smiled. "I'm glad. It's such a nice day for a walk."

They continued on to their favorite spot, the oak tree near the small stream in the cow pasture. Zsuzsi took out her sketchpad while Trudy took off her shoes and socks and walked in the stream. In a few minutes Zsuzsi threw down her pad.

"It's no use," she said. "It's all spoiled."

"What's spoiled?" asked Trudy, walking up the stream.

"The whole afternoon. I can't stay here and draw when I know she's back home, sulking and angry."

Trudy left the stream and sat down next to Zsuzsi. "I'm sorry, Zsuzsi. It's my fault."

"No, it's not. I should have asked her along more often."

"Maybe we should both go talk to her."

"No, I need to do that myself." She sighed and lay back, folding her arms under her head. "I'll go in a few minutes."

Above her the new oak leaves sparkled in the light breeze like gold coins. "It's so beautiful here," she murmured.

Trudy leaned back on one elbow and looked up at the leaves. "Thank you for staying a little while longer," she said. She looked down at Zsuzsi, and kissed her on the cheek. Zsuzsi smiled, and reached up to touch Trudy's hair, which gleamed today like the oak leaves, like gold threads on auburn velvet. Trudy bent over and kissed Zsuzsi on the mouth. Zsuzsi kissed back and stroked the soft hair. She felt Trudy's hand slide up slowly from her waist until it touched Zsuzsi's breast.

"No," Zsuzsi murmured. She pushed Trudy away and sat up, her cheeks burning.

"I'm sorry," Trudy whispered.

"No," Zsuzsi said again. "Don't be. I mean, I let you, and I shouldn't have." She took a deep breath. "I mean, we shouldn't have. Neither of us." She couldn't meet Trudy's eyes. "I'd better go."

"I'll walk home with you," said Trudy, and reached for her shoes.

"No, don't," Zsuzsi said, gathering her pad and pencil. She stood up quickly. "Stay as long as you like. I need to go home anyway, to talk to Jolan."

She walked away. "See you tomorrow?" asked Trudy.

"Of course," Zsuzsi called over her shoulder. She walked quickly, for once ignoring the smell of mint beneath her feet, almost not seeing the fence for the tears in her eyes. It was wrong, wasn't it? It was wrong. Girls weren't supposed to kiss each other like that, to touch each other like that. It was wrong, not that anyone had ever said so, but it was something you just knew, instinctively. Wasn't it? It had to be wrong to do it, to feel your breath quicken and your breasts tingle like that, to feel the sudden moisture between your legs. It had to be even more wrong to like it.

I'll have to go to confession on Saturday, Zsuzsi thought. All I have to say is I committed a sin of impurity. Like the other time, all I had to say was I committed a sin of omission. I just didn't help someone who needed help, that's all I had to say, and I was absolved. Three Our Fathers, three Hail Marys, and it was all fixed, like it never happened. And it's such a small lie, to say you're sorry when the priest asks you. Almost no lie at all, because you're sorry you lied, even if you're not sorry you did it.

But I'm sorry this time.

She ran up the stairs past an astonished Jolan, into the bathroom where she shut the door and ran cold water on her face. I'm sorry this time, sorry I did it, and sorry I wanted to do it, and most of all sorry I didn't want it to stop.

The next afternoon she surprised Jolan even more by asking her to walk home.

"Did you have a fight with Trudy?" she asked.

"No," Zsuzsi said. "I just think you're right, that we need to spend more time together. I talked to Trudy, and she understands."

But when they passed Trudy who was waiting on the sidewalk, even Jolan could see the hurt in her eyes. Still, Trudy's loss was her gain, so she didn't ask questions. In a few days, from Jolan's point of view, everything was back to normal.

For Zsuzsi it was another matter to see Trudy during classes, and to work with her during Chemistry lab, to act as though everything were the same when nothing really was. Zsuzsi would talk only of classroom affairs, nothing else, knowing all the while that Trudy was aching to talk to her of more important matters. It went on for one week, then another.

Jolan was waiting for Zsuzsi on the school steps, as she had for the past two weeks, as she had done ever since they began school. Zsuzsi walked up to her slowly.

"What's the matter?" asked Jolan.

"Jolan, Trudy was absent today."

"So?"

"So I think I should go see her, to find out what's wrong. Come with me, please?"

Jolan pressed her lips together and turned her head. The gesture was so much like Margit's that Zsuzsi almost smiled.

"Please, Jolan, I really want you to come. I'm worried about Trudy, but I do want you along with me."

"If you're going to see her, you don't need me," said Jolan. She walked down the steps.

Zsuzsi leaned against the rail, hesitating. She did want Jolan along, for reasons she could never explain to her, but she was also concerned that something had happened to Trudy. What could happen to her, now that her father was dead, she couldn't imagine. But she had an odd feeling that something was wrong; she had to find out.

Slowly, she walked to Water Street. She hadn't been there since the weather had gotten warm enough to stay outside after school. The street looked as drab as ever, treeless and shabby, but a few dandelions poking out of the dirt made bright spots of color in front of one house. Zsuzsi looked down at her shoes as she approached Trudy's house. It was hard for her to be so close to the river, and she couldn't look at the riverbank without a shiver of revulsion. She walked up the steps and knocked on the door.

After a few moments Trudy opened the door.

"Hello," said Zsuzsi. Trudy didn't answer.

"I was worried," Zsuzsi said, "when you didn't come to school."

"My mother is in the hospital," Trudy said in a toneless voice.

"Oh, no! What's wrong?"

"Do you really care?" asked Trudy. The hurt in her voice made Zsuzsi cringe.

"Of course I do, Trudy. I mean that."

"Come in, then. I'll tell you," Trudy answered.

Zsuzsi followed her down the dark hallway, as stuffy and airless as ever. Inside Trudy's kitchen, though, the difference was apparent. The floor was swept clean and all the dishes were put away. The table had a clean cloth on it and there were no dirty clothes or newspapers anywhere in sight. The living room was equally clean, with some of Margit's doilies on the two shabby chairs. Trudy sat on the edge of her bed, made up with a clean coverlet, and Zsuzsi sat on a chair.

"She went to the hospital last night," Trudy explained. "She collapsed at work, and they came to get me around 11:00. I didn't come home until after lunchtime. I've slept a little but I'm getting ready to go back as soon as visiting hours start."

"What's wrong with her?"

"They said it's exhaustion. She's not sick, but she needs to rest. She can't work two jobs anymore. The doctor said she has to stay in the hospital for at least a week, and then she should rest at home for several weeks after that."

"Oh, Trudy, I'm so sorry. I knew something was wrong; I've had a bad feeling all day."

Trudy's lip began to tremble.

"They won't hold her job at the factory, either the day job or the night one, unless she can come back to work right away. But she can't, so she's going to lose her job. That's all she talks about, how she's going to lose her job."

"Trudy, please don't cry. It'll be all right, as soon as she gets well."

She shook her head. "It's all my fault! She worked so hard for me, and now she's in the hospital!"

Zsuzsi couldn't stand it. She got up to sit next to Trudy, and put her arms around her friend.

"It's not your fault, Trudy, it's what she wanted to do. She loves you, and that's why she worked so hard. In a couple of weeks we'll be out of school, and then you can get a job, too, and she won't have to work so hard anymore. You'll see, everything will be all right. Think how happy she'll be when you graduate, and then you'll be able to work, and be a big help to her."

As she spoke, she cradled Trudy's head on her breast, rocking slowly back and forth. In time Trudy stopped crying, but Zsuzsi didn't let her go. She leaned her cheek against Trudy's hair. "Feel better?"

Trudy nodded. "I've missed you," she said.

Zsuzsi stopped rocking.

"I love you, Zsuzsi."

"I love you, too, Trudy," Zsuzsi whispered into Trudy's hair.

"Love isn't wrong, is it?" asked Trudy.

Zsuzsi let her go and sat up. "No, love isn't wrong, but—"

"But what? Last time we—out in the field—didn't that feel good to you? I—I love it when you touch my hair, or hold my hand, or kiss me. I feel how much you care. I feel like I matter, like I'm someone that someone else can love. And I feel safe, so safe when I'm with you. Can that be wrong?"

"No," Zsuzsi sighed. "No, I don't think so."

She looked at Trudy and smiled. "Safe. That's how I feel with you, too."

She smoothed Trudy's hair back and smiled again. Then she took Trudy's hand, kissed it, and placed it over her own heart. "Safe," she repeated, very softly, as she reached up and began to unbutton her blouse.

Chapter 15
June 1922

St. Brendan's class of 1922 sat on the stage in the high school auditorium, boys on the right in dark suits, girls on the left in white dresses. Zsuzsi sat proudly in her new dress, a graduation present from Eva.

It was cut from a remnant of silk that had been used for one of Mrs. Van Dyke's friends. The low waist and high hem were the latest fashion, and the material was finer than any other girl's. Zsuzsi leaned forward to catch Trudy's eye, but she was listening intently to the opening prayers of Monsignor Daly. Zsuzsi sighed as she leaned back again. Trudy had almost been late for graduation; the graduates were already lining up for the processional when she arrived, and Zsuzsi had not been able to greet her with anything more than a quick smile.

Monsignor Daly finished his benediction and began his speech. Zsuzsi settled more comfortably into her chair; it would be at least half an hour before he finished. She looked out at the audience. Light from the tall windows of the auditorium filtered over the room full of parents, grandparents, brothers and sisters, aunts and uncles. Most of the men wore seersucker suits and balanced straw boaters on their knees. Businessmen and shop owners looked more comfortable in their Sunday best than the factory workers, who sat stiffly, occasionally rubbing a broad finger between a ruddy neck and the starched collar. The women looked like flower petals in pastel dresses of voile and silk, the poorer among them in simple dresses of muslin. There was a curious mix in the auditorium of long dresses and high button shoes with shorter dresses and light, high-heeled slippers that buckled across the arch of the foot. A few of the poorer women wore large flowered hats, made over more than once to approximate the latest fashion, but now hopelessly out of date compared with the newer style whose narrow brim and soft crown slouched prettily on the head.

Zsuzsi was relieved to see that Aunt Margit and Mrs. Bornheimer, while not dressed in the height of fashion that she would have preferred, at least did not look dowdy. Aunt Margit was scandalized by the short skirts worn by the more progressive women in the town, but her own skirt at least revealed her ankles, still slender, in silk stockings. Zsuzsi was grateful that Eva had persuaded Margit to allow both Jolan and herself to dress in the newest style. She caught Jolan's eye and smiled. Jolan smiled back.

While Monsignor Daly droned on, Zsuzsi prevented herself from squirming on the hard folding chair by dreaming up alterations to Mrs. Bornheimer's outfit. Trudy's mother, who seemed to lack any fashion sense at all, had been cajoled into shortening her hem as much as Margit had. Zsuzsi mentally raised the hem even further, lowered the waist, changed the gauzy cotton to a fine silk, and switched the color from white to powder blue before settling on dusty rose.

Forty-five minutes after he began, Monsignor Daly finally completed his speech and stood aside for Sister Patrick to present the diplomas. Zsuzsi clapped politely as each girl received her diploma, but clapped with real enthusiasm for Trudy, who smiled when she took her diploma, shook Sister Patrick's hand, and shook Monsignor Daly's hand. Zsuzsi thought back to the day when she first saw Trudy walk into school like a frightened child, and breathed a small prayer of thanks for the changes in her friend. A few minutes later she walked across the stage for her own diploma.

But instead of handing her the diploma, Sister Patrick first announced, "Zsuzsanna also receives the award for honors in art."

Zsuzsi blushed as Sister Patrick held out not only her diploma but also a small white box.

"Congratulations, Zsuzsanna," murmured Sister Patrick.

"Thank you, Sister," answered Zsuzsi.

Monsignor Daly merely nodded and smiled. Zsuzsi shook his hand and walked back to her seat. She looked out at the audience where Uncle Emil stood, still clapping madly, then she sat down and opened the box. Inside was a silver chain, with a small pendant of Saint Luke, the patron saint of artists.

Zsuzsi closed the box and wrapped her hand around it tightly. She smiled as the rest of the girls received their diplomas, followed by the boys. Then the audience and graduates stood up to sing.

"My country, 'tis of thee, sweet land of liberty, of thee I sing." Zsuzsi formed the words automatically, paying scant attention to verses that usually meant little enough to her, but today seemed full of melancholy. Months ago she had written to her mother, asking if she could possibly, at last, come to America to see the graduation. Only a week ago, she had finally received a reply, a long letter full of news about a country still ravaged by the aftereffects of the Great War. Travel was difficult, they were still poor, but Piros had high hopes that Bela Kun's regime would change the status of the villagers.

Her letter was full of words and phrases Zsuzsi had never heard before: new social order, union of workers, soviet.

"Please try to understand, my sweet one," she had written, "how hard it is for me to tell you that I cannot—I must not—leave dear Hungary at this time. We are just beginning to recover from the War. Our village has formed a collective and together we are making repairs to homes, clearing fields and planting crops, restoring the best of our former way of life while rejecting the old ways that resulted in oppression of the poor by the ruling classes. We are building a new society and I would so much love to have you take part in it. But there is still too much to correct, and until the new order establishes itself, I cannot risk your return.

"And so, my dear love, you see that I cannot leave now and you cannot return now. We must still be apart for a while. I wish you could be here to see what we will accomplish! I know our future will be a bright and productive one. So, too, may your graduation day be bright and happy, for you are now a grown woman taking her place in the world. I know your aunt and uncle take good care of you, and I am grateful every day to know you have enough to eat, and good clothes to wear, and a safe home to live in. But do not forget the struggle here in your true home, and the worthiness of our cause. As always, I send my love to you all. Kiss Jolan for me. Your loving Mama."

Zsuzsi felt tears well up in her eyes and her voice shook on the words "Let freedom ring." If only she were truly free, free to see her mother again! How often she felt torn between her loves—for Uncle Emil, for Trudy, and the security of her life here, against the love she felt toward her mother. Despite her mother's optimism, Zsuzsi had no desire to return to Hungary, but wished with all her heart that her mother and brother would come to America.

The song ended. Clutching her award and diploma, Zsuzsi walked in procession with the other graduates until they passed through the auditorium doors. Once outside, the students broke ranks to find their friends. Zsuzsi hugged and kissed several girls before finally catching up with Trudy. They hugged and kissed each other's cheeks like the other girls.

"Congratulations on your art award," said Trudy in a subdued voice. "I'm so happy for you, Zsuzsi."

"Thank you, Trudy, but—is everything all right?" asked Zsuzsi.

Trudy opened her mouth to answer but just then they were surrounded. Jolan, Mrs. Bornheimer, Uncle Emil, Trudy, and Zsuzsi kissed, hugged, and laughed as one. When they finally separated, Aunt Margit leaned forward and kissed each girl on the cheek.

"Congratulations, Zsuzsanna."

"Thank you, Aunt Margit."

"And to you, too, Gertrude."

"Thank you, Mrs. Molnar."

Uncle Emil stepped up with his camera and made them pose over and over, first Zsuzsi and Jolan with Margit, then Trudy with Mrs. Bornheimer, then Trudy and Zsuzsi side by side. When he was finally finished, Margit asked Trudy, "Will you and your mother join us at home for some refreshment? Eva is waiting with fresh lemonade and sandwiches."

"Thank you so much, Mrs. Molnar," said Trudy's mother. "But I'm afraid we cannot accept. You see, Trudy and I are leaving Hardenbergh today."

Zsuzsi recoiled as though she'd been struck. She looked at Trudy, who looked back with an expression of pure misery.

"Is this true?" asked Zsuzsi.

Trudy nodded. "We're going to live with Mama's relatives in Scranton."

"But why? I thought you were happy here!" Zsuzsi almost shouted.

"Zsuzsanna, lower your voice," said Aunt Margit.

"Come, Margit, Jolan," said Uncle Emil, taking Margit's arm. "Let's give Zsuzsi and the Bornheimers a few minutes together. Come." They stepped out of earshot.

Mrs. Bornheimer smiled kindly but her face was flushed with embarrassment.

"Your uncle is a tactful man, my dear. I am afraid our news is a bit of a shock for you. But you see, we just can't make ends meet living here. I am not as strong as I used to be, so I can't work as much, and even when Trudy gets a job, it will be a long time before she can earn enough to support us both. We simply won't be able to pay the rent. We have no choice." She gave Zsuzsi a hug. "Thank you for everything you've done, especially in the last six months. You and your family have been wonderful to us, and we will always be grateful for your kindness. Now I'll leave you two alone to say goodbye, while I take my leave of your Aunt and Uncle." She squeezed Zsuzsi's hand. "Perhaps they'll give you permission to visit us after we've had a chance to settle in."

In the crowd of jubilant families, Zsuzsi and Trudy stood still. Zsuzsi thought she might never speak or move again. She made no attempt to blink back her tears.

Trudy looked at her with pity. "I didn't know how to tell you, Zsuzsi. Mama decided only a few days ago. It's just not possible to stay. I understand that."

"Do you want to go?" Zsuzsi asked finally, through clenched teeth.

"Please don't be angry with me! Of course I don't want to leave you, but yes, I want to go with Mama. She's been through so much, and she's so frail since her collapse. She needs me, Zsuzsi. I have to take care of her."

"What about me?" Zsuzsi lowered her voice to a whisper. "What about us?"

Trudy handed Zsuzsi a handkerchief. "Do you think this is easy for me? I cried all night when Mama told me. I have to go, Zsuzsi. Like Mama said, we have no choice. Now please, let me say goodbye."

Trudy put her arms around Zsuzsi and murmured, "I love you, Zsuzs. I always will."

Then she was gone. Zsuzsi watched her move through the thinning crowd. She felt a scream building in her throat, and held the handkerchief to her mouth. Then she turned and pushed her way through the crowd. She heard her Aunt call her name, she knew people were staring at her, but she ran even harder, as though she could outrun the pain.

When she could run no more she walked, past the fine stone and clapboard homes belonging to the mayor, to the Van Dykes and other wealthy families, past houses that grew smaller and smaller, until she was in familiar territory. Carefully staying away from her own block, she cut across the neighborhood until she reached the end of Kossuth Street, and walked on to her favorite field, the one where she and Trudy spent many hours.

At this time of year there were no cows in the field, and the grass was tall and fragrant with clover. Wild roses grew along the split-rail fence, and bumblebees fed on the sweet flowers. Zsuzsi hiked her dress up to climb the fence, and walked toward the stream that bisected the field. The water was low in the summer, and many of the smooth rocks were exposed. She took off her shoes and stockings and waded into the stream where the large tadpoles of bullfrogs preyed on smaller ones. Already the bigger tadpoles were growing legs. She sat down on a flat rock at the edge of the streambed and hugged her knees to her chest, watching iridescent blue and green dragonflies dart above the water.

She was still sitting and watching when Uncle Emil strode through the grass.

"Jolan told me I'd probably find you here," said Uncle Emil.

Zsuzsi didn't answer.

"Do you mind if I join you?"

She looked up in surprise as her uncle sat down at the edge of the stream, took off his shoes and socks, and rolled up his pants. He stepped into the water and sat down next to Zsuzsi, dabbling his feet in the mud under the water.

"Be careful. There's a snapping turtle in here somewhere," she said.

"I don't doubt it. This is a fine place for a turtle. Sometimes I envy them."

"What do you mean?"

"Well, think of the simple life they have," Uncle Emil explained. "They swim in a cool stream, they sun themselves on rocks, just like we're doing, and when danger threatens all they have to do is pop into their shells until it passes. Wouldn't it be nice to be a turtle, and have a shell to hide in when something tries to hurt us!"

"Uncle Emil—"

"I have a sandwich in my pocket if you're hungry."

"No, thank you."

"Your aunt made quite a lovely platter of sandwiches, cucumber and onion, tomato and watercress. Very refreshing, and festive. Too bad you weren't there to enjoy them with us."

Zsuzsi began to cry. Emil put his arm around her.

"I'm sorry, Uncle Emil!"

"It's all right, my dear. I'm not scolding. This should have been such a happy day for you! Maybe it was cruel of the Bornheimers not to tell you of their plans sooner, but I think they were trying to spare your feelings. Wouldn't you have been sad, all through the graduation ceremony, if you had known then?"

"I—I suppose so, but..."

"But it was a nasty shock, indeed. And it's quite spoiled the celebration for you. My poor, poor Zsuzsi! I so wish I could spare you all the hurt that life can bring!"

"So do I, Uncle Emil."

"And I wish I could make it better. It's so very difficult, to lose one's best friend."

Zsuzsi bit her lip. She wanted so much to tell him that Trudy was more than just a friend. But how could she? Even kind Uncle Emil would never understand how she felt. She merely nodded her head.

"I could tell you that it will pass, but that won't help you get through today, or tomorrow. What can I do, *lelkem*? Is there any way I can help?"

"Oh, Uncle Emil, you help so much just being here. Only, please, don't make me go back yet. Let's just sit here, please?"

Emil kissed the top of her head. "We'll sit here for as long as you like, my dear. There's nothing I'd rather do than sit here with you."

In a little while Uncle Emil was able to coax her into eating half a sandwich, and when hunger won out over despair Zsuzsi finished the sandwich of her own accord. Finally, she stood up. "I suppose we ought to go home now," she said.

When they arrived at the house, Zsuzsi fully expected to be upbraided for behaving in such an unladylike manner in front of the whole school, but Aunt Margit merely poured Zsuzsi a glass of lemonade and set out the rest of the sandwiches. Zsuzsi wondered what Uncle Emil had said to her while she was gone. Perhaps the lecture would come tomorrow. Jolan and Eva gave her a hug and Ferenc demanded to see her award. Zsuzsi put the necklace around Ferenc's neck.

"Aren't you going to open your present?" he asked.

She looked up at Margit and Emil in surprise.

"What present?" she asked.

Emil smiled and handed her a small box. "From your aunt and me, and Jolan."

Zsuzsi opened the box. "A wristwatch!"

Jolan helped Zsuzsi put it on. "Now you're really a grownup," she said. "How does it feel?"

"The watch? It feels lovely," Zsuzsi said.

But being a grownup felt altogether different.

The next morning, when she opened her eyes, the first thing Zsuzsi saw was her new watch. She smiled, until seeing it reminded her of all that had happened the day before. The hot summer stretched before her, day after empty day. There was nothing for her to do, without Trudy.

She sat up in bed. She vaguely remembered Jolan saying she was going into town with Margit, to buy groceries. Uncle Emil was already in the *Hirlap* office by this time of day. She got out of bed, took a long, cool bath, and went into the kitchen. It was already too hot to eat, even with the curtains drawn to keep the house as cool as possible. She walked upstairs, and knocked on Eva's door, but there was no answer.

Sighing, she went downstairs and out the back door. Even here there was nothing to do. Uncle Emil and Ferenc kept the garden neat and free of weeds. A low hedge ran in a straight line along one fence, and on the other stood a row of tall lilacs, their green leaves dusted with white mildew. No spent flower heads were allowed to stay on the bushes, but only a few weeks ago the lilacs were heavy with purple and white flowers. Zsuzsi had picked a bouquet for Trudy. She sighed again.

Bumblebees flew among the rosebushes, one of yellow flowers, the other pink. Their perfume reminded Zsuzsi of Eva's cologne. Along the back of the yard, in the sunniest part, Emil's tomatoes and peppers flourished. The peas were long gone but cucumbers climbed the back fence. Small pears hung from the pear tree and the sour cherries, so good for pie, were deepening their color. In another month they would be ripe.

Normally, Zsuzsi would have spent the morning helping Aunt Margit and Jolan clean house, but everything had been done ahead of time for graduation. In the afternoon she would have gone walking with Trudy, or to the moving pictures if it rained. Zsuzsi put her hands up as though she could push the memories away, then she turned and fled through the gate to the only place that held no memories of Trudy.

Uncle Emil smiled as she walked into the *Hirlap* office.

"What brings you here today, my dear?" He walked up to her and kissed her cheek.

Zszsui shrugged. "I was lonely, I suppose. Can I help?"

"Sit down. We're just bundling the finished papers now. I'll be done in a few minutes." He walked into the other room.

"It seems everyone has something to do except me!" Zsuzsi sat, but in a moment she stood up and began to pace back and forth. A few minutes later Uncle Emil came back. He had washed his hands and was rolling down his sleeves.

"That's all, then. Are you hungry? It's a bit early for lunch if you had a big breakfast."

"Actually, I haven't eaten yet."

"Then I shall treat you to lunch at the soda fountain."

Sandor stepped in, almost ducking through the door. He'd grown even taller since Zsuzsi had seen him last. She suspected he'd not had regular meals until he began working for Uncle Emil. The work seemed to agree with him—he looked healthy and his color was good, even though he spent all day indoors.

"Is there anything else, Mr. Molnar?" he asked.

"No, Sandor. Not if Geza has gone with the deliveries. We're just going to lunch at the soda fountain. Would you care to join us?"

Sandor's color deepened. "Oh, no thank you, Mr. Molnar. I'm expected at home." He nodded toward Zsuzsi. "Hello."

"Hello, Sandy."

"Well, then," he said. He nodded his head once more. "I'll see you on Monday, Mr. Molnar. Goodbye, Zsuzsi."

"Goodbye," she said. When they were out the door she asked, "Is he always so awkward?"

"Only when you're around, my dear. Otherwise he's most competent."

"Don't tell me he still has a crush on me! Why, he's a grown man now."

"And you are a very attractive young lady. Why shouldn't he, as you say, 'have a crush'?"

"Please don't let's talk about Sandy, Uncle Emil!"

"All right, then. Tell me why everyone has something to do except you."

"Oh, I didn't realize you heard that. But it's true! I—thank you," she said, as Emil held open the door to the soda fountain. They sat down at the counter; its smooth marble surface felt cool under Zsuzsi's hands. They ordered chicken salad sandwiches, with coffee for Uncle Emil and a chocolate malt for Zsuzsi.

Zsuzsi turned toward Uncle Emil.

"I should go to work, Uncle Emil, now that I'm out of school, but I don't know what I should do. I'd rather not work in the factories."

"Your Aunt wouldn't hear of it," said Uncle Emil.

"But I don't know stenography, and I'm not good at anything in particular."

"You're good at art. You won an award, after all."

"But art isn't practical, Uncle Emil."

"Now there you are wrong," said Uncle Emil.

The young man tending the soda fountain brought their sandwiches and drinks. Zsuzsi realized that she was hungry indeed, and said no more until she finished her sandwich.

"Now," said Uncle Emil, after ordering a second cup of coffee. "You say art is not practical, yet look at any newspaper or magazine. Someone draws the illustrations in them."

"But those are real artists, Uncle Emil. They went to school, and studied art. They have talent, and training."

"You have talent, too. Why shouldn't you get the training?"

"Because it's expensive! And besides, the nearest art school of any reputation is all the way in Newark."

"Newark, hmm? That would mean a train ride every day."

"Oh, Uncle Emil, I couldn't do that. Think of what Aunt Margit would say! Besides, I can't even apply. I have no credentials."

"You could get a letter of reference from Sister Thomas."

That was possible, Zsuzsi supposed.

"Let me ask you this," said Uncle Emil. "Would you like to go to art school?"

Zsuzsi nodded.

"Then I suggest you talk to Sister Thomas first thing Monday morning."

"But Uncle Emil, how—"

Uncle Emil put his hand on her shoulder. "First thing's first. Talk to Sister Thomas. Find out what you need to do to apply. Then apply—you have nothing to lose by trying. If they say no, then we'll think of something else. But at least you will have tried."

"And what if they say yes?" Zsuzsi asked.

Uncle Emil smiled. "We'll take that step when it comes."

Chapter 16
September 1922

The locomotive pulled into the Hardenbergh train station with a squeal of brakes and an exhalation of steam. Suddenly enveloped in hot white clouds, Zsuzsi stepped back until the massive engine slid by. When the cars halted, the conductors jumped down and placed footstools on the platform to assist the passengers.

Zsuzsi took the conductor's hand and climbed into the nearest car. She selected the cleanest seat she could find, and sat down on the red plush upholstery with her portfolio balanced on her knees. She looked out the window as the train began to roll, watching the station slide past to reveal the familiar streets below. How odd it was to see them from such a height—the roofs of the clothing store, the shoe store, the men's haberdashery. Then the streets were gone as the train surged across the Lenape River, over the truss bridge that both terrified and fascinated Zsuzsi. This was only her second train ride by herself. The first had been early in July, when she went to apply for admission to the Newark School of Design.

The train was already across the river and flying past corn fields and chicken farms when the conductor came into the car. He punched the ticket Zsuzsi handed him, returned it to her, and walked on. She marveled at his composure, and thought she could never become used to moving along at such speeds every day.

On the previous trip Uncle Emil and Jolan had seen her off at the station, over Aunt Margit's protests that she was too young to travel alone.

"She is a young woman now," Uncle Emil had said, "and if she is to make her way in this world she must do so with a degree of independence. The greater her self-composure, the greater her chances of a successful interview. This is something she must do on her own."

At the time, Zsuzsi had been grateful for Uncle Emil's strong support, but as they walked up the steps to the platform her excitement faded. What if I miss the train, she thought, and then, what if I miss my stop? What if I get lost? She checked her purse for the directions to the school. From the train station she was to take the number 10 omnibus to the intersection of Market Street and Rahway Avenue, then walk two blocks north on Rahway Avenue to the school. She read the directions over and over until she had them memorized. Then she heard the rumble of the locomotive, and the clang of its bell, as it swooped into the station, hissing and squealing like a monstrous dragon.

She kissed Uncle Emil and Jolan goodbye, and then she followed the others onto the train, sat down, and checked the contents of her purse for the umpteenth time: her ticket, the directions, the letter of reference from Sister Thomas. Besides her purse she held a large envelope with her best drawings, eight of them, in black and white and pastel. Sister Thomas had helped her select them from her school assignments and from the drawings she had done so many times while Trudy had waded through the stream or picked wildflowers.

Zsuzsi refused to let herself think of Trudy on this day. She had received a letter from her—she and her mother were settled into her aunt's house, Trudy was to begin work as a housekeeper on the following Monday. She wrote the way she talked, a chatty, breezy kind of letter, but one that never said the important things: whether her heart ached all day as Zsuzsi's did, whether the summer loomed ahead full of loneliness, whether she would ever be happy again.

She blinked away her tears. It wouldn't do to arrive at her interview with puffy eyes and a red nose. She opened her window a crack, enough to feel air on her face but not, she hoped, enough to let cinders fly in. How unfair life could be! Here she was, embarking on a real adventure, and all she felt was sorrow like a great weight in her stomach. Every morning when she woke the weight would descend on her again. Some days she could scarcely get out of bed.

It was hard for her to share Uncle Emil's and Sister Thomas' enthusiasm, yet as they prepared for her interview she began to realize how much she needed something to take her mind off Trudy, something to lift the weight. Until she woke this morning, with the realization that today was the day, her upcoming interview had seemed not just far away but even unreal, something vague that would happen someday to someone else. But it became more and more concrete as she brushed and braided her hair, tied it with a white satin bow, and put on her best dress of white voile. Now here she was, on the train to Newark, less than two hours away from the most important discussion of her life.

Fear and excitement mingled with the rhythm of the wheels as the train sped to its next stop. Zsuzsi knew from the schedule that there were three stops between Hardenbergh and Newark. She didn't know whether to be relieved at each delay, or impatient to go on. At each stop she checked her wristwatch and then looked at the schedule to make sure the train was on time. What she would do if it weren't she had no clue, but it seemed important to know.

Fortunately, the train pulled into Newark Station right on schedule. The conductor helped her down and she followed the disembarking passengers down the stairs. In the station building, she found signs to direct her to the omnibus stop. Bus after bus pulled up to the stop, but never a number 10. Zsuzsi began to worry that she should have taken an earlier train. Finally, the number 10 arrived, and she stepped aboard.

She had wanted to sit up front, to better scan the street signs, but the bus was crowded, and she had to take an aisle seat more than halfway to the rear. To her relief, the bus driver announced each stop as he approached it. She got off the bus twenty minutes later and started toward the school, but realized after a block that she'd turned the wrong way. Hurrying, she retraced her steps. When she arrived at the correct address, she waited for just a moment to catch her breath, then dashed up the steps.

Inside the building, young men and women lounged in the wide corridor or rushed by with large, flat leather packages under their arms. A girl with bobbed hair carried an easel. An older woman, also with bobbed hair but wearing a severe black dress, came out of a door to Zsuzsi's right.

"May I help you?" she asked.

"I'm here to see Miss Eleanor Roberts," answered Zsuzsi.

"Do you have an appointment?"

"Yes, at 10:30."

The woman glanced at her wristwatch. "You're right on time. Follow me."

She led Zsuzsi down the corridor, which was lined with lockers like any school. But here the air smelled of turpentine and oil paints instead of chalk dust. After they passed several closed doors, which Zsuzsi assumed to be classrooms, the corridor ended, but two more corridors opened at either side, forming a tee.

The woman pointed to the right. "All administrative offices are down this corridor. You want the first door on the right."

Zsuzsi thanked her but the woman had already begun walking back. She took a deep breath and knocked on the door.

"Come in," a voice called. It sounded pleasant enough and Zsuzsi opened the door.

"Miss Roberts?"

"No, I'm Miss Martin, Miss Roberts' secretary."

"I beg your pardon. I'm Zsuzsanna Takacs. I have an appointment with Miss Roberts."

Miss Martin, a plump woman with bobbed brown hair and a pleasant smile, motioned Zsuzsi to take a seat. Zsuzsi sat down while Miss Martin finished a piece of typing. The office was small but well lit, with three wooden chairs for visitors on one side and Miss Martin's desk on the other. Miss Martin collected her typing, walked over to the inner door, and knocked once before going in. A moment later she held open the door for Zsuzsi.

On the train Zsuzsi had pictured Miss Roberts as an older woman with gray hair tucked into a neat bun, but after only a few minutes in this building she was not surprised to see that Miss Roberts, like everyone else Zsuzsi had seen here, had bobbed hair. At first glance she seemed Eva's age, but then Zsuzsi saw a scattering of fine wrinkles around her eyes and realized that Miss Roberts was closer in age to Aunt Margit. Unlike Aunt Margit, Miss Roberts was dressed in the latest fashion; her silk dress, the color of sunlit grass, had the shortest hemline Zsuzsi had ever seen. Miss Roberts' lips were colored deep red and she wore spots of rouge on her cheeks.

Miss Roberts shook Zsuzsi's hand and asked her to be seated.

"So, you want to be an artist," she said. She took a lighted cigarette from the ashtray on her desk and inhaled, looking at Zsuzsi the whole time.

"Yes, well, no, not really," Zsuzsi said, trying not to stare at the two streams of smoke that emanated from Miss Roberts' nostrils. "That is, I want to learn how to draw, but I want to become an illustrator, to draw for newspapers, perhaps, or magazines. I need to earn a living, you see."

Miss Roberts stubbed out her cigarette and smiled for the first time. "Well, that's a refreshing answer. Most students come here expecting to be the next Cezanne or Cassatt. You seem to be of a more practical bent."

Before Zsuzsi could reply Miss Roberts said, "You have a letter of reference, of course?"

"Yes," said Zsuzsi, reaching into her purse. "Here it is. It's from Sister Thomas, the art teacher at my high school."

Miss Roberts leaned forward to take the letter. While she read it Zsuzsi glanced around the office. It wasn't very large, no larger than the outer office where Miss Martin sat, but it had a window, with dark green drapes, and a wine colored carpet under the desk and chairs. An oak file cabinet stood in one corner of the room opposite a small table with a china tea service atop it. Two paintings hung on the walls, one a portrait of a young girl, the other a landscape. Zsuzsi thought they were well done and wondered who the artist was.

"Well, Sister Thomas speaks very highly of your abilities. May I see your samples?"

Zsuzsi handed Miss Martin the envelope. Miss Martin opened the envelope and pulled out Zsuzsi's drawings, then she carried them to the window, where she looked at each one, quickly, and then went to the beginning and looked them over again.

"Are these all you have?" she asked.

"Yes, they're my best pieces. Sister Thomas helped me choose them."

"I see." She sat down at the desk again and spread out the drawings. "Some of these are quite good, Miss Takacs. Am I pronouncing that correctly? Good. Well, as I was saying, you have a basic talent. I especially like the way you've caught the texture of the fabric in this drawing. It's really quite well done. But it simply isn't enough to determine your admission to this school at this time. I'm sorry."

"You mean I'm not good enough," Zsuzsi said, trying to keep her voice steady.

"I mean I haven't seen enough to judge. I need more drawings, at least two dozen, before I can judge whether you have what it takes to succeed here. Our school's reputation depends on the quality of our graduates, as I'm sure you can understand."

Zsuzsi nodded. She was afraid to speak, sure that if she opened her mouth she'd start to cry.

"This small group of drawings, how long did it take you to do them?"

"It's mostly the work I did during this last school year."

"There, you see?" said Miss Roberts. "This represents perhaps one drawing a month. If you come here, you must work much harder than that. Our students draw every day, and they paint, and they sculpt. They don't do any of that on a whim, as the mood strikes, but every day, all day. Have you ever worked that hard, Miss Takacs?"

Zsuzsi shook her head.

"Well, then," said Miss Roberts, gathering up the drawings. "Go home and draw, Miss Takacs. When you have enough work for me to fairly and honestly assess your talent, make another appointment. Shall we say, in eight weeks? In the meantime I'll keep your letter of reference on file."

Miss Roberts stood up and opened the door. "Miss Martin, would you give Miss Takacs the grand tour on her way out?"

Zsuzsi shook Miss Roberts' hand and accompanied Miss Martin into the corridor. Miss Martin led her upstairs to the studios, great rooms with high ceilings, long windows, and skylights, but after she'd seen them Zsuzsi couldn't remember what they looked like. She tried to concentrate as Miss Martin described what they were seeing but all she could hear was Miss Roberts' voice repeating, over and over, "It simply isn't enough...I'm sorry. I'm sorry. Sorry."

They walked back downstairs to the classrooms where students wearing paint-spattered smocks drew or painted still lifes and portraits. In one room a young woman stood naked on a platform while the students sketched her in charcoal. Zsuzsi felt her face turn red; that sight, at least, penetrated the haze she was walking in. Yet none of the students seemed embarrassed, or giggled, and the model was perfectly composed. Miss Martin acted as though she saw such things every day. With a shock, Zsuzsi realized that, of course, she did.

She could hardly take it all in. She had never seen anything like it—girls and grown women with bobbed hair, women smoking openly, wearing makeup, standing nude in front of other young women and men! What would Uncle Emil think, or Aunt Margit, or shy Sister Thomas, if they could see this place?

"Well, that's the tour," said Miss Martin. "Do you have any questions before I see you out?"

"Just one," answered Zsuzsi. "What are those leather cases that everyone here carries?"

"They're portfolios, for holding artwork." Miss Martin gave her a pat on the shoulder and said goodbye.

Zsuzsi looked down at her envelope and sighed. A girl passing in the hallway looked at her quizzically. Zsuzsi imagined how she must look, with her old-fashioned braid and her Sunday best dress, so out of place in this working environment where girls wore smocks over sensible skirts and blouses. She felt like a peasant, and she hadn't felt like that since Ellis Island.

To have her drawings dismissed so quickly! Miss Roberts couldn't have spent more than five minutes looking at what had taken days to draw and hours to select. She walked quickly away from the school. She wanted to go home, to get away from this huge city and these sophisticated people, the traffic and the crowds. She swallowed hard and blinked back her tears. She didn't want to seem any more out of place than she already felt.

A number 10 bus pulled up at the stop just as she arrived. She boarded and sat in the first available place, then took out her train schedule. The sooner she caught a train for home the happier she'd be.

But on the train, she went over and over Miss Roberts' words. She hadn't dismissed Zsuzsi out of hand. She'd offered her a second chance. Zsuzsi opened her envelope and took out the drawing Miss Roberts had liked. It was a pencil drawing of Eva as she sewed a hem. With her pencil Zsuzsi had shown the difference between Eva's simple muslin dress and the rich velvet of the hemmed skirt. Zsuzsi had struggled with Eva's profile, and still felt dissatisfied with it, but she could see that the two fabrics were indeed the best things in the picture.

By the time the train pulled into Hardenbergh, Zsuzsi was determined to succeed. She'd begin today, as soon as she got home. But first she needed supplies. She walked to the stationery store along familiar downtown streets, which suddenly seemed narrow and quiet. At the store she bought two new sketchpads, pencils, pastels, and charcoal. She looked for portfolios but the store didn't stock them. A clerk showed her a catalog, and there she found what she was looking for, but the price was more than she'd expected. Disappointed, Zsuzsi left the store without ordering a leather portfolio. Then she had an idea.

There were several barbers in Hardenbergh, but only one store she knew of that specialized in bobbing women's hair. Zsuzsi walked to Miss Brill's Salon, where a sign in the store window read "We buy hair."

And so, by the time she walked back up Kossuth Street, Zsuzsi had bobbed hair and a leather portfolio on order.

Aunt Margit actually dropped a plate in surprise when Zsuzsi walked in the door. Her mouth opened wide but no sound came out. Zsuzsi calmly told her the events of the morning, of her need for a portfolio and more drawing supplies, and her determination to succeed.

Aunt Margit said only, "Your hair! Your beautiful hair!"

Zsuzsi walked to her and kissed her on the cheek.

"It really is most practical, Aunt Margit. And now, I must get to work."

Uncle Emil and Jolan were no less surprised, but neither was rendered speechless. Zsuzsi cut off their exclamations as firmly as she had responded to Aunt Margit's silence. In the end, Uncle Emil conceded she had behaved quite independently and resourcefully. Jolan admitted that bobbed hair suited Zsuzsi well.

Since then, Zsuzsi had drawn, every day. She drew everyone in the family: Aunt Margit embroidering, Uncle Emil proofreading, Jolan in the garden. She drew Eva at work and at leisure, Ferenc playing; still lifes, landscapes, even her home, enough drawings to fill the portfolio that now lay carefully balanced on her lap.

Zsuzsi rested her hands on the cool leather of the portfolio and took a deep breath. Her emotions zigzagged between wild panic and calm optimism. Only last night, panic had won out and she lay in bed restlessly, sure her drawings were terrible, her dress too severe, her dream of becoming an illustrator ridiculous. She tossed and turned, finally slipping into an exhausted sleep only when Jolan reached over and took her hand.

Zsuzsi woke with butterflies in her stomach, whether from excitement or fear she didn't care to guess. She bathed and washed her short hair, rinsing it with cider vinegar to make it shine. She forced down a piece of toast and a cup of coffee, to please Aunt Margit, then finished dressing. When she looked in the mirror she saw a smart young woman who looked cool and professional in a simple dress of navy linen, with a plain white collar and white cuffs on the short sleeves. It had been Zsuzsi's idea to add the collar and cuffs to the plain dress, and she was pleased with the effect. She marveled that Eva, whose hands were so skilled at making patterns and sewing garments, did not think of design alterations that to Zsuzsi were plain as day.

With her new portfolio in hand she felt like an art student for the first time, but would Miss Roberts see her the same way? One minute Zsuzsi was sure her drawings were fit only for the trash, the next minute she thought they had some merit at least, and perhaps a few of them were even good. That they were her best work she had no doubt. That they were good enough, she doubted very much.

Back and forth, up and down, the butterflies of fear and tension flew inside her all the way to Newark, and on the bus ride to the school. As she walked the last two blocks she concentrated on breathing deeply and looking as confident as possible. She made herself walk up the steps of the art school as casually as if she'd done it for years, and she went along the corridor with her head high. This time, no one stared at her. In fact, after a quick glance her way, the students in the corridor ignored her completely. Zsuzsi felt as though she'd passed the first test.

Miss Martin greeted her with a smile and opened the door to the inner office. Zsuzsi walked in with her portfolio tucked under her arm. She removed her white gloves and shook Miss Roberts' hand.

"Good Morning, Miss Roberts, and thank you for seeing me again."

"It's my pleasure, Miss Takacs."

Zsuzsi handed her the portfolio. Miss Roberts opened it and, as she had done the last time, took Zsuzsi's drawings to the window, where she reviewed them one by one.

The room was so quiet Zsuzsi heard the wall clock tick the minutes away, the sound of sketch paper rustle as Miss Roberts took each drawing from the top of the pile and placed it on the bottom, and a dull thudding that she realized was her own heart beating.

Miss Roberts looked at the drawings impassively, a raised eyebrow now and then Zsuzsi's only clue that Miss Roberts had seen something of note, but whether she raised her brow in surprise, admiration, or disgust Zsuzsi could not tell. Finally, Miss Roberts placed the drawings on her desk and smiled at Zsuzsi.

"I can see you've been working hard, Miss Takacs," she began. "These are much better samples than what you brought the first time."

"Thank you," said Zsuzsi, certain Miss Roberts was about to add "But they just aren't good enough." Please, God, she prayed, don't let me cry in her office.

Miss Roberts extended her hand. "Welcome to the Newark School of Design."

Chapter 17
June 1924

Weary but content, Zsuzsi walked the six blocks from the train station to Kossuth Street one Thursday evening, shifting the weight of her sketch pad and art books from one arm to the other. As she came closer to home she greeted neighbors who were sitting on front porches, or taking an after-dinner stroll. When she approached Kossuth Street she stopped for a breath of the sweetly scented honeysuckle air. Despite the excitement of attending a big-city art school, Zsuzsi never failed to enjoy coming home.

She didn't think she'd ever been more satisfied, especially now that she was only a few weeks from completing her course of study in fashion design. Early in her training, her instructors had recognized Zsuzsi's ability not only to draw fabrics and dresses but also to create whole new designs. Zsuzsi laughed to think that she, who couldn't sew a straight hem, was now designing entire garments for others to make. She had even commissioned Eva to sew one of her own designs to wear for graduation, for her final portfolio was to include not only black-and-white sketches and full-color drawings, but even the very outfit she hoped to wear on job interviews: a two-piece suit of champagne-colored peau de soie, with a shawl collar piped in matching satin, and a short, pleated skirt.

She shifted her books once more to open the garden gate. Here she inhaled the fragrance of roses, for Uncle Emil's favorite shrubs were in full bloom. Pink and yellow tea roses unfurled in the center of the garden, and red climbing roses spilled over the fences on both sides. White peonies were so heavy they hung almost to the ground, and bearded irises lined the back hedgerow with frilly blue and yellow blossoms. In the center, pepper and tomato seedlings were thriving among short rows of cabbages and lettuce, onions and potatoes. Uncle Emil had used every square inch of space.

Zsuzsi couldn't decide which garden season she liked best—April's daffodils and cherry blossoms, May's lilacs, or this lush display of summer. If Uncle Emil had been her father she would have known whom to credit for her color sense. She smiled and walked in the door, where supper would be waiting. She rarely came home in time to eat with the others, but Aunt Margit always had a platter made up for her.

Aunt Margit's initial disapproval of Zsuzsi's art classes had been frosty, especially during the first year of classes, when Zsuzsi brought home page after page of nude figures sketched in charcoal. Once her classes took a more practical turn, however, even Aunt Margit saw that Zsuzsi was talented enough to make a decent living from her artwork. When Margit realized that she and Emil would not have to support Zsuzsi until she was married, the climate in the Molnar household warmed considerably.

Aunt Margit and Jolan had finished washing up and were about to sit on the front porch, but they waited for Zsuzsi to change into a comfortable housedress, and kept her company while she ate.

"Is Uncle Emil out walking?" she asked.

"As usual," answered Jolan, who wore her long hair pinned up in a bun now that she was graduated from high school.

"This came for you today," said Aunt Margit, holding an envelope. "From Trudy."

Zsuzsi stopped eating. "From Trudy? I haven't heard from her in months." She picked up the letter, then put it down again. "I'll open it after supper."

When would her heart stop lurching at the mention of Trudy's name? After she began her art studies, Zsuzsi wrote to Trudy less and less often, partly because she was so busy, but also because each letter reminded her just how much she still missed Trudy. Would it never go away, that old dull ache that made it hard to breathe?

She scraped her plate into a pail with the rest of the evening's kitchen scraps. "I'll take this outside," she said. She carried the pail to Uncle Emil's precious compost pile, dumped it out, and then rinsed it under the spigot. She took the letter from her pocket and began to open it, then changed her mind and put it back in her pocket. She walked to the front of the house, relieved to see that Aunt Margit and Jolan were not yet encamped on the porch, and hurried up Kossuth Street. There, past the last of the houses, the scent of honeysuckle was almost overpowering. Along the shoulder of the dirt road, wild raspberries were in bloom with cascades of white flowers under the forest canopy. Across the road, the small herd of Guernseys belonging to the Amwell family grazed in the field where Zsuzsi and Trudy had spent so much time together.

Zsuzsi leaned across the fence, hoping the cows would come over to be scratched, but after looking up briefly they ignored her. She opened Trudy's letter. It began as Trudy's letters always did, with a quick resume of her situation and her mother's health, but the language was a little more careful—at times even stilted—than her usual casual writing. There was a large blank space between the paragraphs, where Zsuzsi could almost imagine Trudy pausing for breath.

"And now, dear Zsuzsi, I must tell you that I have news, good news, and I hope you will be glad for me. I guess there's no way to say it except to say that I am going to be married after the fourth of July. There, I've told you, and I can imagine your face as you read this. His name is William Galfetti, and he is Italian, which Mama has gotten used to. He is a stonemason, and carves memorials for all the cemeteries in Scranton. You can see that he will never want for work! I suppose I shouldn't joke about such a thing, but it means so much to me that he has steady, secure work, and will be able to support me and even Mama. If you knew what it was like living in Mama's sister's house—not that I'm ungrateful, for Aunt Betty has been most generous to let us stay here, but it's very much her house, and she's very strict about so many things. Well, you know all about that. And you know how much I dislike keeping house for other people. Marrying William will put an end to that. He's very kind, and gets along quite well with Mama—now, anyway—and he loves me. He's said so.

"I love him, too, Zsuzsi, although it's not the same as—you know. Please understand that I will always love you, you know that, don't you? But I need someone like William who can take care of me, and support me and Mama, and it isn't as though young men have been knocking on my door all this time. So I have accepted William, and I think we will be happy, but I also want to know that you'll be happy for me, too. Please be happy! And someday you'll find your own William.

"Well, that's the big news from Scranton. I look forward to your reply, because I so want your blessing, and also, because there isn't anyone in the world I'd want besides you to stand up for me on my wedding day. Can you? Will you? Please?

"As always, give my love to your Aunt and Uncle, and to Jolan, Eva, and Ferenc.

"Love, Trudy"

Zsuzsi crumpled the letter into a ball and shoved it deep into the pocket of her dress. The cows looked up in surprise as she wept.

Dear God in Heaven! She had never, ever expected such a thing. To think of Trudy marrying—and was she to stand next to her, smiling, pretending happiness? Did Trudy really have no idea how much the very idea hurt her, how it brought the old ache to the surface, and turned it into a roaring, raging pain? She paced back and forth in front of the fence, so visibly agitated the cows moved further back from the road.

The sky faded from the fuchsia of sunset to the pale lavender of dusk before Zsuzsi had her tears under control. Then she walked back to the house and calmly announced Trudy's news, which was received with genuine pleasure by everyone else.

"What an honor it is to be asked to stand up for your friend," said Aunt Margit. "Of course, you'll do it?"

Zsuzsi gritted her teeth. "Of course," she said. Jolan looked at her oddly, as though she heard the bitterness Zsuzsi tried to keep from slipping through.

That night Zsuzsi turned her back to Jolan, pretending to be asleep, so she wouldn't have to endure any more of the speculations, comments, good wishes, and blessings she was to convey to Trudy in her reply.

The next morning Zsuzsi got ready for school like a sleepwalker, unable to eat breakfast, and so distracted she nearly forgot her sketchpad. At the first street crossing she was nearly run over by the milk wagon. She took a deep breath, collected herself somewhat, and continued to the station, where she boarded the train automatically and sat in her usual seat. When the train arrived in the Newark station, she began to walk toward the exit, but stopped suddenly. All around her people strode purposefully to work or to school, but she couldn't go on.

She felt like a marionette, controlled by some higher power pulling strings to make her move toward the ticket counter. As though some puppeteer in the background were speaking for her, she heard herself ask the clerk for a round trip ticket to Scranton.

While she waited for the train, Zsuzsi argued within herself. Going to Scranton was a crazy idea. What could she hope to accomplish? She should return her ticket and go to school. If she started right now she wouldn't even be late. But then the train arrived, the invisible puppeteer worked the strings, and she boarded. Once the train began to move she relaxed a little. The decision had been made; it was too late to get off.

For the first time she would miss school. Would anyone notice? Yes, but her instructors would merely assume she was ill, and she could catch a return train that would bring her home not much later than usual. Aunt Margit and Uncle Emil need never know.

Zsuzsi leaned back in her seat and looked out the window as the train surged north and west. She had never ridden on the Erie-Lackawanna line, and despite her inner turmoil her artist's eye was captivated by the scenery. Farms alternated with forest as the countryside grew more and more hilly. Small towns nestled in valleys where children stopped playing to wave as the train sped by. Towns gave way to villages and the villages to isolated farms. In the distance, Zsuzsi glimpsed a long green ridge that seemed to grow a bit larger each time the train rounded a curve in the tracks. Then they were speeding north along the Delaware River, which sparkled clear blue in the morning light.

Zsuzsi gasped as the train crossed the river. The bridge was higher than the railroad bridge at home, but more startling was the height of the great ridge the river bisected. Covered with trees, it was so high that Zsuzsi had to open her window wide and lean her head out to see the top. It seemed to go on and on to the east, and when they had crossed the river, it continued westward as far as she could see.

Zsuzsi remembered the mountains of Austria she had seen when she left Europe. This ridge wasn't so high or so steep, but was far longer. She wondered how the train could possibly cross it, when suddenly everything went dark. Zsuzsi started, then realized the train had plunged into a tunnel. In a matter of moments they passed into sunlight again.

As the train traveled farther into Pennsylvania the scenery resembled that of northern New Jersey, but the hills loomed steeper, the villages and towns stood farther apart. Fewer automobiles but more wagons moved along the narrow roads, and the children who stopped playing to wave at the train were dressed more poorly. The farms seemed less prosperous, the fields rockier than any she had seen. Zsuzsi knew little of the area—geography had never been her best subject—only that she was entering an area of coal mines and iron works.

The ride took nearly three hours, and Zsuzsi was glad when the train finally reached Scranton. It was not a very pretty city. The air was smoky from nearby mills, and the narrow houses seemed covered with a layer of grime. Zsuzsi got off the train stiff, hot, and hungry.

The stationmaster gave her directions to the house where Trudy worked as housekeeper and cook. It was more than a mile from the train station, but the walk felt good after such a long ride. In a few blocks the small crowded houses gave way to larger homes with a bit of front yard. They had the decorated gables, turrets, and wraparound porches typical of homes built at the end of the last century.

Zsuzsi stopped in front of a brick house with yellow shutters and a green door. Lace curtains hung in every window, all the way to the attic, and atop the gable end a weather vane shaped like a running horse pointed to the south. The slate path that led to the front steps was lined with geraniums that looked as thirsty as Zsuzsi felt. Now that she was finally here, the nerves she had repressed on the train ride came back in full force, making her mouth dry. She hesitated, on the brink of turning back, but then took a deep breath, walked up to the front door, and rang the bell.

The door was opened by a young woman with short brown hair and pale skin sprinkled lightly with freckles. She wore a blue dress with a white apron and carried a feather duster. The expression on her face changed from cautious curiosity to puzzlement to wonder.

"Zsuzsi?"

Zsuzsi smiled. "I got your letter. I had to come."

"Zsuzsi!" Trudy opened the door wide. "Come in! Come in."

Zsuzsi stepped into the hallway. A staircase with an ornate wooden balustrade climbed up to her left. A small table with a fern and telephone on top of it was the only furniture in the hall.

"I can't believe you came all this way!" exclaimed Trudy. "But I'm so glad you did. It's good that you came today. Mrs. Wheaton has her charity luncheons on Fridays, and Mr. Wheaton eats downtown. Otherwise I'd have to ask you to wait in the kitchen while I served dinner. Are you hungry?"

"Famished," said Zsuzsi.

Trudy led her down the hall into the kitchen, a large, bright room with a table set for one.

"I was just having lunch. I'll make you a sandwich. Is tongue all right?"

"Fine."

Zsuzsi took off her hat and gloves and set them on the table with her sketchbook. She sat down, willed her heart to stop pounding, and fussed with smoothing her skirt. Trudy handed her a glass of lemonade.

"It's fresh. I just made it this morning." She looked at Zsuzsi, who took in every angle and curve of her face. "I guess I'd better make you that sandwich." She turned toward the counter. She seemed at home in the Wheaton kitchen, which had a big, modern stove and a large icebox. Trudy worked with a practiced efficiency Zsuzsi had never seen before.

Zsuzsi couldn't take her eyes off Trudy. Even wearing a frumpy maid's uniform, she still looked slender and lovely. Zsuzsi ached to hold her. To distract herself, she asked, "What's in that other room?"

"Butler's pantry," answered Trudy, "only there's no butler. There's just me." She handed Zsuzsi the sandwich. Her hands looked red and rough.

Trudy sat down, and gestured toward the sketchbook. "May I?" she asked.

Zsuzsi nodded, her mouth full of sandwich.

Trudy turned the pages of the sketchbook, smiling. "These are wonderful, Zsuzsi. Your work was always good, but these are really the cat's meow."

Zsuzsi laughed. "The cat's meow? You sound like a flapper!"

Trudy laughed, too, and suddenly Zsuzsi felt like a schoolgirl again. Why had she been so nervous about coming? Talking to Trudy had always been the easiest thing in the world. They talked about their hair, about Zsuzsi's designs, about Buster Keaton and Charlie Chaplin, and they agreed that *The Ten Commandments* was the best motion picture they had ever seen.

"Oh, Trudy! It's so good to talk like this again! I've missed it, missed you, so much."

"I've missed you, too, Zsuzsi. If only Hardenbergh weren't so far away."

If only you'd never left, Zsuzsi wanted to say. But it wasn't Trudy's fault, nor was it Mrs. Bornheimer's. "This is a beautiful home," was all she said.

"Beautiful, yes," said Trudy. "But I hate every inch of it. If it were mine—well, it isn't, and it's no better at Aunt Betty's. I feel like a servant there, too."

"It must be awful for you."

"Oh, at least here I get paid to dust the furniture and beat the carpets. It's not so bad, I guess; after all, I'd have to do the same things in my own home. But doing it for someone else makes it different. Everything must be done her way, and if I make the slightest mistake she acts as though I'd broken her best vase, or something. Aunt Betty is worse. Mama and I have never felt at home there. But that will soon change."

Zsuzsi felt herself stiffen. "I suppose it must." She tried to keep her tone neutral, but Trudy knew her too well, and her smile faded.

"Don't you want me to be happy, Zsuzsi?"

"Of course I do! More than anything—but I—I wish it didn't have to be this way."

"What other way can there be?"

"Oh, Trudy. I'll be graduated soon—I'll get a job, in Newark, or maybe even New York. I could support us." She reached for Trudy's hand. "And you could find some other job, in an office, so you wouldn't have to work so hard. You could cover your hands with softening cream instead of dish water—"

Trudy pulled her hand away and stood up. "No, Zsuzsi."

"Why ever not?"

"It's just not possible. Be realistic, Zsuzsi!"

Zsuzsi felt her face redden with anger. "Don't tell me you really love this William person!"

"Yes, I love him." She picked up the plates and carried them to the sink. With her back to Zsuzsi, she said, "I know it isn't the same as you and me—but that's over, Zsuzsi, two years ago it was over. It was just something that happened—"

"Something beautiful."

Trudy nodded, and turned toward Zsuzsi. "But it was a long time ago and—and it's something I would never do again. William must never know. Zsuzsi, promise you me you'll never say anything."

Zsuzsi stood up and gathered her things.

"What do you take me for, Trudy?"

"I'm sorry. It's just that this is may be my only chance, to get out of this house, out of Aunt Betty's house, to make a life for myself, and for Mama."

"You haven't said it's your only chance to be happy. Will you be happy, Trudy? Can you be really happy with him—with any man?"

"He isn't just any man, Zsuzsi. He's kind, and gentle, and good to me, Zsuzsi. He treats me like a lady."

"Has he bedded you?"

"Zsuzsi! What do you take ME for?"

Zsuzsi sat down again. She felt tears in her eyes and looked up at the high ceiling, trying not to blink, trying not to cry. "I'm sorry. That was unfair. I shouldn't have said it."

"That's all right. I know you didn't mean to say anything hurtful."

"But I did!" Zsuzsi hit the table with her fists and began to sob. "I did mean it to hurt! It hurts me, Trudy, it hurts me so much to think of you with him. Don't you know how much I've missed you? I think of you every day! Every day! I still love you, Trudy!"

Whether she was weeping from anger or despair Zsuzsi couldn't tell anymore. She wanted Trudy to reach over, to hug her, to kiss her and tell her it would be all better, to do anything that would give her some hope. If only she would reach for Zsuzsi's hand.

But Trudy didn't move.

Zsuzsi wiped her eyes with the back of her hand. "Is there nothing I can say, nothing I can do, to make you change your mind?"

"No," Trudy said quietly, and the resolution in her voice made Zsuzsi wince as though she'd been struck. She pulled her handkerchief from her purse and blew her nose. Somewhere in the house a clock struck the half hour.

"I'm afraid you'd better be going, Zsuzsi. Mrs. Wheaton will be home by two, and it wouldn't do for her to find me entertaining a guest instead of doing the ironing."

"What do you care? Haven't you given your notice?"

"Yes, I've given a month's notice. But it wouldn't do."

"God, you sound so, so conventional. You sound like a married woman already." She took a compact from her purse and powdered under her eyes. Trudy's composure had become downright irritating.

"I didn't know you wore makeup," observed Trudy.

"No? Watch this." Zsuzsi reached in her purse and pulled out a small pot of rouge. She dabbed it lightly on her cheeks and lips.

"Does it make me look fast?"

Trudy nodded, suppressing a smile.

"I can do even better," said Zsuzsi. She reached in her purse again and brought out a cigarette.

"Zsuzsi Takacs! You smoke?"

"I will if you get me a match."

Trudy reached into a holder next to the stove and handed one to Zsuzsi. She scraped the match on the kitchen table, lit the cigarette, inhaled deeply, and blew the match out with the smoke.

"Want one?" she asked.

Trudy waved her hand in the smoke. "You'd better put it out. I don't want Mrs. Wheaton to think I've started smoking when she's not home."

"If I were you, I wouldn't care, but I'll take it outside if you like."

Trudy was visibly shocked. "You'd take it on a public street?"

"Trudy, women have been smoking for more than thirty years."

"Not outdoors."

Zsuzsi blew smoke through her nostrils. "Everyone smokes in Newark."

"This isn't Newark."

"No, it isn't," said Zsuzsi drily. She stood up and walked reluctantly down the hall. So, it was final. No more to say, no more to do, except succumb.

"Tell me," she said when they reached the front door, "what are you wearing to your wedding?"

"Mama's dress. It's old-fashioned, I know, but it will please her to see me in it."

"Then I suppose I shall have to wear something long, as well."

"Zsuzsi! You mean, after all, you'll be there? You'll stand up for me?"

"If you still want me, after everything I've said."

"You know I do."

"What color?"

Trudy smiled. "Peach, because that's what you are." She extended her hand, but Zsuzsi put her arms around Trudy and held her tight. She smelled like laundry soap. Zsuzsi pressed her cheek into Trudy's hair, then let her go. She turned toward the door, changed her mind, took Trudy's face in her hand and kissed her hard on the mouth, forcing Trudy's soft lips open with her tongue. Trudy's face turned white.

Zsuzsi smiled and wiped the lipstick off Trudy's mouth.

"Just to remember me by. Don't worry, I'll never do that again." Then she opened the door and walked past the wilted geraniums, glad for the breeze that blew cigarette smoke in her eyes. It was a good excuse for her tears.

She smoked her cigarette with an outward bravado, ignoring the glares of neighborhood matrons, but her sorrow and anger had left her shaking and weak. She returned to the station and boarded the train listlessly, leaning against the seatback like a marionette whose strings had been cut. All over, all over, all over the wheels seemed to say. All over, her heart echoed, and she didn't think it would ever love again.

With a month to plan for the wedding, she had plenty of time to design a maid of honor's dress. Using Aunt Margit and Uncle Emil's wedding picture as a guide, she produced a simple design with short puffed sleeves, a lace bodice, and a long straight skirt. She dropped the waist to give it a more contemporary look, in hopes of wearing it again. With the sleeves removed and the hem shortened, she could wear the dress to a dance or dinner.

She helped Eva make a pattern and cut it out, but when it came to the actual sewing Eva refused to let Zsuzsi work on it. Eva of all people knew how little skill Zsuzsi had with a needle. With Jolan's help it was done in plenty of time.

The whole family, even Eva and Ferenc, went to the wedding. Ferenc was to be ring bearer, while Aunt Betty's youngest daughter would act as flower girl. The train excursion was a festive one for everyone except Zsuzsi. It had been years since Aunt Margit and Uncle Emil had left Hardenbergh, and neither one had been to Pennsylvania before. They packed a picnic basket with fried chicken, cucumber salad, and apple strudel.

It was hard for Zsuzsi to pretend she had never been on this train before, hard to pretend the scenery was new and exciting, hard to pretend to be thrilled to be maid of honor. By the end of the trip she longed for fresh air, solitude, a cigarette.

They were met at the train station by one of Trudy's cousins, who drove them to his mother's house. Only Zsuzsi seemed bothered by the short, hot trip in an overcrowded automobile. When they arrived they were met by the formidable Aunt Betty, a large woman whose old-fashioned clothes and hair contrasted sharply with her guests, by now all wearing Zsuzsi's designs. Mrs. Bornheimer, sallow as ever, had unfortunately chosen to wear brown. Zsuzsi's spirits fell even further.

But upstairs, after a rest and a cool bath, Zsuzsi couldn't help feeling some of Trudy's excitement. The old-fashioned, off-white wedding gown suited Trudy's figure, and when she put on the long veil she looked like a porcelain doll. They drove to the church with her little cousin Annabelle, the flower girl, and her Uncle Carl. Zsuzsi was determined not to spoil Trudy's day. She had said everything there was to say a month ago, and to try to say more would only cause hard feelings. And so she smiled and concentrated on appearing the perfect maid of honor, while inside she was a turmoil of envy, regret, despair, and love.

After they arrived at the church, Zsuzsi arranged Trudy's train and veil, fussing over the presentation as though she were a full-fledged fashion designer and Trudy her model. When the music started she followed the flower girl up the aisle, remembering to smile broadly at Jolan and the rest of the family, trying not to stare all the while at the groom.

He was, Zsuzsi admitted grudgingly, a good-looking young man, with dark hair and eyes, and broad shoulders that strained the seams of his navy-blue suit. He was not very tall, no taller than Trudy in her heels, and Zsuzsi could picture him growing fat with age, like so many of his relatives sitting on the opposite side of the church. Zsuzsi's hands clenched tightly around her bouquet when she saw his eyes light up as Trudy approached. She was trying hard not to hate him, and failing.

The priest read the opening benediction, and in moments it was over. How few words it took for Trudy to become someone's wife! In appearance she was no different; the fabric of her wedding dress felt just as silky to Zsuzsi as she helped Trudy turn and face the families, yet nothing was the same, or would be, ever again.

Zsuzsi's cheeks ached from smiling, and it was a relief to allow the tears to come. With most of the women dabbing at their eyes with lace handkerchiefs, no one would think Zsuzsi odd for crying. By the time she reached the doors of the church she was composed again, and she smiled through the receiving line and on the short walk to the parish hall. Once inside, however, she walked briskly to the women's rest room. Here, leaning on the sink, she let the muscles of her face relax while she took great, deep breaths. She caught her eye in the mirror, and glowered at her reflection. "If looks could kill..." she murmured, then she locked the door, sat down on the commode, and lit a cigarette.

She inhaled deeply, but was only halfway through the cigarette when someone knocked on the door.

"Just a moment," she called, and taking one last drag she flushed the cigarette down the toilet. She washed her hands and face, set her mouth in an insincere smile, and opened the door.

She couldn't decide which was worse, the wedding itself or the reception. The ceremony was the thing that officially took Trudy from her, but the reception was interminable, a series of dreadful relatives asking her to dance, glass after glass of lemonade raised in toast to the happy couple. Zsuzsi knew most of the men had pocket flasks with them, but she knew she would never be asked to join them for a drink. The only consolation was the dinner of homemade ravioli followed by a roast of veal.

By the third time one of William's cousins had asked Zsuzsi if he could teach her the *tarantella* she'd had enough. She slipped outside, where the night air had finally cooled enough to allow perspiration to dry. Zsuzsi shook out her damp skirt and fanned the bodice of her dress. She longed to take off her hose and sink into a cool bath. Exhausted, she walked slowly across the lawn between the parish house and the church, stopping to rest against the trunk of a large elm tree. Suddenly, she heard murmured voices, and peered though the dark at a couple walking toward her tree. Not wishing to intrude, she began to step away from the tree, but stopped when she heard the voices speaking Hungarian. By the time she realized who the voices belonged to, it was too late to join them without appearing to have eavesdropped. She leaned into the tree's shadow and hoped they would come no closer. She'd had enough pretending for one day.

"What a lovely evening, but what a long day," said Eva. "How much longer do you think the reception will go on?"

"I think we can leave shortly," said Uncle Emil. "Surely even an Italian wedding can't go on all night."

"Don't be too sure," said Eva with a laugh, and Zsuzsi was struck by the joy in the sound of it. "I must admit, though, I haven't had such a good time in years."

"I am sorry the happy times are so few and far between for you. I would wish you nothing but happiness in your life."

"Emil, I didn't mean I'm not happy! I have a good life. I have my work, and Ferenc, and such good friends in you and your family."

"What about a husband?" asked Emil.

"Oh, a husband. I had quite forgotten about one of those." Eva's voice was light and joking.

"You're too young—and too beautiful—to forget such a thing."

"Emil! A beauty I've never been. Zsuzsi and Jolan are beautiful. And Margit is still a lovely, handsome woman."

"There is more than one way to be beautiful, or lovely, or handsome, Eva," said Emil, with such bitterness in his voice that Zsuzsi was startled. "My wife's handsomeness is only external. Inside she is cold as—"

"Emil, you shouldn't talk to me of this," said Eva in a low voice.

Zsuzsi agreed with her.

"But you must know!" exploded Emil. "How can you live upstairs from us and not know?"

"Emil—"

"Eva, we have not lived as husband and wife for many years."

Zsuzsi could feel her cheeks turn red. She imagined Eva's were the same. She should leave, she knew, but they were so close now that if she moved they would hear her, and she didn't know how to avoid an awkward scene except by staying where she was. If she tipped her head, she could just see Uncle Emil and Eva silhouetted by the lights of the parish center windows.

Uncle Emil had taken Eva's hand.

"Emil, don't."

He lowered his voice, but the noise of the reception did not reach this far, and Zsuzsi could hear every word, could hear his voice shaking with emotion.

"I've tried so hard, Eva, God knows I've tried. But a man can do only so much before he gives up. She never loved me, not even in the beginning, especially not then, but I thought she would grow to love me, and for a while I fooled myself into thinking she did. I was wrong, as wrong as a man can be."

"Emil, I am so sorry," said Eva, placing her free hand on top of the one that held hers.

"You are so kind, Eva. That's what makes you different from Margit. Your kindness. And I know you loved Gyula—I know you are capable of love."

"Emil, please don't go on," Eva said, but Zsuzsi noticed that she didn't step back, or pull her hand away when she said this.

"You see, Gyula was like a brother to me, and you a little sister. But seeing you every day, seeing your kindness and generosity, your warmth next to her coldness, your inner beauty against her ugly dried-up heart..."

There was silence. Zsuzsi peered around the tree. She could see one figure, two people embracing so closely they formed one silhouette, two lovers kissing to make one shadow.

She put her hand over her mouth so they couldn't hear her gasp. In a moment—or was it several moments?—Eva pushed Emil firmly away.

"No, Emil. We mustn't."

"I'm tired of doing what I must, and not doing what I want."

"Please, Emil. Whatever is—or isn't—between you and Margit, we must never do this again."

"Was it so terrible?" asked Emil, with a note of despair in his voice that nearly broke Zsuzsi's heart.

"Oh, dear Lord, Emil! It was wonderful! No—don't come any closer, please. If you really care for me, you won't do that again."

"I don't understand."

"Emil, you are married. God doesn't care whether your marriage is happy or not. You made a solemn vow."

"I don't care about God's wishes or his vows anymore, Eva."

"But I do. And even if I didn't, how could I be so disloyal? She has always been good to me and to Ferenc. Whatever may be between you, she has only treated me and my son with Christian charity. I cannot betray her friendship, and may God forgive me for wanting to!"

She ran from Emil back toward the parish hall. Emil stood watching her, and Zsuzsi saw his shoulders droop, his head bow. If she hadn't heard his sobs, she would have thought he was praying. She stood very still, and in a few moments he wiped his eyes and began to walk slowly back.

She waited until he was out of sight before letting out her breath. With shaking hands, she reached into her purse and lit a cigarette. Well, well, well. Poor Uncle Emil! No wonder she felt so close to him—they shared the same kind of pain, and they both had to pretend it didn't exist. In a way, Uncle Emil was luckier than Zsuzsi—at least he could hope that Eva might change her mind. Today, Zsuzsi lost that option forever.

When she finished the cigarette, and her hands stopped trembling, she smoothed her skirt, and walked back to the marriage feast.

Jolan

Chapter 18
February 1926

Jolan leaned against the dais in the assembly hall of the Hungarian-American Social and Athletic Club, fingering the red, white, and blue bunting. Normally the dais was draped in red, white, and green, the colors of Hungary, but this evening's celebration honored both the first president of the United States and its newest citizens. Jolan wished that Zsuzsi had come; after all, it was Zsuzsi who first applied for citizenship, and convinced the rest of the family to do the same.

This morning they had taken the train to Trenton, where they met other applicants at the State Court House. Jolan trembled every time she recalled the room full of people, of all ages and nationalities, reciting the oath of allegiance together. "I swear that I will support the Constitution of the United States," she whispered to herself, "and that I absolutely and entirely renounce and abjure all allegiance and fidelity to any foreign prince, potentate, state, or sovereignty of which I was before a citizen or subject, that I will support and defend the constitution and laws of the United States against all enemies, foreign and domestic, and bear true faith and allegiance to the same."

How wonderful and terrible it was to say those words! Now no one had a right to call her a "hunky." Now she could prove she was as good as any of the young men and women of the town, the ones she had gone to high school with who would not even say hello when she saw them on the street. But how sad to think she had to renounce her own childhood, the part of her that was truly Magyar, the last link to her first home and her mother.

How proud Mama would be of them all! Aunt Margit, Uncle Emil, and even Eva, whom her mother had never met but whose friendship filled Jolan's letters. It had been good to see Eva again on a social occasion. Jolan had enjoyed their evening together, and was sorry Eva had left early to put Ferenc to bed. Even though Jolan saw her daily at the dressmaking shop, it was odd to come home to strangers upstairs. The last family to rent the upstairs apartment had lived there only a few months, and now the apartment was vacant again. She wished Eva would come back, but Eva had rented a storefront for her dressmaking shop, with an apartment of her own upstairs. It was true that Eva needed more space, but she'd made do for years, and Jolan never understood why she'd insisted on leaving so abruptly, not long after Trudy's wedding.

Jolan shook her head. So many changes—Trudy married, Zsuzsi living and working in New York City, Eva moving and opening up the shop, and she herself, now working as Eva's assistant. Each change, when she thought about it, was for the better; even though she missed Zsuzsi terribly, it made sense for her to work in the city, where career opportunities were the best. But she missed the evenings spent talking with Eva, or baking cookies with Ferenc. Aunt Margit was as involved as ever in charities for the church, and Uncle Emil had his newspaper, now published daily, his garden, his violin. Only Jolan felt restless, at loose ends.

Her thoughts were interrupted by Sandy Hegedus, Uncle Emil's lead pressman.

"May I offer you a glass of punch, or a cup of tea?" he asked.

"Punch, thank you, Sandy."

They walked to the refreshment table, where only a few pastries remained on the trays of *kifli*, *kalacs*, and *fank*. Sandy handed her a glass of punch, and smiled.

"And how is your sister these days? I thought she would be here."

You hoped, more like, thought Jolan, with more pity than malice. She didn't think Sandy would ever stop carrying a torch for Zsuzsi. He was a personable young man, and it was a shame that Zsuzsi had never even noticed him.

"She's fine, thank you, but quite busy. She works most evenings, you know."

"She shouldn't work so hard," said Sandy with a frown.

"Well, her career is important to her, and she's trying to make a name for herself."

"She could make a name for herself by marrying."

Jolan nearly laughed out loud at the idea, but fortunately was stopped from making a reply by the tinkling of a spoon against a punch glass.

"Ladies and gentlemen," announced Georg Nagy, president of the Magyar Savings and Loan and also of the Social and Athletic Club, "in a few moments we will have music and dancing—the *csardas*, not the Charleston—but before we do may I extend, on behalf of the Hungarian-American Social and Athletic Club, our sincerest congratulations to our new United States citizens."

His audience applauded with enthusiasm, and the Magyar Men's Marching Band began to play. Jolan sang with the rest. "My country, 'tis of thee, sweet land of liberty, of thee I sing..." Tonight the song brought tears to her eyes.

After the song finished she danced a *csardas* with Sandy, then excused herself. She had no intention of becoming a surrogate for Zsuzsi, and though Sandy was a pleasant enough young man, nothing about him made her want to encourage his attentions. And so it happened that when Jolan walked back to the refreshment table, she passed in front of Monsignor Andrassy just as he dropped his coffee cup.

Warm coffee splashed on her ankles, and she looked down in surprise, then up at the Monsignor, a short, plump, white-haired old man who never seemed to change with the passing of years. But now she saw an odd, surprised look in his eyes. He reached toward her with his left hand, but his right hand hung limply at his side. His face seemed to belong to two people—the left side completely normal, the right somewhat slack, with a droopy eye and a line of saliva forming at the corner of his mouth.

"Monsignor?" she asked.

He grunted something unintelligible, and then he fell forward, his right leg buckling at the knee.

Jolan reached for him, as did several other people, and together they managed to keep the Monsignor from hitting his head on the hardwood floor.

"Get Dr. Hajdu! Quickly!" said one of the men. Jolan got to her feet and looked around. Dr. Hajdu, talking to Uncle Emil and two other men across the room, hadn't yet seen the problem.

"Dr. Hajdu! Dr. Hajdu!" Jolan called his name as she ran to him. He turned his head, looked beyond her, and saw a group of men kneeling around a prostrate figure.

"Get my bag," he said to no one in particular, and hurried to Andrassy's side. One of the men ran to get the medical bag from the doctor's car.

"Jolan, what's happened?" asked Uncle Emil.

"It's Monsignor Andrassy. He's collapsed."

"Wait here." Uncle Emil, too, hurried across the room.

Jolan watched as the doctor knelt by the old priest's side. He looked at him only briefly, and then gestured to the men standing around him.

They picked Andrassy up and carried him outside. Uncle Emil walked back to Jolan.

"The doctor says it's a stroke—they're taking him to the hospital. Where is Margit?"

"I don't see her. She must be in the kitchen, seeing to the refreshments."

"Find her, and tell her what happened. Then go home. I'll be at the hospital, and will call when I have word of his condition."

Jolan nodded, and went into the kitchen. As she thought, Aunt Margit was there. As head of the Social and Athletic Club Women's Auxiliary, it was her job to organize the refreshments and supervise the cleaning up.

"Aunt Margit?"

"Yes, Jolan?" She turned around. "What's wrong? Don't you feel well?"

"It's Monsignor Andrassy. He's had a stroke. They've taken him to the hospital. Uncle Emil's gone with them."

"Oh, dear Lord!" Aunt Margit blessed herself and recited a quick prayer. "I must go there as well." She began to hurry out of the kitchen.

"Uncle Emil said we should go home," protested Jolan.

"I must go to Monsignor," said Margit, hurrying into her coat. "You go home and wait."

"But, Aunt Margit—"

"I said go home." She rushed out of the hall.

Bad news spreads quickly, and the hall emptied quickly, except for the band members putting away their instruments. Jolan returned to the kitchen to help the women of the Ladies' Auxiliary clean up. Afterwards, she walked home, alone.

The night was very cold and clear. Jolan hurried home, almost falling where a patch of ice from the past week's snowfall covered the sidewalk. She hoped Aunt Margit would have come home already, but the house was dark, and when she got inside, chilly. Without taking off her coat she turned on the lights and went into the basement to shovel coal into the furnace. She came back upstairs and started a pot of cocoa. Only when she heard the radiators clang with the rushing steam did she remove her coat and hat.

It was odd to be home alone after dark in an utterly quiet house, except for the comforting hiss of the radiators. She put a record on the Victrola, and curled up on the couch with a cup of cocoa. "I hate to see that evening sun go down," Bessie Smith sang mournfully, and Jolan agreed. She enjoyed her work as a seamstress, spending her days with Eva in the dressmaking shop, listening to Ferenc tell about school when he came home in the afternoon. He was like a little brother to her, and if he still lived here he would want to stay up with her, reading or playing a game of checkers. She'd had no idea how lonely life would become after she graduated high school. Somehow she had pictured life going on the same as before, with evenings spent at home, but she had never pictured home as empty as this.

She had made few friends at school. Of course she had friends at the Social and Athletic Club, but many of the girls were already married, and the none of the boys she knew there had sparked any interest within Jolan, though a few seemed interested in her. She sighed. Sandy was typical—a nice young man, with a steady job—but Jolan couldn't imagine getting romantic with him, or any of the others. She sighed again, leaned her head against the couch, and dozed off.

The rasp of the phonograph stylus woke her. She rose and pulled the stylus off the record, then turned off the parlor light to go to bed. To her surprise, it was nearly dawn. Faint morning light shone from the edge of the draperies. She drew them back to look outside, and saw Aunt Margit, weeping and supported by Uncle Emil, walking slowly up the stairs. She hurried to open the door for them.

Aunt Margit stepped inside and walked past Jolan without saying a word. Jolan turned to her uncle.

"Uncle Emil, you look exhausted. Let me take your coat."

"Thank you, my dear."

He sat down heavily and rubbed his face.

"Shall I make some coffee?" she asked.

"No, Jolan, but thank you. I must go to the *Hirlap* office. Monsignor Andrassy passed away not long ago."

"Oh, Uncle Emil, how sad!"

"Is it? He was old, and he went quickly. I don't think he was conscious at all after the stroke."

"He tried to say something to me, just as it happened...."

"I am sorry you saw that. Death is not something a young girl should have to face."

He turned his head at the sound of Margit weeping. His jaw clenched as his expression changed from pity to something else Jolan could not name. He spoke in a tight and strained voice. "Your aunt is obviously quite upset. We have some difficult days ahead of us, Jolan. Do you think Eva can spare you today? Your aunt should not be left alone."

"Of course, Uncle Emil. I'll telephone her later this morning. Poor Aunt Margit! She was so fond of him."

"Indeed," said Uncle Emil. "Well, I must wash up and then go to the office. We'll have to print a special issue today, with his obituary on the first page. Don't expect me home for lunch."

"All right. Are you sure you're not too tired to write?"

Uncle Emil smiled in a way that was both sad and grim. "I've had Andrassy's obituary written for a long time."

He walked toward the bathroom, leaving Jolan puzzled and somewhat shocked. She knew her uncle had no great love for the old priest, but his tone made him sound almost glad the old priest was dead. But that wasn't possible. Uncle Emil was the kindest of men. It must be tiredness that made him sound so odd.

While Uncle Emil got ready for work, Jolan checked on Aunt Margit. She seemed to be asleep, lying face down on the bed. Jolan took off her shoes, and draped a blanket over her, then shut the door. After Uncle Emil left she quietly bathed and dressed, cleaned the kitchen, and telephoned Eva. Then she lay down on her own bed and drifted to sleep.

Aunt Margit woke her at midmorning. Wearing a severe black wool dress, with her face pale and lined with grief, she looked at once fragile and forbidding. "I am going to church to say a rosary for him. Aren't you late for work?"

"Uncle Emil thought I should stay with you, Aunt Margit."

"There's no need, Jolan, I am perfectly all right now, although you are welcome to join me at church when you are ready." And with that she walked out.

By the time Jolan had dressed, brushed her teeth, and put on her hat and coat, Aunt Margit was a block away. Jolan hurried to catch up. Aunt Margit walked swiftly and silently to the church, as though Jolan were not by her side. When they arrived at church the front pews on one side were already filled with parishioners. Across the aisle the sisters of Saint Elizabeth sat in a group, fingering their rosaries. There would be no school today. Jolan blessed herself with holy water and walked up the aisle behind Aunt Margit. They genuflected, slipped into a pew, and knelt.

Jolan took out her rosary beads and joined the prayers. She liked saying the rosary, hearing the repetition of the Paternosters and Aves, feeling the smoothness of the white beads, which she had received at her first communion. It was one of the few possessions she had brought with her from Hungary, along with her prayer book and the few embroidered linens she had made, and she thought of home every time she used it. On the day she received the beads, the small village church had overflowed with flowers. Warm sun had streamed in the open windows, and the prayers were full of joy. What a contrast the church was this day—cold, dark, and somber, with only the red sacristy light glowing, the statues covered with purple cloths for Lent. Jolan shivered. She tried hard to feel properly sad, but Monsignor Andrassy had always seemed a stern figure of authority to her. She had never been at ease on the evenings when he had dinner at their house, and she had always tried to avoid confessing her sins to him, preferring Father Biro, who was kindlier—and less likely to recognize her voice.

Jolan did not see Father Biro. He must have said morning Mass, but he was not in the church now. She wondered if he would become the new pastor, then realized with guilt how far her mind had wandered from her prayers. She lowered her head and continued the rosary. When they had completed the five decades, Jolan expected Aunt Margit to kiss the small crucifix attached to her beads and put them away, but she continued to finger the beads. Jolan groaned inwardly, then felt contrite. Monsignor Andrassy had done so much for the parish, she could hardly balk at saying a full rosary for him. Two more times around the beads. Her knees would get sore and her back would ache, but these were small discomforts compared with the suffering of Monsignor Andrassy the previous night.

When at last the prayers were done, Jolan leaned back against the pew. Her stomach was growling and she felt lightheaded from missing breakfast. Aunt Margit took out her prayer book, still kneeling ramrod straight.

"Aunt Margit?" Jolan whispered.

Margit shook her head and put a finger to her lips.

Jolan sat back in the pew. Most of the parishioners had gone, leaving only the nuns and a few older women. The men had work to do, the younger women homes to keep. Jolan's stomach growled again. She rubbed her knees, wondering how a woman Aunt Margit's age could kneel upright for so long. Uncle Emil had asked Jolan to stay with her aunt, but she was getting dizzy from hunger. It was already past lunchtime. Finally, she stood up. Aunt Margit, kneeling with her eyes closed, ignored her. Jolan genuflected and walked down the aisle. At the rear of the church, she put a penny in the offering box and lit a candle for Monsignor Andrassy.

The cold, fresh air outside the church revived her enough to walk home, where she made herself a sandwich and drank two glasses of milk. Afterwards, she briefly considered going back to church, but could not face an afternoon in the cold, dark building. She was sure Aunt Margit would do nothing else. She went to the *Hirlap* office instead, where she explained the problem to Uncle Emil.

"I don't mean to say that prayer is useless, Uncle Emil," Jolan concluded, "but I can't see the point of staying there all day, when Eva needs me to work."

Uncle Emil kissed Jolan on the forehead. "It's all right, my dear. I've seen her like this before. She'll be there all day, as you say, and no doubt tomorrow and the next day as well. I'll bring her home when I've finished here. Go to work."

Aunt Margit did, indeed, stay at church all afternoon, and the following morning, but transferred her praying to the Devine Funeral Home the next afternoon, at the first viewing for Monsignor Andrassy. Though a steady crowd of parishioners, nuns, and clergy from surrounding parishes and congregations filled the funeral home, Aunt Margit was the first to arrive, and one of the last to leave.

Jolan had never been to a wake before. In Hungary, when her infant brother Wendel had died of diphtheria, his small coffin had sat in the front room of the house for only a few hours before burial. When her youngest brother Tomas had died of the influenza, his body had been taken like so many others to the village schoolhouse until burial could be arranged. Now Jolan was appalled to see the open coffin, surrounded by sprays and bouquets of sweet-smelling flowers, on display in front of rows of chairs, as though an audience had come to see a picture show.

She followed the line of mourners to the front of the room, and knelt briefly before the figure of Monsignor Andrassy. His waxy, lopsided face seemed too small to belong to the authoritative priest whose forceful sermons used to echo in the church.

Jolan stood up, trembling, and turned to Uncle Emil, who put his arms around her and led her to a seat.

"How awful this is!" she said in a low voice. "He looks so—so horrible!"

"Yes," said Uncle Emil.

"But it doesn't look like him at all! How can all those people say he looks like he's sleeping—that he looks peaceful? It's grotesque!"

"I know," said Emil. He took her hand.

"Uncle Emil, I don't think I can stay here very long."

"That's all right, my dear. You've made your duty call. I'll see you home, and then come back. I, unfortunately, should stay a while longer."

"Then stay, Uncle Emil. I can walk home by myself. It's only a few blocks."

"Are you sure? You look very pale."

She kissed him on the cheek. "I just need to get outside. It's hard to breathe in this stuffy room, and the flowers make my head ache. Please, stay with Aunt Margit. I'll be fine as soon as I get some fresh air."

She stood up and walked into the hall. One of the morticians walked past her, carrying yet another large bouquet, and she was overwhelmed by the spicy fragrance of carnations. Suddenly she heard a ringing sound, the hall went gray, and she began to fall.

She was only half aware that strong arms caught her, and that she was carried onto a couch. Someone put a cushion under her feet and placed a cool, wet cloth on her forehead. In a few moments the ringing in her ears faded and she could see again, but she still felt weak and dizzy.

"Are you all right?" asked a baritone voice.

"It was the flowers," Jolan murmured, turning toward the voice, and looked into the brownest eyes she had ever seen. They were surrounded by long, dark lashes, set in a handsome face, with a straight, somewhat aquiline nose, and soft-looking lips pressed together in concern. The young man's high cheekbones and dark, curly hair gave him the look of a gypsy.

"I'm sorry, what did you say?" she asked.

"I only said that it was very close in here. The scent of the flowers is overpowering. It's no wonder you fainted."

"I didn't faint!" said Jolan. She pushed herself up, but the dizziness grew stronger. "I never faint," she said.

The young man grinned. "Pardon me. I didn't know it was the custom here to lie down in the hall of a funeral home."

"I did no such thing!" protested Jolan. "I just felt dizzy for a moment, that's all."

"Of course," he said, still grinning. "My mistake. May I help you sit up, if you're feeling better?"

"I can sit up myself, thank you very much."

He stood back as Jolan pushed herself up. She swung her legs over the side of the couch and tried to stand, but the effort made her giddy.

"Why don't you stay here a moment, and let me fetch a glass of water? You still look rather pale."

"All right," said Jolan. While he was gone she patted some color into her cheeks, and pinned up the hair that had gone astray while she lay on the couch.

"Here," he said, holding out a glass.

"Thank you," said Jolan. He sat down while she sipped the water. "Better now?"

She nodded. "Yes, thank you, Mr...?"

"Forgive me! Tibor Nemeth. Uncle Kalman was my great uncle."

"Uncle Kalman?"

"Monsignor Andrassy."

"Oh! Oh. I didn't know he had family in this country."

"He doesn't, except for me. My mother, his niece, passed away in 1918, during the epidemic. He has no other living relatives, I'm afraid."

"I'm sorry."

"And you?" he asked.

"Me?"

"Your name?"

"Oh! Pardon me—Jolan Takacs." She held out her hand. "How do you do."

He took her hand in a firm grip.

"Your hand is cold," he said, covering it with his other hand. Jolan thought she'd never felt anything so warm in her life.

"Is that better?" he asked, releasing her hand.

"Much better." She could still feel the warm imprint of his fingers on her hand. *I knew the moment I looked in his eyes.* She could almost hear her mother's voice, telling again how she had fallen in love with Jolan's father. *And then I passed him a piece of cake, and our hands touched. It was like fire, Jolanka! Like fire racing up my arm from my hand straight to my heart. Like fire.*

"Jolan? You are still here? Is something wrong?" asked Uncle Emil.

"Hello, Uncle Emil. No, I just felt a bit faint, and Mr. Nemeth brought me a glass of water."

The two men shook hands. "I'm Emil Molnar. Thank you for taking care of my niece, Mr. Nemeth."

"He's Monsignor Andrassy's great nephew, Uncle Emil."

"Please accept my deepest sympathy, Mr. Nemeth."

"Thank you, sir."

"Have you come a long way?"

"I'm from Detroit, Mr. Molnar. I just arrived a few hours ago. I left as soon as I could make arrangements. I'm in my last semester at the university, you see."

"Ah. And what are you studying?" asked Uncle Emil.

"Classical literature, Latin and Greek."

"Do you plan to teach, then?"

"Eventually, I suppose I will," Tibor said.

"Eventually?" asked Jolan.

He turned to her and smiled in a way that was almost apologetic. "Yes. I have a bit more studying to do. In the fall I am going into the seminary."

Jolan's cheeks burned as though she'd been slapped. She stood up. "If you will excuse me, I'll go home now. I'm feeling much better. Mr. Nemeth, it was a pleasure meeting you. I wish it could have been under happier circumstances."

He took her outstretched hand. "Thank you, Miss Takacs."

She kissed Uncle Emil on the cheek. "Goodbye, Uncle Emil. I'll see you when you get home."

Jolan walked swiftly to the door. Once outside, she leaned against the column of the funeral home. A light snow fell, painting the street white and bringing an early twilight to the afternoon. She buttoned her coat, pulled on her gloves, and began walking home, berating herself all the way. "How could I have given him my hand? Twice! I'm never so forward.

What possessed me? He's so handsome! I'm so embarrassed! Fainting, of all the silly things to do! I acted like a child, an absolute child. But when he took my hand—" Within the glove it seemed her hand still felt his warmth. "Oh, put him out of your head, Jolan Takacs! The seminary! Lord, why must it be that the first interesting man I meet is going to be a priest? It's so unfair!"

With such thoughts whirling in her head, Jolan came home, for the second time in a week, to a cold and empty house.

Chapter 19
March 1926

A robin sang from the pear tree as Jolan walked into the garden after work. She stopped for a moment to listen. All around her were the sounds and sights of spring. Daffodils had burst into bloom only a few days before, their yellow heads looking like little suns. New pea vines climbed the brush Uncle Emil had poked into the moist ground, and the pear tree itself was fat with buds that soon would open. The warm air caressing her cheek as she walked toward the house made a pleasant change from the unseasonable chill of the past few days. She called a greeting to the robin, glad to pass through this vitality on her way home from work. Like the spring breeze, the green and yellow garden was a welcome change from winter's drab brown yard.

Aunt Margit was already preparing dinner as Jolan walked in the kitchen door.

"Hello, Aunt Margit," said Jolan. "Dinner smells wonderful. Is it chicken?"

"Hello, Jolan. Yes, thank you, roast chicken. Hurry and wash up so you can help me. We're having company tonight."

"All right," Jolan said, walking into the bedroom to hang up her hat and coat. "Who is coming?" she called.

"Tibor Nemeth."

Jolan stood still, her hat in hand. No, impossible. She couldn't have heard right. She walked to the bedroom door.

"Whom did you say?"

"Tibor Nemeth. He's the great-nephew of Monsignor Andrassy, God rest his soul. Mr. Nemeth was at the funeral. Do you remember him?"

Jolan remembered all too well. Her embarrassment from fainting at the wake returned in full force. "Oh, no," she muttered.

Slowly, she walked to the bathroom to wash her hands.

"Hurry, please, Jolan. He'll be here shortly."

Jolan washed her face and smoothed her hair. Unlike her sister, Jolan refused to have her hair bobbed. She knew that vanity and pride were sinful, but she was very proud of her thick, brown hair. She made sure it was tucked neatly into a bun, and that all her hairpins were in place, before walking into the kitchen.

"Shall I set the table, Aunt Margit?"

"Yes, in the dining room. I've already put on the tablecloth and napkins."

The tablecloth was Aunt Margit's best linen, embroidered with pink roses and blue forget-me-nots. Jolan opened the cupboard to get out the fine Hungarian bone china Aunt Margit had brought with her when she came to this country. She took out white dinner plates, each with a cobalt-blue border around the edge surrounded by a circle of gold. Next to each plate she set out bread-and-butter plates, cups, and saucers.

"How did you happen to invite Mr. Nemeth for dinner?" she asked casually.

"I saw him at church. He's here collecting the Monsignor's things."

"I thought he was attending college in Michigan," said Jolan.

"He's on holiday. Easter vacation."

Aunt Margit walked in and put a linen runner on the sideboard. "He's staying at the Voorhees Hotel, and eating in restaurants. I thought he'd like a home-cooked meal for a change."

She returned to the kitchen while Jolan finished setting the table with water goblets and Aunt Margit's silverplated flatware. All the table needed was a centerpiece.

"Shall I cut a few daffodils for the table?" she asked Aunt Margit.

"Good idea."

Jolan went back into the garden with a bud vase. She didn't want to pick too many flowers and ruin Uncle Emil's display, but three or four daffodils would brighten the dining room.

She heard footsteps coming up the path, followed by the gate unlatching.

"That gate still squeaks, Uncle Emil," she said, bending over the flowerbed.

"It does indeed, but I'm not Uncle Emil."

"Oh dear!" Jolan straightened up and turned around. She could feel her cheeks reddening at the sight she must have presented to him. "Mr. Nemeth! I thought you were my uncle—he always comes in the back way."

"Forgive me for startling you, Miss Takacs. I would have come in the front door but I saw you in the garden and wondered if I could be of help."

His smile made her knees go weak. "Thank you, but I'm quite finished. I'm just picking a few flowers for the table."

"They're beautiful," he said, but he was looking at Jolan, not the flowers.

Her mind went completely, utterly blank. She couldn't think of a single polite, meaningless phrase to continue the conversation. Being rendered speechless was a new experience for her—according to Aunt Margit she was far too outspoken for her own good. Yet here she was, tongue-tied as a schoolgirl, unable to make even the smallest of small talk. And so she smiled.

At that, Nemeth's own smile became a broad grin, and that's how Emil came upon them, staring and grinning at one another over a vase of daffodils.

"Care to let me in on the joke?" asked Uncle Emil.

Jolan was so startled she nearly dropped the vase.

"No joke, Mr. Molnar, I was merely admiring the flowers," said Nemeth, smoothly extending his hand to Emil. "Tibor Nemeth."

"I remember. It's a pleasure to see you again. Will you join us for dinner?" asked Emil.

"Yes, sir, your wife invited me today." Unlike Jolan, Tibor Nemeth seemed perfectly capable of carrying on a conversation, and he continued to talk as they walked inside. He held the door open for Jolan. As she walked past him she smelled the clean fragrance of shaving soap and the spicy aroma of bay rum. Her heart beat faster at being so close to him.

She wished she had had time to bathe and change into clean clothes. Her skirt was covered with snippets of thread and bits of fabric.

Aunt Margit welcomed Nemeth into the kitchen graciously but Jolan knew she was flustered at having him there. No doubt she had wanted him to come into the front parlor, to sit on the sofa and listen to music before dinner, but Nemeth won her heart by sniffing heartily at the pots on the stove and then kissing her hand.

"Mrs. Molnar, you have no idea what a treat it is to be in a real kitchen with a real family and a real dinner on the stove. I usually eat in a cafe or dining hall, and I am hopeless when it comes to cooking. Bless you for asking me!"

Aunt Margit preened and fussed and shooed him into the parlor with Emil while she and Jolan set out the platter of roast chicken with bread stuffing, potatoes that had been roasted in the chicken juices, green peas, and Aunt Margit's best green-tomato and cauliflower pickles. After they took their seats around the table, Uncle Emil said grace.

"In the name of the Father, and of the Son, and of the Holy Ghost, amen. Bless us, oh Lord, for these thy gifts, which we are about to receive from thy bounty, through Christ our Lord, amen. In the name of the Father, and of the Son, and of the Holy Ghost, amen."

Uncle Emil carved the chicken with great ceremony, passing the plates to Margit for the vegetables. Tibor Nemeth ate with a hearty appetite that visibly pleased Aunt Margit, but Jolan was so quiet and ate so little that Aunt Margit asked if she were feeling well.

"I'm fine, Aunt Margit," said Jolan. She forced herself to eat a little more, but for some reason she was not the least bit hungry.

Uncle Emil and Tibor Nemeth discussed his studies, and his life in Michigan.

"What made you decide to take a degree instead of entering the seminary right from high school, if you don't mind my asking?" said Uncle Emil.

"Not at all, sir. It's a natural question. It's to fulfill a promise I made to my father. He was not so convinced as my mother that I should become a priest, and he wanted me to have a classical education. My mother, of course, always had in her heart that one of her sons should become a priest."

"I thought becoming a priest was more a matter of having a vocation, rather than fulfilling a family obligation," said Jolan.

"Jolan!"

"Well, Aunt Margit, isn't it true?"

"You're right," said Nemeth. "But in many families, it is traditional for one son to become a priest. Unfortunately, my older brother was killed in the war, and my younger brother died of croup when he was only three. Despite all that, I do sincerely believe I have been called to the priesthood. I am fortunate that I can please my mother and my father, may they rest in peace, and please God as well."

"Where will you study?" asked Uncle Emil.

"At St. Isidore's on Long Island, a few miles east of Brooklyn. It's a lovely place, right on the ocean, the perfect site for prayer and meditation. And because St. Isidore is the patron saint of farmers, all seminarians work on the seminary's farm. I am looking forward to it."

"From the university to a farm—that's quite a change," observed Aunt Margit.

"The priest in charge of the seminary, Father Alphonse, believes that manual labor is good for the health of the soul as well as the body. I'm inclined to agree with him. I've done farm work in Michigan every summer."

"And will you do so this summer?" asked Uncle Emil.

"No, sir. I enter the seminary as soon as I am graduated."

"Well, then," said Uncle Emil. "I should like to toast your success in entering the seminary."

"Emil—" protested Aunt Margit.

"He's not in the seminary yet," said Emil. "Besides, I doubt if many fully ordained priests really support Prohibition in their heart of hearts."

Tibor grinned. "I must agree with you there, Mr. Molnar."

"Then let's go down to the basement," said Emil, pushing back his chair. "I have a little homemade brandy, nothing very good, not much better than *palinka,* to tell you the truth, but better than nothing at all. Ladies, if you'll excuse us."

Margit began to gather the plates. "Look at this, Jolan. You've hardly touched your food. Are you sure you're not coming down with a cold? This changing weather can do it to you."

"No, Aunt Margit, I'm quite well. I'm just not hungry. I—I ate some cookies with Ferenc when he came home from school. I suppose it spoiled my appetite."

"Really, Jolan, you should know better. You'll probably be hungry in two hours."

Jolan helped Aunt Margit do the dishes, wondering what prompted her to tell a white lie about the cookies, for she hadn't eaten any, and was actually quite hungry when she first came home. Then Tibor Nemeth walked in. Why should that simple fact change anything? Yet it did. Somehow it changed everything.

In fact, it was Aunt Margit, not Jolan, who ended up suffering from the seesawing temperatures. By Saturday her sniffles had developed into a cold so bad that she went to bed. On Sunday, she missed Mass for the first time in years. Uncle Emil insisted she stay in bed. Every winter, rumors circulated that another bout of influenza was coming, and though none of them had gotten more ill than a cold or bad cough since Jolan and Zsuzsi first arrived, Uncle Emil wanted to take no chances.

"But I wanted to put fresh flowers on Monsignor Andrassy's grave," Aunt Margit whispered hoarsely.

"I can do that for you, Aunt Margit," said Jolan.

She went downstairs and picked a half-dozen daffodils, but the bouquet seemed meager to her, so she walked to the Amwell farm where daffodils grew wild, and only when she had a thick bouquet did she go to the cemetery. Monsignor Andrassy's grave was easy to find, marked by a square marble column five feet high that was topped by the figure of an angel with outspread wings. The new marble gleamed bright in the sunshine, but as she walked toward it a cloud covered the sun, darkening the marble and sending a shiver down her spine. Someone was kneeling in front of the stone, so Jolan waited a few feet away, not wanting to intrude on a parishioner's prayers.

Then he stood up and turned. Tibor Nemeth.

"Why, Miss Takacs," he said with surprise. "I didn't expect to see you here. Did you know my great-uncle well?"

"No," she said, aware she was blushing for no reason but unable to prevent it. She looked down at the flowers in her hand. "Your uncle was loved by many people in the parish. These are from Aunt Margit."

"How kind. Please tell her I'm very grateful. Shall I put them in a vase for you? Someone left one here."

"A lot of people have brought flowers, these past few weeks. Here, let me take off this wet cloth. I didn't want them to wilt."

She pulled off the wet dishtowel she'd wrapped around the stems, and handed him the bouquet. His fingers wrapped around hers as he took them. To Jolan it felt as though an electric current had passed between them.

It was like fire, Jolanka!

"These are quite lovely," Nemeth said. His voice was soft yet deep. Jolan imagined it would sound beautiful chanting a High Mass. "Are they all from your garden?"

"No, some are wild. You can see how different they are—the cups are divided, they look almost shaggy."

"Someday I'd like to see where they came from," he said with a smile.

"I can show you today, if you like. The farm is just down the road from our house."

"Thank you. I'd like that." They began walking toward the cemetery gate. "I have enough time for a short walk before the train comes."

Jolan inhaled sharply. "You're leaving today, then?"

"Yes, I must get back to my classes."

"That's too bad," she blurted. "I mean, Aunt Margit was hoping to see you again before you left, but she has a cold, and—and it will be several days before she'll be well enough for company."

"I am sorry to hear she's ill. Please let her know I wish her a speedy recovery, and tell her that I'll write when I get back to Michigan."

Michigan! How far away it sounded. Since she had come to this country Jolan had never been out of New Jersey, except for the trip to Scranton when Trudy was married. That trip had taken hours; how much longer must it take to get to Michigan! Suddenly Jolan's eyes filled with tears. She bit her lip to stop them but couldn't, and when she turned her head away to hide the tears she stumbled on a half-buried marker, a small square of granite with the letter "K" on it.

"Are you all right?" asked Nemeth. "Why, you're crying! What's wrong?"

Jolan shook her head and wiped fiercely at her eyes with the heel of her hand.

"Please, Miss Takacs, tell me what's wrong."

Jolan was torn between humiliation and despair. "You're leaving," she said, finally. She looked up at Tibor Nemeth and saw, through the tears, everything she did not want to see on his face: surprise, dismay, and worst of all, pity.

"Oh, Miss—Jolan. Jolan, I am so sorry. I didn't realize. I hope I haven't done anything to encourage these tears—it's quite impossible, you must know."

Jolan could feel him pulling back from her, though he hadn't moved a step. The extreme gentleness of his voice, the polite denial, put a distance between them as great as the distance from here to Michigan. She groaned, and did the only thing she could think of to prevent herself from running all the way back home. She leaned her head on Nemeth's chest and sobbed.

At first he stood still, arms half raised in surprise, but slowly he raised one hand and placed it lightly on her hair, and then he put his other hand on her shoulder. But she continued to cry, so he held her close and stroked her hair, saying "Hush, hush now," in a voice so soft and sweet she wanted to hear it forever. Gently he retrieved a handkerchief from his breast pocket and handed it to her. It carried the faint smell of bay rum. She wiped her eyes, then clutched at his lapels, whispering, "Don't go! Please don't let me go!"

"Jolan—" he began, but she tightened her grip and looked up at him. "Don't say you didn't know. Don't say you haven't felt anything. In the garden, the other day, when you looked at me and smiled, I felt it go right through me. You must have seen, you must have felt it, too!"

"Jolan," he said again, through clenched teeth. He took her wrists and tried to lift her hands away.

"Don't say you feel nothing, holding me like this."

She was close enough to feel his heart beating, to feel the hardness of his erection pressing against her leg. She smiled. "You see? I knew it!"

And then he was kissing her, his left hand kneading her hair, his right moving up to grip her shoulder, and Jolan could not have cared if the whole of Hardenbergh saw them. But he broke off, suddenly, and held her at arm's length, taking a deep breath before letting her go.

"You don't play fair, Jolan Takacs," he said with a shaking voice.

"Neither do you, Tibor Nemeth, if you can kiss me like that and still go on to your seminary."

He clenched and unclenched his fists. "It was wrong of me to do that. You must understand. I've made promises—to my parents, to myself, to God."

She wiped her eyes again and took a deep, unsteady breath. "Well, I certainly can't compete with God, can I?"

Tibor shook his head. "The point is, you shouldn't even try."

"I can't help it. I'm falling in love with you, Tibor, and if you think I'm 'fast' for saying so, or easy for kissing you, then you think wrong."

He bowed his head. Jolan wondered if he was trying to form his words, or praying for guidance.

"I'm sorry, truly sorry, if I did anything or said anything to mislead you, Jolan. I never meant to do anything, anything, to make you think my intentions went beyond friendship." He looked up at her then. "Until today. But I'm only a man, Jolan, and you're a beautiful girl. I can't help what just happened." He spread his hands in a gesture of apology and resignation. "It will not happen again."

"You can just ignore your feelings? Pretend there's nothing?" she said, feeling the tears come back.

"I must. And so must you, if you really feel some—fondness—for me, then you must let me go."

"Oh yes, I see that!" she said, with a bitter edge to keep the tears from overtaking her again. "But the question is, will you be able to let me go, after what's happened today?"

He winced, as though her words hurt him physically, and she turned away, walking fast, with the pressure from his lips still making her own lips tremble, and the taste of his mouth filling hers. On Saturday, in confession, she would have to find it in herself to be sorry she had tempted a would-be priest, but no penance could possibly hurt as bad as knowing she would never feel his mouth on hers again.

Chapter 20
January 1927

The Hungarian-American Social and Athletic Club Orchestra, made up largely by members of the Magyar Men's Marching Band, began a Brahm's waltz, led by Emil Molnar on violin. The groom at the wedding feast, Sandor Hegedus, led his bride around the dance floor with more enthusiasm than grace, at least to Jolan and Zsuzsi's eyes. Zsuzsi nudged her sister's arm.

"Let's go to the ladies' room," she whispered, "before any of these charming young gentlemen ask us to dance."

Jolan nodded, and the two of them left the hall. Zsuzsi held the door open for Jolan, then followed her in and locked the door.

"Cigarette?" she offered.

"Why not?" said Jolan, taking it between her fingers.

Zsuzsi raised an eyebrow but lit the cigarette. "Well, it's a relief to have Sandy finally married, isn't it? No more stares and sighs from that direction."

"You've been safely in New York all this time," said Jolan. "After you left he tried to transfer his attentions to me."

"Well, he might not have made such a bad husband after all, for you, I mean. He's perfectly nice, just not my type."

"Nor mine. I assure you, any feelings I ever had for him were strictly of the sisterly variety."

"Are you going to smoke that cigarette or let it burn out in your fingers?" asked Zsuzsi.

Jolan took a puff on the cigarette, then broke into a fit of coughing.

"I do believe that's your very first, little sister." She inhaled deeply, then blew the smoke out of her nose.

"Show off," said Jolan, in a hoarse voice. "Don't worry. I'll get the hang of it." She took another, smaller, puff, and coughed smaller coughs.

"Jolan, I know there's something wrong. What is it?"

"Nothing. Nothing at all."

"Then why are you so thin? I hate to see one of my dresses hanging on someone like a sack. You've lost weight since I last fitted you. There are circles under your eyes, and you're positively quiet. You never were such a mouse! Are you ill?"

"No," said Jolan, successfully drawing smoke into her mouth, where she let it float for a moment before blowing it out. "There. That's better."

"Who is he?"

Jolan started. "What do you mean?"

"I mean I recognize the symptoms," said Zsuzsi. "How long ago did he break your heart?"

Every day, she wanted to answer. "You needn't be so flip, Zsuzsi Takacs. I didn't see you on the arm of Mr. Right today. Why, you never mention anyone, even casually, in your letters."

"I'll have to fix that," said Zsuzsi, half to herself. To Jolan, she smiled and said, "I have my work, you know. When an artist is establishing her reputation, she can't waste time on frivolous affairs."

"What rot you talk! There must be millions of young men in New York. Surely you date."

"Oh, of course, between shows. But seriously, first there's the fall line, and then the spring, and then the cruise wear. It never stops." She flicked her cigarette in the toilet and flushed. "We'd better go. We'll have been missed, or there's a line outside the door, one or the other."

Jolan tossed her cigarette in the toilet and followed Zsuzsi. Her sister spoke lightly about being an artist, but Jolan knew that Zsuzsi took her work very seriously, and it was beginning to pay off. In just a few years, she'd worked her way up to assistant to the head designer for a New York fashion house. Her specialties were dresses and formal wear, and though she was able to bring Jolan and Margit only the previous season's leftovers, her own clothes were always the very latest style. Today she wore a stunning gown of pine green velvet, unaccented beyond a simple gold brooch. Her hair was freshly bobbed, and her red lip rouge gave her a vampish look unmatched by any of the Hardenbergh girls.

It pleased Jolan to see how poised and self-assured Zsuzsi had become. She epitomized the modern career woman, in Jolan's eyes, and Jolan sometimes envied the exciting and glamorous life her sister must lead in the city, surrounded by fashion models and wealthy clients. But then she thought Zsuzsi's life must also be a lonely one, with no family nearby. And how did anyone live in a big city, without cow pastures, or pear trees, or daffodils?

They sat down at their table, where Jolan opened her purse and took out a crumpled handkerchief. She pressed it to her nose, inhaling the faint fragrance of bay rum, and hastily put it back in the purse. She hadn't realized, that day, until she was almost home that it was balled up in her fist. Of course she should have washed and pressed it and returned it to him, but a combination of embarrassment and longing kept her from doing so. It was all she had of him, this unwashed square of linen that she carried everywhere, lest Aunt Margit find it and ask where it came from.

Jolan felt her cheeks redden, that she behaved so childishly. She had thought that as time went by, she would think of Tibor less, she would hurt less, she would grow used to his absence. But Aunt Margit had written to him, and he'd returned her letter, and now the two of them corresponded. He wrote infrequently, no more than once every three or four weeks, but every time his letter arrived Aunt Margit would read it aloud. The letters were polite and somewhat formal, as would be any letter written to an older friend of a deceased relative: brief accounts of his progress in the seminary, tales of farm work, anecdotes about other seminarians. Jolan wished that either Aunt Margit or Tibor would stop writing, but Tibor would never be so rude, and Aunt Margit was delighted to hear from a relative of her beloved Monsignor. So the letters continued, as did the pain of separation, the memories, the longing.

"Is he here?" asked Zsuzsi.

Jolan's heart skipped a beat. "Is who here?"

"You know who I mean."

Part of Jolan wanted to blurt it all out. She and Zsuzsi were as close as sisters could be, at least they used to be, but since Zsuzsi moved to New York they rarely had time for the heart to heart talks they once had. But this was not the time, and certainly not the place.

"No," she answered. "I'm going home."

"I'll go with you."

It took twenty minutes to extricate themselves from the wedding reception, to say goodbye to the bride and groom, the parents, the wedding party, Uncle Emil and Aunt Margit. When they finally stepped outside they were astonished to walk into a snowstorm.

Almost an inch of snow had already accumulated, and it came down in the swift, tiny flakes that mean a lengthy and heavy snowfall. They slipped and slid in their dress shoes, holding each other up, laughing and sticking out their tongues to catch snowflakes. They gathered snow off shrubs and threw it at one another as though they were children. It was so good to have Zsuzsi home!

By the time they arrived home they were soaked. Though it was not even eight o'clock, they put on warm nightgowns and robes, and made hot cocoa. They were just settling down for their talk when Aunt Margit and Uncle Emil arrived. Jolan made more cocoa, and the four of them sat and discussed the wedding and the snow until Jolan could no longer stifle her yawns and went to bed. She fell asleep almost immediately, without ever having the opportunity to speak with Zsuzsi alone.

She woke to a world made of crystal. Sometime during the night the snow had changed into ice, but the storm had passed, leaving the sun to rise on a dazzling world. Every branch, every twig was covered with a silvery glaze. The sidewalks and gardens were blanketed with snow under a thin crust of ice. Everything shone and gleamed so cleanly that Jolan understood why winter was the beginning of the new year. No other season had such crisp air, such fresh and pure scenery.

There was no question of Zsuzsi's return to New York; it would be at least a full day before the railroad tracks were cleared. They walked to church, stepping carefully over the treacherous ice, then came home to breakfast. Zsuzsi and Jolan took turns shoveling snow. They made a snowman in the backyard, beneath Uncle Emil's pear tree, and then came inside to dinner. In late afternoon they visited with the upstairs neighbors, a middle-aged couple named Kish whose grown children lived in their own apartments in town. Mrs. Kish shared Aunt Margit's passion for needlework, though not her exceptional talent, and Mr. Kish worked in the Van Dyke plant as a shop foreman. They were good company for Aunt Margit and Uncle Emil, and the two couples often came together for a late supper on Sundays.

It was not until Jolan and Zsuzsi were in bed that Zsuzsi had her idea.

"Come with me tomorrow," she said.

"What do you mean?" asked Jolan.

"Come to New York. You've never been, and the change of pace will do you good."

"I have to work, and so do you."

"Then come next weekend. We can shop, or go to the theater, or the museums—there's no shortage of places to go and things to do."

"You don't have any room," said Jolan.

"Nonsense! Alice and I have had overnight guests before. We've two beds, and a comfortable sofa. It's no trouble. What do you say?"

"I say I need some sleep if I'm to sew a straight seam tomorrow. Let's talk in the morning."

"Okay." Zsuzsi leaned over and gave Jolan a kiss on the cheek.

"It will do you good, you know."

"Mmm," was Jolan's only reply.

Zsuzsi rolled over and was soon asleep, but now Jolan was wide awake. New York! She had never been there. It would be an adventure, and pleasant to see where Zsuzsi lived. When Zsuzsi first moved to the city she took a room in a women's residential hotel, but since October she shared a flat in Greenwich Village with a friend of hers, a painter. She'd asked Jolan to visit almost immediately, but with clothes to make for the holiday season Jolan was too busy to get away. Now that Hardenbergh's wealthy ladies were no longer going to parties round the clock, the workload would settle back to normal. Perhaps Eva would even give her a day off. On that thought she fell asleep.

In the morning Jolan and Uncle Emil walked Zsuzsi to the train station, then Uncle Emil left for the *Hirlap* office and Jolan for Eva's dressmaking shop. Jolan enjoyed the cozy atmosphere of the shop. The front room, where Eva greeted customers, was small, holding only a sofa and two chairs, and a small table on which she served coffee. In each of the two storefront windows a mannequin stood, dressed in a seasonal outfit. Behind a curtain, on the right, was the fitting room, and on the left, Eva's office. Behind that was the workroom, with its clutter of fabric, thread, and trim. Although to an outsider it would seem disorderly, Eva and Jolan knew exactly where everything was, and since the work never stopped, there was always a pattern laid out, parts of a dress on fitting dummies, and the previous day's work neatly pressed. Three sewing machines were always threaded and ready to hum into action; during the holiday rush Eva employed temporary help, but for the rest of the year she and Jolan divided the work between them.

This morning Jolan worked on a woolen skirt, an Irish tweed that mixed threads of brown, gray, and green. She loved working with the supple fabric. The design was a simple one, of soft pleats, yet the imported fabric alone cost more than any skirt Jolan would ever wear.

Jolan quickly became engrossed in her work, and did not mention the New York trip to Eva until midmorning.

"I think it's a wonderful idea," Eva said. "You and Zsuzsi see each other so rarely now. It would be lovely to visit her."

"Do you suppose, now that the holidays are over, that I could take an extra day, a Monday or a Friday? I would so like to see where she works."

"I don't see why not, as long as they don't hire my assistant away from me!"

Jolan laughed. "No chance of that, Eva, don't you worry!"

Eva smiled. "The trip will do you good, I think."

Jolan looked up from her work. "Funny. That's what Zsuzsi said."

"Well," said Eva, snipping a thread and turning a sleeve right-side out, "you have been working very hard lately. Too hard, maybe. You have gotten rather pale. And you've lost weight. I can't use you to try on Joan Regan's dresses anymore. When are you planning to go?"

"Soon, I think. Weather permitting, of course."

"Of course."

But the weather did not permit. Ever since Sandy's wedding, the weather had perversely been clear at midweek, but threatening or snowy by the weekend. Week after week the same pattern prevailed. Jolan, now that she had a trip in mind, found herself more and more irritable at the delay. Finally, in mid-February, a solid thaw and weekend without the threat of snow allowed her to take the train to New York on a Saturday morning.

Zsuzsi met her at the Pennsylvania Railroad Station and led her to the subway. Jolan had never been on an underground train before; she was startled by the noise of it, the screech of brakes, the way the lights sometimes flickered. But it was cheaper than a taxicab, and according to Zsuzsi, just as quick as the streetcar, and sometimes quicker, especially at this time of year, when the streetcar tracks were often covered with snow.

When the subway stopped they walked upstairs and emerged into a narrow street. Brick houses stood in rows on either side, with no room at all between them. Though the light was flat and shadowless on this cloudy day, Jolan could see that one side of the street received more sunlight than the other, because one sidewalk was mostly clear, but the other, where Zsuzsi led, still had patches of ice and piles of dirty snow on it.

"Here it is."

The house was like the other houses on the street, with a heavy carved door and a bow window to one side. A wrought iron rail led up half a dozen granite steps. Once inside they climbed a staircase, four flights up to Zsuzsi's apartment. Jolan was relieved to see that the staircase was clean and brightly lit. She had half expected a dingy hallway smelling of stale cabbage, with a shadowy figure slouched against the wall on each landing. Although Zsuzsi's way of life may have been quite Bohemian by Hardenbergh's standards, it was obviously so normal that even Aunt Margit would approve. The house had been one residence some time in the past; now it was divided into flats. Jolan imagined what it must have looked like when it was one person's home: the staircase full of young ladies in ball gowns at night, and during the day young men leaving calling cards on a silver tray.

"It's like something in an Edith Wharton novel, isn't it?" asked Zsuzsi when they reached the top landing.

"You read my mind."

Zsuzsi smiled and unlocked the door. Jolan walked into a large studio. An easel stood in the middle of the floor, draped with a cloth whose color was impossible to determine, it was so spattered with paints. One wall was almost all windows; the opposite wall was plain except for a door.

"The staircase opens into the front of the building, where there's a north exposure, so Alice had to make this the studio. We live behind that door, in the rear of the building." Zsuzsi pointed the way.

Jolan stepped through the door into a kitchen, which held an old-fashioned gas stove, an icebox, and a soapstone sink. Against one wall a table was covered with bright yellow oilcloth. Beyond this room was the living room, furnished with a hodge-podge of chairs and a sofa, almost all of them draped with throw rugs or squares of fabric.

"Alice is in the bedroom, the last room behind this," Zsuzsi said in a low voice, apologetically. "She'll still be asleep. We were out rather late last night."

"You must be tired, then, to have gotten up so early to get me," said Jolan.

"No, I've been up for hours. We were at a party I found dreadfully boring, and I'm ashamed to say I fell asleep while we were there. Alice woke me up to come home, and I've been awake all morning. Would you like something to drink? Tea? Coffee?"

"Actually, I'd like to use your bathroom."

"Through the kitchen. It's that ell you saw cutting into the studio—added in after the building was converted to flats. Go freshen up, then tell me where you'd like to go."

Jolan wanted to go everywhere, but settled for a walk up Fifth Avenue from Washington Square Park. It was a perfect day for walking; a full thaw had set in, with the temperature so mild Jolan soon unbuttoned her coat. Melting snow made the sidewalks wet and everywhere she heard the sound of water flowing through gutters and into storm drains. Soon they reached the shopping district. Jolan laughed to think of Hardenbergh's six blocks of "downtown" compared with the tall buildings of New York. Here were B. Altman & Co., taking up an entire city block; Best & Co.; Russeks; Franklin Simon & Co., Bonwit Teller; Arnold Constable, and then Saks, which like the other large stores stretched a full block. They window shopped, as they had done when they were girls, but these windows held dresses Jolan knew she could never afford to buy.

"One hundred seventy-five dollars!" she exclaimed. "How can one outfit cost so much?"

"Well, it's an ensemble, Jolan, coat and dress combined. And that looks like exquisite georgette. Notice that navy blue is still a good color for spring, though it's not as big as last year."

Jolan shook her head. "It's so funny to see spring clothes already. The dress shop in Hardenbergh won't display them for another month."

They walked on. "That's the difference between Hardenbergh and New York," said Zsuzsi. "Look here—these dresses aren't so expensive as that ensemble."

"Well, I like the embroidery on that jacket," said Jolan, "but still, Zsuzsi, ninety-eight dollars! For a daytime frock!"

"There was one in Avedon's for thirty dollars, in crepe, remember that one? It was very smart—all the spring dresses are tailored this year. No more ruffles and tucks like last season."

"Tailored or no, thirty dollars for a frock is what Eva charges her customers, not what I can pay."

"Well, you and Eva make almost all your own clothes anyway. I'll tell you what—let's cut over to Park, and walk down to Broadway. It's not far from the flat, and you'll like John Wanamaker's. The prices are very reasonable."

"By whose standards?"

Zsuzsi laughed. "By our standards. Do you think I would pay over ninety dollars for a frock? But mark my words," she said as they waited to cross Fifth Avenue. "One day you'll see my designs in the windows of Saks and Bonwit Teller! And they won't be imitations of Paris designs, either—they'll be my own!"

They continued window shopping as they walked. Zsuzsi pointed out the number of sweater ensembles on display.

"Now that's very new this season. Last year you didn't see a single one."

She chatted on about horizontal stripes and zephyr weaves, collarless necklines, the newest shade of yellow. Although Jolan had a good eye for fabric, and could tell a well-made piece of goods from a cheap one, she knew that without a pattern to follow, or directions from Eva, she could never design a sweater, or dress, or ensemble. She marveled that Zsuzsi could dream up a design from scratch, figure out where to put pleats, how to drape a shoulder, choose the right fabric and texture and color. Already her designs were sold in J. Bamberger's, the most fashionable store in Newark. Though the design house she worked for, Jourdain's, was small, Jolan didn't doubt that one day Zsuzsi would indeed be working for one of the biggest fashion houses or department stores in New York.

"Now there you go," said Zsuzsi as they walked into Wanamaker's. "Under twenty dollars."

"I do like this one," said Jolan of a simply tailored street frock, with a pleated skirt and blouson top. A wide band of contrasting fabric at the hip made it look like a two-piece outfit.

She looked at the label. "Pierre Jourdain—why that's your firm. So that's why you brought me here."

Zsuzsi smiled. "Would you like it in rose or green?"

"I didn't bring enough money to spend on clothes," said Jolan.

Zsuzsi laughed. "It's one of mine! I'll get you one, wholesale. And in rose, I think, to set off that lovely skin of yours."

"Zsuzsi, thank you. How wonderful to see this hanging here, and know that it's your creation. How happy you look! You've positively glowed, all afternoon, talking of the latest fashion."

She squeezed Zsuzsi's hand. "Are you hungry? That bag of chestnuts we had hours ago was all I've eaten since breakfast."

Zsuzsi apologized for keeping Jolan from lunch and led her to the tearoom, where finger sandwiches and cinnamon toast took care of her hunger.

"Let me pay for this," said Jolan, opening her purse. Something white fell out and plopped onto the floor next to her seat.

Zsuzsi reached for it, and shook it out. "A man's handkerchief? Hasn't Aunt Margit embroidered enough feminine hankies for you? What are you doing with one of Uncle Emil's? Why Jolan, you're blushing." Zsuzsi looked down at the handkerchief, and again at Jolan, and then handed it to her.

"It's not Uncle Emil's, is it?"

Jolan shook her head and stuffed the handkerchief into her purse.

"Tell me about him," said Zsuzsi, waving away the waitress who had seen them reach for their purses.

So Jolan told her.

"Oh, my dear," said Zsuzsi, holding Jolan's hand. "I do understand how you feel, I really do. I'm so sorry. But a priest!"

"He's not a priest yet. Do you think it's a sin to pray he never becomes one?"

"No doubt. Not that knowing it will stop you. Oh, Jolan, I know it's hard, but sometimes you do have to give up. No matter how much you love someone."

"I'm not ready to do that yet."

"My poor Jolanka! It's not as though he loves another girl—he loves God. How can you compete with God?" She put two dollars on the table and stood up. "Come on, let's go home. This isn't the place for a good cry."

When they arrived at Zsuzsi's flat, Alice was awake, and painting. Zsuzsi's flat-mate was small, with dark curly hair and a heart shaped face so well proportioned that even her slightly prominent nose seemed to fit perfectly. She stood before a canvas a foot taller than she was, using a palette knife to dab on broad patches of color. She didn't mind company while she worked, and so Zsuzsi and Jolan sat down on a sofa to watch. Jolan was so fascinated by the process that soon her spirits improved. To her, the canvas was filled with splotches of color, though a few rectangular shapes seemed to predominate. After a while Jolan realized that Alice was painting a cityscape, and that the rectangles were buildings, but she had never seen buildings with such colors before—reds and purples juxtaposed with yellows and greens. Zsuzsi looked on with approval, so Jolan assumed it must be well executed, but she felt terribly ignorant.

Finally, Alice decided to quit for the day. She sat down with the two sisters, lit a cigarette, and put her feet up on the arm of the couch. "My mother would have a conniption if she saw me working on the Sabbath, but I figure if inspiration comes from God then He shouldn't mind." She smiled at Zsuzsi and reached for her hand.

"Alice's parents are orthodox Jews," Zsuzsi explained. "They've practically disowned her because she doesn't keep kosher and she paints on Saturdays."

"I'm sorry," said Jolan, who was not entirely sure what "keep kosher" meant. Old Mr. Weiss from the poultry shop was the only Jewish person she'd ever met before.

Alice laughed. "Actually, they're most upset because the philosophy of Vanderbilt and Rockefeller appeals to me more than that of Marx and Engels. But let's not talk family, or politics. It's more important to decide what we should do tonight."

After some discussion, in which Jolan could take little part, they settled on a supper club that Zsuzsi and Alice both liked. After putting on evening clothes—Jolan had to borrow a dress of Zsuzsi's—they took a streetcar uptown to Mack's Place. As they walked down the steps to the basement entrance Jolan thought they were entering a private home, since there was no sign. But once inside, through the dim lighting and the haze of cigarette smoke, she saw small tables, a dance floor, and a Negro band. The jazz music was so loud conversation was all but impossible. Zsuzsi ordered for them and the waiter set down glasses of water. Jolan nearly choked when she took a sip.

"What is this?" she shouted to Zsuzsi.

"Gin!" She laughed at Jolan's shocked expression. "Don't worry! We won't be raided!"

Jolan was glad, when dinner arrived, to see that it was perfectly normal steak, with a baked potato and green salad. She had never been in a blind pig, or seen a Negro band, or women dancing the Charleston and drinking gin. Jolan sipped the gin slowly, until she could swallow it without shuddering. Zsuzsi offered her a cigarette, and she realized that having a cigarette improved the taste of the gin, so she sat and smoked and drank like the others, and at one point even found herself on the dance floor.

She looked down at her watch, but had a hard time focusing. Could it really be after midnight?

"Zsuzsi, we should leave!" To talk she had to put her mouth close to Zsuzsi's ear.

"Whatever for? Tomorrow isn't a work day!"

"Church!"

Zsuzsi put down her drink. She started to say something then thought better of it. Instead, she put her mouth against Alice's ear and shouted something Jolan could not make out. But Alice laughed, and said "You're kidding!" Zsuzsi shook her head. "I'll stay a while!" shouted Alice. "See you later, alligator!"

Zsuzsi and Jolan left, weaving a little. Zsuzsi put her arm through Jolan's and led her to the streetcar, where they talked and giggled the whole ride home.

The next morning Zsuzsi handed Jolan a glass of something fizzy.

"Not before Mass," said Jolan.

"It's just water with sodium bicarbonate."

"Thanks." It tasted vile to Jolan, but she was sure anything she put in her mouth would taste the same. She hoped the walk to church would clear her head. The day before, a walk to St. Patrick's Cathedral had seemed an excellent idea. This morning, she was not so sure.

"Oh, come on," said Zsuzsi with a groan. "Consider it penance for last night."

By the time they arrived either the fresh air or the sodium bicarbonate had cleared Jolan's head, and she was able to appreciate the sweet, rich sounds of the organ floating through the vast cathedral, whose windows, even on a cloudy day like this, were tributes to both the artistry of man and the inspiration and glory of God. Jolan had never been anywhere so beautiful.

After church and brunch, they strolled up to Central Park. They walked so much Jolan was grateful to take the subway back downtown, and to spend a quiet evening listening to the radio. Alice, who had been asleep face down on the studio couch when they left for church, was also glad to stay home. She had an ugly bruise on her cheekbone.

"Mack's was raided last night," she said. "You just missed it. I managed to slip out the back but not before I caught an elbow in my face. Just missed my eye, thank goodness."

"Does this happen very often?" asked Jolan, trying not to sound shocked.

"Never there," said Alice. "Oh, a speakeasy gets raided almost all the time, you see it in the papers every weekend. But not one we've ever been to."

"That's right," said Zsuzsi. "I would never have taken you there if I thought it was possible."

"No harm done," said Jolan, then she laughed. "I had a marvelous time. You're right. This trip has done me good."

She sat back, and they listened to a program of Civil War music, a tribute to Abraham Lincoln in honor of his birthday. Then she went to bed, though Zsuzsi and Alice stayed up for a while. Jolan left them side by side on the couch, with Alice's head on Zsuzsi's shoulder.

On Monday morning Jolan packed her overnight bag, and went with Zsuzsi to Jourdain's on Seventh Avenue. Zsuzsi wanted to give her a tour of the building before Jolan left for the train station. But when they arrived Zsuzsi had to meet with her boss, so she left Jolan in the hands of the secretary, Miss Marshall, who asked one of the clerks to show her around.

They were nearly finished their tour of the building when Zsuzsi burst into the cutting room.

"Oh, Jolan, I've been looking all over for you! I've wonderful news—I'm to go to Paris with the head designer!"

Jolan squeezed Zsuzsi tight. "How marvelous! When will you go? For how long?"

"We sail in a week—a week, so little time—but we'll be there nearly a month, and then there's the trip back. But Jolan, I have some vacation coming. I'm going to try to see Mama!"

"Mama! Can you?"

"Well, once I'm over there it's not so far, really, is it? Oh, I wish you could come—I know, I know, there's never enough money for it but still, I wish you could."

"So do I. But a week! Is that enough time to get a passport, the right visas?"

"I don't know—I'll find out. But Jolan, if it all works out—think of it! Seeing Mama again, after so many years!"

Jolan hugged her sister again. "I am so happy for you! And if you see her, give her my love. Tell her—oh, tell her everything!"

Chapter 21
April 1927

Jolan walked home from work slowly one fine spring evening. The morning's rain, followed by broken clouds and sun, left a warm, muddy smell in the air. The sights and fragrances of spring bloomed: crocuses beneath hyacinths, daffodils clustered at the base of trees and in window boxes. Every bright yellow flower reminded her that a year ago she'd lost Tibor Nemeth. They had stood in the garden over a vase of daffodils... she'd brought daffodils to his great uncle's grave...they had kissed, one year ago.

Jolan sighed. She knew she should forget him, but it seemed with every passing day she was more and more obsessed. How many times had she told herself he'd forgotten her by now? How many times had she reminded herself it was impossible? And yet she felt sure, more now than ever, that she loved this man she had kissed only once and hadn't even seen in nearly a year. Yet she knew him so well, from his letters to Aunt Margit, letters that always closed with his regards to her family. They never once mentioned her by name.

She walked into the house wearily. Aunt Margit was not at home, but she had left the afternoon mail on the kitchen table. Jolan smiled when she saw it. News from Zsuzsi at last! She hadn't heard from her, beyond a postcard sending her greetings and their mother's love, since Zsuzsi had left for Hungary. She took the letter outside and sat down on the back porch to read it.

"Vienna, April 7

"My dearest Jolanka,

"First, my apologies for not writing sooner. I send my love to you and Uncle Emil and Aunt Margit. I miss you all! But I must say it is so good to be in a real hotel again, with a big tub for soaking, and such wonderful strudel for breakfast! I arrived last night, and though I'd intended to write as soon as I got here, I was so tired I merely fell into bed, and slept.

"The last time I wrote—really wrote—was when I left Paris for Budapest. The trip itself was wonderful—the most marvelous scenery, especially through Switzerland and Austria, and then Budapest, but I was so eager to see Mama I stayed there only the one night. Then a train to Eger, and a bus to Barackfalu, but it took ages, stopping at every tiny village, and sometimes just a crossroads. The roads are very bad.

"I was quite nervous, the closer we got to Barackfalu. Some things are so much the same, like farms that looked as they always had, with teams of horses plowing and flocks of geese being fed by little girls. Others were so different—whole towns where there were none—and yet what had really changed was me. I felt so funny, handing the border patrol my United States passport. And my Magyar is not so good as it once was. I hadn't noticed when I started thinking in English, and of course in New York I never get the chance to speak Magyar, only when I visit Hardenbergh. I had to ask people to repeat things, and I'm sure I mispronounced words, or at least spoke with an American accent. I really felt like a stranger.

"But Barackfalu! Tell Uncle Emil that the apricot trees are still there, and the schoolhouse. Our own house looked just the same, though smaller than I remember. Mama and Deszo were waiting for me. He's all grown up now, Jolan, and he's the image of Papa. And Mama—how we hugged each other, and cried!"

Here Jolan had to stop as tears filled her own eyes. If only she could have been there!

"It seemed like hours before we could do more than cry and say 'Mama' and 'Zsuzsi,' over and over again. Mama kept touching me—my hair, my cheek, my hand, as though she couldn't believe I was really there. Oh, Jolan, she is so changed! The war years were bad enough but what followed was very hard on her. She has aged—her hair is completely gray, and she looks older than Aunt Margit. Her face is lined from worry and sorrow. She showed me the graves of our little brothers and sisters. She has never gotten over the fact that Papa is buried in Germany, somewhere she doesn't even know. And her hands! She works in the fields, like a peasant. All the land around the village has been taken into what they call a 'collective,' a huge farm owned by the state. Everyone works there—they've become some kind of model project. She had to give up her own land, Jolan, hers and Papa's, and what should have passed to Deszo belongs to no one. Poor Mama works as hard as any farmer. Her hands are red and rough, her back is bent, but the worst is she never laughs anymore. Remember how often she used to laugh? Whenever she looked at Papa, or us, she seemed to laugh with sheer joy. There was so much love, and so much happiness! But last week, the most I ever saw was a smile, almost a shy one, as she spoke of Deszo and his important position within the 'party.' It seems he's become some sort of minor official, I never knew what exactly. Oh, Jolan, he struts around so. I quite disliked him. Imagine my writing that about our brother! That's why I couldn't send more than a brief card from Barackfalu. I'm sure Deszo, or someone, read every word. I know that sounds crazy, but people are watched there.

"So many people died, after the war, as one faction or another took over. There was so much violence, but no one really talks about it now. Mama told me a little, looking over her shoulder the whole time. It made me shudder to think she lives that way. And Deszo—when he found out what I do for a living, why he had nothing but scorn in his voice. I am 'bourgeois,' it seems, for catering to the wealthy. As if I design for the Vanderbilts! Honestly! I tried to explain that my clothes are in department stores, where anyone can buy them, but he argued and kept parroting Karl Marx. I think he has memorized *Das Kapital.* It became terribly awkward. I think he was actually embarrassed to have me there. Maybe I am such a blatant example of capitalism that I jeopardized his own position. I don't know. It was horrible. I only felt comfortable when he left, and soon enough he stayed away from us altogether. But that made Mama so upset—she dotes on him, and after all, he's all she has over there—she was miserable when he went away.

"So I stayed less than a week. I'm so ashamed, but things were so changed, and Deszo was so insufferable—it was clear he was making Mama choose between us, so finally I left. I tried to talk to Mama, to ask her to come with me, but she was afraid to speak of such things. She seems so passionate about this farm experiment—at least she talks as though she is—but I think it's more for Deszo's benefit than from conviction. I don't think she'll ever leave. She wants so much for Deszo to succeed, and how could she ever leave the one child she has left there?

"Life is funny, isn't it? I never really wanted to go back to Hungary, and yet I did. And when I got there I saw for certain that it isn't home anymore. Not for us. And I so wanted to see Mama, and have a happy reunion, but even that wasn't possible, after all. I don't think I can bear the sorrow of it, Jolanka! There's nothing left for us in Hungary, not even the mother we knew.

"I am sorry to bring such unhappy news. I hope you, at least, and Uncle Emil and Aunt Margit are well and just as you were when I saw you last. I now look forward to coming home, more than I thought possible. We sail from Cherbourg in three days. By the time you get this, I shall be on my way home. Love, Zsuzsi."

Jolan let the pages fall into her lap. How was it possible that people could change so much? Even during the worst of the war years, their mother had always smiled for them, made them laugh. It was true, after their father's death, that something had changed in Piros, diminishing her, altering the quality of her laughter and her smiles. She was like a pitcher that had broken and was mended, never to be filled to the brim again. Yet still she smiled, and laughed, and Jolan understood it was for her sake, and Zsuzsi's, and Deszo's. But now she and Zsuzsi were gone from home, and Deszo was grown up, so nothing remained for Piros but pride in her son, and the so-called collective farm.

What a funny word "collective" was. Jolan had heard about such things from the speakers who came to the Social and Athletic Club. They were almost always young men, not much older than Deszo, usually one or two a year. They spoke of the satisfaction of working for the collective, of the evil of private property, the equality that would result when all men worked for the good of the state. Jolan had attended one or two such speeches, but they bored her, and by the polite but unenthusiastic applause she knew she was not alone. To be sure, a few of the younger people in the audience were moved by the speeches, but most of the older men and women remembered life in the fields, the hardships of sunup to sundown toil. Here they worked six days a week but had their evenings free to attend concerts or go to the cinema or just to stay home and listen to their new five-tube radio. These were people for whom property was not an evil word but a good one, property bought from their own wages. The zealous young speakers would not gain much support here.

Jolan folded the letter carefully and put it in her pocket. She suddenly felt very alone. Looking across at the neighbors' yards, she could see signs of spring everywhere, but no one gardening. Most people would be indoors having supper. She wished Aunt Margit and Uncle Emil were home. Zsuzsi's letter reminded Jolan how far away her sister was, and the rest of her family seemed even more remote. She shivered a little, though the evening was still warm.

She went into the house for a sweater before going out again to find Uncle Emil. She met him walking up Cherry Street. He smiled and waved as soon as he saw her, and quickened his pace. His obvious pleasure at her company made Jolan feel quite herself once again. She kissed his cheek, he offered his arm, and together they walked the rest of the way home.

"This is a nice surprise," he said.

"I was lonely. Aunt Margit isn't home. Do you know where she is?"

"Yes, didn't she leave you a note? She must have been in a hurry. She called this afternoon—*Puskasz-neni's* daughter-in-law is having a baby, and your Aunt Margit is minding the children until their father comes home. He works the second shift, so she won't be home until after midnight."

"I thought Aunt Margit didn't get along with *Puskasz-neni.*"

"Well, you know your aunt. She likes to feel useful, and she and *Puskasz-neni* get along much better now that we aren't neighbors anymore."

"What shall we do for dinner, then? You must be hungry, Uncle Emil."

Uncle Emil laughed. "I'm sure I am not half as hungry as you, my dear. I am far more used to the Lenten fast, after all. Don't worry, your aunt left us fried chicken in the icebox."

They paused in the garden. The light was beginning to fade, paling the sky and suffusing the daffodils with pastel shadows.

"What a lovely evening," murmured Uncle Emil. "It seems a shame to go inside."

"Then let's picnic. We can eat here on the back porch."

While Uncle Emil washed up Jolan spread a cloth on the porch. She set out the fried chicken, sliced bread, a dish of pickled cauliflower, and a bottle of milk. She and Uncle Emil sat down on either side of the cloth, their feet resting on the steps below.

After Uncle Emil had eaten two pieces of chicken he leaned against the porch rail and began to fill his pipe. Jolan said, "I had a letter from Zsuzsi today, quite a long one. I'd like you to read it."

She handed him the letter and began to gather up the food.

"Put the porch light on, would you, Jolan?" asked Uncle Emil as he put down his pipe and took out his reading glasses.

Jolan flicked the switch when she walked into the house. She put the food away, rolled up the picnic cloth and placed it in the clothes hamper, and made a pot of coffee.

Uncle Emil came in as she was setting out cups and spoons.

"I am sorry, Jolan," he said.

She turned to him with tears in her eyes. He folded his arms around her, holding her tight while she cried. When her sobs diminished he kissed her, led her to a chair, and poured the coffee.

"People do change, Jolan," he said.

"I know, but I had always hoped—I had always counted on sending for her, after Zsuzsi and I had worked a while and saved enough. I had wanted to bring her here, to live, where life wouldn't be so hard for her. I thought we could all be happy together."

"Your Aunt and I have some savings. You could have asked for that."

"No, Uncle Emil. You and Aunt Margit have taken care of us all these years. I couldn't have asked anything more of you. No, this was something I wanted to do for Mama, to thank her for sending us here, for sacrificing all those years away from us, because it was for the best, I do understand that. And now she sounds so unhappy, at least that's what Zsuzsi says."

"Maybe you need to see for yourself. I could give you the money for that."

"Uncle Emil, you are such a good man! But I can't take that from you, and besides, I'm—I'm not so sure I want to see how things really are there. It's terrible of me—I'm such a coward, but I don't think I could stand to see Mama old and gray and sad. She's so pretty in my mind, so happy, and young. I don't think I can give her up, not yet."

Uncle Emil placed his hand over Jolan's. "You're no coward Jolan, not if you are facing what is truly in your heart. But don't ever avoid going just because of money. We can always find a way to deal with that."

Jolan almost cried again, but this time from gratitude. Uncle Emil was the kindest, most generous man she knew. He was always so understanding, always comforting, when she was young and unhappy over school, or now when her heart grieved over changes she could not control. She was tempted to tell him about Tibor Nemeth, but she remembered how Uncle Emil celebrated Nemeth's entrance into the seminary, so she said nothing. She could not face his disappointment in her, any more than she could face her fears about her mother.

Meanwhile the daffodils continued to bloom, bursting into bright yellow flowers, followed by red and pink tulips. Easter came and went in a flurry of pastel dresses and white lilies. As Uncle Emil's vegetable shoots pushed through the rich garden soil, and everywhere the cycle of renewal was heralded by flowers and bird song, Jolan felt herself cocooned in loneliness. She knew it was her own fault, that she was cheating herself out of her favorite season, but she could take no joy in the robin's nest in the pear tree, or the new family of kittens next door, when her own life stretched before her as one of stitches and hems, with young Ferenc and Uncle Emil her only male companions.

Soon the pear tree bloomed like a white cloud in the corner of the yard, and then it was Ferenc's twelfth birthday. When he came home from school that Wednesday Eva had waiting his new suit, his first with long pants, which she had made of the finest navy blue gabardine. Jolan's present was a set of vacuum tubes with which he could build his own radio, and Zsuzsi had sent a model aeroplane from F.A.O. Schwartz. Uncle Emil and Aunt Margit came over in the evening, something they rarely did these days but always on Ferenc's birthday, and gave him a leather wallet.

Jolan watched Ferenc blow out the candles on his chocolate cake. He was a tall boy, already nearly his mother's height, but with none of her slenderness. Jolan had seen pictures of his father and knew that Ferenc resembled him closely. Not for the first time Jolan wondered if that was why Eva never remarried. Maybe if Ferenc looked less like his father she would feel more free to wed. Silly thoughts, idiotic romantic thoughts, the kind she always had anymore. Jolan sighed. Maybe that was the function of an old maid, to try to match up everyone else.

When it was time for bed Ferenc hugged and kissed everyone in turn.

"Thank you for the radio tubes, Jo-Jo," he whispered as he hugged Jolan. She held him tight for a moment. Soon enough he wouldn't want hugs or kisses from any of them, especially now that he would wear long pants. It had been two years since he'd last called her Jo-Jo, his pet name for her when he was just a little boy. It brought tears to her eyes to hear it. She shook her head. She cried too easily these days.

Ferenc was more like a brother to her than Deszo. Jolan had a hard time even picturing her brother now, yet she had vivid memories of Ferenc: walking him to school, playing soldier with him afterward, baking cookies on cold winter evenings. Now, on Saturday, he was to be confirmed, wearing his first grownup suit, being accepted into the church as an adult. Jolan had been helping him with his catechism for months.

Over and over they drilled through the questions the bishop of Trenton might ask him: *Who made you? God made me. Why did God make you? To know, love, and serve him in this world.* How Ferenc would serve Him Jolan didn't know, but she fervently hoped it would not be as a priest.

On Saturday afternoon they all sat in church, Eva on the end so she could see Ferenc in procession, then Uncle Emil, Aunt Margit, and Jolan. Zsuzsi was not able to get there in time for the ceremony but had promised to come home for the celebration afterwards. When the organ began the processional march they all stood, and watched as the bishop, preceded by altar boys and Monsignor Czigany, walked slowly up the aisle. Two of the altar boys carried beeswax candles in tall gold candlesticks; a third carried the gold crucifix. The Monsignor himself swung the censor full of incense, sending puffs of sweet smoke from side to side. The bishop, in red robes and tall pointed hat, carried the gold crosier symbolizing his office as a shepherd of souls. Behind him came the sisters of St. Elizabeth's, walking two by two, and then the girls in white dresses, and the boys in blue suits.

When the children were in their pews the congregation knelt. Jolan had not been to a confirmation since her own, many years before in Hungary. That had taken place at a small village church, with scarcely a dozen children from the surrounding countryside. This church, though totally familiar, still impressed Jolan with its marble-faced pillars, stained glass windows, and ornately carved altar. On the altar lay the cloth made by Aunt Margit, looking plain white from this distance, but Jolan knew it was embroidered the whole length with the chi-rho symbol in white silk.

She held her breath as the bishop began asking questions of the boys and girls, and pointed almost at once at Ferenc. He stood up, answered his question in a clear voice without making mistakes, and sat down again. Jolan wanted to applaud, but clasped her hands instead. After the catechism was recited to the bishop's satisfaction, the students lined up at the altar rail to be anointed with holy oil, and to receive the ceremonial slap on the cheek that symbolized the struggle of the early Christians. Uncle Emil, as Ferenc's sponsor, stood behind him, his right hand on the boy's shoulder. When the bishop asked what Ferenc's confirmation name was to be, Emil said "Istvan," Steven. Ferenc Istvan Farkas was duly received into the church.

Back home, with a mouthful of cake, he gleefully observed that he was probably the only boy in the church to have two parties in one week. This time, however, his presents reflected the solemnity of the occasion. From his mother he received a gilt-edged missal, from Aunt Margit and Uncle Emil a hand-carved crucifix to hang over his bed, from Zsuzsi a book about the life of St. Steven, and from Jolan a new rosary of black and silver beads.

Jolan was carrying cake plates into the kitchen when Eva burst into tears. "My little boy is all grown up," she sobbed.

"Well, I think he looks very handsome in long pants," said Jolan. "But don't worry, Eva, it will be years before a lovely young girl steals his heart from you."

"Thanks," said Eva bitterly. "It could happen in only four or five years, did you think of that? What will I do without him then?"

Jolan looked to Aunt Margit for help, or some logic at least.

"Perhaps God has already claimed him," Margit said. "You could do worse than have your only son dedicate his life to God."

"A priest?" Jolan and Eva said in unison. Eva laughed. "Oh, Margit, I can't imagine such a thing! He likes to cook too much, for one thing, and to play with radios and aeroplanes. Not my Ferenc!"

"You never know," said Aunt Margit.

Jolan slammed down her tray so hard the cups and plates rattled.

"Really, Aunt Margit! Why should every young man waste his life that way? Better he should build radios, or fly aeroplanes, or even cook lunch at Woolworth's. There are enough priests in this world, don't you think?"

She stalked out the back door, letting it slam behind her, leaving Aunt Margit and Eva sitting in perfect astonishment, while in the parlor Ferenc put his favorite Al Jolson record on the Victrola.

The following morning Jolan was still out of sorts, not the best mood for churchgoing. Nothing seemed to go right for her. She spilled the jar of tooth powder on the bathroom floor, she put her thumb through one of her best stockings, and she could not find a single dress in her closet that satisfied her. One was hopelessly out of fashion, another needed hemming, another had a spot on the bodice. She decided that pink was too childish, green made her look ill, and yellow couldn't be farther from the way she felt. Only at Aunt Margit's impatient call did she finally decide to put on a navy blue dress whose dark color suited her mood.

The walk to church seemed to take longer than usual. Aunt Margit was silent, still irritated at Jolan's outburst from the night before. She radiated disapproval in every step. Uncle Emil had gone on ahead as he always did when it was his turn to usher at Mass. During the service Jolan knelt, stood, and sat mechanically, her mouth forming the words of the prayers but her mind and heart disengaged. She dutifully placed her offering in the basket Uncle Emil passed to her, and sat in seeming—but feigned—attention during the sermon. When Aunt Margit nudged Jolan to go to communion, Jolan sat back to make room for her aunt to pass by. Aunt Margit nodded and went to the communion rail while Jolan sighed with relief. Apparently her aunt agreed that Jolan was hardly in a state of grace this morning.

After the final benediction she stood with the rest of the congregation and made her slow way out towards the sun. Her stomach growled and the thought of breakfast was the only thing on her mind. She followed Aunt Margit down the steps, and then almost collided with her as Aunt Margit stopped suddenly.

"Why, Mr. Nemeth, what a pleasant surprise," said Aunt Margit as she held out her hand.

Jolan felt her heart stop. By the time Nemeth and her aunt finished greeting one another she was fairly certain she had control over her face once more, but she doubted her dry throat would allow her to make a sound.

"Hello, Jolan," he said.

For a moment Jolan was nearly dizzy. She imagined they were standing in the garden once again, alone, instead of on the crowded sidewalk in front of church.

Jolan cleared her throat. "Hello, Mr. Nemeth."

"So tell me, Mr. Nemeth, what brings you to Hardenbergh?" asked Aunt Margit. Jolan never thought she could be so happy to have her aunt monopolize a conversation. It gave her a chance to compose herself and to observe Tibor indirectly. He looked the same as he did a year ago, except for faint smudges under his eyes, probably the result of hard studying. But his smile, his cheekbones, his tan skin and dark hair were all as Jolan remembered, as she had pictured him in her mind every day. She held her breath when Aunt Margit invited him to dinner and was relieved to hear him decline. She couldn't bear the thought of sitting through a whole meal with him at the same table.

"Perhaps later in the week," he said.

"Before you return to the seminary?" asked Aunt Margit.

He hesitated. "Yes, before I return to Long Island."

They exchanged goodbyes. Jolan, whose heart had seemed to stop when she first saw him, now felt it hammering so hard she thought it would burst from her chest. Breakfast was out of the question now. She told Aunt Margit she would wait for dinner, and used the torn hem of her white dress as an excuse to retire to her room.

"The Lord's day is not a day for work, Jolan," protested Aunt Margit.

"I'm sorry, but I can't very well mend my own clothes during work hours, and the last thing I want to do when I come home at night is pick up a needle. I won't be long, Aunt Margit."

But in her room, she sat with the dress in her lap, staring out the window at the pear tree and the pink and white peony buds opening beneath it. At dinner, she ate so little that Aunt Margit felt her forehead.

"You don't have a fever. Is your stomach upset, Jolan?"

"I suppose it is, a little."

"You should lie down, then."

"I will help your aunt clean up," said Uncle Emil.

"Thank you both but I think maybe I need some air right now."

Jolan left the room as quickly as she could without actually running. She felt as though she were suffocating, the way she had felt at Monsignor Andrassy's wake. Once outside she stood for a moment, gulping in the soft air, fragrant with lilacs, then she turned, fleeing up Kossuth Street as though she were being pursued.

She practically ran into Tibor Nemeth as he stood on the corner.

He reached out to steady her but she pulled back sharply.

"What are you doing here?" she asked, aware of how rude she sounded, but unable to stop herself.

"Actually, I was waiting for you."

Jolan's heart lurched. "How could you know I was coming out here?"

He smiled. "Not knew. Hoped."

She felt the flush rise in her cheeks. "You might have had a long wait."

"I know. But I hoped I could speak with you in private, without your delightful but ever-present aunt and uncle."

"Why?" The question came out much more harshly than she intended.

"I thought you might want to show me that farm where the daffodils grow wild."

"The daffodils are all dead now." She walked past him, wanting to get away, yet heading for the very farm he asked about. Again her heart pounded like a hammer. For so long she had wanted to see him again and inhale that never forgotten scent of bay rum! Now that he was here his presence was almost unbearable.

He walked beside her, with his hands in his pockets. "Not many people are about," he observed.

Jolan could hardly believe he wanted to make small talk. "I expect they are still having dinner. Like Father Biro, whom you said you were visiting."

"Father Biro had to call on a parishioner," he said.

They walked past the houses that were so much like the one Jolan lived in, and then stepped off the last of the sidewalk onto the road itself, next to a verge of tall grass dotted with fleabane and buttercups. The road narrowed into the familiar country lane that she and Zsuzsi had walked so many times. The woods on the north side of the road were full of birdsong. On the other side was the cow pasture and its stream, where a month ago vibrant daffodils had blossomed. Jolan stopped walking, but felt like she would burst if she stood still. Although she was still in her navy blue dress, she climbed the split rail fence. Tibor put his hand on the top rail and vaulted over.

"Is this it?" he asked.

"Is this what?" She wished she could ease the tightness in her voice, but knew if she did her words would come out shaking and weak.

"Where the daffodils grow," he said softly.

"Yes, actually, it is, Mr. Nemeth."

"Please, Jolan. You kissed me once. Don't you think you should call me Tibor?"

She stopped walking. She hadn't expected him to remind her of that. Her heart, which she had only calmed by focusing on the forest and the birds and the pasture, began hammering again. She shaded her eyes with her hand, telling herself it was only the bright sunlight that made her eyes tear up. He was standing very close to her now, but she couldn't look at him.

"I didn't come here just to see Father Biro, Jolan. I've been sent away from the seminary. The term doesn't end until June. But it was apparent to everyone, especially my confessor, that although I worked hard and studied hard and prayed harder than I've ever prayed before, that top grades in Latin are not enough to make a man a priest. Not when that man is in love."

As though his words had the power to knock her down, she knelt in the tall grass. Suddenly the air was full of the fragrance of mint, sweet and fresh, and full of hope.

Tibor knelt beside her. "You were right, Jolan, when I saw you last, when you said I couldn't ignore what happened between us. You haven't been out of my mind—or my heart—since that day. I can't tell you how many times I tried to pray—and instead, saw your face, and remembered how your lips tasted." He laughed, a sharp, sudden laugh that held pain as well as humor. "Don't you see? My body told me what my mind and heart refused to believe. I love you, Jolan." He took her arms, and turned her toward him. Then he moved his hands up to her shoulders, her neck, and finally cupped them over and through the masses of hair she still wore in a loose bun at the back of her head. She felt his fingers caressing her hair, cradling her head, and heard in his voice the intensity her eyes were too full of tears to see.

"I love you, Jolan, I've always loved you," and then his lips were on hers, his tongue was in her mouth, and she reached for him so eagerly she pushed him down into the grass. How long they kissed she had no idea, but suddenly he stopped, and held her face in his hands.

"Will you marry me, Jolan?"

Jolan hadn't thought any words could surpass "I love you" for bringing happiness. She was wrong.

"Oh, yes, Tibor! Yes!"

It was she who stopped the kiss the second time. "Not in a cow pasture!"

He laughed, and put her hand to his lips and kissed each of her fingers. "Not until we're married."

He stood and helped her up, then they brushed off each other's clothes.

"We're lucky you didn't shove me onto a cowpat!" he said, and Jolan laughed, delighting in the sound of his voice, in the touch of his hands as he reached for her again, in his words as he whispered, "God knows I want you right now." A thrill ran through her body like nothing she had experienced before, as though his kiss was a lightning bolt running through her very soul. When they separated long enough to walk out of the pasture, she knew that everything would be different in her life from this moment on.

Everything, that is, except Aunt Margit.

They walked home with their arms around each other until they reached the first houses, then Tibor gently let go of her. She was absurdly grateful for his tact; had anyone seen them walking that way on a public street she would have been branded as "easy." And so they walked up to the house in perfect decorum, not even holding hands. Margit and Emil, enjoying the fine weather by sitting on the porch, looked at them with surprise as they walked up the stairs.

Tibor explained that his first year in the seminary showed him that he did indeed lack the vocation he once thought he had, but even this preparation was of no benefit once he formally asked Emil for Jolan's hand in marriage.

"NO!" Aunt Margit's reaction was explosive. "Jolan, how could you!"

"It's not Jolan's fault, Mrs. Molnar. God does work in mysterious ways, and there are many ways of serving Him. I think it's clear He intends that I serve Him by becoming a husband and father, instead of shepherd to a flock."

"But you made a promise to your parents! How can we let Jolan be the instrument by which you break that promise!"

"I have agonized over that very point, Mrs. Molnar. I have come to agree with my confessor that perhaps it was not fair to expect me to live up to that promise. And under the circumstances, I can do God's work better by being a good husband than by being a bad priest."

"Nonsense—"

"Margit," interrupted Uncle Emil. "Please. The young man has made his request most properly. But Mr. Nemeth, you must give us time to

276

think about such a serious decision. It has been a very sudden one, after all."

"Not to me, Uncle Emil."

"Nor to me. But your uncle is right, Jolan," Tibor said. "We must give him and your aunt time to think and talk about it. When may we expect your decision, sir?"

Uncle Emil looked nonplussed. Aunt Margit's lips were compressed into a hard line all too familiar to him and to Jolan.

"Come to my office tomorrow morning. In the meantime the three of us will discuss these—circumstances."

"Until tomorrow, then," said Tibor, with a bow.

Uncle Emil stood up. "Just one question, before you go."

"Yes, sir?"

"Do you truly love her?"

Tibor smiled at Jolan. "With all my heart and soul."

Uncle Emil looked at the two of them. He nodded. "Tomorrow."

Jolan started down the steps, but her uncle put his hand on her arm. "We need to talk, don't you think?"

Jolan sat down on the top step, once again in turmoil. She followed Tibor's progress with her eyes while Emil went back to his chair, and began filling his pipe. Margit sat still as a statue, looking as if she had stepped in a puddle of vomit.

When the pipe was lit, Emil asked one question.

"Do you love him?"

"Yes, Uncle Emil!" The expression on her face was as convincing as her words. Emil turned to Margit, who would not meet his eyes.

"Well, that settles it," he said.

"Does it indeed?" asked Margit. "A priest! Seduced by this—this Jezebel!"

"That's not fair, Aunt Margit!"

"Isn't it? I suppose that's not grass on your skirt, or in your hair! What were you doing, making love in a hayfield?"

"Margit!"

"No, Aunt Margit. We kissed, that's all. He told me he loved me and he proposed to me and we kissed. We've done nothing wrong."

Uncle Emil held up his hand before Margit could open her mouth.

"Marriage is as much a holy sacrament as ordination," he said. "God will surely bless their union, as long as there is love between them." He looked again at Margit, who this time met his glance with a cold stare.

"However, marriage is also not something to rush into, or to do on an impulse. How much time have you spent together? Only a few hours?"

Jolan started to answer, but Emil held up his hand again. "You don't want to do something you may later regret, my dear. You may well love this young man, and he you, but do you know each other? Do you even like each other? Finding that out takes time."

"Time will only strengthen our love."

Emil smiled. "I'm sure it will. But what do you really know about Tibor Nemeth right now? Can you tell me his favorite food? His favorite color? His favorite flower? Can he tell me the same things about you? My dear, I would be a fool to doubt your love for each other. One look at your faces tells us how you feel. But marriage should provide, not just love, but also friendship, companionship, partnership. You can't be friends with someone you don't know."

Jolan rubbed her head as though it ached. There was logic in everything Uncle Emil said, but what good was logic when there was love? Still, a brief engagement would give her time to ready a trousseau. She had some things already, but—she looked up her uncle. "How long must we wait?"

"Oh, a few months would seem appropriate," said Uncle Emil. He put his pipe in his mouth.

"One year," said Margit.

As Emil and Jolan began to protest, she stood up.

"It took him a year to decide he was not to be God's priest. Let him take the same time to decide to be a husband. I will not give my consent to this marriage without a year's engagement."

"A whole year! Please, Aunt Margit—"

"A year is not such a long time, Jolan," interrupted Uncle Emil. "It is not an unreasonable request."

Jolan clenched her fists. A year! She had already waited a year. She looked at her aunt and uncle. Uncle Emil's expression was sad, but Margit's was full of spite. For what reason? What had Jolan ever done to deserve it? She could not understand it, nor could she fight it. Aunt Margit had a will of iron, and in a matter like this she would never back down. If Jolan objected, she would lose her aunt's permission entirely. It wasn't fair, but then Margit had never been concerned with fairness.

278

Jolan unclenched her fists and stood up. "Very well, Aunt Margit, Uncle Emil. I will wait one year. But at the end of that year Tibor and I will be married, and that's a promise." She walked to the front door and opened it. "And by the way, Uncle Emil, his favorite flower is the daffodil." She let the door slam shut behind her.

Chapter 22
June 1928

Jolan looked in the mirror to adjust her veil one last time. Her veil was a long one, reaching to the hem of her gown, and topped with a circlet of silk flowers. Her gown was a long one, too, made of white lace over an ivory silk underdress that Eva had made according to Zsuzsi's design. On her hand was the ring Tibor had given her at Christmas, a square-cut emerald in a filigree of gold, which had been his mother's.

She marveled that a year whose days passed so slowly could have, as a whole, gone by so quickly. She had seen little of Tibor for a month after they announced their intentions to Uncle Emil and Aunt Margit. While he made arrangements to move to Hardenbergh, she alternated between energetic excitement and a lethargy that all but immobilized her. One day she would wake early and practically run to Eva's dressmaking shop, to stitch and plan and talk; then the next day she could barely get up from her bed, she was so full of missing Tibor. On those days she walked to work distractedly, clutching his handkerchief and imagining all sorts of disasters that would prevent his coming back. When he cabled the date of his return Jolan counted the hours, so eager was she to see him again, yet while she waited for his train she paced in fear that he had changed his mind, that his feelings had diminished, that he would stop only long enough to tell her goodbye.

Then the train arrived, and he leaped down to the platform almost before it had stopped, with such a smile of joy on his face that Jolan thought she would never be so happy again in her life.

She smiled, remembering, as she pulled the veil over her face. How many times in the past year had she felt that way, and here she was feeling it all over again.

It had been a difficult year. To save money, Tibor lived in a single room in a crowded boarding house, but he and Jolan could never meet privately there. He came to dinner at the Molnars' two or three times a week, but there Aunt Margit, at first cool, later merely vigilant, was as obtrusive as any boarding house owner. So they went to the cinema, stopping afterwards for ice cream, or to the library, or concerts, or just took long walks, talking, always talking. It wasn't long at all before Jolan could report to Uncle Emil that Tibor's favorite food was *palacsinta*, with pot cheese filling, and that his favorite color was the bright yellow-green of a new leaf. Since they were now officially engaged they could walk hand in hand, even downtown; Jolan loved the feeling of his warm, strong hand around hers.

But it was their walks in the country she liked the best, even in winter, when the cows stayed in their barns and the dirt road was frozen into ruts. Then Tibor walked with his arm around her, stopping to kiss her often, holding her close. Jolan loved the taste and feel of his tongue in her mouth; his kisses made her breathless and weak, so that she leaned against him and wished she could slip under his coat to be even closer. Yet she felt guilty about such thoughts, and wished she could talk to someone, but Aunt Margit was unapproachable, and she was too embarrassed to ask Eva. June seemed so far off....

Zsuzsi arrived on Christmas Eve. After Midnight Mass they returned home to a meal of *kolbasz* and sauerkraut, then to bed, where, in the dark, Jolan was able to tell Zsuzsi of the way her body responded to Tibor's kisses, and the very unchaste desire she felt for him.

"Have you ever felt like that?" Jolan whispered.

"Yes, I have. Everyone does, at one point or another."

"Then it isn't wrong?"

Zsuzsi reached for Jolan's hand and gave it a squeeze. "No, it isn't wrong, Jolanka, it's normal and healthy. You love each other! What could be more natural?"

"But to think of waiting until June—I don't think I can bear it."

Zsuzsi was silent for a moment. "Well, not everyone waits for marriage."

Jolan sat up. "Zsuzsi! Do you mean to say we should? And that it's all right? Surely you haven't—"

Zsuzsi also sat up. "Jolan, not all of us are destined for marriage. You are. Anyone can see that and how much you love him. Your faces positively glow when you look at one another. I am so happy for you! I think you and Tibor have been given a gift and I wish you a long and happy life together, with children and a home and all that goes with it. But I have my work, and that, too, is a kind of gift." She sighed. "Who knows? Maybe someday I will feel differently, but I just don't think marriage is for me. Does that mean I must live like a nun?"

"But it's a sin. Isn't it?"

Zsuzsi laughed softly. "I have a very hard time imagining that the most natural of acts, the act of love, can really be a sin. Not when there is love…but if marriage is what you want, then I suppose there's no harm in waiting. It will make the moment seem even more wonderful when it finally arrives. After all, opening your present on Christmas morning is much more fun because of the wait, don't you think?"

"I suppose so! But it's so hard!"

"Most things are, Jolanka." She reached over and hugged Jolan. "It will all work out. You'll see."

Winter crawled toward spring, and finally Jolan was able to show Tib his daffodils in Amwell's field. Soon the days began to tumble together, as the dress took shape and arrangements were made for the church, the hall, the reception, the honeymoon. Jolan embroidered sheets and pillowcases. Aunt Margit thawed enough to crochet a tablecloth. The trousseau was finished with a month to spare.

Jolan and Tibor were to move into the first floor apartment of the building Uncle Emil owned—the very apartment where he and Aunt Margit had spent their first years in Hardenbergh. Jolan and Aunt Margit scrubbed it from floor to ceiling, and Tibor and Jolan painted and wallpapered. Only a week ago they moved in their furniture—a couch and two chairs, a kitchen table, a wardrobe, a new bed. Once, while Jolan was hanging curtains, she tumbled off the ladder, and Tibor caught her. His hand slipped under her skirt, resting on her thigh with a feeling like an electric shock that she felt to her core. She put her arms around Tibor, who kissed her hard and began lowering her to the floor, when they heard Aunt Margit at the door, calling for help with an armload of kitchen things. It was the closest they had come. Now all the waiting—the year of loneliness, and then the long engagement—was over, and her new life was about to begin.

Jolan smiled at her reflection and picked up her bouquet of white peonies from the garden. She was ready.

Zsuzsi, dressed in a gown the color of new leaves, was waiting in the living room. She had, of course, helped Jolan dress, but stepped out when Jolan asked to be alone for a moment. Uncle Emil, who had been fussing with his cravat, stopped with his hands in midair.

"Mother of God," he whispered. "You look like an angel."

Jolan reached for his hands. "Dear Uncle Emil," she said, choking on the words.

"No tears, no tears," said Zsuzsi, "at least not until we're in church. We can have a good cry then, but I want no tears on that lace until after the ceremony."

Aunt Margit, in a new dress of ice-blue silk, came in from her bedroom, pulling on matching gloves. She stopped short when she saw Jolan.

"You look—perfect," she said.

"Oh, my," whispered Zsuzsi. No one, but no one, had ever heard Margit call anything perfect. There could be no higher compliment from her.

"Well, then," said Uncle Emil, offering Jolan his hand. He led her outside, to the car he had hired as a wedding present. The upstairs neighbor stood next to it on the sidewalk.

"You look beautiful, dear," said Mrs. Kish. "Do you have everything— something old, something new, something borrowed, something blue?"

"My ring is old, my dress is new, I've borrowed a necklace from Zsuzsi, and I have a blue ribbon on my flowers, Mrs. Kish."

"Wonderful! We'll see you at the church, then," she said, and hurried to join her husband, who was already halfway down the block.

With a maximum of fussing Jolan was installed in the car for the short drive to the church. It took an equal amount of fussing to get her out of the car, and even more to arrange her veil and train in the church vestibule. Tibor's college roommate, Ronald Armstrong, came into the vestibule in his capacity of best man to see if Jolan was ready. They had met only a few days before, but Jolan felt as if they were already old friends. He stared at Jolan, and wolf-whistled softly.

"You are the loveliest and calmest bride I've ever seen," said Ronald. "Tib is pacing back and forth like a tiger in a zoo."

"Then I suggest you get him in front of the altar," said Zsuzsi drily.

He held out his hand to escort Margit into the church. Zsuzsi held Jolan's train aside so that Uncle Emil could move into position, then she made her final arrangements of gown, train, and veil. Jolan reached for her hand.

"Thank you, for everything," she whispered. Zsuzsi smiled and gave her hand a squeeze before stepping in front of her.

Uncle Emil held tightly to the hand that gripped his sleeve. The night before, he and Jolan had gone for a walk, their last companionable walk and heart-to-heart talk. Though she would be living only a few minutes away, he would miss their evenings together. He repeated the words with which he had ended their talk the night before.

"God be with you, my dearest," he said as the organ began to play. "I wish you happiness and love for all your life together."

"I love you, Uncle Emil," was all she had time to say before Zsuzsi began walking up the aisle, and then she and Uncle Emil stepped from the vestibule into the church. It seemed that half of Hardenbergh was there, mostly friends of Uncle Emil and Aunt Margit, with two or three school friends of Tibor's from Detroit, and one young man in a cassock, Tibor's closest friend from the previous year. Only Trudy and William were missing—they had sent their regrets, because Trudy was expecting their third child—and Mama as well, who though she sent her love and best wishes was not able to leave Hungary.

Halfway up the aisle Jolan was finally close enough to see Tibor clearly. In his long coat with tails he looked more handsome than she had ever seen him. He never took his face from hers, and she trembled to see the play of emotions on it, love and desire, joy and solemnity. She wished, when Uncle Emil stepped away and put her hand in Tibor's, that she could lean against Tibor and feel his strong arm supporting her as it had done so many times before.

Monsignor Czigany began the opening words of the wedding ceremony. Aunt Margit had tried to persuade Jolan and Tibor to have a Mass, but they insisted a simple ceremony was all they wanted. Privately Jolan thought it was tasteless of Aunt Margit to suggest that Tibor should watch a Mass being said on the day he gave up all hope of ever being able to say one himself. She was in awe of what he had given up for her.

They exchanged rings, then he lifted her veil and they kissed for the first time as husband and wife. Tibor grinned when Zsuzsi reached over, shaking her head, to rearrange the veil into more suitable folds. Then came the walk down the aisle, handshakes and hugs, photographs, the ride to the Social and Athletic Club for the reception.

For Jolan, the reception was a blur of food and music, cake and punch, one *csardas* after another as she danced with Tibor and Uncle Emil, Ronald Armstrong, Tibor's college friends. It was many hours—though it seemed like only minutes—before Jolan threw her bouquet, and she and Tibor left the hall to change for the train ride to Niagara Falls. At Aunt Margit and Uncle Emil's for the last time, Jolan went into her bedroom to change from her wedding gown into a street-length dress of pale green linen. In Aunt Margit and Uncle Emil's room, Tibor exchanged his coat and tails for a seersucker suit. Ronald and Zsuzsi drove them to the train station, where to their surprise the rest of the wedding guests were waiting. Jolan was both delighted to see everyone, and dismayed at having to say goodbye all over again. Somehow they managed to hug and kiss their way to the train just before it pulled out.

At last they were on the train, in a half empty car that gave them the illusion of privacy, but when they sat down and Tibor kissed her Jolan heard the cheers of their friends and relatives on the platform. The cheers faded as the train pulled out of the station, but still Tibor kissed her.

The conductor cleared his throat. Jolan felt her face turn red as Tibor handed the conductor their tickets. She had never been kissed in such a public place before, and a few hours of marriage were not enough to make it seem less of an impropriety, no matter how much she enjoyed the kiss! She had not felt such a confusion of feelings since the day she met Tibor.

Tibor grinned at her embarrassment. "I promise to behave myself for the rest of the journey, Mrs. Nemeth."

Jolan flushed again at hearing her new name. "I think I'm sorry to hear that!" she murmured. Tibor laughed and kissed her hand.

"It won't be long, my love."

"But it's hours and hours to Niagara Falls."

"We're not going straight through to Niagara tonight. We're stopping in New York City."

"Tib!"

"It's Ron's wedding present—one night at the Seneca Hotel. We'll go on to Niagara tomorrow morning."

Jolan felt her face turn even redder. What had been furtive and forbidden this morning was now sanctioned and very public. A few words, an exchange of rings, a signature on a piece of paper—suddenly everything was different. How could such a thing be? Even her name had changed, yet Jolan felt no different from the girl she was this morning, having her last breakfast in Aunt Margit's kitchen. Now, she sat on this speeding train, with Tibor holding her gloved hand, yet she no longer needed to pull her hand away, or sit a few inches apart, and if he kissed her again in front of the rest of the passengers it might shock an elderly lady but the ring on her finger made it nothing more than a lapse in manners at worst.

They sat together, talking quietly, but mostly lost in thought, as the train stopped at New Brunswick, Metuchen, Rahway, Elizabeth, Newark, and finally entered the tunnel to New York City.

They emerged into the Pennsylvania Railroad Station, still crowded with people and open shops even though it was after eight o'clock. Tibor, carrying most of their bags, led the way to the busy street, where they took a cab for the short ride to the Seneca Hotel on Fifth Avenue. Jolan felt very small and self-conscious as they entered the marble-paneled lobby and walked to the front desk. She watched Tibor register them as Mr. and Mrs. Tibor Nemeth, then glanced up at the desk clerk, sure he would be leering at them, but his face was bland as he handed Tibor the key and called "Front!"

A bellboy dressed in a maroon uniform with gold braid took their bags and led them to the elevator. When they got off at the 10th floor, he took the key from Tibor and opened the door onto a room more lavish than anything Jolan had ever seen. A bouquet of flowers stood on a credenza near a double bed with a blue satin bedspread. Jolan tried to look anywhere but at the bed as the bellboy turned on the lights and closed the drapes and handed the key back to Tibor. He touched his hand to his cap as Tibor tipped him and walked briskly to the door. Finally, Jolan and Tibor were alone.

Jolan stepped over to the bouquet and looked at the card. "It's from Ron," she said, her voice sounding artificially bright.

"Of course," said Tibor, his voice very close.

Jolan turned away from his outstretched arms. "I need to—um—freshen up," she said, thinking it was a ridiculous phrase for needing to use the toilet after a long train ride.

She went into the bathroom, mortified at the level of intimacy she was now thrust into. She felt as exposed as if the door had been made of cardboard. After using the toilet, she splashed cold water on her face, and rinsed her mouth, wondering if she should take her dress off, or let her hair down. And what was Tibor doing all this time?

How silly she was to feel this self-conscious after so many months of wanting and waiting. She took a deep breath and opened the door. Tibor was standing at the window. He had shut off all the lights but one and opened the drapes. He had taken off his jacket and removed his tie. And he had turned down the bed.

He turned from the window and smiled at her. "Come see the view," he said in a soft voice.

She took his outstretched hand and joined him. Below them, automobiles and taxicabs passed by looking like children's toys. The light of the street lamps far below, and the neon lights of stores and hotels, gave the sky an odd glow, even though it was fully night.

Jolan felt Tibor's hands on her shoulders, and experienced both a thrill of desire and an attack of shyness.

"Let me take your hair down," he whispered. She stood still as he removed the hairpins one by one, and then used his hands like a brush to lay the hair over her back and shoulders. She felt him rub his cheek against her hair and felt her body go weak as he began to kiss her hair, then he gently brushed it aside to expose the side of her neck. When he kissed her there she moaned and gripped the windowsill.

"Come with me, Mrs. Nemeth."

He led her to the bed, where he reached down and turned off the light.

"Better?"

"Yes, thank you." The room seemed totally dark at first, but her eyes quickly adjusted to the neon glow coming from the windows, and though he was silhouetted she could clearly see Tibor remove his shirt. With trembling hands she reached for the buttons at the back of her dress.

"Let me," he said, and putting his arms around her he fumbled with the tiny pearl buttons, chuckling at his own clumsiness. "My hands are shaking, too," he said, and she could hear the smile in his voice. And then he was serious. "I've never done this, you know."

Jolan smiled and put her hands on his chest. "I'm glad."

He slipped the dress down past her shoulders, letting it fall to the floor, then he did the same with her slip. She was wearing nothing but a silk teddy, a secret gift from Zsuzsi, and her rolled stockings. "Sit down," he said, and he knelt to pull off her stockings.

At the touch of his hands on her legs Jolan thought she would faint. It was like the day she had slipped from the ladder—like lightning running the length of her leg. *Like fire, Jolanka.*

"Oh, Tib," was all she had time to say before he was kissing her, as he had done so many times, but this time they didn't have to stop, and when he slipped the straps of her teddy off her shoulders to reveal her breasts it seemed the most natural and wonderful thing in the world for him to kiss her there.

And when they lay next to one another, naked, in the city lights, the rightness of it made all sense of shame go away, and she marveled at the feel of the hard muscles under his soft skin, at the smoothness of his chest and the roughness of the hair on his legs.

When he touched her she nearly cried with joy, but when he entered her she nearly cried out in pain.

Afterwards, as they lay in each other's arms, Tibor kissed her cheek and said, "I'm sorry I hurt you."

"It didn't hurt."

Tibor sat up. "Don't ever do that, Jolan. Don't lie to me about something like that. I know it hurt you—I hurt you—and that's bad enough without the lie."

"I know you didn't mean to, Tib. It just happens, at first. I'm sure it will feel better the next time."

He bent down to kiss her, and in a little while Jolan learned that the second time hurt, too, but not nearly so bad as the first, and the third time hardly hurt at all; in fact, by the third time it was beginning to feel very good indeed.

Chapter 23
July 1930

To Jolan, nothing in the world smelled as good as a baby fresh from the bath. She rubbed her nose on Aranka's soft back, and dusted her round bottom with Van Dyke's baby powder. Turning the baby over, Jolan kissed each small foot before pinning on a fresh diaper. She slipped an undershirt over the baby's head, and kissed each arm as she drew it through the armhole. She wrapped Aranka in a light cotton blanket, crocheted by Aunt Margit. It was too hot to put anything more on her, even though she would spend most of the day shaded by the hood of the baby carriage.

"Let me take her while you get ready," said Tibor.

He held the baby with the practice brought on by two and a half months of parenthood. Smiling, he lay Aranka in her carriage while Jolan changed from her housecoat into a summer dress. As she belted it she could see that she had regained most of her waistline. She doubted her stomach would ever lie as flat again, but the roundness of her abdomen was more than balanced by the fullness of her breasts. A fair trade, she thought. She put the bag holding Aranka's spare bottles and diapers over her shoulder, picked up the strawberry pie she had made the night before from the last of the season's berries, and joined Tibor on the porch.

With Tibor pushing the baby carriage, they walked the six blocks to Aunt Margit and Uncle Emil's house. Though it was not yet noon, heat made the sidewalk shimmer. By the time they arrived for the Fourth of July picnic Jolan's dress clung to her back and her feet felt like they were on fire, even though she wore open-toed shoes. The air had the sultry, dead feel to it that promised a thunderstorm later in the day.

Zsuzsi had arrived the night before, so they were all together for the holiday. Jolan went inside to put the pie in the icebox, and when she came out her daughter was being passed from Zsuzsi to Mrs. Kish, who cuddled and fussed over her until Uncle Emil took her. He smiled broadly at Aranka's chubby face, while Aranka stared at his beard, more flecked with gray than when Jolan had first seen it. Tibor brought Jolan a glass of lemonade, and they stood arm in arm, watching as Uncle Emil took the baby down the garden rows. What little lawn the garden had room for was covered by chairs and a grill Uncle Emil had made from cinderblocks and a piece of iron grate. A narrow walk of slates led from the grass to the garden proper. Jolan loved the garden at every time of year, but especially in summer, when it seemed ready to burst with beans and cabbages, tomatoes and peppers, small pickling cucumbers, summer squash. This year, thanks to a wet spring, the garden seemed especially green and lush. On either side the flower borders were vibrant with zinnias, cosmos, balsam, marigolds. At the very back of the garden, between the pear tree and lilac that marked the corners of the yard, forsythia made a solid wall of green. And at the very center of the garden stood Uncle Emil's pride and joy, his roses: one yellow with an edge of salmon, a second deep pink, a new bush pure white. Along the fence were the bushes he called Seven Sisters, which bloomed in clusters of small, dark red flowers. Their combined fragrance filled the yard with a sweet, fruity perfume.

"Emil, are you going to show that child every single cabbage, or are you going to start the fire?" asked Aunt Margit.

Emil kissed his great-niece before surrendering her to Jolan. While he got the fire started, the women brought out plates of sliced cucumber and onion, loaves of rye bread, and pickles. Next came a slab of *szalonna*, Hungarian bacon to grill over the fire, and a platter of the seasoned pork cutlets called *pecsenye*. Tibor cut the *szalonna* into squares and Mr. Kish impaled them on grilling forks, then the three men took charge of the cooking, turning the *szalonna* until it was crisp, letting the drippings soak into slices of Aunt Margit's homemade rye bread.

"I'll go in and feed Aranka while the men cook," Jolan said to Zsuzsi. She walked up the back stairs into the house, and went into the bedroom she and Zsuzsi had shared for so many years. She sat down on the double bed, unbuttoned her dress, and held Aranka to her breast, humming the song she remembered from her own childhood. "*Az a szep, az a szep,*" she hummed, "Sweet one, sweet one..."

In the kitchen, she could hear Mrs. Kish and Aunt Margit making iced coffee.

"Such a darling baby," said Mrs. Kish. "And doesn't Jolan look well!"

"It will be a miracle if that baby doesn't get prickly heat with this muggy weather," said Aunt Margit.

"They're predicting rain again for this evening. That should cool things down."

"Aunt Margit," called Tibor from the yard, "do you want your *szalonna* bread with cucumber or onion?"

"Both!" she answered. "Honestly! Shouting for all the neighbors to hear."

Mrs. Kish laughed. "Oh, he's a young man. What does he think of the neighbors! And he's a good young man. Married a whole year, and as in love now as the day they married. You can see it in their eyes, the way he looks at her, and she at him."

"Just like her mother," sighed Aunt Margit.

"Ah, to be young again..." Mrs. Kish's voice faded as she followed Aunt Margit out the back door.

And what was that supposed to mean, wondered Jolan as she moved the baby to her shoulder and patted her back. Aunt Margit so seldom mentioned Mama. Of course Mama looked at Papa the way she looked at Tibor. So what?

Aranka belched, so loudly that Jolan laughed. "Oh, sweetie, I wish you could meet your Grandmama. We sent her your picture, yes we did, and soon she'll write back to us. But it's not the same."

Jolan hugged the baby and kissed her cheek. No, it wasn't the same, but it looked like all they could do for the time being. Times were hard, and getting harder. Tibor taught Latin at St. Brendan's, and in the summer he did farm work, but they were just getting by. She knew she should be grateful he had a job, when so many men had lost theirs, but she'd hoped they could save enough money to bring Mama here. Jolan was beginning to think she'd never get to see her mother, not in the foreseeable future.

But today was not the day for thoughts about faraway relatives or the disastrous economy. Jolan buttoned her dress and walked outside, where the smell of *szalonna* competed with the scent of roses.

Zsuzsi took the baby from Jolan so she could eat. Tibor handed her a plate with a slice of *pecsenye* between two pieces of bread. The bread was rich with drippings, and the grilled and seasoned pork so flavorful that Jolan ate two sandwiches, followed by a slice of chocolate cake baked by Mrs. Kish.

By midafternoon Uncle Emil and Mr. Kish were dozing in their chairs while the women talked quietly among themselves, and Tibor grilled one last piece of bacon, slicing off the meat as it cooked. Jolan gently rocked the baby carriage with one foot, and Zsuzsi fanned herself.

"Why isn't it any cooler?" she wondered aloud, "if the sun is behind the clouds?"

Jolan squinted up at the sky. "How can you tell, with all the haze? The sky looks just as milky to me as it did an hour ago."

"No, it's getting quite gray." As if to punctuate Zsuzsi's observation, a distant roll of thunder grew louder and then faded.

"Well," said Aunt Margit. "Let's get everything into the house before it rains."

"It was just one little thunderclap," protested Jolan. "Maybe the storm will go the other way."

But a second boom of thunder sounded, louder than the first, making Uncle Emil stir in his sleep.

"That's that," said Aunt Margit getting up. "It's coming this way."

"More rain!" said Zsuzsi. "Just what we need. Wake up, Uncle Emil, your garden is about to be drowned again."

By the time they had brought the food inside and folded the tables and chairs, the first drops were falling in half-dollar-sized splashes. Mr. and Mrs. Kish thanked Margit and Emil and then went upstairs to their own apartment. Everyone else gathered in the living room as the raindrops fell faster and faster. Within moments it seemed that a solid wall of water pounded against the house. A flash of lightning, followed almost immediately by the crash of thunder, frightened Aranka. Tibor rocked her in his arms while Jolan and Zsuzsi shut windows, and then they watched the rain, listening to the roar of the water that was nearly as loud as Aranka's cries.

Then, as though some angel had turned off the heavenly tap, the rain slowed to a trickle, and stopped altogether. Thunder continued to rumble in the distance, but sounded fainter and fainter with each moment. Uncle Emil opened the living room windows again.

Jolan and Tibor said their goodbyes, taking advantage of the lull to go home. Outside the air was slightly cooler, though steam rose from the wet pavement, and the air had the sweet smell of city streets after a rain. So much water flowed toward the storm drains that Tibor and Jolan took their shoes off to cross the street. By the time they reached their own apartment a light rain was falling again, and more thunder had begun to sound.

While Tibor stowed the baby carriage in the hallway, Jolan went inside to change Aranka's diaper. Then she fed the baby once more, and put her in the crib for a nap, while Tibor took off his wet shirt and dried his hair.

"Here," he said, holding up a towel. "Unpin your hair and I'll dry it for you."

Lightning flashed as he gently rubbed Jolan's hair dry. Then he kissed her shoulder and cupped his hands around her breasts.

"I like the way your dresses fit these days."

Jolan smiled. "Enjoy it while you can. Once the baby is weaned I'm afraid everything will go back to normal."

He kissed the back of her neck. "The doctor said to wait eight weeks. It's been nearly ten."

"I think this is the first time we've both been awake at the same time she's been asleep."

"How can she sleep with this thunder and lightning?" he asked, unbuttoning Jolan's dress.

"She takes after her father," said Jolan.

"Who loves her mother very, very much," said Tibor, taking her into his arms, and they made love while outside lightning flashed and thunder crackled and rumbled, and Aranka thankfully slept through it all.

The next morning, Tibor went to work at the Staats farm, bicycling five miles up Kossuth Street. Beyond the city limits its name changed to Somerset Road, and it curved south and west to merge with the highway that led toward Trenton. Only the year before it had been paved for the whole length, and though the joints in the concrete made for a bumpy bike ride the surface was at least passable even on a rainy morning. Before the road was paved, Tibor would have to dodge the puddles, and arrive at work covered with mud, or else get up extra early to walk the five miles. They couldn't afford a car.

Jolan often wished he could find work closer to home, but the Amwells, whose field held their beloved wild daffodils, had a son and daughter and didn't need an extra hand. These days, Tibor was lucky to get any summer work at all. He enjoyed the milking, the haying, even learning to repair Mr. Staats' tractor. Last summer, when Jolan was pregnant, it was hard for her to get up before dawn to make him breakfast, but this summer Aranka was up and hungry so early that Jolan was awake regardless, and because she was busy feeding Aranka Tibor had begun to make their breakfast himself. Jolan, who had never been an early riser, now enjoyed the quiet moments the three of them shared before Tibor left for work.

After Tibor was on his way Jolan bathed the baby and put her down for a nap, then she cleaned the apartment, which was so small she was done with her chores by midmorning. On Monday she would do laundry, and soon enough Aranka would demand more of her time and attention, but for now she had nothing that needed doing. Before the baby came she had continued to work part-time at Eva's shop, and that occupied her afternoons; since the baby was born she'd had a steady stream of visitors. Aunt Margit stopped by every afternoon, and Uncle Emil visited on his way home from work. Neighbors often dropped in, all of whom helped with the baby and the chores while Jolan regained her strength. Yet except for being tired from lack of sleep, with a hungry infant to feed several times a night, Jolan was fully recovered now, and feeling well, to the point of restlessness. If the rain stopped she would put the baby in the carriage and walk to Eva's to visit.

But the rain didn't stop. Indeed, it rained so hard that Aunt Margit telephoned to say she was staying home. Jolan spent the afternoon dozing, or listening to the radio, until the third floor neighbor, Mr. Racz, came home from work and discovered that the roof was leaking. When Tibor came home he went into the attic to repair the roof.

On Sunday morning the rain continued. Aunt Margit and Uncle Emil went to the early Mass so they could watch Aranka while Jolan and Tibor went to church. They stayed all day, listening to the afternoon concert on the radio until lightning made the radio crackle with static.

"I've never seen so much rain," said Aunt Margit. "When is it going to stop?"

"They're predicting more for tomorrow," said Uncle Emil. "The river is already running high after two days of this. They're afraid it may flood."

"Is it prone to flooding?" asked Tibor. "Surely the river bank is high enough to prevent it."

"I'm told that it last flooded about thirty years ago," said Uncle Emil. "It gets high during a bad rain, but I've never seen it overflow the banks, myself. Yet it's been such a wet spring and summer that the ground is saturated. I suppose the water has to go somewhere."

"It's been a good year for mushrooms, I'll say that," said Tibor. "I'll stop on the way home tomorrow and pick some more."

296

Aranka began to cry.

"What's the matter, little one?" asked Jolan. "I just fed you an hour ago, and your diaper's dry."

"It must be the heat and humidity," said Aunt Margit, "making her fuss. Can you blame her? If this rain doesn't stop we'll sprout gills."

"Maybe it's time to build that ark, Tib," said Jolan.

Tibor looked out the window. "Maybe it is."

When it was clear the rain would not abate, Aunt Margit and Uncle Emil decided to leave. "We'll get wet no matter what, so we may as well go now," said Aunt Margit. "We have umbrellas so it won't be too bad."

They kissed and said goodbye, leaving Jolan and Tibor with Aranka, who still fussed so that Jolan picked her up to nurse.

"I guess she was hungry after all," said Tibor.

Jolan shook her head. "I think she's just bored. This gives her something to do."

Tibor sat on the couch next to them. "You look like a madonna," he said. He touched the baby's cheek, which was clammy and moist. He watched as a drop of perspiration rolled between the curves of Jolan's breasts, and wiped it off with his fingertip.

"Don't get ideas, I'm busy," said Jolan.

Tibor put his arm around her shoulder and kissed her earlobe. "She'll have to sleep sometime. I can wait."

Jolan smiled at Tibor's obvious desire for her. The physical part of being married to him was a source of joy she had never imagined. It was a luxury, this sensuality, to sit here with a baby suckling at her breast, and this tan and fit man she loved so much watching her with both love and lust in his eyes. Nothing could be more arousing than being wanted like this. She turned her head to him and opened her mouth for his kiss.

A small grunt from Aranka and an unmistakable odor put a quick end to that.

Tibor groaned. Jolan stood up, laughing, and went into the bedroom to change the baby's diaper.

The next morning Tibor put on his oilcloth slicker and bicycled to work. The morning was so dark with rain and clouds that Jolan carried the baby into bed to nurse her, and soon dozed off with Aranka in her arms. She was startled awake by the sound of Tibor's voice. She got up and walked into the living room, where her husband stood holding the telephone. He smiled at her and waved her in.

"Mr. Staats? Tibor Nemeth. I'm afraid I can't make it in, sir. Piscataway Creek has overflowed, and the state police have closed Somerset Road.... Yes, it was well over the banks. There must be two feet of water in the low part of the road. I couldn't even see the bridge surface....Yes, I expect so....Hello? Hello? Operator?"

He looked up at Jolan. "The line's gone dead."

"Your pants are soaking. Change your clothes or you'll catch a cold."

"I doubt that'll happen in this heat but I'm always happy to undress for you, ma'am."

Jolan took his wet clothes and draped them over the edge of the tub. "I'll wash these with the rest of our things, but first I have to do the diapers."

She was walking toward the diaper pail when the lights went out.

"Oh, no! How can I use the washing machine if there's no electricity?"

"Let's wait and see. It may come on in a few minutes," said Tibor.

Jolan made a fresh pot of coffee. "I'm glad stoves use gas. We'll have to heat water later for Aranka's bath if we don't get the power back."

But an hour and several cups of coffee later the power was still off. Jolan looked at Tibor in dismay. "We can make do with our own clothes until Thursday, but the diapers have got to be done today." Since the three residents of the building shared the single washing machine in the basement, Monday and Thursday were Jolan's washing days, while Tuesday and Friday were Mrs. Szabo's, and Mr. Racz washed on Wednesday and Saturday.

"I guess we'll have to do it the old fashioned way, by boiling them on the stove," said Tibor.

It was a smelly and unpleasant task. Tibor filled the metal washtub at the outdoor pump and carried it to the stove. While the water came to a boil, Jolan scrubbed the diapers on a washboard in the sink, put them in the tub to boil, and then rinsed them in bluing. After a batch was finished, Tibor carried them to the basement, where he put them through the wringer and hung them up in the light of a kerosene lantern. When the diapers were finished they had the rest of the baby's clothes to do. Aranka woke from her nap and fussed for most of the day, so that one of them was always trying to soothe the baby, while the other was either hauling water or clothing or scrubbing or stirring. The hard work, the heat in the kitchen, and the baby's cries put Jolan's nerves on edge and strained Tibor's good nature.

They were nearly done when Tibor stumbled in the dark basement and dropped a load of clean clothes on the floor near the coal bin. He brought them back upstairs as Jolan was changing Aranka. The sight of them made her burst into tears.

"Don't worry, I'll do them over myself," snapped Tibor. Then he rubbed his back and walked over to Jolan. "I'm sorry. I'm angry at my own clumsiness. I shouldn't have spoken that way to you."

"It's not just that!" sobbed Jolan. "It's everything—the everlasting diapers, and the heat, and the rain, and she keeps fussing." Tibor took her in his arms. "This is the worst day of my life! When will it stop?"

Tibor kissed her hair and held her tighter. "It makes haying look easy, I'll tell you that. And I'll never think teaching Latin is hard work, ever again."

He kissed her once more and went back to the stove. Jolan wiped her face with a wet washcloth and went back to the baby. By the time the laundry was done and the baby bathed and fed, Jolan and Tibor were too tired and hot to even think of cooking. She pulled some cold meat from the icebox and sliced some bread for sandwiches.

Uncle Emil stopped by, despite the rain.

"You two look exhausted," he said. "What have you been doing?"

"Diapers," Tibor and Jolan said in unison. Uncle Emil grimaced.

"I came to tell you that the whole city is without power, and it looks like we'll be without it until the rain stops. The river has overflowed the banks and Water Street is flooding. So is every street east of here that's low enough. I've seen it. A terrible thing."

"Are the telephones still out?" asked Tibor.

Emil nodded. "And the telegraph. But before it went out a message came through that it may stop raining tonight, and if so, the worst of the flooding will be tomorrow. How the river can get any higher I don't know, but it will."

"What about the people who live next to the river?" asked Jolan.

"They're being evacuated. The Red Cross has them going to the high school for tonight. I've never seen such a thing, I tell you."

He kissed Jolan and shook Tibor's hand. "I must be going. Stay dry, if you can."

After he left, Tibor and Jolan sat on the couch, holding hands, while the dim daylight faded into dusk, and then darkness, punctuated by an occasional flash of distant lightning. Sometime during the night, Jolan woke. They were still on the couch, Tibor slumped in the corner, Jolan leaning against his shoulder. She lay still for a moment, thinking Aranka must have cried out, but she heard nothing. Then she realized it was the silence that had awakened her.

"Tib!" she whispered. "Tib, wake up."

Tibor stirred and reached for her.

"Tib—listen!"

"What is it? What's wrong?"

"Nothing—just listen."

He opened his eyes. "I don't hear anything." Then he sat up. "It's stopped!"

They stood up and walked through the kitchen to the back porch. Drops fell from the roof, landing with a plop on the wide leaves of the hostas on either side of the porch. All around them they could hear water dripping from the leaves of trees, from the eaves, and a slow trickle in the downspouts, but the incessant pounding of raindrops was finally over.

"Ah, the air smells good tonight," said Tibor.

"Maybe the sun will come out tomorrow," said Jolan.

"Maybe. I'll get up at the usual time and try to get to work. I doubt I'll get through, but I should try."

"Then we should go back to bed. But let's open all the windows first."

They tried not to waken Aranka, but the wood was swollen on many of the windows, so they squeaked as Tibor forced them open. Jolan changed and fed her, and then they all fell asleep for the remainder of the night.

Tibor left the house without waking Jolan, but by the time he came back she was awake—and the lights were on.

"Somerset Road is still closed, as I suspected. When did the power come back?"

"About half an hour ago. The light woke me up. Isn't it wonderful?"

"It is indeed."

After breakfast Jolan gave Aranka a bath, and suggested they go for a walk. They met Mr. and Mrs. Szabo in the hall.

"Are you going to see the flood?" Mrs. Szabo asked. "Everyone's going down there."

Jolan looked at Tibor. "Well, I had planned on just a walk around the block, but we all need an airing out today."

"Let's go," said Tibor.

They went out together, onto the street where many families were walking toward the river. Hardenberg was built on a hill, with St. Brendan's church the high point of the city. Its steeple was visible for miles to anyone coming toward the town. To the north and east the city blocks sloped gently toward the river, to the flood plain where the city was founded nearly three hundred years before. Several square blocks of houses and shops, including Water Street, constituted the oldest part of the city. Houses were built right up to the riverbank, a small bluff on the Hardenberg side, but considerably higher on the northern bank.

It was the oldest and poorest part of town, an area Jolan hadn't been to since Trudy moved away. It was odd to see roadblocks set up by the sheriff's men, with a crowds of onlookers gathered to see beyond them. Jolan led Tibor, who was pushing Aranka's carriage, to the roadblock at the very end of Water Street.

Tibor whistled in surprise. "Now I know why it's called Water Street."

Jolan remembered the street as a narrow one, with only about a dozen houses on either side, no front yards, only a few weedy trees to break up the monotonous pattern of lopsided porches. Trudy's house was only the third from the riverbank, and Jolan remembered walking on that bank, looking down at the dirty river that flowed smoothly from west to east with the outgoing tide.

Trudy's house was gone. There was no riverbank. Instead, a swirling mass of brown water swept past just yards from the roadblock. Maybe half a dozen houses still stood on either side of the street, the furthest in water higher than the first-floor windows. Debris piled up against the houses: pieces of lumber, whole trees, household goods; the water carried more of it downstream, moving faster than any river Jolan had ever seen.

When she could take her eyes from the scene she looked up at the low clouds, blowing in gray shreds, getting thinner by the moment. Soon the sun would be visible, and a blue sky, but when Jolan looked at the river swollen to nearly three times its normal size she saw nothing but a brown horror, sweeping away possessions and livestock, even entire homes. An act of God, they called it.

It hurt Jolan to think that God would have any part of this.

Tibor

Chapter 24
June 1934

Tibor collected the last of the senior English exams and stuffed them into an already overflowing briefcase. He closed the windows and lowered the shades, then stood for a moment looking at the room before shutting off the lights. Every June he felt the same way, both melancholy and relief at the end of the term. He had come to love the smell of chalk dust, the way the radiators clanged every winter, the neat rows of desks, each with an inkwell in the upper right-hand corner. In September he was full of zeal for the coming year, another class of young minds, another round of Latin declensions and bad translations of Caesar. By the end of the school year his zeal was long since overtaken by frustration, only partly at the young minds that were not always receptive to his teaching, but also at his own failure to accomplish all he wanted. Would he never be satisfied? Probably not. He shook his head, smiled at his own foolish desire for perfection, and turned off the lights.

His steps echoed in the empty hall as he left St. Brendan's. Outside, he loosened his tie and walked toward home on a sidewalk that shimmered with heat. He had only to grade this last set of examination papers and attend graduation. In the past he had always looked forward to the summer recess and work on the Staats farm. He'd always liked physical labor, didn't mind working long hours, and enjoyed country air that smelled of hay and cow manure. Dairy cows were easy to work with; most had gentle dispositions, and a love of routine. All the farm animals had traits that Tibor liked, even chickens, among the silliest creatures God made. One of them liked to perch on the handlebars of his bicycle, and Tibor often took it for a short ride before leaving at the end of the day. But there would be no bike rides for chickens this summer.

Last summer Mr. Staats had lost his farm. In March, one of his sons had been killed when the tractor rolled over on him, and after that Mr. Staats lost all desire to work the farm. When the bank foreclosed, his remaining son persuaded the old man to move west with him, and they left for California that July. Luckily Mr. Amwell employed Tibor two days a week for the remainder of July and August, though he really didn't need the help, paying him with milk and eggs instead of cash. But this summer he couldn't use Tibor at all. He'd had to sell off half his stock to keep the farm, and with a teenaged son and daughter had all the labor force he needed after that. Tibor had taken odd jobs, when he could find them—a dollar for sweeping out the corner grocery store three times a week, a dollar fifty for pumping gas at the Somerset Esso when the regular man was ill. But odd jobs were scarce this year, when more and more men were out of work, and fewer shopkeepers could afford to pay. Van Dyke's had cut wages. Even Uncle Emil had had to cut back. Many of his advertisers had gone bankrupt, and he could afford to publish his newspaper just twice a week instead of daily.

Times were harder than Tibor had ever known. Now two years since Roosevelt took office, the Depression still had a firm grip on the economy. And the current drought made things worse. Crops that only a year before were plowed under in an attempt to raise prices were expected to fail throughout the Midwest. People already stood on lines at soup kitchens—what would the winter be like?

A small form bursting out the front door and down the steps distracted Tibor from his gloomy thoughts.

"Daddy!" shouted Aranka. He picked her up and hugged her close.

Jolan stood in the doorway with Vendel in her arms. Tibor smiled. This was what he lived for, his family that filled him with such happiness. Every day he woke with a prayer of thanks for his wife and two children. To think he had almost missed having them!

He walked up the steps with his daughter in his arms. Vendel reached out to him and Tibor took him from Jolan, while managing to give her a kiss at the same time.

"I'll get your book bag for you," she said, while Tibor cuddled his four-year-old daughter and two-year-old son. They walked inside together, and Tibor sat down on the couch with a child on either side. This had become a ritual, Aranka pulling at his jacket and Vendel tugging at his tie until he removed both and sat back, looking like their familiar father again. Jolan brought him a glass of lemonade.

"If you're finished with being a playground for your children, are you ready to listen to your wife? I have good news, and I've been waiting just as eagerly as they to have you home."

"Well, I can always use good news," said Tibor.

"A man from the PWA office stopped by today. He said they can use you on the new dam. You're to go to their office tomorrow to find out when to start, and where."

306

Tibor reached for Jolan's hand. "That is good news indeed. I've been dreading another summer of odd jobs."

"I know. He said they can use only a few men who are not on relief, and only men with families. He said the dam will not only prevent another flood, it will create a small lake right here at Hardenbergh, and so the railroad and highway bridges will have to be lengthened. It'll mean several years work, so that's why they can take men like you."

"Thank God! But where is there room for a lake?" said Tibor, as he put his arm around Vendel.

"Where the houses used to be, on Water Street. The ones that washed away in the flood. It will be a long narrow lake, but still wider than the riverbed. One block of old warehouses will have to be demolished, and the water will cover the whole low-lying area beyond, that marshy pasture land east of town."

"Even that land is pretty dry, this year. It seems funny to worry about the river flooding again with such a bad drought."

"That's the best part about the project—people's homes will be protected, and the city can use the lake as a reservoir for water. There's something about it in the evening paper, but I haven't had time to read it yet. That reminds me—Uncle Emil called this afternoon, to say he'll be stopping by later on."

Tibor lifted Aranka onto his lap and she rested her head against his chest. "Someone didn't take a nap this afternoon?" he asked.

"No—it was so hot she couldn't sleep."

Tibor began rocking Aranka while Vendel slid off the couch to get his blocks.

"Funny that Emil called," he said. "He stops by often enough without calling first."

"I think he just wanted to make sure you would be home this afternoon. Is she asleep? Let's put her to bed and then I'll fix you something to eat."

Tibor stood up carefully and carried Aranka into the bedroom. He put her in the middle of the bed and kissed her forehead. At night she slept in a small trundle bed that was rolled underneath their own bed during the day. Vendel slept in her old crib, in a corner of the bedroom, but since he'd already napped he was happily building towers of blocks in the parlor.

Emil arrived shortly after Aranka woke from her nap. She did not make the transition from sleep to wakefulness well, so that when Emil walked in she was crying, and that made Vendel cry, which made for a few chaotic moments.

"Everything all right?" he asked once the children were given milk and graham crackers.

Jolan patted Aranka's head. "She's just out of sorts because it's hot and she didn't get her nap on schedule. How are you, Uncle Emil? You look tired. What can I get you?"

"Nothing, thank you, my dear. Why don't you sit down? You don't have to treat me like company."

Aranka climbed in his lap. "Cookie?" she offered.

"Why thank you." He took a bite of the soggy graham cracker. "Mmm. Very good."

He made a face over Aranka's head, and Jolan laughed. "Let me get you some lemonade to wash that down."

As soon as the children were finished with their snack, Jolan sent them into the yard to play. She and the two men sat on the back porch to supervise.

"What is it, Emil? You look worried," said Tibor.

Emil pulled out his pipe and began to fill it from the pouch of tobacco he always carried. Tibor recognized this as a delaying tactic and looked over at Jolan, who frowned and shook her head. Something was wrong.

Finally Emil had the pipe lit. He folded the tobacco pouch and returned it to his pocket, puffed on the pipe for a moment, and then sighed.

"You both know, of course, that your aunt and I lost all our savings in the crash."

"Yes," said Jolan.

"I'm not complaining, you understand, it happened to many, many people. Everyone is in the same boat, so to speak. And really, it hasn't been so bad for us. God has watched over us, and we have enough food on the table. Oh, we've had to cut back here and there but nothing drastic. But now...." He paused.

"What is it, Emil?" asked Tibor.

"It's the press. It breaks down practically every day. It's so old, you see. I bought it used, it's over thirty years old. I can't get parts for it anymore, and to fix it is just to throw good money after bad. It just doesn't make sense. If I want the *Hirlap* to continue, I'll have to buy a new press."

"Of course the *Hirlap* must continue!" said Jolan. "It's an institution now."

"Well, my choices are to retire and close the *Hirlap*—no one would buy it, not these days—or to get a new press."

"The community needs your voice, Emil," said Tibor. "What would it take to buy a new press?"

"Several thousand," said Emil. His voice shook. "I can't borrow that kind of money. I've tried—the Savings and Loan said they couldn't risk it. Not until the Depression eases. But Georg Nagy did make me one offer." He looked first at Jolan, then at Tibor. "He is willing to buy my share of the house."

"That's good, isn't it?" asked Jolan.

Emil took two or three puffs on his pipe. "He doesn't want to keep these old apartments. He's just interested in the property." Emil stared at the small grassy yard. "I'm sorry. Once the property is his, you'll have only thirty days."

Tibor felt as though a chunk of ice had grown in the pit of his stomach. Where would they live? They couldn't afford a house of their own, and apartments were scarce. Plus they'd never find one that would accept the nominal rent he paid Emil and Margit. And with the building of the dam, and so many men coming to work on it, it would be even more difficult. He looked at Emil, who had tears in his eyes.

"I just don't know what else to do," whispered Emil.

Jolan looked stunned. She stared at the children playing in the yard. Tibor wondered if she felt the same panic he did.

He cleared his throat. "Emil, I understand. The paper is important, especially in times like these. I know you don't have any other choice." He took the older man's hand. "We'll manage. Don't worry about us. You do what you have to do."

"Yes, Uncle Emil, we'll be fine," said Jolan, but Tibor could hear the insincerity in her voice.

Emil stayed only a few more minutes, then left to inform their upstairs neighbors. Tibor saw him out, and then came into the kitchen, where Jolan was rinsing their glasses. He picked up a dishtowel.

"It's not such a bad thing," she said in a falsely bright voice. "We're already crowded in this little place, and I seem to be late again."

"Late for what?"

She looked at Tibor with a raised eyebrow. "Tibor, this month, it's late. I—I missed last month, too, but I thought it might just have been from worry, or something." She nodded as his eyes grew wide. "I don't have any morning sickness, you see, so I wasn't sure, but missing two months in a row must mean number three is on the way."

Tibor wrapped his arms around her. The last two times she had announced she was pregnant his reaction had been unqualified joy. This time, the joy was tempered by fear. He tried not to let it show in his voice.

"We'll manage. I have the PWA job, and we'll find a place. It'll be fine, everything will be fine," he said, as Jolan began to cry.

Tibor woke the next morning thanking God and President Roosevelt for the PWA. He repeated his thanks every morning as he boarded the bus that drove him and the other local workers to the construction site. A tent city had been erected to house many of the workers who came from farther away. Hundreds of men were involved in the project. Since Tibor had no engineering background or experience with heavy equipment, and since he was not in a union, he became one of a small army that hauled dirt by wheelbarrow. The men worked a six-hour day in two shifts to take advantage of the long summer days and to employ as many men as possible. Tibor was on the first shift, and spent his afternoons at home, reading the paper for apartment ads, occasionally going to see apartments, always coming home disappointed. Most apartments were no bigger than the one he and Jolan lived in now, or were in a rundown section of town, or were large enough but cost too much rent. Tibor's salary as a schoolteacher was low, and as an unskilled worker on the dam he made only fifty cents an hour.

Mr. Racz moved out of the building at the end of June, to a rooming house where his meals were provided and his rent was lower. Mrs. Puskasz came downstairs every day to fret and complain. Her husband was to retire at the end of the year. Where would they go? What would they do? Every day, the same questions, but no answers.

"For goodness' sake, she's driving me crazy," said Jolan one afternoon as Tibor rubbed her back. "I cringe when I hear footsteps on the stairs."

"I know, me too," said Tibor. "Let's be patient, my love. Something has got to come along. I know it will."

But in spite of his words Tibor was worried. Each day brought them closer to the start of school, when his days would be filled, with no time left to look for a place to live. Jolan could hardly take over, with the little ones and another coming. This pregnancy seemed harder on Jolan than the first two. She'd had no morning sickness at all, but then the backaches had started, making it difficult for her to keep up with the children. By the time Tibor came home from the construction site, Jolan was so weary she needed to lie down. Tibor would rub her back, and then take over with the children, making their lunch, putting them down for a nap. While they slept he would go out for an hour's worth of house hunting, but he could accomplish little in such a short time.

The heat made it even harder. He and Jolan were both short tempered, and the children were cranky. There had been no new apartment ads in the morning paper. He couldn't ever remember feeling so helpless.

All the while construction continued. Tibor had never seen anything built on such a large scale. Though his point of view was limited to the contents of a wheelbarrow, all around him mountains of dirt were constructed or pulled down. So the dam's foundations could be laid down, a temporary earthen dam had to be constructed to divert the river. Steam shovels and other heavy equipment were used as well as hundreds of laborers like Tibor. He imagined that from the air they must look like a swarm of ants streaming over an anthill. That anyone had a plan for this chaos, a vision of what the final product would look like, and an understanding of each step in between, was incomprehensible to him.

The contents of one wheelbarrow were easier to understand, or working with a pickaxe to dislodge clumps of heavy clay. The need that drove the men to this kind of work was also easy to understand. On the bus that ferried them to and from the work site, or during their break, he got to know the men he worked with. Probably three-quarters of them had families, some locally, some much farther away. Some of the men were so thin from hunger Tibor wondered how they could even swing a pickaxe. Their desperate gratitude for this hard and dirty work frightened him.

In mid-July Emil told them that settlement would take place by the end of the month. That night Tibor dreamed that he and Jolan had become hoboes, living in a boxcar with two children in rags. A chilly wind blew through the open door of the car, and as the train sped through the night Tibor looked out but he could see no lights at all. Suddenly,

Jolan screamed in pain. "The baby is coming!" she cried. "Tibor, help me! Help me!" "I can't," he whispered, and then he jumped.

Tibor woke with his heart drumming in his chest. The gray light of dawn shone through the open windows. He got up, and leaned on the windowsill, taking deep breaths of the warm and humid air. Then he knelt down, suddenly ashamed that for weeks he'd been thinking only of what he could do, instead of asking for help. He'd let his pride in being a husband and father overwhelm him, and had almost forgotten that he was also a son. Tibor bowed his head and prayed, then went to work that morning at peace, knowing that the solution to his problems was in far more capable hands.

That afternoon Emil called after supper, asking Tibor to come over. Jolan elected to stay home since the walk was too much for her back, so Tibor kissed her and said he'd be home as soon as possible. Emil was waiting on the porch when he arrived.

"Come," he said, walking down the steps. "Let's go up the street."

His eyes twinkled in a way that Tibor had not seen all summer. "Has something happened, Emil? Some good news? You seem so...eager," said Tibor.

Emil nodded. "I've been trying and trying to think what we can do, especially now that Jolan is expecting. How is she, by the way?"

"Her back hurts."

"Hm," Emil said. This was a subject far away from his expertise. "Well, give her my best wishes, and when you go home give her a back rub. So, let me tell you what I've been doing. I know how difficult it has been for you, but all this apartment hunting is no good, no good at all, not with a third child coming."

"It's all we can afford," said Tibor. "Surely you're not suggesting I look at houses? I can't afford the rent on a house, even if one were available."

"No, no, too costly, I know. But there may be a third option. I have been going over the proceeds from my share of the building, and I compared them with the purchase price of the new equipment. And, thank the Lord, there's a small surplus."

They stepped off the end of the sidewalk and onto the street at the edge of the woods near Amwell's farm. Tibor always took a deep breath when he walked here, in part because the scent of honeysuckle was so strong at this time of year, but mostly because it felt so good to leave behind the houses and sidewalks of Hardenbergh.

He waved to Henry Amwell, who was walking across the pasture toward them.

"What are you going to do, Emil? Expand the paper back to a daily?"

"No, my boy, I'm going to buy you an acre of land."

"What?" Tibor could not keep the surprise out of his voice.

"Hello, Mr. Amwell!" called Emil.

"Mr. Molnar. Tibor."

The men shook hands.

"I was just telling Tibor about the acre you're willing to sell."

"That's right," said Amwell. "Tibor, you know how small my herd is these days, so I can afford to lose a bit of pasture. But I need some ready cash right now. I need a new cultivator, because mine is so old if I try to sharpen the disks anymore they'll disappear. Your uncle tells me you're looking for a place to build a house."

"Build!" Tibor looked at Emil with astonishment.

"Of course," said Emil. "It costs too much to buy, but you need a house for a growing family. So you'll build one."

"Wait a minute! It's not so easy as that! And," he lowered his voice, speaking in Hungarian. "I can't take your money, or have you spend it on me."

"Nonsense. I owe it to you. But we'll discuss that later," Emil said, then more loudly, in English, "Where exactly did you say the land was, Mr. Amwell?"

Amwell pointed to his left. "Right here, along the fence, would do fine. It's flat enough for a house and garden, and if you'll help me fence off the other two sides, Tibor, I'll let you have the wood from that old barn, the one the roof collapsed on last winter. The roof's a total loss but the siding will do nicely for you."

"But—"

"That's a kind offer, Mr. Amwell," said Emil. "Mr. Nagy and I will complete our business within a few days. With your permission I'll have a deed drawn up, and you and I can complete this transaction as soon as possible."

"Fine with me," said Amwell. "Tibor?"

"I don't know what to say. I—thank you, I—"

"It's fine with both of us," said Emil. "We'll work out the details on the way home. Thank you, Mr. Amwell." He held out his hand. Amwell shook hands with Emil, and then with Tibor, and then touched his hat as he turned away.

"Emil, I can't possibly—"

"Make an old man happy, Tibor. It's the only solution, and it will get Margit out of church for a change. I've lost count of the novenas she's said for you and Jolan."

As Tibor opened his mouth to object again, Emil put up his hand. "It's not charity. Since I'm the one who's evicted you in the first place, I feel responsible. You're my family, Tibor. Besides, you'll have to do the work almost single-handed, although I'm sure Sandy will be willing to help. I'm afraid I'm too old for heavy construction work but I'll do what I can."

They walked along in silence. "You're far from old, Emil," Tibor finally said, but his voice broke on the words, and he turned away, trying to blink away the tears in his eyes. "I was getting desperate," he whispered.

Emil patted him on the shoulder and walked toward the fence, where he leaned back and made a great show of filling his pipe.

When Tibor was able to look up he saw Emil watching a robin hunt for worms on the grassy shoulder. Emil smiled after exhaling a cloud of pipe smoke, and the smile reached his eyes until they gleamed. Tibor hadn't seen him this relaxed and happy in months. Emil's solution was good not just for Tibor and his family, but also for Emil himself.

"Thank you, *Kerris Papa*," said Tibor. "You're a good man, Emil. You're like a father to me."

Emil grinned and clapped Tibor on the back. "Let's go home."

On the way they began making plans. Tibor could work on the house each afternoon, of course, and the days would be long for several more weeks, allowing Sandy to help out after work, if he was willing. They would start small, to have a roof overhead before the weather turned cold. A kitchen, a parlor, a bedroom for the children and one for him and Jolan would be enough to get started. They would add bedrooms as the children grew. Tibor would have to excavate at least two feet for the foundations, forgoing a basement; it was just too much work to dig deep enough in the rocky clay. The city sewer lines did not extend this far, but an outhouse would serve temporarily, and Tibor could put in a cesspool the following summer. The one thing he couldn't do by himself was drill a well. But the solution to that problem would come in time, he had no doubt. Not after what happened today.

Chapter 25
September 1934

Tibor swore as he nicked his finger for the third time. He was, on this fine late-summer afternoon, not working on his own house but instead was in the basement of Emil's house, helping Margit stretch curtains. This was something Jolan would normally help with, but she was having a difficult pregnancy, and so Tibor was "volunteered" to help. It wouldn't take too long, he reasoned, and it would give him a break from house construction. As much as he liked the smell of freshly cut wood, and the feel of a hammer striking true on a nail, he sometimes felt as though the project would never end. But he hadn't bargained on this.

He sucked the tip of his thumb, not willing to risk Margit's wrath if he should bloody one of her freshly washed sheer curtains. Then he continued to stretch the thin material on the wooden frame that was studded with nails, points facing out. According to Margit and Jolan this procedure was necessary to keep the curtains from shrinking, but Tibor thought it was a contraption meant to torture any man who attempted to use it. The spacing of the nails was clearly intended for the thinner—and more practiced—fingers of a woman. He couldn't believe that Margit and Jolan went through this process every spring and fall.

"What did you say, Tibor?" asked Margit as she walked by with another armful of curtains.

"Sorry—I didn't realize I'd spoken aloud. I was thinking that you do this for spring and fall cleaning."

"Ha! I should be so lucky," said Margit. "It's been once a month, all summer. Leave the windows open and in comes dust and dirt from that dam and bridge construction. My house is filthy."

Tibor knew Margit's house was spotless, as usual, despite the dirt she imagined coming through the windows. In the winter she'd complain about soot from coal furnaces blowing in every time the door was opened. He wondered how she would manage if she were living as he and Jolan were doing right now. The Amwells generously let them have a room in their farmhouse, but Tibor had also erected a tent, and on fine summer nights it was cooler to sleep outdoors than in the farmhouse. "Living like hoboes," Margit complained. The children, of course, thought it great fun, and Jolan said she didn't mind, but Tibor was anxious to make a home for her and the children. It had taken most of August to dig deep enough to set the foundation piers, once he'd finished digging postholes for Mr. Amwell's fence. The house plans hadn't seemed large, but when Tibor began digging out what would become the crawlspace, he felt like he was excavating for Mr. Van Dyke's mansion.

Every afternoon, after putting in his morning at the dam, Tibor would begin work on his own construction project, with help from Sandy or the Amwells two or three evenings a week. Even Ferenc had pitched in, the last time he was home on leave from the army. Tibor had lost count of the wheelbarrows of rocks he'd hauled away, but at last the concrete foundation piers were in place, and then the floor joists.

They'd had to vacate their old apartment by the end of August. Amwell allowed them to store much of their furniture in a corner of his barn, and their few valuables—some china and silver pieces—were safely in Emil's attic. The new owner did have their old building demolished, but Tibor was able to salvage the kitchen appliances for use in the new house. These, too, were stored in the barn. In the meantime, he and Jolan and the children were either squeezed into a small farmhouse bedroom or were literally camping on their land. It would be all right for another few weeks, as long as the weather stayed warm. Tibor thought that he could finish the framing and have a roof overhead by the end of October. The house would be far from finished, but at least they'd have shelter when the weather turned cold.

He wiped his brow. On a day as warm as this it was hard to imagine winter. He finished stretching the curtains and gave Margit a kiss goodbye. "I'm glad you don't have any more curtain frames, Margit. I don't think I'd have any fingertips left if you did."

"Practice will make perfect," she threatened. "I'll let you know when they're dry and you can help with the next batch."

"I look forward to it," Tibor said with a straight face. But when he escaped outside he grinned. He'd rather hammer a nail than stretch a curtain on it. He walked out past Emil's garden, whose plants had wilted somewhat in the strong sunlight. But the soil was fertile, thanks to Emil's religious composting, and the plants would perk up when the sun went down, although he knew Emil would welcome more rain for the tomatoes and peppers. More rain would not benefit Tibor, though, and he felt guilty about preferring the lengthening drought. He didn't like to think about how a rainy autumn would delay construction.

It took only a few minutes for Tibor to ride his bicycle to the new house. He felt a mix of pride and trepidation when he saw the former pastureland now fenced in for his family, and the floor joists of his new home. By this time next year there would be a garden, and perhaps a fruit tree or two, Oxheart cherries, like the ones he'd had growing up. As he got off the bicycle and opened the gate, he smelled the pleasant, astringent fragrance of freshly cut wood. The physical work was always a joy to him, whether he was sawing a joist or hammering a two-by-four into place. Yet he was doing most of the work by himself, and the magnitude of the task was daunting. Of late, his morning and evening prayers had been most fervent.

Jolan was watching the children as they played in the brook. She stood up when she saw Tibor, and walked slowly toward him, her right hand bracing the small of her back. He waved and began to nail down the first floorboard. He had nailed down three boards by the time she walked through the back gate. She stood for a moment, leaning heavily on the gatepost. She was at the midpoint of her pregnancy, but not yet showing as much as she had with the other two children.

"How did you do with the curtains?" she asked.

"I have more holes in my fingers than this board has," he answered. He looked closely at her. "Are you all right?"

"It's just the heat," she said. "And I think lunch disagreed with me. I'm just going to the outhouse."

Tibor nodded and went back to nailing floorboards. The outhouse was the very first thing he'd constructed on the site, but he wanted to install a cesspool before the ground froze, if he could manage it. The children—once they were persuaded to use the outhouse at all—thought it rather an adventure, but he hated for Jolan to use it, though she'd never once complained. Just a few more weeks, he thought. A bathroom will be the first room with walls and a door.

He paused to wipe his brow, and then walked over to the outhouse. Jolan had been in there too long, and it was brutally hot inside. He knocked on the door.

"Jolan? Are you all right?"

The door opened and Jolan stepped out. She stumbled, and Tibor grabbed her to keep her from falling. Her face was gray.

"Tib—help me—I'm bleeding."

Tibor eased her to the ground, trying to ignore the stab of fear in his gut.

"I'll go in the house and call the doctor. I'll only be a moment."

She nodded, crossing her arms over her stomach. "Hurry."

He vaulted the fence and raced for the farmhouse. "God, please God..." he thought. He leaped onto the back stoop and opened the screen door.

"Mrs. Amwell! Help!"

Mrs. Amwell came into the hall, wiping her hands on her apron. "What on earth?"

"I must use your phone—the doctor—for Jolan." He was already past her and in the kitchen by the time he finished speaking.

"I'll go to her," said Mrs. Amwell.

Tibor took the earpiece off the hook and cranked the handle of the old-fashioned telephone. "Operator? Get me Doctor Hajdu. He's on the Kilmer exchange."

He leaned against the wall, waiting for the doctor's office to answer. He'd interrupted Mrs. Amwell's canning; a dozen jars were arranged on the kitchen table, packed with string beans, ready for their lids. Tibor noticed all this with one part of his mind while another part screamed for the doctor to answer the phone.

Finally the doctor's office answered. "It sounds like a miscarriage. Get her to the hospital right away," Doctor Hajdu said when Tibor explained what was happening.

"I have no car—wait! I'll borrow Amwell's truck."

"I'll meet you there," said Doctor Hajdu, but Tibor had already hung up.

He ran into the yard, where Mrs. Amwell knelt beside Jolan.

"Mrs. Amwell, I must get Jolan to the hospital. Your husband's truck—"

"Take it," she said. "Hurry."

Tibor picked Jolan up. "You'll be all right—we're going to the hospital now."

Mrs. Amwell held the gate open for him.

"It's a good thing you're so strong. She'd never be able to walk," said Mrs. Amwell. "And don't worry about the children. I'll take them into the house with me as soon as you're gone."

She chattered on, out of nerves, and Tibor wished she would go away, but he needed her to open the door of the truck. By the time he placed Jolan on the seat and gotten the truck started his hands were shaking. He wiped his face on the rolled-up sleeve of his shirt and drove as quickly as he dared.

It wasn't more than two miles to Hardenbergh Hospital, but there were several stoplights on the way. Tibor leaned on the horn and swerved to get past the traffic. Jolan sat silently, gripping the seat with one hand, the truck door with the other.

"Just a moment more, love, and Doctor Hajdu will take care of you."

Jolan began to weep. "What can he do? We're losing it! We're losing our baby! Oh!" she screamed as he stopped in front of the emergency entrance.

"Help me, please!" he called. "My wife is in pain!"

Two orderlies came out with a stretcher and together they lifted Jolan onto it.

"We'll take her in—you need to move that truck," one orderly said.

Tibor ground the gears as he slammed the truck into reverse. He moved it to a space on the street and ran back to the hospital, arriving at the same time as Doctor Hajdu.

"Doctor, she's bleeding, badly! You've got to save her!"

"I'll take care of her," the doctor said. "You need to sit down with a cool drink and wait. You look like you're going to drop from heat prostration, and that won't do your wife any good. I'll let you know as soon as I can."

Tibor sank into a chair in the corridor and held his head in his hands. The front of his pants were stained with blood. So was the seat of Amwell's truck. So much blood! How much could she lose and still be all right? *Dear God, let her be all right,* he prayed. *Don't let her hemorrhage. Women could die when they hemorrhaged during childbirth. Don't take her from me. Please don't take her. Don't.*

But this wasn't childbirth. In all probability it was a miscarriage. Yet all his prayers were for Jolan, none for their child.

With horror, he realized that he wanted the baby to die, if it meant saving Jolan. If he was praying for her life, then he was also praying for his own child's death.

He began to weep. It had all gone wrong, right from the start. They should have loved this baby, wanted this baby, instead of worrying about the apartment. It was a baby, a blessing, a gift, yet all they thought of was money and a roof overhead, as though the baby were an obstacle to be overcome. And Jolan had had so much trouble with backaches...now God was punishing them for being ungrateful for His gift. They'd been so selfish. So many people were in desperate straits, truly homeless, itinerant, out of work. He and Jolan were wealthy in comparison, not in dollars, but in family. Until now...

Tibor pressed his hands to his eyes. *It's my fault! My fault, my most grievous fault! Oh, God, punish me, not her. Take away her pain. Let her live, just please, let her live. I was so arrogant to think I knew what was best. After all my training! And now I beg you...instead of trusting you...oh, God, forgive me! But please...if you have to take one of them tonight, don't take my wife!*

He rocked forward and back, forward and back. What was taking so long? He heard footsteps hurrying down the corridor, saw a nurse go in the same doors they took Jolan through.

"Pardon me, nurse?" But she was gone, and the doors swung shut. He looked up and down the corridor. At one end was a window, glowing yellow with sunlight. At the other was a wooden box, like a coffin standing on end. A phone booth. He ran down the hall, fumbling in his pockets for a coin. He reached for the telephone, put the nickel in the slot, dialed CH for Charter, then the numbers.

"*Hardenbergh Hirlap.*"

"Emil? Emil!"

"Is this Tibor? What's wrong?"

"Emil, it's Jolan. We're at the hospital. She's—she's losing the baby. Please come."

"I'm on my way." The line went dead. Tibor slumped against the wall of the phone booth, relief momentarily washing away fear. Emil, dear, comforting Emil was on the way. He opened the door to the booth, stepped into the hall, and only then realized he should call Margit, too, and wondered briefly why he hadn't called her first. But when he reached in his pockets he found nothing. He'd left his wallet in the tent, emptied his pockets, in fact, so he'd be more comfortable while he worked. Only that one coin had remained.

He walked slowly down the corridor, stopping in front of the double doors. Each door had a window in it, but one of frosted glass. He couldn't

322

see anything, couldn't hear anything, couldn't *do* anything. No, that was wrong. There was one thing he could do, the only thing to do. He leaned against the wall, directly opposite the door, then let his back slide slowly down the wall until he was sitting on the floor with his knees drawn up, his hands folded on top of them, and he began to pray.

"*Confiteor Deo omnipotenti, beatae Mariae semper Virgini, beato Michaeli Archangelo, beato Ioanni Baptistae, sanctis Apostolis Petro et Paulo, et omnibus Sanctis, quia peccavi nimis cogitatione, verbo et opere: mea culpa, mea culpa, mea maxima culpa. Ideo precor beatam Mariam semper Virginem, beatum Michaelem Archangelum, beatum Ioannem Baptistam, sanctos Apostolos Petrum et Paulum, et omnes Sanctos, orare pro me ad Dominum Deum nostrum. Amen.*"

He heard footsteps again, looked up at Emil and Margit hurrying down the hall. He stood up and began to weep again. Emil put his arms around Tibor, and Margit held his hand. They sat down, and Margit took out her rosary. Together, the three of them continued the prayers Tibor had begun.

They were halfway through the rosary when the time the double doors opened again. Tibor stood up as soon as Dr. Hajdu came out.

"Jolan?" he asked.

"She'll be fine."

"Oh, thank God!" Tibor reached for the doctor's hand. "Thank you, Doctor Hajdu. You don't know how grateful I am."

"And the baby?" asked Margit.

"I'm sorry," the doctor said. "We couldn't save it."

"Oh, no," said Emil.

"It was God's will," said Margit.

Tibor said nothing.

"These things do happen, Mr. Nemeth," said the doctor. "Usually because something is seriously wrong with the baby. It's nature's way, and there's nothing we can do. But you brought Jolan in quickly, so we stopped the bleeding, and she'll be fine, and she'll be able to have children again, just not right away. We've given her a sedative, and she's almost asleep, but if you want, you can see her for a few minutes."

"Thank you, doctor." Tibor put his hand on the door. "Doctor Hajdu, can you tell me if it was...if you could tell...a boy, or a girl?"

"A boy."

Tibor nodded, and pushed the door open. He stood in a room filled with equipment. A nurse pointed to another door.

"She's in there, Mr. Nemeth." Tibor went into the next room. Jolan lay under a white sheet, her face an odd sallow color that Tibor realized was pallor beneath her suntan. She looked like a woman who had just given birth. He took her hand and kissed it.

"Mmm," she stirred, and opened her eyes. "Tib."

"Shh, don't try to talk, my love. You're going to be fine, did the doctor tell you that?"

She nodded, and began to cry.

"Shh, don't cry, sweetheart, please don't cry. It will be all right."

"Oh, Tib, it's my fault! I didn't want it enough."

Tibor sat down carefully and cradled her head in his arms. "Hush, darling, hush. Don't cry." But he was crying, too, because no rational, scientific explanation from Doctor Hajdu could take away the guilt that he felt. Like Jolan, he hadn't wanted this child enough. But worse was the choice he made this day, which tainted his relief and happiness that Jolan would be all right.

Some other day, he hoped he would be able to mourn the death of the son whose life he had so easily forsaken for his wife's.

Chapter 26
May 1936

The parade of black sedans draped with red, white, and blue bunting halted in front of a red ribbon stretched across the entrance to the new bridge. In the first car rode the honorable Patrick J. Riley, mayor of Hardenbergh, and his wife Margaret. In the second car was the widow of the previous mayor, the one who had signed the agreement with the PWA authorizing the bridge and dam construction project. Mrs. Wheatstone, who still wore black even though her husband had passed away more than sixteen months ago, held a large pair of scissors in her hand. She and the mayor and Mrs. Riley left their cars and arranged themselves in front of the ribbon while news cameras flashed and the mayor began to speak.

Beneath the bridge, water had been rising slowly since the completion of the dam three-quarters of a mile downstream. The new Lake Lenape would fill in the low-lying, marshy waste fields that bordered the river and was beginning to cover what had been Water Street and Trudy Bornheimer's old neighborhood. On the barren shore, once the lake was near capacity, a park would be constructed. This work would be done with local labor and local funding; most of the men who had worked on the dam and the bridge had already moved on to the next project, a sewer system somewhere in Pennsylvania, perhaps, or construction of a town hall in West Virginia. Or they simply hopped a freight train and headed south hoping to work as field hands. Those who remained were men who already lived in Hardenbergh, men like Tibor, for whom the construction project had meant the difference between making do and not making it at all.

Precisely on the stroke of noon Mrs. Wheatstone lifted the large scissors and sliced the red ribbon, which fluttered to the pavement in graceful arcs. The Magyar Men's Marching Band, the Sons of the Shillelagh Brass ensemble, and the German-American orchestra joined together to play the opening bars of "America the Beautiful." Mrs. Wheatstone, the mayor and his wife, and the town councilmen got into their respective cars for the ceremonial first drive across the bridge.

"From every mountainside, let freedom ring," sang Tibor in his strong baritone. Like the rest of the crowd, he cheered and clapped his hands when the cars passed over the two-lane span and crested the rise on the other side. A few moments later, the cars turned around to come back across the bridge. The crowd began to disperse.

Tibor looked around for his children, who were somewhere closer to the marching bands with their Great-Aunt Margit, waiting to help Great-Uncle Emil carry home the banner of the Magyar Men's Marching Band. He couldn't spot them yet, with a sea of summer dresses in front of him, but in a moment he noticed someone waving at him.

Tibor smiled. "Ferenc!" he called. Ferenc made his way through the crowded street, and stepped up onto the sidewalk. He had grown in the past few years into a tall, good-looking young man. Fit and energetic, he still carried himself with the exaggerated straight posture of a soldier.

"Tibor, how good to see you again."

They shook hands. "I didn't expect to see you here, Ferenc."

"I came in on the 10:30 train. I had to come, when I got mother's letter. You've heard the news, I suppose, from Jolan?"

"Yes. We're very happy for her."

"I think it's wonderful, too. For lots of reasons. I'm on my way to see her now. Will you walk with me?"

"I'm waiting for my children to appear. They're with Margit and Emil, somewhere over there. When the crowd thins a bit more they should be in sight."

"I'll wait, then," said Ferenc. "It will be good to see them."

He took a pack of cigarettes from his pocket, and offered one to Tibor. The two men smoked for a moment, watching the crowd.

"You look as though school agrees with you," said Tibor.

Ferenc grinned. "It agrees with me more than the army did. I'd rather make ten souffles in an afternoon than march ten miles under a full pack."

"Oh, I think the army did you good."

"Sure, it gave me the biceps I need to whip egg whites by hand, all day long."

Tibor laughed. "Well, I'm sure your experience as an army cook helped you get into culinary school," said Tibor as he ground out the cigarette.

Ferenc nodded. "I'm sure it did, though I still shudder at the sight of a potato peeler. And I got to see more of the country than most people do, thanks to Uncle Sam."

"Not to mention Hawaii."

"Mmm. Nice beach, there, though Honolulu isn't much of a town. Too many drunk sailors from Pearl! But you know, it's good to be home, and I like New York all right. That reminds me—Zsuzsi sends her love. Say—where's Jolan? With the kids?"

"She's home, resting. We're not taking any chances this time."

Ferenc scanned the crowd. "Oh, gee, is she okay?"

"She's fine. She's having a much easier time with this one, thank God, no back pains or sickness. It's just that, well, after what happened last time, we're being extra careful." Tibor took a deep breath, and let it out slowly. "We really want this baby." He didn't speak the words "this time."

"There they are. Over here!" He waved. Aranka came running up to them, but Vendel hung behind, unwilling to let go of his end of the rolled-up banner.

"Uncle Ferenc!" she called. "What did you bring me?"

"Aranka!" protested Tibor, but Ferenc laughed and held out a Baby Ruth. "Share it with your brother," he said. He hugged Emil, and kissed Margit on the cheek. "You look wonderful, both of you."

They walked up the street, stopping at Margit and Emil's house, mostly so the children could use the bathroom, and then Ferenc left for his mother's a few moments before Tibor took the children home.

He didn't mind the walk home but it was too much for little Vendel, especially after the morning's excitement. He hoisted his son onto his shoulders and walked home with one hand on Vendel's ankle and one holding Aranka's hand. Their slow progress suited him on such a pleasant day. They heard the hum of bumblebees, listened to the calls of robins and bluebirds, and stopped to pick a bouquet of dandelions for Jolan.

His heart still beat faster when he saw the house he had built almost entirely with his own hands. Small and practical, it sat on the property with plenty of room behind to add on as more children came. He had built a low porch on the front, with two steps leading up to it, roofed and wide enough for chairs. It was a pleasant place to sit, shaded in the afternoon and warmed by morning sunlight. Best of all, it faced the pasture where he had proposed to Jolan. In front of the porch, on either side of the step, he had planted his Oxheart cherry trees. They were still saplings, like his own children, and would grow with them. Next year they might have cherries enough for one pie.

Jolan was outside in the pasture, sitting on her favorite rock, her bare feet in the creek. With her skirt hiked up above her knees she looked like a teenager, and Tibor grinned. The children ran ahead, pulling off their shoes, and were already splashing in the water by the time Tibor sat down next to his wife.

"You look beautiful," he said. He put one arm around her and rested his other hand lightly on her stomach. He gave her a long kiss, then pulled away and smiled. "If I'd known you were looking this good I would have left the children at Margit and Emil's."

"Tibor Nemeth! What a thing to say to a woman in my condition."

'Your condition won't last forever," he said, and kissed her on the neck. "I love you," he whispered, lifting his hand up to her breast.

"Tib!" she whispered back. "Not in front of the children."

He kissed the back of her neck and began to unbutton her blouse. "They can't see what I'm doing from there."

He had just finished with the last button when Aranka shrieked and ran toward them. Jolan pushed Tibor's hand away, and buttoned her blouse again.

"Mama, Mama, we found a crayfish but it got away."

"Did it? Well, you can catch another one later."

"What is Papa laughing at?" asked Aranka.

"You know Papa. He always thinks he's funny. Will you help me stand up, Papa? Then we can give the children some cookies I made while you were gone."

Tibor took her hands and gently lifted her up. As they walked toward the house, he silently gave a little prayer of thanks for their good fortune. He believed the worst of the Depression was over for them. This summer he would stay home and take care of the children, and do the heavy housework, and tend the garden, while Jolan rested. He would let nothing jeopardize this baby. Not this time.

They spent the rest of the afternoon sitting quietly on the porch, while the children played in the yard. And after supper Tibor explained yet again that it was too early in the season to catch fireflies, then he bathed the children, letting them splash in the tub more than Jolan would, and put them to bed. When he was finished mopping up the bathroom floor, he joined Jolan on the porch step.

"The air smells so good tonight! It seems like summer already," she said as he sat down beside her.

"It's sure to be a hot one," he said, putting his arm around her shoulder. He kissed her on the cheek, then on the mouth, then on the neck.

"Oh, Tibor, what do you see in me when I look like this? I feel like an elephant!"

"You are a beautiful woman," he said. "You are a beautiful mother, and I've wanted to kiss you all evening."

Only later, when they were in bed, did he remember to tell her about seeing Ferenc that afternoon.

"What did he say about Eva? Have they set a date yet?"

"I don't know."

"Didn't he say? Didn't you ask?"

"No, and no."

"Men!" she said in a voice full of exasperation. "You never remember the important details."

"I thought I did pretty well with that tonight," Tibor said, yawning. Jolan shut the light off. He couldn't see her smiling, but he heard it in her voice.

"I love you anyway," she said.

"I love you, too."

The next morning Tibor borrowed Mr. Amwell's pickup truck so they could all go to church. The Amwells went to the Methodist Church on Wilson Street, in their venerable model-T, and generously had offered the use of their truck as soon as they knew Jolan was pregnant again. Tibor was grateful for the use of the truck, because the city trolley lines did not extend this far, but it irked him, too, that he could not afford a vehicle of his own. He looked over his shoulder at the two children sitting in the open bed of the truck. He didn't like leaving them there but there wasn't quite room enough for four in the cab—and soon there would be five.

They left early enough to find a parking space close by, and walked up the church stairs while the bells rang their warning that Mass would start in ten minutes. One by one they genuflected and made the sign of the cross, then slipped into a pew on the left side of the center aisle, first Jolan, then the children, and finally Tibor.

He knelt and folded his hands in prayer, first in thanks, and then in supplication, that somehow money would be found for a car of his own. Then Father Eszterhazy walked onto the altar, and Mass began.

Tibor loved the ceremony of the Mass, the solemnity of the Latin prayers mixed with the songs of the choir and the celebration of the Eucharist. When he was first married, he wondered, once or twice, what his life would have been like if he had stayed in the seminary, what it would be like to stand in the vestments and hold the gold chalice and paten. But those had been idle thoughts. Tibor knew he was far better as a parishioner than he would have been as a priest. Every time he looked at his wife and children he knew that.

At communion he let Jolan out of the pew first, while he waited with the children, and when she came back he went to the altar rail to receive the host. It was for him the most joyous moment of the Mass to kneel afterwards while the host slowly melted on his tongue, to lose himself in prayer and feel the sense of renewal that came from being in a state of grace.

After Mass, they joined other families in front of the church for a few social minutes. Jolan immediately looked for Eva.

"There she is," she said, leading the way. The crowd parted before her like the Red Sea.

"Eva," she said as she drew closer, and the two women hugged. Tibor kissed Eva on the cheek, and shook Ferenc's hand. Standing on Eva's other side was the object of Jolan's interest, Bela Jelinek, who owned the butcher shop on Cherry Street. Two years ago his wife had passed away, of cancer, Tibor thought. He was not a tall man; in her heels Eva stood nearly eye-to-eye with him, but he had broad shoulders, and muscular arms. He took Tibor's hand in a strong grip.

"So?" said Jolan. "Have you set a date yet?"

Eva laughed. "You always get right to the point, Jolan! But it depends on you, dearest. I want you to stand up with me. Can you do that as you are, or shall we wait until after the baby comes?"

Jolan flushed. "Eva, how sweet of you to ask, but I couldn't possibly, not like this."

"Why don't we talk about it later?" suggested Eva. "It's not something we can discuss in detail standing in this crowd. "

"Come by this afternoon," Jolan suggested. "We can have rhubarb pie."

"Rhubarb? That's my favorite," said Bela.

"Then you must come," said Tibor. "Jolan's pies are wonderful."

"I use Aunt Margit's recipe, of course," said Jolan later, when they sat on the porch with slices of pie and glasses of lemonade for the women, cold beer for the men. "So you should really give her credit for the crust."

"It's delicious," said Bela. He leaned back in his chair and patted his stomach. "As good as my dear mother used to make, God rest her soul."

Tibor smiled. He liked Bela, who was direct in his enjoyment of life's pleasures—a piece of pie, a cold glass of beer, a comfortable chair. He looked at Eva with a mixture of affection and awe that was charming, and Tibor thought he would be a good husband for her. He was glad for Eva. Her first husband dying so young, raising Ferenc by herself, and years of hard work had taken their toll. Her hair was going gray, and she wore glasses all the time now, not just for work. But she was only 39, after all, and though Bela must be near 50, he was a strong and healthy man. The match would be good for both of them.

"So what do you think, Jolan?" she asked. "Shall we wait until after the baby is born?"

Jolan blushed. "I hate to think of you waiting for such a thing—you have your own happiness to think about."

Eva smiled and took Bela's hand. "We have many happy years ahead of us, dear Jolan, so waiting a few months will be no hardship. We very much want you to stand with us at the altar, and we also want to be sure your little one is safe."

"It's not such a little one at that," said Jolan. "I show so much already."

Bela cleared his throat. "I've always thought September would make a nice time for a wedding," he said. "After the heat of the summer is over, but when the weather is still fine enough to be outdoors."

Jolan looked at Eva. "Why, we could have the reception here, then, in the yard."

Eva smiled. "That would be lovely. We can borrow folding tables and chairs from the church hall...."

Tibor waved his arm at Bela. "Let's take a walk. Unless you want to be involved in all the details to be discussed here this afternoon. They'll be at it for hours." They walked down the steps and toward the pasture fence.

"I'm happy to have settled, more or less, on a date," said Bela. "I will leave all the details to Eva."

"You were very tactful back there. Thank you."

Bela shrugged. "It's nothing. It wouldn't be right to ask your wife to stand up with us in her condition. And it will give us time to make other arrangements, as well, for moving Eva's things to my apartment above the store, for her to finish her current orders."

"She's giving up dressmaking?" Tibor asked.

"Of course. I do a good business at the butcher shop," said Bela, with a nod toward the car parked in front of Tibor's house. "And that work is terrible for her. Hurts her back, her eyes, her fingers. A woman like that shouldn't have to work. Not my wife."

"Of course. I'm a bit surprised, that's all. Eva is such a good seamstress, with important customers."

"She should have fine things of her own, and not have to sell them to rich women. Mrs. Van Dyke and her cronies will have to go elsewhere from now on." He stopped walking, and faced Tibor. "It's not just my feelings, understand. I'm not that kind of man. But she's worked too hard for too long. I'll give her the kind of life she deserves."

Tibor smiled. "I'm sure you will."

It was a fine Saturday in September when Tibor sat in a pew in St. Elizabeth's church, with Aranka and Vendel fidgeting next to him, and a five-week-old baby in his arms. At the altar, Jolan stood in a dress the color of lemon frosting, and Bela's son, Ignacz, stood on the right, while between them Eva and Bela exchanged vows. Afterwards, he felt like a guest at his own house, while Jolan and Zsuzsi orchestrated the reception.

Zsuzsi had driven down in her new convertible. She had designed the dress Eva wore, but Eva made it herself, of sky blue silk so light it seemed white in the sunlight. Ferenc baked the cake, a tower of white frosting with blue and yellow roses cascading down the tiers. Bela of course supplied the main course, a suckling pig. Tibor had felt superfluous until now, when armed with a champagne bottle he could refill glasses and at least be of some use.

He looked around to see whose glass might still be empty. A few yards away, Emil stood leaning against the fence. Tibor walked up to him.

"Emil, more champagne?"

Emil started. He looked the other way, and Tibor thought he wiped his eyes. "No, I'm fine," Emil said.

"Is something wrong?"

"No, of course not."

"Were you thinking about the news from Spain?"

Emil sighed. "No, actually, I was not, not today. It's just—it's not something I can explain. Maybe it's just my age, and a bad habit of thinking of what might have been."

"What do you mean?"

Emil shook his head. "Nothing at all, Tibor. I'm just being a foolish old man. Don't mind me. It's a good party. Let's go enjoy it."

They walked back to the rest of the guests, who asked Emil for a song, so he took up his violin and began to play.

Tibor took advantage of the interlude to check on the baby. Laszlo was in his carriage in the dappled shade of a young elm, sound asleep, with a small bubble on the corner of his mouth. Tibor gently wiped it away with his pinky. Laszlo didn't stir. People said he took after Tibor, not just his eyes and mouth, but in the strong way he kicked at his blankets. When he slept he looked as fragile as any infant, but awake he was full of energy. Tibor already pictured him captain of the high school football team.

Laszlo was wide awake when the last of the guests had gone and Eva and Bela went to the train station to spend a brief honeymoon in New York City. Most of the cleanup was done; only one table remained with its tablecloth and a last bottle of champagne. Jolan fed the baby, using a bottle, because the doctors said it was healthier than the breast, though Tibor privately doubted it would make much difference. The other two children were napping, so it was just the four of them. Zsuzsi rested her feet up on one of the chairs, and Tibor leaned over to pour her another glass of champagne.

"That's plenty!" she protested, waving him away. "I've had far too much as it is."

"You're not going back until tomorrow, though, so drink up," said Tibor. "It's a wedding. People are supposed to get drunk at a wedding."

"It was a lovely, lovely day, Jolan," said Zsuzsi. "You've done a wonderful job."

"Indeed," said Tibor. "To my lovely wife." They clinked glasses.

Jolan put the bottle down and put the baby against her shoulder. They all waited while she patted his back until Laszlo gave a satisfying belch.

"My, he's good at that," Zsuzsi said.

"He takes after his father," Jolan said. "He's already very much a boy."

"To my new son," said Tibor. They clinked glasses again.

They sat in a slightly dizzy, overfed, comfortable silence as the sunlight changed to amber. "Mosquitoes will be coming out soon," Jolan said, yawning. "We'll have to go in before it gets dark."

"But it's so lovely sitting here right now," said Zsuzsi. She lit a cigarette and inhaled deeply.

"I wonder if they've arrived in New York yet," said Jolan.

Tibor glanced at his watch. "A good half hour ago, I'd say."

"Speaking of New York," said Zsuzsi. "I have a favor to ask of you two." She took her feet off the chair. "May I hold him?"

"Of course," said Jolan, handing her the baby. Zsuzsi kissed him and rubbed his back.

"Was that the favor?" asked Jolan. "You can hold him anytime you want."

Zsuzsi looked at Jolan as she spoke, but Tibor had the distinct feeling she was speaking mainly to him.

"You know I am going to Paris again," she said. "Well, this time I may be there for a while. At least six months, maybe even a whole year. I know, I know, I'm going to miss this little man. But work is going so well for me right now I can't pass up the opportunity. It means working with top designers, and well, you know all that already. So I'm going to sublet my apartment, to Ferenc actually—he can't afford it entirely, so I'll be subsidizing him, anything to get him out of that roach-infested place he's in now. But what am I to do with that automobile?"

"Garage it," said Tibor. "Sell it. Let Ferenc use it."

"Sell it? I just bought it. And as for garaging, have you any idea what that costs in the city? It just doesn't make sense. And Ferenc couldn't afford the upkeep. So there you have it. Will you take care of it for me?"

Tibor almost choked. "Take care of it? What are you talking about?"

"I know it's an imposition but it would help me so much."

"Zsuzsanna, you are so transparent!" said Jolan. "It's out of the question."

"Absolutely," said Tibor. He gulped down the last of the champagne and tried to swallow his anger as well. He knew that Zsuzsi was well off, but he never envied her for it. She worked hard for every penny, and he was proud of her success, and he didn't even mind the generous birthday and Christmas gifts she gave the children. But to accept her charity, to admit that he couldn't afford even a used car—

Zsuzsi looked from one to the other. She put out her cigarette. "All right then. Here's the way it is. We're family. I respect your pride, Tibor, and I am not in any way suggesting that you are not a good provider. My God! Just look at this place, and what you've accomplished, literally with your own two hands. It's beautiful, and your children are healthy and Jolan is radiant and your life is very, very good. But you have three small children, and it's almost a mile just to the outskirts of town. How is Jolan to shop? Must she walk into town every other day for groceries? What happens if God forbid someone gets sick while you're at the school?"

Tibor made an effort to unclench his jaw. "Thank you, Zsuzsi, but—"

"No buts. I'm not giving you a car, Tibor, I'm lending you a car, there's a difference. It will be convenient for you and very convenient for me, and when I come back I will take it back to New York with me. In the meantime, you have the use of it. You'll have to pay for gas and oil, of course, and have repairs made if need be, but think what it will mean for Jolan."

"Zsuzsi," she said, "I don't even know how to drive a car."

"It's easy. You'll learn."

"Zsuzsi, I know you mean well," Tibor began.

She stood up. "I'm going inside to take a long, soaking bath. You two can discuss it all you want, but I'm not taking no for an answer. Tomorrow, if I must, I will walk to the train station and leave the keys here and you'll be stuck with it, whether you want it or not. I don't care if you don't use it once while I'm gone. At least it will be out of the city. All I ask is that you put the top up if it looks like rain."

And with that she walked into the house.

Chapter 27
August 1937

"There's blue frosting on the ceiling," said Tibor, leaning back in the kitchen chair. "And on the ceiling light, and in your hair." He yawned.

Sitting across the table, Jolan looked up and yawned as well. "There's some in your hair, too."

"I suppose we have to clean it all up," he said.

"In a minute."

"We wouldn't be this tired if it hadn't rained, you know."

"I know." Jolan put her feet in Tibor's lap. "But it did rain. It's still raining."

"Pouring, I'd say," said Tibor, rubbing Jolan's feet. And it was. Fat drops gathered on the edge of the porch roof and splattered down on the steps. The cherry trees drooped with the weight of the water. Tibor felt like one of those trees. He had hoped for a sunny day, so they could take the children to Lake Lenape, where they could run and swim and use up their energy. Instead, they were cooped up in the house for their brother's first birthday. During this long day the children had fought over who would open Lazlo's birthday presents, then they fought over who got the bigger slice of cake. Right now they were in their room, to nap whether they wanted to or not, while the guest of honor slumped in his high chair, sound asleep.

"Tomorrow, please God, let it be sunny," said Tibor.

Jolan stood up slowly, and began to collect the dirty plates. "I hope so."

Tibor's prayer was answered. The sky the next morning was clear azure. Jolan packed a picnic basket and they drove to the lake, stopping first to pick up Aunt Margit and Uncle Emil. Jolan opened Laszlo's present from his great aunt and uncle, a crocheted sweater just big enough to fit him through the coming winter. At the lake Jolan and Margit spread a picnic cloth, where Margit sat while the others bathed. Margit thought it undignified to put on a bathing suit but she relaxed enough to take her shoes off and run her feet through the sand that had been trucked in to form a small beach. Emil wore an old-fashioned suit with a singlet but Tibor wore just a pair of swimming trunks. He carried the baby while Jolan stepped into the water with the other two children.

They splashed in the cool lake until Laszlo swallowed some water and began to cough and cry. Tibor gently patted him on the back until it was clear he was all right, only frightened. It seemed a good time for the picnic, then, so they left the water and toweled themselves dry. Jolan and Margit passed around plates of fried chicken and pickles and sweet and sour coleslaw. There was iced tea for the grownups and lemonade for the children, and for dessert Margit's excellent peach pie.

"This is much nicer than yesterday," said Tibor, who leaned against a tree with Vendel's head in his lap. He rubbed his son's back in slow circles. Aranka sat nearby watching her younger brother, who napped on his stomach, legs curled beneath him like a little frog. Emil smoked his pipe while Margit crocheted yet another baby sweater, and Jolan merely sat with chin resting on her knees, watching the water and all the families splashing in the lake.

Then they heard the sound of an airplane, and everyone looked up. It was a blue biplane, droning above them, so high it looked like one of Vendel's toys. Biplanes flew overhead almost every day now, almost commonplace, only ten years after Lindbergh's heroic flight. Tibor smiled to think that he was in Detroit on that day, making arrangements to move to Hardenbergh. It was such a wonder, then, that a solitary man could fly so far, could travel in thirty-three hours a distance that normally took at least a week. After Lindbergh, the Atlantic didn't seem so vast anymore. It seemed anyone could get in an airplane and fly off to France, or Italy, or Spain.

Spain. Tibor tried to imagine an airplane like that one, so innocent looking, dropping bombs over there. How long could Madrid hold out against the forces that attacked her? This conflict was so much worse in many ways than the Great War. The bombs killed civilians, ruined cities, seemed to be on the verge of destroying a whole country. Newspaper editorials warned that another large-scale war was about to erupt. Tibor shivered suddenly. He knew people were suffering in Europe, but it was so far away, and this was too sweet a day for sad thoughts.

He caught Jolan's eye, and smiled. Today was, without doubt, the tranquil and happy birthday they had hoped for.

A week later, he was sitting on the front porch, enjoying another fine afternoon with the Sunday newspaper, when he heard Laszlo crying. He assumed it was time for either a diaper or a bottle, but when Laszlo didn't stop crying after several minutes, Tibor put the paper down and walked inside.

"What's wrong?" he asked.

Jolan held her hand on the baby's forehead. "He's burning up. Can you get me the thermometer?"

Tibor opened the medicine cabinet and took out the thermometer. He shook it down as he walked back to Jolan, who had the baby's diaper off already, and inserted the thermometer with the finesse of a trained nurse. Laszlo howled for the next three minutes, and cried even after the thermometer was removed.

Tibor held it to the light. "One hundred and one," he said. "I'd better call the doctor."

Tibor's heart began to thud in his chest. Such a high fever, to develop so quickly! It was probably nothing to worry about, but he couldn't help worrying. He'd known school children struck down by scarlet fever. And this summer the newspapers had been filled with horrifying stories of children afflicted with polio. Tibor fought against his panic. It was probably just a summer cold. There was no sense in being an alarmist.

The doctor agreed. "Rub him down with alcohol to bring the fever down. If the fever doesn't break by morning, then bring him in."

They rubbed him with alcohol right away, and again before they went to bed. But they got no sleep; their baby fussed and cried most of the night. They took his temperature twice more, and it showed a steady climb. By dawn he had a fever of one hundred and three.

Doctor Hajdu's office was in the first floor of a two-family house, a few blocks away from Margit and Emil's street. When they knocked on the door at seven a.m., they could see the doctor had just awoken. He received them in his bathrobe and slippers.

"What seems to be the trouble, here?" he asked, reaching for the baby.

"We hope it's no more than a summer cold but his fever keeps climbing, doctor," said Tibor.

The doctor raised his eyebrows. "Has he been sneezing or coughing?"

"No. It's just the fever, such a high fever," said Jolan.

Doctor Hajdu frowned. "A high fever. Let's take a look."

The doctor moved so slowly toward the examining room that Tibor wanted to shove him. He fought against a rising panic. Laszlo was so young—just a year old, practically an infant. And they called it infantile paralysis. He walked over to the examining room window, leaned his head against the glass, and began to pray.

Laszlo cried through the whole examination, almost screaming when the doctor moved his arms and legs. Out of the corner of his eye, Tibor watched as the doctor took the baby's temperature, listened to his heart, and finally touched Laszlo on the cheek, very lightly. He rubbed his eyes and said to Jolan, "You can dress him now."

Tibor was too terrified to speak. He looked at the doctor, who took a long time to make eye contact. When he saw the doctor's expression, he felt faint for the first time in his life.

"He has it, doesn't he?" Tibor whispered.

Doctor Hajdu looked down at his slippers and nodded once. "I think so."

Jolan looked up at his tone. "Has what? Doctor Hajdu, Tib? What are you talking about? It's just a summer cold, isn't it? Why, we were at the lake just last week. He could have gotten a cold from anyone there, couldn't he?" She picked Laszlo up and hugged him to her chest.

"Mrs. Nemeth, I'm sorry, but we'd better get this little boy to the hospital right away. I want to have another doctor take a look at him, but I'm pretty sure he'll come to the same conclusion I did. I think your little boy may have contracted..."

Don't say it, Tibor prayed, please God, don't say it.

"...infantile paralysis."

Tibor began to cry.

Jolan's face went white. "Infantile paral—? You mean polio? No! My God, no! Please, no!"

Tibor reached for her but she pulled back, then sat in the wooden chair next to the examining table, rocking her son. "No," she said. "No, no, no."

The doctor cleared his throat. "I'll go upstairs to dress, then we'll go to the hospital together. I'll drive." He sighed and left the room.

Tibor knelt down at Jolan's feet and touched Laszlo's back. He could feel the fever's heat through the baby's clothes. "It will be all right. It will. He can recover—he's strong, and children do recover."

Jolan looked at him as though he were crazy. "And the ones that do? They're on crutches, with horrible braces on their legs, or in wheelchairs. Crippled!" Her voice broke. "My God, not our Laszlo! Not our baby!"

A few moments later the doctor stood before them, hat in hand. "Come, let's take him where he'll get the best of care."

He led Jolan and Tibor to his car, opening the door so they could get into the back seat. Tibor ached to hold his son on the ride to the hospital but Jolan clutched him tightly. Laszlo sounded tired. His cries were weaker, but then, he'd been crying almost all night, and hadn't eaten, or sucked at his bottle. Tibor took out his handkerchief and blew his nose. For the first time in his life he felt utterly alone.

They rode through familiar streets but he recognized nothing, and he was surprised when the car halted in front of the large, red brick building of the hospital. He felt as though everyone he passed looked at them with pity, and already counted his baby among the dead. He couldn't look at their faces.

Jolan was reluctant to give Laszlo to a nurse. "Can't I go with him?" she asked.

"It's just for a little while," said Doctor Hajdu. "You'll see him again soon."

So they waited, empty handed, for how many minutes or hours Tibor couldn't tell. Once he tried to hold Jolan's hand, but she pulled away and shook her head. He was bereft. He knew he ought to comfort her somehow, but he wanted comfort from her instead, to lay his head in her lap, to have her stroke his hair and tell him everything would be all right.

When the two doctors finally came into the corridor, he looked at their faces and lost all hope.

Doctor Hajdu introduced the other physician as Doctor Kraft. Tibor shook hands mechanically.

"Well," said Doctor Kraft. "I'm afraid it is bad news, after all. Your son does have polio."

"How bad?" whispered Jolan.

"It's much too soon to tell. Doctor Hajdu tells me that he is otherwise a healthy and strong baby. We'll do what we can to make him comfortable but, frankly, there's not much we can do except wait and see how much of a fighter he is."

"Is he—paralyzed?' asked Tibor.

Doctor Kraft shrugged. "It seems to be affecting his legs now but it's just too soon to tell how the disease will progress."

"We should have brought him in last night," said Tibor.

"It wouldn't have made any difference, Mr. Nemeth. There's nothing you could have done," said Doctor Kraft. "This disease follows its own course."

"Can we see him now?" asked Jolan.

"Of course. Follow me."

They walked down the hall toward the children's ward. "He's not in the ward," said Doctor Hajdu. "We're keeping him in isolation. You'll have to put on a mask and gown."

When they were gowned, Tibor and Jolan were led into a small room with one crib in the center. Laszlo lay on his back, quiet, not moving.

"We gave him something for the pain, and he'll sleep now," said Doctor Kraft. "Rest is probably the best thing for him. Stay as long as you like, but try not to wake him." He and Doctor Hajdu left the room.

Tibor and Jolan stood on either side of the crib, looking down at their son. He was pale, but for the first time in hours he looked peaceful. After a few minutes, Tibor said, "I'd better call Mrs. Amwell and tell her she'll need to watch the children a while longer. I'll call Margit and Emil, too." Jolan barely nodded as he walked out.

He paused in the doorway. "I won't be long."

In the corridor, he took off the mask and the gown, and walked down the hall to the telephone booth. He sat on the small bench, and closed the door. What would he say? What could he say? What help could anyone give?

Worse than the doctor's sympathetic but essentially objective manner were the reactions from Mrs. Amwell and Margit. He hung up the phone hurriedly after each call, drained of energy and trembling. Finally he stood up and walked back to where his son and Jolan waited, as still as a tableaux.

Margit and Emil were not allowed to visit Laszlo. After speaking with Tibor briefly in the corridor, they went back to Tibor and Jolan's house to take care of the children. Tibor and Jolan took turns lying, restlessly, on a cot that Doctor Kraft had sent in to the room, but neither one slept. All night, it seemed, a parade of nurses and doctors came in, solitary figures dressed in ghostly white, who checked on their son and left again without saying a word.

In the morning, when Laszlo began to have trouble breathing, Doctor Kraft placed him in an oxygen tent. Tibor walked into the corridor when Doctor Kraft left the room.

"Doctor, be honest with me. How bad is he, that you have put him inside that thing?"

Doctor Kraft rubbed the back of his neck. He looked unshaven, and Tibor wondered if he had been up all night as well. The doctor gave him an appraising look, and then shook his head.

"It doesn't look good, Mr. Nemeth. His legs are definitely paralyzed, and the polio is affecting his lungs. It's as though the disease is moving up his body. The oxygen will help, some, but I can hear fluid in his lungs. If the fluid keeps building up, there's nothing I—or anyone—can do. Ultimately, if the paralysis moves up further, it will affect his neck muscles, and he won't be able to swallow."

"What then?"

"Mr. Nemeth, are you a praying man?"

Tibor almost laughed. He was more tired than he thought. "Yes, Doctor."

"Then I suggest you pray, because hope and prayer are all we have working on our side right now."

The doctor put a hand on Tibor's shoulder. "I'm sorry," he said. He turned and walked away.

Tibor watched the doctor as he walked down the hall. It was not the doctor's fault, he knew that, yet anger made him want to run after the man and knock him to the floor. *How dare he say my son is so bad as that? Laszlo is a vibrant, smart little boy who looked right at me only a few weeks ago and said "Da. Dada." Then he laughed when I lifted him out of the high chair and covered his face with kisses. And he's strong. He's been standing up for weeks, strengthening his legs. Any day now he would take his first steps.*

Tibor gasped for air as though he felt Laszlo's agony. To walk! What a small thing it was, to put one foot in front of the other, to push your weight forward, to balance on the ball of your foot and swing the other leg ahead. So easy to walk, so natural.

Tibor looked down at his own footsteps as he walked back to the isolation room, but instead of going in he walked past it, and down a flight of stairs, to the hospital chapel. It was a small, non-denominational room, with a half-dozen pews, a bare cross at the front of the room, a bouquet of pink and yellow flowers on a stand. Sunlight filtered in through a stained glass window above the cross and played in primary colors across the gray carpet. Tibor knew the chapel well; he'd spent hours in here when Jolan was in labor just one year ago. He was glad no one else was there.

He walked to the front of the chapel, knelt, and blessed himself, but before his lips could form the words of any prayer he broke down and sobbed, at first with a tight attempt at control, like a man ashamed of crying, and then he wept openly.

"Why?" he asked aloud, when he could finally speak. "Why do you want his life? What purpose can you have for him in heaven? Why do you need him now? Isn't one of our children enough for you? And what am I to pray for? That you spare his life, but leave him a cripple? That you take him swiftly, without pain? I don't want my son to die! Please God, not my son!"

The chapel door opened, and someone sat in a pew somewhere behind him. Tibor wiped his eyes and sat back, drained of energy, drained even of anger. He could not understand it. Was God as arbitrary as that, to take two babies from one couple? Was the Old Testament Jehovah still demanding sacrifice? Were Tibor's sins so evil God must punish him this way? Where was the mercy of His Son? It made no sense. He stood and stared at the cross above the altar. "Not my will but Thine be done," he said through clenched teeth. It was a lie.

He walked back to his son's room, with a hollow in his gut, an emptiness he had never felt before. Through every loss—his brothers, his parents, his miscarried son—Tibor's faith had sustained him, provided a guidepost to help him through dark days and nights of grief. But this felt like robbery. For the first time in his life, Tibor felt nothing of faith.

Jolan had not moved. She stood sentry over the crib. The odd cellophane bag ballooned with oxygen over the struggling body of Laszlo. Tibor stood next to his wife and put his hand on her back. "How is he?"

"Worse," she whispered. "The doctor was here while you were gone." Her voice broke. "He doesn't think Laszlo will last the night."

"Not last!" Tibor was shocked. "So soon?"

Jolan began to cry. "It happens that way...he said...sometimes...I'm almost glad...Seeing him suffer..." She turned and leaned against Tibor, who held her but knew he gave no comfort when he himself felt only anger and despair.

"At least we can thank God he won't grow up with wasted limbs," she said finally, "watching other children play. Oh, Tib! This is wrong! We've given up on him already, even the doctors. We should be praying and thinking of him getting well, instead of giving in to this nightmare. We should be helping him fight!"

Tibor held her closer. She was right, but she was wrong, too. The last thing Tibor wanted was a lifetime of paralysis or pain for his son. But was it really a mercy to take such a young life? Was it asking too much to be allowed to watch him grow? To play catch? To go fishing? To see him become a young man, and marry and have children of his own? Why was that asking so damn much?

Heart, mind, and body screamed the question, why? Why? But there was no answer except the hiss of oxygen, his son's labored breathing, and footsteps hurrying past in the hall.

Chapter 28
January 1938

Tibor knelt down and brushed snow off the shoulders of the reclining lamb atop the very small headstone marking Laszlo's grave. The grave was set into a small rise, and was one of too many very small plots with very small headstones in this section of the cemetery. Some of the stones were plain, others were adorned with tiny angels; all had the short span of dates that marked the unyielding presence of polio, diphtheria, scarlet fever, typhoid, whooping cough.

Tibor hated coming here, yet he stopped by almost every day. In the fall he took some solace in seeing the grass grow green and thick around the headstone, and he had planted a yellow mum, which he watered and pinched back until it was a full mound of sunny flowers. When the frost came Tibor had cried to see it go brown and shriveled. He cut it back almost to the ground, wondering if resurrection were possible.

At Christmas he and Jolan had placed a small blanket of evergreen boughs over the grave, and this was still fresh looking, with a small red bow that would have seemed festive anywhere else.

Tibor brushed his gloved hands together and the snow sprinkled onto the evergreens, where it sparkled like mica in the noon light. Jolan refused to come here today, the first day of the new year; she shook her head when he asked if she wanted to come with him, saying she wasn't sure she would ever come back. Tibor thought he understood. The place held so little comfort, and so much loneliness. He wished she were here to hold his hand.

They'd held hands so little in the past months, hardly touched one another, and hadn't once made love in the long, bleak months of autumn. What's the point, Jolan would say, in trying to create another life to be taken away? And she would roll over in bed, her back to Tibor, who wanted to tell her how much it would comfort him, that all he really wanted was to hold her close. But she was right. If he put his arms around her, felt the curve of hip and breast, he'd be lost in her softness, and another baby would be on the way. Too soon.

He stood up, folded his hands, and bowed his head. To a passerby he would seem lost in prayer, but Tibor was merely lost. He had not prayed since Laszlo died. He had tried, and felt like a hypocrite. He went to Mass every Sunday, hoping for, not anything so obvious and unsophisticated as a sign, but at least a lightening of the grief, however small, that might allow hope to flourish again. He knew despair was a dreadful sin, one of the seven called deadly, and if he should be struck by a car and killed he would suffer eternal torment in hell. Yet even the knowledge that his own death would separate him from Laszlo forever—for surely his little soul was in heaven—even that knowledge could not crack the shell of hopelessness he wore. He couldn't do it alone; he needed Jolan's help, but she had withdrawn into a sorrow so deep he thought he no longer existed for her. If he didn't have two other children to care for, he would have even considered suicide.

He kissed his fingertips and placed them on top of the little lamb's head, then walked to the car. He'd taken good care of Zsuzsi's car all this time, polishing the outside and tuning the motor at the slightest hint of roughness. It started on the first try, and he pulled smoothly into the city traffic.

Zsuzsi had not been able to come to the funeral, of course, and was in fact staying on in Paris longer than she had planned. She was a success there, her designs now part of a famous fashion house, her line "Mlle. Suzanne's." But her letters, at first a welcome distraction from bad times, were increasingly filled with worrisome news. A trip to Berlin had been "shocking, the great city full of marching soldiers and that red and white flag with its ugly black swastika."

Rome was little better, she wrote, with its own posturing dictator to hold the people in thrall. But she had been to the Vatican, and the Sistine Chapel, where Michelangelo's genius had filled her with awe:

"I wish I could describe to you both the scope and the grandeur of the frescoes, dim as they are under centuries of candle smoke. For the first time I felt a kind of jealousy, that my own talent is so slight, no matter how much I am flattered by those who say I paint with textiles. I wish you could see these works—the Pieta, especially, which is so fluid and alive. The look on Mary's face quite broke my heart, when I thought of all the mothers who have lost their sons, and you, too, dearest Jolan and Tibor...."

The driver behind Tibor beeped his horn when the traffic signal changed. He took his foot off the brake pedal and drove on. Funny how everything came back to his son's death.

When he arrived home, the children had changed out of their church clothes and were lying on the floor by the Christmas tree, which drizzled pine needles every time one of the children brushed against it. They were absorbed in a game of Parcheesi, scarcely looking up to say hello. Jolan claimed to need no help yet in the kitchen, where the aroma of roast pork meant that dinner was imminent.

"I'll need you to mash the potatoes in a while," she said, "but not right now." They could talk about something so trivial, but he could not get her to talk about their son.

He sat down on the couch with a library book, *The Saint in New York,* but in the half hour until he was called to the kitchen the book stayed open to the same page. It felt good, when he was finally summoned, to press so hard with the potato masher he almost pushed the pot off the stove.

Dinner was a quiet one, as dinners had become. Tibor's heart ached to see his children so subdued. He and Jolan made an effort to make their Christmas a happy one, but the effort had been exhausting, and they couldn't keep it up through the whole holiday season. If he were a superstitious man he'd be concerned that their behavior today was a harbinger of the year to come, but he was sure a thaw would come in their hearts. If he had to wait a few more weeks, another few months, even, there would surely come a time when they all could smile again without feeling guilty.

It was the longest winter Tibor could remember in a long time. The children could not help but enjoy the snow, and he joined them, making snowmen, and throwing snowballs, until they almost forgot. They would come onto the porch, stamping the snow off their shoes, laughing at one another, briefly joyous, until Jolan opened the door. Then the warmth of the house and of the cocoa that was waiting for them only made her chilliness more noticeable. The children would go back to Parcheesi, and Tibor to another book, while Jolan sat in the rocking chair, mending. Some days the mending lay in her lap as she stared out the window, occasionally wiping at the condensation with the sleeve of her sweater.

If she had ever cried, or grieved openly since the funeral, it would be easier for them all, but she was so stoic, so neutral, she reminded him very much of Margit in one of her moods. Not even the invasion of Austria provoked her into expressing fear or anger, though Tibor felt a wave of revulsion that almost made him ill. They listened to the news on the radio, sitting at opposite ends of the couch.

When the special announcement was over, and "Fibber McGee and Molly" came on, he turned the radio off, and suggested they go for a walk. It was hard to sit still after hearing such news. "Come, Jolanka," he said. "We both have cabin fever." He helped Jolan with her coat, grabbed a flashlight, and they went outside.

In the starlight their breath made small silver clouds, though spring was only a week away. The grass crunched with frost beneath their boots, and the metal latch on the gate burned Tibor's hand with cold. They stepped into the pasture, walking toward the frozen creek. Neither spoke.

The ground was uneven, pocked with hoof prints from the late-winter cycle of freezing and thawing. At this time of night the cows were snug in the barn on the other side of the pasture. Tibor shone the flashlight along their path, not wanting Jolan to step on cowpats, even though they were frozen.

They were almost at the creek when they saw it. At first it looked like a shadow, then like a rock, and then like a coat tossed carelessly onto the grass. A few steps later and they could finally identify what it really was: a newborn calf, dead.

Tibor could see that it wasn't breathing; still, he took off his glove and placed his hand along the tiny ribs to be sure. The calf's flank was ice cold. Its open eyes were clouded over; a small film of frost covered the whiskers of its nose and chin. The umbilical cord lay beneath it, and a few feet away, the dark mass of afterbirth.

"Poor little thing," he said, then he heard a sound that made him look up. Jolan was sobbing.

He dropped the light and caught her as she fell, easing her to the ground. In his arms she cried out loud, huge, wrenching sobs that tore at her body. Tibor rocked her, patting her hair gently with his hand. It used to hurt him when she cried, when anything made her sad, but tonight he felt a rush of relief. He held her close, not wiping his own eyes, not wanting to speak, not wanting to interfere in any way with the flood of grief that was so overdue.

Thank God, he thought, then no, thank *you*, God. He bowed his head until his lips touched her hair, and silently prayed his thanks.

When her sobs turned into shudders, he kissed the top of her head and helped her stand up. She wiped at her face with her gloved hand, and he took out his handkerchief to do the job properly. She blew her nose into the linen, and he was reminded of the day she first declared her love for him. He had vowed never to see her again, yet he dreamed about her every night after that. How much more he loved her now!

"Let's go in, my love, you're shivering," he said. He put his arm around her, and they walked home.

They checked on the sleeping children when they walked into the house, then Tibor helped Jolan to the bed, and wrapped her in the blankets. As soon as she lay down she began to cry again. Tibor put his arms around her, and cradled her to him. He would hold her all night if need be.

When she finally could speak, her voice was shaky and hoarse.

"What an awful mother I am," she whispered, "to weep so bitterly over a an insignificant creature, when I couldn't squeeze out a tear for my own son."

Tibor kissed her hair again. "You don't think you're crying for him tonight?"

She shrugged. "I don't know. It was just the sight of it—newborn—not even a chance to live. Why must it be the little ones? What purpose can God have to take a newborn calf?"

"Maybe He wanted to give our Laszlo something to play with in heaven. I know it seems cruel but, oh, my dearest love, there must be a reason, there must. How can we bear to live if there isn't?"

He heard Jolan swallow hard. "I wanted to die. I wanted to die in his place."

"I know. Me, too."

He rubbed his face against her hair. This was the closest they'd been, body and soul, since the summer.

He held Jolan until she fell asleep. He eased her head onto the pillow, and then lay next to her, awake for a long time afterwards. When the deep darkness of the room began to lighten, he got up quietly, dressed, went outside. He saw the palest glow on the eastern horizon, but the sun was far from rising, and it was bitter cold. He began to walk. No one drove by at this hour on a Sunday; only the song sparrows were awake, and the first of the robins, calling in the woods across the street.

He turned toward Hardenbergh, listening to the robin's promise that spring was truly coming.

Very few parishioners came to the 6 a.m. service, but Tibor arrived at the church so early no else was there except Monsignor Czigany, still in his cassock, not even in his vestments yet. Tibor could see his own breath as he walked through the vestibule and dipped his hand in the cold font of holy water. He made the sign of the cross, genuflected, and approached the altar. Monsignor Czigany heard his footsteps, turned around, and smiled.

"Tibor, what brings you to the church at this hour on such a cold morning?"

"Monsignor, I've come today hoping you can hear my confession before the service."

"Of course." The priest stood and bowed toward the altar, then turned to Tibor. "Would you be more comfortable in the confessional, or shall we sit here?"

Tibor extended his hand toward the first pew. "This will be fine, Monsignor. I am deeply ashamed, but I have no need to hide in the dark."

"Sit down then, my son. I will be right back." The priest walked into the robing room, returned in a moment wearing narrow purple stole around his neck, and sat down next to Tibor.

Tibor took a deep breath before beginning. "Bless me, father, for I have sinned. It has been nearly seven months since my last confession."

He glanced at Monsignor Czigany, who merely said, "I know," and nodded for him to go on.

"Father, after Laszlo—after Laszlo died, I committed the mortal sin of despair. I felt abandoned by God, but now I understand that it was I who abandoned Him. You know I still came to church with my family, and that I have not taken communion. What you do not know is that in all this time I could not and did not pray. At first I was too angry. Then I was without hope. And then I think I felt nothing at all. For a long time I rejected every gift that God gives a man. I doubted God's existence. And even, when this burden seemed unbearable, thought of taking my own life. I have sinned grievously, Father, and I am so very, very sorry." His voice broke as he began to cry.

"What has brought you back, my son?"

Tibor took out his handkerchief and blew his nose. He took a deep, shuddering breath. "I'm not sure. A small thing, maybe, that showed me the mercy of God. Last night, He reached out to me, even though I had turned my back to Him all these months."

"Is there anything else you need to confess?"

Tibor shook his head. "Only that, in my despair, I haven't been a very good husband, or father."

"Tibor, you have been through a most difficult time. God has tested you as he once tested Abraham, but this time, He took the sacrifice, for reasons we humans cannot begin to imagine. Do not be too hard on yourself. Other men have broken under the weight of such grief, and if you no longer despair, and are truly sorry for your sins, then God forgives you."

Tibor blew his nose again. "Thank you, Father."

"Say a rosary for your penance, Tibor. Ego te absolvo..." The priest traced the sign of the cross in front of Tibor, then stood up and placed his hand on Tibor's shoulder. "Welcome home."

Tibor's hands shook as he took the rosary out of his pocket. He used to love the repetition of the Hail Mary's and Our Fathers, the plea for a mother's intercession and the affirmation of faith. Sometimes, like everyone, he said the rosary quickly, by rote, but this morning he said each prayer with care and humility. He stayed for the early Mass, and when Monsignor Czigany offered communion to the few nuns and elderly parishioners who were regulars at the morning service, Tibor gratefully went up to the altar rail and closed his eyes as the host was placed on his tongue.

For the first time in seven months, mourning was tempered by the comfort of prayer. When he walked home, it seemed as though the sun's warmth rose in his own soul.

The children were just stirring when he got home. He put a pot of coffee on the stove while they took turns in the bathroom. Then he walked into the bedroom where Jolan still slept, curled on her side like a child.

He sat on the bed and rubbed her back gently until she woke. He watched the play of emotions on her face, as she remembered the night before.

"It's all right, my love, everything will be all right," Tibor said. She reached out to him.

"Why are your clothes so cold?" she asked.

"I've been out. I went to confession."

She opened her eyes wide and sat up.

"I thought it was time," he said. She took his hand in hers. "I'm glad."

He knew they still had much to think about, to talk about. Nothing so hurtful could be put right with one night's tears. And sometime, maybe soon, they might do more than just hold hands. But they were holding hands now, for the first time in a long time, and the touch of Jolan's fingers filled him with the promise of hope. Whatever was to come, a small piece of the rift in their hearts had finally begun to heal.

Chapter 29
February 1940

It was a simple enough exchange: Tibor handed Attila Vörös five crisp twenty-dollar bills, and Janos handed Tibor the keys to a 1935 Hudson with whitewall tires. A quick signature on the back of the title made the transaction official, and Tibor walked, grinning, out of Vörös's office. Snow crunched under his feet and he wrapped his muffler more tightly around his neck as he walked toward the gleaming black automobile, his first. His very own.

The driver's side door creaked a bit as he opened it, and Tibor made a mental note to lubricate the hinges. He sat on the beige horsehair seat and closed the door, which thumped solidly to his satisfaction, as it had last week when he came in for a test drive. He started the motor, stepped on the clutch, shifted into first gear, and pulled slowly out of the car lot.

It had been an inconvenient couple of weeks since he had driven the convertible up to New York for Zsuzsi, who thankfully got out of France before the "sitzkrieg" began. To avoid the hazards of the war in the Atlantic, she had crossed overland into neutral Switzerland, and from there into Yugoslavia, where she boarded a merchant ship that sailed down the Mediterranean to pass through the Suez Canal. Her ship had docked briefly in India, spent a week exchanging cargo in Australia, and then had come across the Pacific to Hawaii and finally San Francisco. No doubt her designs for the coming season would have an Oriental influence.

But for Tibor, delightful as her homecoming had been, the important thing was to return the car she had left in his care. She tried to talk him out of it, but since she left for France he had put away a bit here and a bit there until he had enough saved for a used car. When it was time to drive Jolan to the hospital, this time he would do so in his own car.

It had been a nerve-wracking time to be carless, with Jolan so nearly due. But on her last visit to the doctor, just one week ago, they were assured that she would carry for at least two more weeks. So Tibor had returned Zsuzsi's car the first weekend after her return, and now, he had his very own transportation. He would commemorate February 18 as his personal independence day from now on.

He drove home the long way, savoring each mile, and pulled in front of the house with three beeps of the horn. The children came running from the house, pulling on hats and scarves, while Jolan stood in the doorway, shaking her head and smiling.

"Aren't you coming for a ride?" he asked, as the children climbed into the back seat.

She patted her stomach. "I'll wait until we have a destination. But I'll make cocoa while you're gone. Don't be too long."

"We won't be," said Tibor. He beeped the horn and turned the car toward the street.

"Daddy, is this really and truly ours?" asked Aranka. She bounced up and down on the seat.

"Really and truly it is," said Tibor.

"Daddy, will you teach me to drive?" asked Vendel.

"In a few years, I'll be happy to."

"Daddy, can we go to the park?" asked Aranka.

"No, just a quick ride so I can get home to your Mama. I don't like leaving her when she's so close to having the baby."

"I want a brother," said Vendel.

"Believe me, kiddo, we are very aware of that. But it's not up to us. We'll have to wait and see."

"Mommy says it's a girl," said Aranka.

"Mommy may be right," said Tibor. "She looks just like she did when she was carrying you."

Vendel stuck his tongue out at his sister. "I don't understand how a baby gets in there."

"God plants a seed," said Tibor. "Just like when we plant seeds in the garden."

"Does Mommy have dirt in her tummy?"

Tibor chuckled. "No, son, a baby doesn't need dirt to grow. Just love."

He pulled back up to the house and they all got out. Before climbing the steps to the porch Tibor turned around to admire his prize. For a five-year-old car it was in remarkably good shape: a small dent in the right rear fender—a parking mishap, according to Attila—was the only external flaw. The previous owners had kept it in fine repair. Tibor imagined how nice it would be in a few months, to polish the gleaming hood on a warm Saturday morning.

At Jolan's call he went inside. She handed him a mug of cocoa and helped him off with his coat.

"So? How does it feel?"

"Wonderful!" He kissed her cheek.

"Not quite so splendid as Zsuzsi's?"

"I don't care," he said. "It's mine—ours—and that means more than all the chrome on all the roadsters in America." He put his arm around her and helped her toward the couch. "Here, sit down and put your feet up."

"It's nearly time to fix supper."

"I'll take care of that. Good cocoa. What am I making, by the way?"

"Lentil soup, already done, in the big pot," she said. "All you have to do is heat it up. With bread and butter it makes a good Lenten meal for Saturday night."

"I'm happy to oblige," Tibor said.

He wasn't much of a cook himself—that was definitely Ferenc's strong point—but he could at least heat up soup without burning it. He worked happily in the kitchen, whistling the theme from "Gone with the Wind." He set the table with one of Jolan's best tablecloths, the ecru damask embroidered with roses in the same color. He found a candle they kept in a drawer for when the electricity went out, but since they had no candlesticks he lit the candle, dripped a bit of wax onto a dessert plate, and stuck the candle down.

"Dinner is served," he announced when all was ready.

He helped Jolan off the couch, an awkward procedure that took a few minutes, and then he led her into the kitchen.

"Why, what's the occasion?" she asked in surprise.

"It's Hudson Day."

Jolan rolled her eyes.

He helped her settle into a chair, checked the children's hands for grime, ladled the soup, and then said grace.

Jolan put down her spoon after eating only a few sips.

"What's the matter, dear? Soup not warm enough?"

She shook her head. "Just indigestion. Even though I'm carrying lower now, the baby presses on my stomach so much there's hardly room for a mouthful. I'm all right. No need for everyone to stop eating."

They continued their dinner, with Jolan picking up her spoon every few minutes, but after a while she grimaced and put the spoon down. "It's no use. I just can't get comfortable tonight. I can't believe I have at least another week of this."

Tibor reached for her hand. "I love you very much, you know."

She smiled. "I know."

He collected the dishes and ran water into the sink. As he did the dishes he glanced over his shoulder at Jolan. She sat still, rubbing her stomach. The baby had indeed dropped. He couldn't imagine having all that weight pressing on internal organs. The discomfort at this stage must be appalling, but she rarely complained. Vendel couldn't understand how the baby got in there, but Tibor couldn't understand how it ever got out.

He finished washing up and called to Aranka. "Hey there, kiddo, how about drying the dishes so I can help Mama into the living room?"

Aranka came into the kitchen with some reluctance. "Do I have to?"

He knelt down in front of her. "We've had this talk before, young lady. Right now your Mama needs all our help. Be a good girl for me, okay?" He handed her the towel as she turned toward the sink with an exaggerated sigh.

He stood up and looked at Jolan. She had stopped rubbing her stomach, and sat with one hand on either side of it, and her head tilted slightly, as though she were listening, very intently, to what the baby had to say.

He frowned. "Jolan? Are you all right?"

She looked at him and nodded. "Yes, but I don't think we have to wait one more week."

On the way to the hospital Tibor allowed himself one flash of pride in the Hudson before he concentrated on driving safely. The children sat quietly in the back seat, clearly apprehensive, and it was Jolan who reassured everyone as they drove.

Tibor parked at the entrance to the emergency room and told the children to stay in the car while he helped Jolan out. He just had her upright when two things happened at once: an orderly came out with a wheelchair, and Jolan's water broke. Tibor suppressed a wave of relief that it hadn't happened while she was in the new car, and eased her into the chair.

"One more week indeed," said Jolan, grimacing. "You'd better park the car right away and come in. This one's in an awful hurry tonight."

A few minutes later Tibor and the children walked into the obstetrical waiting room. He helped them off with their coats and lit a cigarette. He was glad Jolan had had the presence of mind to suggest the children each bring a toy or a book. Vendel amused himself with a tin truck, while Aranka read aloud from *The Voyages of Dr. Doolittle*, leaving Tibor free to pace.

After an hour a nurse opened the door long enough to smile and assure him it would be only a little while longer. At this hopeful news Tibor called Emil and Margit. By the time they arrived, Tibor had finished half a pack of Lucky Strikes, Vendel was curled up in a chair, asleep, and Aranka was playing milkman with the truck.

"Any news?" Margit asked. She unbuttoned her coat, but kept her babushka on. Aranka got up and gave her great-aunt a kiss, then she went over to Emil and gave him a hug as well as a kiss. Emil rumpled her hair, and when he sat down Aranka sat on his lap.

Tibor shook his head. "They said it would be soon, but that was almost an hour ago."

"When did she start?" asked Margit.

"We were having supper. It can't be more than three hours all together."

"Oh, then we could be in for a long night."

"Well, her water broke when we got here. That's a good sign, surely?" He walked to the door and listened, stepping back suddenly as it opened.

A nurse poked her head through and smiled. "Not long now," she said, and closed the door.

Tibor threw up his hands. In the course of the next two hours he finished all his cigarettes, Emil and both children fell asleep, and Margit crocheted what seemed to be at least three pairs of booties. Although she seemed perfectly calm, at one point she made a small sound of frustration, pulled out several rows of stitches, and started over.

Tibor watched as the crochet hook flew in her hands. She moved the hook and wrapped the yellow yarn around it so swiftly he couldn't follow the stitches at all. He marveled that she had such dexterity for a woman her age, but then, she was only somewhere in her late fifties, wasn't she? It was the harsh lines running from her nostrils to the corners of her mouth, and the compressed lips, turned down at the corners, that made her seem so much older. He wondered what in her life made her look so unhappy. Emil was certainly a good provider; while not rich, they lived comfortably enough. Maybe it was the fact that she never had children, although to be honest, she never seemed fully comfortable around them, either.

He pulled out his pocket watch, shook his head, and then sat down next to Emil, slouched in the uncomfortable chair with his head tilted back against the wall, snoring quietly. His mouth was open slightly, with a slackness in the jaw that made him look quite elderly. He was at least ten years older than Margit, Tibor knew, but he had none of the frailty of an aging man. He still worked every day at the *Hirlap* office, and gardened from the time the ground warmed up enough in March until the last leaves had fallen from his beloved pear tree.

Tibor had seen photographs of Margit and Emil when they first arrived in America. They made a handsome couple, yet Tibor wondered what sort of marriage they'd had. It was none of his business, of course, yet he wondered about a couple who touched so seldom. When he had first met them, Margit was only in her forties, yet he never saw Emil kiss her, not even once. Tibor knew that Emil was, at heart, an affectionate and kind man. What had happened between him and Margit? God forbid that he and Jolan should ever get that way! The months after Laszlo died had been bad enough.

He sighed and looked toward the door again, willing it to open, and to his surprise, it did. The same smiling nurse looked in and said, "Congratulations, Mr. Nemeth! Would you like to see your daughter?"

Tibor almost knocked her down in his eagerness. The nurse led him to a large window that looked onto the nursery, where pink- and blue-wrapped bundles lay in cribs. She pointed to the nearest pink bundle. "There she is."

Tibor drank in his daughter's pink and wrinkled face. Her eyes were shut tight against the light, and her mouth was set in a pout that told him she would be a handful if given a chance. She had a fine fuzz of short blond hair on her head, and Tibor thought she was the most beautiful sight under heaven.

"How is my wife? May I see her?"

"Of course," said the nurse. "Follow me."

Jolan's room was down the hall, a typically drab hospital room brightened only by the knowledge that this was a floor of birth, not of disease or injury.

Jolan turned her head as Tibor walked in.

"I was waiting for you," she said in a sleepy voice. "They gave me something..."

Tibor took her hand and kissed her on the cheek, on the mouth, and then on the cheek again. He sat down gently on the bed, stroked the fingers of her hand and held it to his face.

"How are you? Was it very bad?" he asked.

Jolan shook her head. "Not really. I've had practice." She smiled. "Have you seen her?"

He nodded. "She's gorgeous. Just like her mother."

Jolan smiled again, half asleep. "Does Erzebet suit her?"

"Your grandmother's name? I think it does. She looks like a rosebud. An American Beauty. Let's make it Elizabeth, shall we?"

"Elizabeth Ann Nemeth. Mmm."

He kissed her cheek again. "Go to sleep, my darling."

He put her hand down, and carefully stood up. Then he knelt by the bed and folded his hands to say a prayer of thanks.

In the corridor, Emil, Margit and both children were arrayed against the nursery window. Vendel looked up. "Daddy, she's so ugly!"

Margit opened her mouth to scold but Tibor laughed. "Beauty is in the eye of the beholder, Margit." To his son, he added, "and I think she is very beautiful."

"But Daddy, she has almost no hair! And she's all red and wrinkled."

"Her head is shaped funny, Daddy," added Aranka.

Tibor squatted down between them. "Well, that's about the same way you both looked, and I thought you were beautiful, too. Just give her a chance. In a day or two she won't look so red, and the wrinkles will fill in, and she'll be cuter than you could ever have thought."

"How is Jolan?" asked Margit.

"Tired. They gave her something to make her sleep, but I'm sure you can go in for a few minutes if you like."

"No, let her rest. She's worked hard enough for it."

"Have you chosen a name?" asked Emil.

"Elizabeth Ann, after your mother, Margit."

"Mama would be very pleased," she said.

"It's late. I should get the children home to sleep. Can I give you a ride home on the way?"

"You have your new car, then?" asked Margit.

"Indeed I do."

"Thank you, Tibor, that would be very nice. We're all rather tired, I'm sure," said Emil.

After a last look at Elizabeth, they took the elevator down to the lobby, and Tibor had the added pleasure of showing off his new car once again.

The next morning, after church, Margit and Emil took the children while Tibor went back to the hospital. On the way he made a brief detour to the cemetery. He stood in the snow in front of the stone lamb, and told his dead son about his little sister.

"I wish you could see her," he said. "I wish we could all be together on this earth. But you and the brother you never knew are both in my heart, always, and in that way we are together, and a family, and shall always be."

When he got to Jolan's room she was awake, and nursing the baby.

"I thought you were supposed to use a bottle," he said, after kissing her. He touched the baby's cheek with his little finger.

"Bottle feeding never felt right to me. I had to fight a bit against the newfangled nurse, but I won."

He sat down and watched. He never got over the beauty of seeing his wife and child in this form of communion. How blessed they truly were. "Just keep her safe," he prayed silently. "I'll do everything I can for her, but please, God, watch over this new life, and let her flourish."

At Margit and Emil's house, the children read the Sunday comics in the *Hardenbergh Daily News* while Margit prepared a Sunday dinner of stuffed cabbage. She had braised the cabbage leaves to make them soft, placed a large spoonful of ground beef and rice on each leaf, then rolled it into a tight packet that she placed in the pan. Now the stuffed cabbage simmered in a broth of tomato juice and chicken stock that she stirred gently with a wooden spoon.

Emil walked into the kitchen with his coat on.

"I am going to re-fasten the burlap around the roses," he said. "It worked loose in the wind the other night."

Preoccupied with her cooking, Margit merely nodded.

Emil walked out the door and onto the back porch, rubbing his left shoulder, which had ached ever since he got up. He must have slept on that side too much during the night. He took a ball of twine and a utility knife from his pocket and bent over the first rosebush. By the time he finished securing the burlap he was slightly out of breath. He stood up slowly and moved his left arm in a slow circle. The ache was becoming a full-fledged pain. His collar felt tight and he loosened first the top button of his overcoat, and then the top button of his shirt. He walked slowly to the next rose bush, wiping perspiration off his forehead.

As he bent over and reached for the loose burlap, the pain came with such force he staggered. He dropped the twine and the knife and reached for his chest with his right hand. He had time only to think "Eva!" as he fell, and then the pain blotted out all thought.

By the time Margit put the lid on the stuffed cabbage and set the table, Emil was in pain no more.

Betsy

Halloween was only three days away, but Betsy couldn't decide whether to be a chicken or a frog. On the one hand, the chicken was comical, with floppy red wattles and tail plumes stiffened with old coat hangars. On the other hand, the frog costume was really cute, with sequined eyes that bulged like a real frog's. Her mother and Aunt Eva had sewn both costumes years ago for her older sister Ronnie. Then Del used each costume, which had been carefully folded and put away until it was Betsy's turn. But Betsy just couldn't make up her mind.

The real problem was her fear that either costume was just too childish to wear. Betsy wished she were closer in age to Del and Ronnie. Del was eighteen, a senior in high school, a track star who could run faster than anyone Betsy had ever seen. And Ronnie was twenty, a typist at Van Dyke and Sons, engaged to an Air Force pilot named Larry Sinclair. Betsy was only ten and a half, and while she was glad her age finally had climbed up into two digits, she was still by far the baby of the family, and stuck with being either a chicken or a frog.

Although Del hadn't worn a Halloween costume in years, Ronnie was going to a costume party this very evening, dressed as a flapper in a fringed red dress. She had a beaded band to wear around her hair, a long string of beads, and a cigarette holder. She was going to look just like the picture of Aunt Zsuzsi in Mama's old photo album.

"Betsy, come help with the laundry," Ronnie called.

Betsy laid the costumes on her bed and walked downstairs. Hanging up laundry was not her favorite chore. She was not quite tall enough to reach the clothesline comfortably, so her job was to shake out each item of wet clothing and to hand Ronnie the clothespins. It was boring, but not as boring as drying dishes.

She put on a sweater and walked into the back yard, where the clothesline was strung from a back window to the elm tree. Next to the clothesline was the rectangular garden where their mother grew vegetables. At this time of year it was an untidy plot, with just scraggly tomato plants and a couple of rows of fall spinach. Theirs was the biggest back yard in the neighborhood. Beyond it was the fence that led to a narrow marshy area, where the old creek trickled by, smelling faintly of sewage, and on the far side of the creek sprawled a large neighborhood of small Cape Cod houses.

Ronnie was already pulling towels out of the wicker laundry basket when Betsy walked up to her. As usual, Ronnie managed to look pretty even when she was hanging up clothes. She had their mother's thick, wavy hair and their father's prominent cheekbones. Betsy envied her sister's slim, grown-up figure, and wondered how long it would be before she, too, wore a bra, girdle, and hose.

Not that Ronnie was dressed up to do laundry. Like Betsy, she wore plain dungarees, a gingham blouse, and a cardigan sweater. Ronnie had tied her long hair back with a scarf, and she wore lipstick but otherwise no makeup. Still, Betsy thought she looked lovely with gold and red leaves falling around her. They went with Ronnie's brown hair, with her beige sweater, and the green scarf that picked up the hazel highlights in her brown eyes.

"Hi," she said, smiling even though she was biting down on an extra clothespin.

"Hi." Betsy picked up a bath towel and handed it to her sister. "You're in a good mood today. You must really love doing the wash."

"I got a letter from Larry in this morning's mail."

"How old is it? Could he tell you anything? Was it censored? Did he get the package of cookies we sent him?"

"Uh fing at uh tie," said Ronnie, taking the clothespin out of her mouth. "It was three weeks old, and no, it wasn't censored, but he doesn't usually write about the war, anyway. He doesn't want to worry me. He just wrote about how he feels and how much he misses me and how he's counting the days till his tour is over and he can come home and we can get married."

"Oh. Mush."

"Well, you won't think it's mush when you're my age."

"I wish I were your age right now."

"Shoot, there's nothing wrong with being ten years old. You have great times when you're ten."

"I'm ten and a half, and I don't think hanging up laundry is a great time."

Ronnie picked up the laundry basket and moved along the clothesline. The towels they'd already hung up snapped in the breeze, leaning toward the southeast like the clouds that spread shadows on the yard. Betsy handed her another clothespin.

"Why, that looks like the Sinclairs' car!" said Ronnie, peering over the clothesline at the green Buick that was pulling into their driveway. "I didn't know they were coming for a visit. How nice!" She smiled and waved as Mr. Sinclair got out of the car.

"He looks like he's dressed for church," said Betsy. Mr. Sinclair wore a gray suit with a white handkerchief in the breast pocket. He carried a fedora in his hand but didn't put it on as he walked around the car to open the passenger door and help his wife from the car. She stood slowly and brushed smooth the skirt of her dress. It was a dark dress, a navy blue print, with a white peter pan collar. She wore a navy blue hat as well, with a veil in front of her eyes that she pushed up and out of the way. She and Mr. Sinclair looked at each other. Neither one looked at Ronnie.

Ronnie stood very still.

Betsy looked up at her sister. Ronnie's face had gone white, and her hand gripped a clothespin so hard the knuckles were white, too.

"What's wrong?" Betsy asked. She heard the screen door squeak open as her mother stepped onto the porch.

"John, Abigail. This is a surprise. Have you driven all the way from Montclair?" asked Jolan.

Mr. Sinclair nodded. Betsy had only met him once before, but she didn't remember him looking so glum.

"We came to see Ronnie," said Mrs. Sinclair in a shaky voice. She held a wrinkled handkerchief, which she waved as though she were shooing a mosquito. "Oh, John. I can't." She began to cry.

Jolan looked quickly at Ronnie as she walked up to the Sinclairs. She put her arms around Mrs. Sinclair and led her to the porch. "Come in, Abigail. Please." She looked at Ronnie again as they walked towards the porch. "Aranka, darling, please come here," she called.

"No," Ronnie said whispered. Her jaw was clenched and her eyes were filling with tears. "No."

"Ronnie? Come on," Betsy said. She reached up and tugged on Ronnie's hand, which pushed the clothespin onto the towel, a white one with a blue stripe down the middle. She was pressing so hard Betsy thought the clothesline would snap. She stood on tiptoe to unclench Ronnie's fingers. "Come on, Ronnie."

"No!"

Betsy didn't know what to do. She couldn't leave Ronnie, who looked as though she was about to run away, but Betsy wasn't strong enough to pull her toward the house. Not that she wanted to go into the house herself. Her heart hammered and her stomach felt the way it did when the dentist told her she had three new cavities. Something must have happened to Larry. And it must be bad if his parents drove all the way from Montclair without even calling first.

Footsteps crunched the fallen leaves and Betsy turned toward the sound. "Daddy!" Daddy would take care of everything. He walked toward them slowly, saying Ronnie's name in that low, gentle way he had, the voice he used when Betsy scraped her knees and the iodine hurt even though he was extra careful with it.

He put his hand on Betsy's shoulder. "Go in the house, Betsy."

"Daddy, what happened?" she asked.

"Go in the house. Stay with your mother." He walked past her toward Ronnie, who shook her head and whimpered, "No, Daddy, no, please, Daddy, no," as he reached for her.

"I am so sorry, my dear love," he murmured, and took her in his arms.

Betsy turned away and walked slowly toward the house. She didn't want to hear whatever she would hear when she got inside, but she couldn't stand to hear her sister's sobs and cries in the backyard where the golden leaves swirled down and down.

She went to the living room and leaned against the doorjamb. This was worse than going to the dentist, much worse. Her mother and Mrs. Sinclair were sitting on the couch, Jolan rocking the other woman as though she were a small child. Mr. Sinclair stood a few feet away, running the brim of his hat through his fingers, around and around.

"It's bad news, sweetie," said Jolan. "Come sit down."

But Betsy was afraid to go near the weeping woman or the man who stood silently and still, except for the hat twirling slowly in his hands.

"Larry's plane was shot down, over North Korea," said Jolan.

"Was he hurt?" she asked. A dumb question, but she hoped the answer was yes. If he was just hurt, it wouldn't be so bad. He might limp like Uncle Frank, but that would be okay.

"Oh, *honicam*. He was killed." When she said the word *killed* Mrs. Sinclair began to howl, and Mr. Sinclair made a noise as though he were choking. Betsy took a step backward, and then ran upstairs to the bedroom she shared with Ronnie. She shut the door and locked it, then climbed into bed and drew her knees up to her chin. She reached for Raggedy Ann and hugged the doll as hard as she could.

She had never known anyone who died. Lots of people died in The War—that's what her father called the Second World War—but none were her relatives, and she was so small then that she barely remembered gold stars being hung in window after window in town. Uncle Frank had been hurt, but he came home, and now he was fine. He just limped a little, especially on rainy days or when he was tired.

"Larry's dead," she said to herself, trying out the words. They were just words. She didn't even know him very well. Ronnie had bumped into him, literally, one evening in March when she and her friends had gone into New York to see *South Pacific*. Ronnie was walking out of the theater, talking to her friends, and didn't watch where she was going. Typical Ronnie. When she bumped into Larry, he caught her arms to keep her from stumbling, and that was that.

He'd been to their house only once or twice before he'd been sent to Korea. More often than not, Ronnie had had to drive to see him at the Air Force base where he was stationed, somewhere way below Trenton. The few times Betsy had seen him, he'd been nice to her, but it wasn't as though they'd become friends. Still, she sort of knew him, at least from his letters, the way he sounded when Ronnie read parts of the letters to her.

How could he be dead if Ronnie just gotten a letter this morning?

She wished Del were home instead of at a track and field meet. She wanted her parents, too, but they were so busy with Ronnie and the Sinclairs that Betsy felt invisible.

It seemed like hours before she heard them go, and then, finally, her father's footsteps on the stairs.

She ran to the door, opened it, and hurled herself at him. "Oh, Daddy!"

Tibor picked her up and carried her back to the bed, where he sat and cradled her as he had done outside with Ronnie.

"You okay, sweetie?" he asked. He kissed the top of her head.

"I got scared," she whispered.

"That's okay. It's pretty scary when grownups cry."

"Is Ronnie okay?"

"No, but she will be, some day. She's with your mother now, downstairs."

"What happened, Daddy?"

"There was a big battle on the 19th. Over a city called Pyongyang. That's the capital of North Korea. And during the battle, Larry's plane was shot down. Another pilot saw it happen."

"He couldn't get out?"

"He didn't have time, sweetie. The plane he was flying exploded. It happened so fast, he probably didn't even know it. He never felt a thing, you can be sure of that."

"But Ronnie just got a letter from him today."

Tibor sighed. "I know. That's what made it such a shock for her. But you know how long it takes his letters to get here. He had written it weeks ago. And sometimes it takes a while for the military to notify the parents. They should have been told right away, we don't know why it took so long. But the chaplain told them first thing this morning, and they were nice enough to come here to tell Ronnie in person. That must have been very hard for them to do. They're good people."

"Daddy, will there be a funeral?"

"I'm sure there will be a service of some kind."

"With a coffin?" She shuddered at the thought. Coffins were so creepy.

"I don't think so, honey. There was an explosion. And when that happens, there isn't anything left. Larry's just gone."

Betsy tried to imagine being gone. Just gone. There one minute, flying, alive, and then boom. Nothing. No one. She shivered.

"I'm glad you never fought in a war, Daddy."

They went downstairs together, and Betsy walked over to where Ronnie and her mother sat on the couch. It was the first time Betsy had ever seen Ronnie look almost ugly. Her cheeks were red and raw, and her eyes and lips were swollen. Betsy didn't know what to say so she leaned over and kissed Ronnie on the cheek. That made Ronnie start to cry again.

"It's okay," their mother said, but Betsy couldn't stand to be indoors one more minute. She ran outside and across the street to the woods. There was a place a few yards down the road, clear of poison ivy, where someone Betsy's size could duck under the brambles and emerge out of sight of the road and passing cars. She crawled beneath the underbrush and then stood up, brushing a daddy-long-legs off her sleeve. She walked past the tall brown trunks of maples and oaks until the noise of passing cars was almost too faint to hear. Ahead of her was a small clearing, with a large granite boulder in the center. Part of the boulder had split off and fallen down, years before Betsy was born, and it made a convenient seat for the tea parties she used to have for her imaginary friends when she was very small.

She sat down on the chilly rock and rubbed her fingers against its rough edge. Del told her the rock was put there by a glacier, eons ago, and marked the farthest south the ice had come in this part of New Jersey. She tried to imagine enough ice to tumble a huge boulder, but it wasn't cold enough to imagine snow at all. White and purple asters still bloomed at the edge of the woods, and all the honeysuckle vines were as green as they were before school started. A cricket chirped in the shade of the boulder, but otherwise the woods were silent. The summer birds had already flown south.

How can someone just not be, she wondered. And when it happens, do you know it? Do you feel like you're floating, and could Larry be hovering over Ronnie right now, like a ghost? Was he in purgatory? Did Episcopalians even go to purgatory?

She remembered the day Ronnie told them Larry wasn't Catholic. Their parents had been so upset, and she was just dating him then; they weren't even engaged. It took a while for Daddy to get over it. But when Larry asked if he could marry Ronnie, while Ronnie and Betsy eavesdropped at the top of the stairs, he promised he would convert, and everything was okay after that. Was he baptized yet? And if not, could he go to heaven? Were Protestants allowed? If not, then where did they go when they died—to Limbo like the pagan babies? It was horrible to think of Larry barred forever from heaven just because he was Episcopalian.

Betsy heard the snap of a twig and she peered out carefully from behind the rock.

"Del!" she hollered. "I'm over here." Her big brother came over. His dark brown hair was damp from showering. He wore the green and yellow varsity jacket he'd won the year before, and beige chinos. He sat down and gave her a hug.

"Hi, Peanut," he said. "What are you doing here all by yourself?"

She shrugged. "I didn't know where else to go." She looked up at him. "Did you tell them this is where I probably was?"

"Nope. This is our special place, you know that." It was Del's special place, really. He had found it when he was a little boy, younger than Betsy, and used the rock first as a play area, and then as a quiet place to find some privacy. He'd shown it to Betsy when she was seven, when she was first allowed to cross the street by herself. It was their secret. Ronnie would never come into the woods—she was too afraid of spiders.

"How did you do at the meet?"

Del smiled. He looked so much like their father when he did so that Betsy always felt glad.

"I came in first in the sprints," he said. "Nobody can run as fast as me." He picked up a pebble and tossed it into the woods. "You ready to come home, or do you want to sit here a while? It'll be dark soon, and it's getting chilly. You don't want to worry Mama, do you? Especially not today."

She shrugged again. "I guess not. Let's just sit a minute longer, okay?"

"Okay."

She rubbed her finger along the edge of the granite again, feeling the sharp smooth surface getting colder with the setting sun. "Del, do Protestants go to heaven?"

"Sure they do," he said. "I guess."

"Do you think Larry is in heaven or in purgatory?"

Del sat up straight and ran his fingers over his crew cut. "Gosh, Peanut, I don't know. Maybe when you fight in a war, the way Larry is—I mean was—and you're fighting evil Communists, maybe you go straight to heaven. I mean, they don't believe in God, so it's like we're fighting for God, like a Crusade."

"I hope so."

He stood up and held out his hand. "C'mon, let's go home."

After church the next morning, they went to Kettimama's and Grandma's house for a light breakfast, as they always did, but Betsy could see that nothing would be as they always did for quite some time. Kettimama solemnly kissed each of them on the cheek, a feathery light touch, before pouring tea and coffee and setting out plates of apple *retes*. But Grandma gave each of them a hearty kiss and a hug, and then she took Ronnie aside and spoke quietly to her, touching Ronnie's cheek, holding her hand.

Grandma spoke very little English. She'd been found in a displaced person's camp after the war. Her son, Betsy's Uncle Dezso, had been killed in battle, so she had no one to take care of her, except Kettimama and Betsy's parents. She'd only been in America since Betsy was six. It was doubtful that Ronnie understood her words, but her meaning came through clearly enough. Ronnie began to weep, and Grandma took a handkerchief out of her pocket and dried Ronnie's eyes as though she were a little girl.

No one had much appetite, but they all ate a little of the strudel, so they wouldn't hurt Kettimama's feelings. Kettimama said something to Grandma in Hungarian, in a cool tone that Betsy could not understand, even though she was taking Hungarian lessons at school. Kettimama was a moody woman, so different from Grandma it was hard to believe they were sisters. Grandma and Ronnie came to the table, where Grandma fussed and fluttered, patting cheeks and murmuring endearments alternating with prayers.

"Yoy, Istanem," she finally sighed, and sat down next to the radiator, shaking her head. She took her black rosary beads from her pocket and began to pray.

On a normal Sunday, the kitchen would be full of conversation. The adults would speak Hungarian, and the children would speak English, and they'd fill up on retes or palacsinta or sometimes just rye bread and butter. Then Betsy and her family would go home to read the Sunday papers, listen to the radio, and prepare dinner.

Today there was little conversation, and Betsy wondered how long things would be like this. After what seemed like hours of pushing retes crumbs across her plate, she was relieved to hear her parents say it was time to go.

On the way home, it started to rain, so Betsy was stuck inside all day, with no escape from the sorrow. She felt guilty even reading the Sunday comics.

By Monday morning she was actually eager to go to school, where everything would be normal and she could laugh out loud without being shushed. It was good to sit in a nice, neutral classroom, to think about safe things like decimals and penmanship, to play jump rope after lunch and to wash off the blackboard at the end of the day. Then all Betsy needed was something to put off going home as long as possible.

When the bell rang she hesitated on the school steps for a moment, then she had an idea. Uncle Frank would be at his restaurant. He wasn't really Betsy's uncle, but he and his mother Eva and stepfather Bela were such close friends of the family that she had called him Uncle Frank all her life. Uncle Frank never treated her like a kid. She ran downtown to his restaurant and opened the heavy door beneath the green awning. She timed it right, between the lunch and dinner crowds, and Uncle Frank waved as she walked in.

"Are you hungry, kiddo?" he asked. "Come into the kitchen."

He made two of his special chocolate parfaits with pistachio ice cream, which they carried out to the bar. Betsy loved sitting on the tall bar stool. It made her feel very grown up. She liked the smell of cigar smoke that clung to the leather bar stools, and the deep maroon carpet on the floor. All the tables had white tablecloths on them, with maroon napkins folded into a tent at each place. On each table was a small platter of black and green olives and celery sticks.

Uncle Frank grunted a little as he sat down. His leg still bothered him, more when he was tired, or on cold, damp days.

"Uncle Frank, how did you hurt your leg, during the war?"

"My souvenir of World War Two?" He ate a big spoonful of ice cream before answering.

"I'll tell you a little secret." He spoke in a quiet voice and looked around, even though the restaurant was empty, except for two businessmen sitting at a table across the room. Betsy leaned closer to him. "Most of the people who come here, who know me, think I was injured in combat. But it happened in a mess tent. Can you believe that? Geez, I spent enough time in a mess tent during my first tour back in the thirties, and when I re-upped they put me right back in with the spuds. Anyway, there I was, making a special dinner for the general and his lady friend, and an artillery barrage started, just as I was making the gravy for a pheasant the general had shot himself that very afternoon. I'm stirring the demi-glace when ka-boom! A shell hits just outside the mess tent. Pots and pans go flying. I was lucky a cleaver didn't hit me. Instead, this piece of shrapnel from a garbage can tears right through the tent and gets me in the hip."

"That must have hurt an awful lot," Betsy told him.

"Nah, it wasn't too bad," he said. "It got me discharged six months early, gave me a Purple Heart, and I had to walk with a cane for about a year. Girls really liked that, let me tell you. They said it made me look suave, like Fred Astaire. They thought I was a war hero or something."

"You never told anyone what really happened?"

"Well, my mom knows, and Bela knows, and your mom and dad know, and now you know, but that's about it. What am I going to tell people, I got nailed by a garbage can?" Betsy giggled. "I don't tell people my real name is Ferenc, either. Who would come to a steak house called Ferenc's? Now Frank's is a good name for a restaurant. Easy to spell, one syllable, fits great on a sign."

Betsy scooped up the last of the chocolate syrup and sighed. "I guess I'd better go home now."

"Kinda grim at home these days, huh? It'll get better. I promise. And don't tell your mother I gave you that ice cream—she'll say I spoiled your supper."

"I won't. Thanks, Uncle Frank."

He held the door open for her and she walked into the glare of afternoon, which seemed even brighter after the dim interior of the restaurant. Betsy shifted her schoolbooks from one arm to the other and began the long walk home.

She chuckled to think of Uncle Frank getting hit by a flying garbage can. If only something like that had happened to Larry, everything would be just fine.

That evening, the family gathered around the kitchen table to carve a jack o'lantern, everyone but Ronnie, who went to bed shortly after supper. Del wielded the big kitchen knife to cut off the top of the pumpkin, and he and Betsy scooped out the seeds and pulp with their hands.

"Daddy, can we still go trick-or-treating tomorrow?" asked Betsy.

"Well, I don't know what Emily Post says at times like these, but I don't see what harm it would do. Have you decided what to wear?"

"The chicken, I guess."

"Good choice."

But the next night, when she put the chicken costume on, Betsy didn't think she looked funny, or even cute. She felt like the saddest chicken that ever lived. She took a grocery bag from the kitchen cabinet and walked onto the porch where Tibor and Jolan waited.

"Now that's a fine looking chicken," he said. "Shall I get the camera?"

"Not this year, Daddy. I don't want my picture taken."

"You sure? All right." He reached for her hand and they walked down the steps. "See you later, Mama."

"Have a good time," Jolan said.

Betsy and her father walked down the road and turned left into the first street, bright with street lamps and jack o'lanterns. Groups of costumed children walked from door to door, shouting "Trick or Treat!" Betsy recognized some of her school friends by the costumes they had been discussing for the past few weeks—the vampire, Larry, Moe and Curly, Little Orphan Annie. But she had no desire to join them tonight, even though she loved Halloween, the costumes and the candy and ducking for apples. This year, it just didn't seem right to have too much fun. After walking only three blocks, she looked at her bag, not even half full, and said, "Daddy, let's go home."

They walked down the middle of the street, hand in hand.

"Will things ever feel normal again?" she asked.

Tibor squeezed her hand. "Yes, it just takes time."

"How much time?" She thought about the small stone in the cemetery that marked where her other brother lay, the one she never knew, except from the photo album. He had died before she was born, years and years ago, but her father still went to the cemetery every Sunday afternoon, unless it was raining hard or snowing.

"How much time, Daddy?"

"It depends. It's hard to say, because it's different for everybody. I can't say it will be so many weeks, or months, or even years. It's in God's hands, now. We're all in God's hands."

Weeks, months, years. And it was all in God's hands. Larry was in God's hands, too, right up until he died. Just how much security was there in God's hands, anyway?

Chapter 31
June 1951

"Where are you going, Daddy?" asked Betsy as Tibor opened the front door.

"To get the ice," he said.

"Can I go with you?"

"May I," he corrected automatically.

"May I go, Daddy, please?"

Tibor flipped the car keys in his hand, making a noise like little bells. "Sure."

Betsy ran to the car and opened the door. Her taffeta dress swished as she slid onto the bench seat. She disliked the prickly feeling of a starched petticoat against her legs, but her mother insisted that she wear her Sunday best today. "It isn't every day that your brother graduates from high school," Mama had said as she piped buttercream frosting in swirls and stars on Del's favorite chocolate walnut cake.

Betsy loved going to the icehouse with her father. It was a strange building on Cherry Street, tucked under the railroad overpass, dark and mysterious like a cave. The iceman would go inside with a big pair of tongs and come back out with a large cube of solid ice, more than a foot square. At home, Tibor would chip at it with an ice pick, making shavings to cool all the soda bottles in their galvanized tub. Left in the shade of the big elm tree, the ice would last all day, a big crystal with bubbles and milky intrusions, slowly melting its sharp edges smooth.

It was a perfect day for a picnic, almost cool enough for a sweater this early in the morning, with a deep blue sky that promised fluffy white clouds later in the day. A fat turkey was already roasting in the oven, and a big bowl of potato salad chilled in the refrigerator. Graduation wasn't until 11:30, so they had plenty of time to pick up the ice. They took a roundabout route, with the windows rolled down, and Betsy held her hand out the window, feeling the wind push against her palm.

Tibor drove into town and turned right on the Lincoln Highway.

"Daddy, the icehouse is the other way," said Betsy.

"I know. I want to do something first."

Tibor turned left on Jefferson Street and then Betsy realized where they were going. She pulled her hand in. It didn't seem right to play hand airplane on the way to the cemetery.

Her father parked in the usual spot and they got out of the car. The cemetery smelled of freshly cut grass that anywhere else would make Betsy want to go for a long walk. They went first to Kettipapa's grave, as they always did. Kettipapa died when Betsy was a baby, but Ronnie and Del told her stories about how he tended his garden, how he always had a fresh stick of chewing gum for each of them, and how funny his beard felt when he bent down to hug them. She was sorry she never met him.

Tibor made the sign of the cross and Betsy followed suit. She said a quick Hail Mary and watched while her father picked a few dead blossoms off the purple and white pansies in front of the granite headstone. Then he took her hand and they walked over to the children's cemetery, where Laszlo was buried.

It was odd to think of a year-old-baby as her older brother. He looked just like them—Del, Ronnie, and Betsy. If you looked at pictures of the four of them when they were babies, they all looked alike. Tibor had taken the same photo of each child, the same embarrassing pose: lying on their stomachs on the chenille bedspread, propped up on their elbows, no shirt, no diaper, just a chubby, smiling face and fat little buttocks. Betsy cringed every time she saw them.

But there were lots more pictures of her, and of Ronnie and Del, only a handful of Laszlo.

His grave had pansies, too, sunny yellow faces that almost made the little headstone look cheerful. Tibor knelt and bowed his head. He stayed that way so long that Betsy put her hand on his shoulder.

"Daddy, are you okay?"

He placed his hand over hers and nodded. "I just want him to know he isn't forgotten." He stood up and they walked back to the car. "He would have been a high school freshman by now. He would have been an athlete like Del, too. He was such a strong baby."

Her father loved playing baseball with Del every summer, and tossing a football every fall. He went to every home track meet, and sometimes accompanied Del as he practiced running down the shoulder of their street. Even Ronnie enjoyed playing football with them, and before Larry died, she used to jitterbug with her friends every Saturday night.

Betsy wasn't very good at playing catch, she wasn't much of a runner, and she didn't know how to dance. She had never lost her baby fat, for one thing; she was on the plump side, like her mother and grandmother, and she preferred to spend her time with a thick coloring book and a full box of crayons. Lately she had begun to draw, using a soft pencil to doodle in the margins of her notebook when she was supposed to be doing homework. She'd much rather be doing that right now, in fact, instead of walking through the cemetery. Her parents spent more time in the cemetery than anyone else, and they made the whole family come every holiday and holy day of obligation.

"Please don't be sad, Daddy," she said. "This is supposed to be a happy day."

Her father squeezed her hand. "I promise not to be sad for the rest of the day."

He kept his promise. He whistled "Pomp and Circumstance" when they finally picked up the ice, he cheered and clapped when Del received his diploma, and he made a toast when they got back home and began the picnic. Even Ronnie perked up for the party. She'd been quiet and withdrawn all winter, almost like she wasn't there at all. She had grown so forgetful that when she went to work in the morning, she sometimes came back in the house two or three times, for house keys or a scarf or a record she had borrowed from a friend and needed to return.

A few weeks ago Ronnie was supposed to keep an eye on supper while Jolan and Tibor attended the parent-teacher conference at school. Instead of watching the stew, she put on an Andrews Sisters record and played "I Can Dream, Can't I?" again and again, until Betsy put cotton in her ears. But by then the song was stuck in Betsy's head, the words playing over and over:

Can't I pretend that I'm locked in the bend of your embrace?
For dreams are just like wine
And I am stuck with mine
I'm aware
My heart is a sad affair
There's much disillusion there
But I can dream, can't I?

And when the odor of burned chuck wafted upstairs, it was Betsy who turned off the stove, dumped the thick brown sludge into the trash, and tried to scrub out Mama's good Dutch oven.

But today the record player was stacked with Perry Como singing "Hoop-Dee-Doo" and Frank Sinatra's "You Do Something to Me." Del even managed to get Ronnie dancing again. School was over, and the long, lovely summer would unfurl like a pretty flag, offering trips to the beach, Fourth of July fireworks, and hours of daylight to play in after supper. For the first time in a long time, everything was perfect.

Three weeks after Del's party, Betsy came home from the movies. She picked up the mail on her way in, tossed the letters on the kitchen table, and went upstairs to change into shorts. The house was quiet, with everyone at work except Betsy and her mother, who was tending the tomatoes in the garden. This summer, Del was helping their father paint houses, to save money before starting college in September.

Jolan stood and waved when she heard the screen door slam.

"Hi, honey. How was the movie?"

"Good! There was a space monster like a giant carrot in the North Pole that ate all the sled dogs, and then they killed it with electricity."

Jolan rubbed the small of her back. "It sounds horrible! Don't tell your father I let you see a movie like that."

"Oh, Mama, it's just science fiction."

"It will probably give you nightmares."

"No, it won't. It was really good. It will probably give Mary Alice nightmares, though. She screamed every time the monster attacked someone."

Jolan shook her head and bent over the tomato plants, pinching back the topmost shoots. "I don't understand why you'd even want to see such a movie."

"Because it's fun. What do you need me to do?"

"You can help me pick some spinach for supper."

"They showed a Popeye cartoon today, too."

"Well, that's more like it."

Betsy whistled the Popeye song as she pulled out the spinach plants. When they picked enough, they walked back to the house together, holding the spinach like dark green bouquets. Jolan put them into the sink to rinse them.

"The mail came," said Betsy.

"I'll look at it in a minute," said Jolan.

Betsy sat at the kitchen table and began to sort through the pile of letters. Not that anyone would be writing to her, but she could always hope.

"Here's a postcard from Aunt Zsuzsi. A picture of the Eiffel Tower, and it says, 'Hello, everyone. Arrived safely after bumpy flight. Three days of shows, then a little sightseeing. Back next Monday. Love, Z'. That's yesterday. She must be home already. See?"

Jolan wiped her hands on a dishtowel and smoothed her hair back into its bun. Betsy handed her the card and went back to the stack of envelopes.

"Telephone bill, a flyer about a dress sale at the Tog Shop, something from the St. Vincent De Paul Society. And a letter for Del."

"For Del?" asked Jolan. "Let me see it."

Betsy held onto the white envelope. "Mama, it's addressed to Del."

"I'm not going to open it, I just want to see who it's from."

Betsy read the return address. "It says Selective Service Center." She held out the envelope.

Jolan stepped backwards until she was leaning against the sink.

"Mama, what's wrong?"

Jolan had to swallow before she could speak. "Selective Service. That's the Draft Board."

Betsy felt her eyelids open wide. "Del's being drafted?"

Jolan rubbed her hands against her apron. It was an old apron, one she'd made from scraps of material from housedresses that had worn out, with a pattern of purple and pink flowers.

"Mama?"

"What time is it?" Jolan asked. Betsy looked at the clock hanging above her mother's head.

"Four thirty."

"They'll be home soon. Go wash up so you can help me with supper."

"But Mama—"

"I said wash up!"

Betsy went into the bathroom and washed her hands and face. She dried her hands slowly, then she went back into the kitchen. Her mother wasn't there.

"Mama?" Betsy looked first in the living room, then in the small room that had once been Del and Ronnie's bedroom, and now served as a study for Betsy's father to use when he graded student papers in the evening. Both rooms were empty. She opened the door to the porch, and there she saw her mother, sitting in one of the Adirondack chairs her father had made, with the unopened letter in her lap, staring at the street. Betsy shut the door, and began to set the table.

She was finished, and sitting in the other porch chair, when Tibor and Del came home. Tibor tooted the car horn as he always did, and the two of them got out of the car. Tibor rolled up the sheet that protected the car seat from their paint-splattered overalls, and they walked up to the house. Tibor's smile faded when he saw Jolan's face.

"What's wrong?" he asked. Jolan shook her head, and stared at Del.

"This came for you today," she said, and held out the letter, "from the draft board."

Del frowned and took it from her. His mouth opened a little as he exhaled. Betsy heard the little "huh" sound he made, and she squirmed in her seat. Del looked up at her then, and smiled and winked. The three of them watched as he ran his thumb under the flap of the envelope. They heard the sound of the paper tearing, and the soft rustle as he slipped the letter out and unfolded it. He tapped it with his fingers. "I guess you all know what this says without my even reading it out loud."

"How much time do you have?" asked Tibor.

"I'm to report to Camp Kilmer in October," Del said. "October 19, to be exact."

Betsy's eyes opened wide. October 19 was the very same day one year ago when Larry had been killed over Pyongyang.

"You're our only son!" cried Jolan. "Isn't there some sort of rule about only sons? And you're going to college in September!"

Tibor put his hand on her shoulder and squeezed it. "The rule only applies to families who lost a son in the last war."

Jolan began to cry. "We've lost two sons! I don't want to lose the only one I have left!"

Betsy looked at her mother and frowned. Two sons? Did she think of Ronnie's dead fiancé as a son?

Del knelt in front of Jolan and put his hands on her shoulders.

"Don't cry, Ma. The war could be over before I even join up. And there's no guarantee they'll send me to Korea. I could be stationed anywhere. Japan, maybe, or even somewhere stateside. Please don't cry."

"Del, take your sister inside, please," said Tibor.

Betsy held his hand tight as they went into the living room and sat on the couch. She wrapped her arms around his bicep and leaned her head against his shoulder. He smelled like paint and sweat. She wanted to smell it forever.

"Do you really have to go?" she asked.

"It's the law, Peanut. And it's my duty. If I don't go, someone else will have to go in my place. That wouldn't be fair."

"But can't you tell them you're a what do you call it, that it's against your principles, or your religion?"

"It's called a conscientious objector. But I'd be lying if I told them that. I hate the commies and I don't want them in Korea or anywhere else."

"But you'll have to leave home."

He rubbed her hands. "I know. I don't want to leave home, but I have no choice. And it's not like it's forever. Just a couple of years."

A couple of years! Betsy could not imagine Del being gone for a couple of weeks, let alone a couple of years. It was hard enough to think of him going to college, but that was at least still in New Jersey. He would have come home on weekends, and been home for holidays. But this—he could be hurt, or even end up like Larry.

"I'm glad you're not a pilot," she said.

Del sighed. "Listen, Bets. You're a big girl now, and I'm not going to kid you. It won't be any picnic if I get sent over there. But I promise I won't do anything dumb, and if I see any of those commies coming at me, well, you know how fast I can run. The second they call for a retreat I'll be gone, and no one's gonna catch me." He kissed the top of her head. "C'mon, let's get supper ready so Mama doesn't have to do that. You'll have to be extra nice to her when I'm gone. You know how worried she's gonna be."

Del changed out of his work clothes and into clean dungarees. He put on one of Jolan's aprons and made a big show of slicing the leftover ham from Sunday dinner. Betsy tore the spinach and put it in a pot to boil while Del peeled potatoes. "I'd better start practicing, from what Uncle Frank tells me," he said.

Betsy leaned against the counter and watched him. "Del, what did Mama mean when she said she'd lost two sons?"

Del glanced at her before he picked up another potato and started peeling it. "I guess she never told you, but she and Pop had another baby, or they almost had one. It was a miscarriage. You know what that is? Where the baby dies before it's actually born?"

Betsy nodded.

"Well, Ma had to go to the hospital, and I guess the baby was far enough along that they could tell it would have been a boy. So that's what she meant."

"Why wasn't he buried with Laszlo?"

Del made a face like he smelled something bad. He dropped the white potato into a bowl of water and reached for another. "I don't know. I guess they don't do that."

"So what happened to him?"

Del shrugged. "Don't know."

Now Betsy had another soul to worry about. Was he in heaven, or was he forever in limbo with all the heathen babies that had died over the years? And what was the big secret? Wasn't she was old enough to know about these things? Would she ever be old enough in her parents' eyes?

The next evening, Uncle Frank came over with a stack of *palacsinta*, just in time for dessert. Betsy loved the rolled crepes and their sweet-tangy filling of pot cheese and cinnamon. She wished she had room for more than one, but at least she could look forward to leftovers for breakfast.

She helped her mother wash the dishes, and then she went onto the porch, where her father, brother, and Uncle Frank were smoking cigarettes. A rumble of thunder sounded to the northwest as she sat on the porch steps. A few minutes later her mother came out, with a pot of coffee, followed by Ronnie, who was pulling on a pair of white gloves. Ronnie's friend Louise turned into their driveway as Jolan refilled the coffee cups.

"See you later," said Ronnie as she walked toward Louise's Buick.

A flicker of lightning made Betsy look up. She counted one-one thousand, two-one thousand, and reached twelve-one thousand before thunder boomed. More than two miles.

"Where is she going tonight?" Tibor asked Jolan.

"To the movies."

"She shouldn't stay out so late on a weeknight," he grumbled.

"Well, I think it's good to see her going out with her friends again," said Jolan. "She's spent too many nights away from the company of young people."

There it was again. Ronnie home, listening to mournful records, Larry dead, Del drafted. Betsy shivered a little.

"So Uncle Frank," said Del. "You were telling us about what I can expect."

"Yep." Though he was answering Del, he directed his comments to Tibor and Jolan. "What happens is, Del goes to Camp Kilmer, but that's just for processing. Haircut, shots, uniform, that sort of thing. Where he takes basic training depends."

"On what?" asked Tibor. "Surely as a local boy he'll go to Fort Dix?"

"No telling with Uncle Sam," Frank answered. "That may seem like a logical place to you and me, but they could send Del to Timbuktu for his basic. There's no telling."

"How bad is basic, really, Uncle Frank?"

"For a strapping kid like you? Piece of cake."

"Really?" asked Jolan. The wind began to pick up, rustling the leaves of the elm tree.

"Sure. It's the ones who are out of shape who have trouble. You've got yourselves a track star here. Ten-mile hike, double time, with full pack? No problem for our boy Del."

Lightning again. One-one thousand, two-one thousand, three-one thousand, four—BOOM!

Jolan stood up. "I think it's time to go inside." She picked up the coffeepot and cups. Tibor held the door open for her. "Don't stay out here too long." He followed Jolan inside.

A gust of wind bent the top of the elm tree, and a moment later the first drops of rain began to land on the porch steps. Betsy watched the splash they made, big as quarters. She stood up and went to the door, holding it open against the wind, but Uncle Frank and Del continued to talk, heads bent toward each other, and she went inside.

Betsy never particularly wanted school to begin, but this year was worse than ever. It didn't matter that she was starting sixth grade, and would no longer have to play in the small children's section of the school playground. Every day closer to October brought her closer to losing her brother. The family picnic on Labor Day highlighted not only the end of the summer season and Sunday trips to the beach, but also the end of how things had always been. Even shopping for a new pencil case and notebook, which always made her anticipate the new school year, seemed to fill her with dread.

But Del was excited to be leaving Hardenbergh. On the night before school started, he'd given her a sketchbook and a set of charcoals, and they went for a walk. The evening was crisp and she shivered in her sweater, so Del draped his varsity jacket over her shoulders, while he tried to explain his hopes for the future.

"The war can't last forever," he'd said to her, "and from what Uncle Frank tells me, I may even want to make a career of it. You know I'm not like Pop—gosh, he reads so much I wonder that his eyes still work. I'm not sure I'm really cut out for college, but I'm not sure what I want to do with my life, except see things and do things that I can't see or do here at home. There's a lot more to the world than Hardenbergh, New Jersey, Peanut. Don't be mad at me for wanting to taste it."

"I'm not mad, Del," she had said. And she wasn't mad. To be honest, she even envied him a little. She just wished she could go with him.

The only good thing about any of this was being permitted to skip school on the day Del had to report for duty. Ronnie was unable to get the day off, so she said goodbye to him as she left for work that day. Del walked her to the bus stop, and when he came home a few minutes later, he went straight upstairs to finish packing his suitcase.

They were all dressed in their Sunday-best clothes, everyone but Del, when he came downstairs with his suitcase in hand. Del was wearing his varsity jacket and a plain white shirt, but no tie. He stood on the porch between Jolan and Betsy, and Tibor took their picture. Then Tibor handed the camera to Betsy, and she took a picture of him with her parents. Funny how she'd never really noticed, until she saw them through the viewfinder, that Del was taller than their father.

When they walked to the car, Betsy expected her brother to stop at the door and take a last, long look at the house, but he got into the rear seat without looking back. He held her hand during the short drive through town, over the Wheatstone Bridge, and into Stelton. They stopped at the bus terminal, directly across the street from Camp Kilmer, where the other draftees were gathering in twos and threes, some talking, some smoking cigarettes, all looking both nervous and excited at the same time.

Betsy looked across the street toward the Camp gate. Beyond it, she could see long, two-story buildings with white clapboard siding, and farther down the road, the white steeple of a church. One building had the sign "Post Exchange" over the door. She wondered what that meant. Soldiers were walking along the road inside the camp, and men drove along the street in jeeps. Except for the color of the uniforms and the jeeps, the Camp could have been almost any small town on a busy afternoon.

Saying goodbye was as bad as she had feared. She didn't want to cry but she couldn't help herself, especially when Del knelt down on one knee to hug her close. "I'll see you in eight weeks, Peanut," he murmured.

"You won't be home for Thanksgiving!"

"No, but with luck I'll be home for Christmas. You be good, okay? Don't give Ma or Pop a hard time."

"I won't."

"Del, your shoelace is untied," said their mother.

Del tied his shoe, still half-kneeling, and then for a moment he put his hands on the ground in front of him, in the ready position. Betsy half expected him to shift his weight forward, as though he were on a track, set to start a race. And he was, in a sense, running not in a race with anyone else, or running away from her and their family, but running toward a future all his own, and suddenly what Betsy felt was not sorrow at all, but pure envy.

Chapter 32
June 1953

The cardboard box was nearly full, but Betsy managed to tuck several packs of Juicyfruit between the peanut butter cookies, the new deck of playing cards, the letters and photos, and the folded Sunday paper.

"We have room for a chocolate bar," she said.

"We can't mail chocolate in the summertime," said Ronnie. "It will melt." Betsy held the flaps closed while Ronnie taped them shut. Betsy carefully addressed the package with a grease pencil, proudly addressing it to Cpl. Wendel Nemeth, 62nd MP Service Company, writing the APO numbers as neatly as she could, and best of all, finishing the address with the word "Germany."

She would never, ever forget how relieved she had been the day Del told them where he was being sent. Betsy thought even the living room walls were listening, it got so quiet, and she was sure everyone could hear her heart thud while she held her breath and tried not to cry when he said "Korea."

Except he didn't say Korea. He said Germany. A wave of relief washed over her, like an eraser wiping a chalkboard clean, leaving her lightheaded and laughing. Betsy knew that the prayers she had said, every night since Del was drafted—please God, let him be safe, don't let him go to the war—her prayers had really been answered. The nuns were right. Prayer did work.

She put the parcel in the basket of her bicycle and began pedaling to the post office. They'd had two Christmases without Del, but not this year. This was one summer she couldn't wait to have over, to be that much closer to his homecoming, even though today was going to be a great day, not just because school was out and she was sending a "care" package to Del, but because she and Ronnie were going to have an adventure all their own. For one whole week, Betsy and Ronnie would be staying with Aunt Zsuzsi in New York City, while their parents celebrated their 25th wedding anniversary by traveling back to Niagara Falls for a second honeymoon.

Betsy had never been to New York. Her parents had taken Ronnie and Del to the World's Fair, but that was a year before Betsy had even been born. She'd seen pictures of the skyscrapers and the Statue of Liberty, but now she would see them in person. And maybe even ride the Staten Island Ferry. None of her friends had ever done that.

Normally, after dropping a parcel at the post office, she would take her time going home, stopping at Uncle Frank's or meeting Mary Alice at the soda fountain. But today she hurried home to pack for her first real vacation. Breathing hard, she coasted to a stop in the driveway, rolling past her father, who was mowing the lawn.

Jolan had already retrieved the suitcases from the storage area upstairs and was wiping the dust off when Betsy bounded upstairs. These were the same brown leather cases Jolan and Tibor had taken on their honeymoon, a wedding present from Kettipapa. Ronnie and Betsy were going to share one suitcase, and their parents would have the other.

"I can do that, Mama," Betsy said. "You have to pack your own things."

"I want to be sure you don't forget anything," said Jolan.

"Betsy's right, Mama," said Ronnie. She wet her finger to test the iron. "Ouch! That's hot enough. I'll be done ironing in a few minutes, and then I can help Betsy pack. It's not every day you get to go on a second honeymoon. Be sure to pack that pretty nightgown Daddy bought you."

"Why did daddy buy her a nightgown for their anniversary?" Betsy asked when their mother went downstairs. "Shouldn't he have given her a necklace or something?"

"You're very young, Betsy. You'll understand someday."

If there was one thing that irked Betsy it was being told that "someday" she would know what everyone else was talking about. It was so unfair being the youngest. Sometimes she thought being grownup was like being in a private club, with special privileges and a secret code. She wanted to be caught up with everyone else, to get the jokes and to go to movies the Legion of Decency rated for adults only. She began to stuff her clothes into the suitcase, but she couldn't hold on to a bad mood while she was packing, not when tomorrow morning she would be on a train for New York.

It wasn't her first train ride, of course. Every August, Betsy and her mother took the train to Newark, to shop at Klein's department store for new school shoes and a new Sunday dress. She always wished they could keep going. New York was just one tantalizing stop away from Newark, but her mother wouldn't waste the trip by sightseeing when they had come to shop. How wonderful it was to finally stay on the train when it arrived in Newark, and to hear the conductor shout "New York! Next stop New York!" as the train pulled out of the station.

She stared out the window as city buildings gave way to the swampy wetlands that bordered the Hudson River. Her father pointed out Staten Island and Snake Hill, a lone outcropping of solid rock, like one gigantic boulder, sticking up out of the marsh grasses just before the train rounded a curve and dipped into the tunnel.

With a whoosh the train grew dark, and Betsy tried not to think about how quickly they were plummeting beneath the riverbed. Suddenly the train sped out of the tunnel into daylight, but a moment later they were underground again, in the Pennsylvania Station.

Tibor pulled their suitcases down from the overhead rack and they slowly made their way out of the train to the platform, a mass of people and noise and color, but too much of it was khaki. Soldiers everywhere, even here. Then Aunt Zsuzsi was waving at them and with a flurry of hugs and kisses they said goodbye to their parents, who were taking the subway to Grand Central Terminal to continue their trip north. A few bewildering minutes later, Betsy was sitting on the warm, musty seat of a taxicab, whose driver honked the horn as he pulled away from the station.

She rolled down the rear window of the cab, leaning out as far as she dared to stare up at the great skyscraper canyons, their steep gray walls filled with windows, where millions of people worked.

"Betsy, put your head in," said Ronnie. "You look like Mr. Pilecki's beagle."

Aunt Zsuzsi smiled and squeezed her hand. "Let her be. It's her first trip to the city."

The taxi swerved and zoomed down the street, stopping suddenly as the traffic light turned red. Then it sped forward again, weaving from lane to lane. Betsy was pushed one way and then the other, holding onto the seat with one hand and the armrest with the other, trying not to squash Aunt Zsuzsi. It was almost as much fun as the scrambler ride on the boardwalk.

They worked their way through the traffic, moving past small grocery stores, jewelry stores, clothing stores, appliance stores, pawn shops—just one or two blocks contained all the same kinds of stores in all of downtown Hardenbergh. Even more amazing was the sheer number of people: women pushing baby carriages down the sidewalks, old men in sleeveless T-shirts hanging out of windows and shouting to one another in foreign languages, a bearded man preaching on a street corner. Then the stores gave way to art galleries, antique shops, and booksellers. These streets were much quieter than the others they'd driven on, blocks filled with brick or stone row houses, four stories high, without front porches. The taxicab stopped in front of one of them.

They climbed out of the cab, rumpled and hot. Betsy could smell exhaust fumes on her dress. She longed for a cherry cola.

Aunt Zsuzsi led them up the front stoop, where she unlocked a heavy wooden door that had a single window covered by a wrought iron grille. They crowded into a small entryway with a tiled floor. The inner door was made of frosted glass. Aunt Zsuzsi didn't use a key for this door. She opened it and stood aside. "Come into the living room."

Betsy gasped. This was like no living room she had ever seen. It extended the whole length of the apartment, a long, narrow room with a high ceiling, wood parquet floor, and a wrought-iron spiral staircase in one corner. Artwork covered the walls. A few of the paintings were recognizable as landscapes or still lifes, but most were abstract shapes and splashes of color, like something Betsy would have done in kindergarten. There were statues, too, in the room, and here, too, some were obviously of people, or at least parts of people; others were just forms. Best of all, at the end of the room closest to them, stood a television set.

"Wow, Aunt Zsuzs!"

Betsy wasn't sure where to sit. This one room had more furniture than her family had in their whole house. She waited to see what Ronnie would do.

Ronnie sat down on a black leather couch that stood against one wall, beneath a large painting that seemed mostly swirls of red and yellow and black. In front of the couch was a low, kidney-shaped coffee table made of the lightest wood Betsy had ever seen. She sat gingerly on the other end of the couch.

Aunt Zsuzsi came from somewhere in the recesses of the apartment with two bottles of beer and a bottle of Coke.

"Here you go," she said. She passed out the drinks and sat on chair that seemed to be made of chrome and air. She took a long drink from the bottle. "Oh, that's so much better!"

Aunt Zsuzsi acted hot but she didn't look it. She was wearing a sleeveless linen sheath and open-toed heels in matching beige. Her dark brown hair was curled into a bun on top of her head, and would have looked prim if it weren't for the fringe of bangs on her forehead. Somehow, she managed to look ten years younger than their mother, whose hair was fading to gray, and whose figure was round and soft. Ronnie was as slender as Aunt Zsuzsi, and if she wore her hair up instead of in a pageboy, she and Aunt Zsuzsi would look more like sisters than Ronnie and Betsy.

"How does lunch at the Automat sound?" asked Aunt Zsuzsi. "You can leave the unpacking until later. And then we can go shopping. Or would you rather see the Statue of Liberty?"

"The Statue of Liberty, please, Aunt Zsuzs?" asked Betsy.

"Okay, let's get going, so we can be back in time to change. I'm having a few guests over for dinner tonight. They're dying to meet you."

Betsy was skeptical about the guests and their desires, but she was thrilled with the automat. She put her nickel into a slot and opened a little door, and there was a plate of macaroni and cheese. Another nickel, open the door, and there was a slice of apple pie. This was fun.

More fun than seeing the Statue of Liberty, it turned out. Betsy thought half of Manhattan Island must have had the same idea. The ferry was crowded, the temperature soared, and her stomach hurt from eating too much. People pushed and shoved as they got off the ferry. Betsy craned her neck up at the statue that towered over them. The statue's uplifted arm was so muscular it seemed to belong to a man, not "Lady" Liberty. She would fit right in on a roller derby team.

The observation deck in the statue's crown was so crowded and hot they opted not to climb the stairs all the way to the torch.

"What was it like for you, the first time you saw this?" asked Ronnie, after they'd descended and bought ice cream cones.

"Oh, my, that was such a long time ago," Aunt Zsuzsi answered.

Betsy licked halfheartedly at her vanilla cone, sending a rivulet of melted ice cream down her wrist.

"I was what, 14, 15 years old," Aunt Zsuzsi continued. "Your mother and I could hardly see the statue for all the people crammed against the rail of the boat. And we were so frightened! We didn't speak a word of English, and we didn't know anyone except the Jelineks, the couple who had watched out for us on the trip over. Some people cheered when they saw the statue, some people cried. I cried. I thought I would never see Mama again, and I had no idea what Uncle Emil and Aunt Margit would be like, or where they lived. And of course, we had to go through Ellis Island, and they treated us like—well, they weren't very kind. So my first impression of America wasn't so good. But then we were finally standing on New Jersey soil, and this man stepped out from the crowd and welcomed us in our own language. I remember looking at him, and he was so happy to see us, I mean, you could just see the kindness and joy in his face, and he kissed us both and I just knew that we were going to be okay."

Aunt Zsuzsi wrapped the remains of her chocolate cone in a napkin.

"So I hate to say it, but this statue doesn't mean half as much to me as dear Uncle Emil." She glanced at her watch. "What do you say we go back?"

Betsy was glad when they finally returned to the apartment. Her stomach still hurt, and she needed to use the bathroom, but Aunt Zsuzsi wouldn't let them use the restroom on the ferry. "Disgusting," she had called it.

Aunt Zsuzsi directed her to the bathroom on the second floor. Betsy sat on the toilet with relief, and waited for the inevitable result of eating too much rich food too fast. The last thing she wanted was to have diarrhea in Aunt Zsuzsi's nice clean bathroom, but to her surprise, nothing happened. Finally she wiped herself and stood to pull up her underwear.

It was when she turned to flush the toilet that she saw the blood. What the heck? She grabbed another piece of toilet paper and dabbed at herself again. It came away spotted bright red. Her throat went suddenly dry. What was wrong? What was she going to do, away from home, away from Mama? She dropped the toilet paper into the toilet and flushed the awful mess away. She had to find Ronnie, and right away.

"What is it, Betsy?" asked Aunt Zsuzsi when Betsy ran downstairs. Her aunt was in the basement kitchen, setting out a plate of finger sandwiches.

"Where's Ronnie?"

"She went to get some coffee. I'm all out. What's the matter, Betsy? Don't you feel well?"

Betsy shook her head. "I need to talk to Ronnie."

Aunt Zsuzsi wiped her hands on her green apron and walked over to Betsy. She put her hand on Betsy's forehead.

"I don't think you have a fever. What's wrong, dear? You look so pale. Please, let me help."

Betsy's lips began to tremble. "Aunt Zsuzsi, I don't know what's wrong. I'm bleeding."

Aunt Zsuzsi looked her up and down. "Have you cut yourself, darling?"

"No, I haven't. It just started." She pointed to her crotch. "Down there."

"Oh-h-h," Aunt Zsuzsi said. And then she did the oddest thing—she smiled. She put her arms around Betsy and held her close. "It's all right, darling, you aren't sick, and nothing's wrong." She held Betsy at arm's length and smiled again. "Growing up so fast! I suppose your mother never said a word about this? So like her! Come upstairs, and I'll take care of it."

"What is it, Aunt Zsuzs?" she asked as they went upstairs.

"You're having your first period, Betsy. Haven't any of the girls in your class talked about it? Maybe something about 'that time of the month,' or even 'the curse'?"

"Well, yeah, once or twice, I heard some of the girls say they had the curse, but I just thought they had a stomach ache or something."

"Does your stomach hurt?"

"A little."

Aunt Zsuzsi went into the bathroom and rummaged in the vanity. "Here we go." She handed Betsy a rectangular white pad about the size of her shoe sole, but easily twice as thick, and a contraption made of elastic. "You hold the pad, and I'll show you how to put it on the belt. You wrap this end through the little buckle, see? And you wear it like this—your legs go through here—and you wear it under your panties. Got it?"

Betsy nodded.

"You put this on and I'll make you a nice cup of tea. If you need to, you can rinse your panties out and hang them here."

Aunt Zsuzsi shut the bathroom door behind her. Betsy stood for a moment, holding the pad and belt as if she were holding a spider. In five minutes she'd gone from thinking she must have something horrible, like cancer, to—to what? Aunt Zsuzsi certainly didn't act as though anything bad was happening, and she had this—thing—right at hand. Betsy shook her head and looked at the white pad. It was big and thick, almost like a large bandage. Well, maybe that wasn't so far wrong. She peeked in the vanity at the bag Aunt Zsuzsi had taken it from. "Feminine napkins," it read. She'd seen a bag like this before, once when she was very small and her mother had come home from the pharmacy. "Just napkins" her mother had said, and Betsy assumed they were just a different brand from their usual table napkins. She'd never even thought about it after that.

She pulled the belt up around her hips. It wasn't very comfortable, and she wasn't sure she did it right. She sat down. It seemed secure enough, but it felt like she was sitting on a pillow. She stood up again, trying to look at the back of her skirt in the mirror, but she couldn't see well enough to be sure it didn't show. She put on fresh panties, and went downstairs.

Aunt Zsuzsi handed her a glass of water and two aspirin. "This should make you feel better."

"Why does my stomach hurt?" Betsy asked.

"You're having cramps," Aunt Zsuzsi said. She handed Betsy a cup of hot tea. "I know it's warm today but drink this. It's very soothing."

Betsy sat down on a stool and watched Aunt Zsuzsi cut up carrots and celery.

"I hope you don't mind if I work while we talk." Aunt Zsuzsi smiled at Betsy again. "You're not sick, Betsy. It's a perfectly normal thing that's happening to you. The bad news is that it will happen every month from now on. The good news is you won't always have cramps. Honestly, hasn't your mother told you anything at all about this?"

"Nope."

Aunt Zsuzsi shook her head. "Well, what's happening is that your body is getting ready for you to have babies. You have an organ called a uterus, and every month it fills with blood, to make itself all soft for a baby. And then, when you don't get pregnant, all the blood has to go somewhere, so it comes out as your period."

"But Aunt Zsuzsi, I'm only thirteen!"

"I know, that's much too young to think about having babies, but your body is getting ready anyway. It happens to all women, like clockwork." She began slicing celery again.

"So that's all there is to it?"

"More or less."

398

"But what keeps me from getting pregnant every month?"

Aunt Zsuzsi put the knife down again. "I suppose your mother hasn't said anything to you about that either? How she managed to have so many children and be so—so prudish I don't understand." She tapped her fingers on the cutting board. "Bear with me, *honicam*. I don't have any children myself, so I never expected to have to tell anyone about the birds and the bees."

"What about them?"

"Haven't you ever seen animals—oh dear, I suppose you don't even remember when the Amwells had cows behind the house."

"I remember all the houses being built, but I don't remember any cows." What the heck did cows have to do with this?

"This would be so much easier if you had a dog or a cat."

"Mama's afraid of dogs."

"I know. And your father is allergic to cats. So you've never even had kittens around the house, or watched them being born."

Cows, dogs, cats, birds, bees—would Aunt Zsuzsi never get to the point?

Aunt Zsuzsi wiped her hands on a dishtowel and sat down next to Betsy. "I don't suppose you've ever seen your father or your brother without any clothes on."

"Of course not!"

"But you realize that men and women are built differently. Like, women have a bustline and men don't."

Betsy nodded.

"Well, men are different in lots of ways. For one, they have an organ called a penis. Have you ever heard that word?"

"I don't think so. How do you spell it?"

"P-E-N-I-S."

"Oh! I saw that on a stall in the ladies room at the movie theater. But I thought it was pronounced pen-is, like a pen."

Aunt Zsuzsi stifled a smile and went on. "Well, if any of your friends have a male dog, you've seen one. It's between their legs. All male animals have one. Dogs, cats, cows, horses, people..."

"Oh!" Betsy almost spilled her tea. She set the cup down on the counter. She remembered the day. She was little, only five or six, and she was in the car with her father. They were driving in the country for some reason, and there were horses in a field. And one horse was on top of the other. They separated just as the car went by. 'What are they doing, Daddy?' she had asked. And her father had answered, 'Just playing.' But Betsy looked back, and she just caught a glimpse of something, bright pink and dangling almost to the ground, but before she had a chance to ask about it her father had started talking about the Yankees, and she forgot all about it. Until now.

She looked at Aunt Zsuzsi. "I saw a horse once. It was all pink, and really big."

Aunt Zsuzsi cleared her throat and nodded. "Yes, that was a penis all right, but don't worry, they're a lot bigger on a horse than they are on a person." She stood up and walked back to the celery.

"The one horse was on top of the other horse."

"Making a baby horse." Aunt Zsuzsi began to arrange the celery and carrots on a tray. She let Betsy put two and two together.

"So the penis goes inside...you mean Mama and Daddy–?" Aunt Zsuzsi nodded.

Ronnie walked in with a grocery bag in her hands. "Mama and Daddy what?"

Betsy looked from Aunt Zsuzsi to Ronnie and back to Aunt Zsuzsi. "Aunt Zsuzs?"

"We've been having a little talk about the birds and the bees. Your sister just got her first period."

"Oh-h-h-h," Ronnie said, just like Aunt Zsuzsi had done. She put down the grocery bag and gave Betsy a hug. "You're all grown up," she whispered. She smiled and tugged at Betsy's braid.

Betsy hadn't thought about it that way. All this talk of what her body was doing and why had distracted her from the fact that she was, apparently, as of today, not a little girl anymore, and never would be again. Finally! It was about time.

"Betsy, did Mama ever talk to you about this?" Ronnie asked.

Betsy shook her head. "No, but Aunt Zsuzsi just filled me in. About everything."

Ronnie looked at Aunt Zsuzsi. "Everything?" Zsuzsi nodded, and Ronnie's cheeks turned pink. "I see." She took the coffee out of the grocery bag and studied the label.

Betsy looked at the red bag of coffee, but she couldn't get the image of the horses out of her mind. The one horse—the female—had shrieked, she remembered hearing that. So did it hurt? But if it did, then who would do such a thing? Daddy would never hurt Mama, would he?

"Well, you girls had better get ready," said Aunt Zsuzsi. "And you know, I think Betsy deserves a more grown-up look tonight, don't you? Certainly she shouldn't wear her hair in braids for a party. Why not take a look through my things to see if we can find something a little more sophisticated for her to wear than that dress?"

"Oh, Aunt Zsuzsi, may we?" asked Betsy. Any questions she had about this new information could wait.

"Sure. I'll be up in a couple of minutes."

"Thanks!" She ran toward the stairs. Aunt Zsuzsi's closet was a whole room in itself, with racks of dresses on two sides and built-in drawers on the other. Betsy was afraid to touch anything, but Ronnie riffled through the garments as though she were in the Tog Shop back home. She kept shaking her head no, no, no, but finally, after consulting with Aunt Zsuzsi, they settled on an apple green silk dress with a long skirt.

"It will only take a few minutes for me to hem this," said Ronnie.

"Better you than me," Aunt Zsuzsi said. She pulled out a set of evening pajamas with black pants and a red top. "This for me. Ronnie, you can wear anything you like. We're the same size."

Ronnie chose a long black skirt with a white sleeveless top. They took turns showering, and then Betsy put on the lovely soft dress, and sat at Aunt Zsuzsi's vanity table while Ronnie brushed her hair.

"Ronnie, can I ask you a question?"

"May I ask."

"May I?"

"Sure."

"Well, about what Aunt Zsuzsi was talking about downstairs..." Ronnie's hand paused in mid-air. "Is making babies something everyone does?"

"No, just married people." She began brushing Betsy's hair again.

"Do you think it hurts?"

"No, of course not. No one would ever have babies if it did. And besides, people don't just do it when they want to have a baby."

"Why?"

"It's what grownups do, once they get married. What do you think Mama and Daddy are doing tonight? Playing rummy?"

"Oh." Betsy thought a moment. Mama's new negligee! So that's what that was all about. Mama had looked so happy on the train, and Daddy kept holding Mama's hand, and smiling at her, like they shared a big secret.

"There." Ronnie gathered Betsy's hair with a tortoise shell comb just as the doorbell rang.

"Here." She sprayed Betsy with a mist of Evening in Paris. "Gosh, you look pretty, Betsy."

Betsy certainly felt prettier than she ever had before, though she was dismayed at how curly her hair was on such a humid day.

"Are you sure no one can see the, you know?" she asked, trying to see the back of her dress in the mirror.

Ronnie shook her head. "Don't worry. No one can see a thing."

The party, like everything else this day, was nothing that Betsy's experience had prepared her for. Aunt Zsuzsi let her have a small glass of sherry, for one thing, and for another, the food was amazing. Aunt Zsuzsi made a steak that was at least two inches thick and as wide as a platter. Served rare, with sautéed mushrooms and fresh Brussels sprouts, it was the most delicious meal Betsy had ever eaten. Aunt Zsuzsi served it buffet style, and everyone ate with plates balanced on their laps. Some guests even sat on the floor, though they were all dressed up.

Ronnie played one record after another, so there was always background music, but nothing like the pop tunes their mother listened to, or the classical music their father always played on Sunday afternoons. Betsy had never listened to Miles Davis or Dizzy Gillespie before. After dinner she sat on one of the funny leather chairs in the living room and listened while everyone else spoke of art galleries and the theater. It was almost like being at the theater, in fact, and Betsy was impressed that Ronnie was able to talk to people as though she weren't just a girl from New Jersey. There was at least one celebrity there, a composer Betsy had never heard of, and an art gallery owner, a writer—a funny little man wearing a white cape—and several artists. Betsy couldn't keep track of them all. Nor could she follow the many conversations punctuated with "darling" and "honey" and "my dear," or keep track of all the people she'd met. The only one she whose name she could remember was the woman named Alice, Aunt Zsuzsi's friend with the funny mannish haircut. She was one of those people who touch all the time, her hand always on Aunt Zsuzsi's arm, or her back, or even around her waist.

She wanted to stay up as long as everyone else, but by midnight she couldn't stop yawning. She said goodnight and went upstairs, reluctant to take off her party dress. But she had cramps again, and it felt good to climb into bed and stretch out on the soft sheets. She was flipping though the pages of her sketchbook when Aunt Zsuzsi came upstairs to say goodnight.

"May I see this?" she asked. She sat on the edge of the bed and laid her cigarette on the edge of the night table so she could turn the pages.

"It's just something I do for fun," said Betsy, after a couple of minutes, because Aunt Zsuzsi was so quiet, staring down at a sketch of the big elm tree in the yard at home.

Aunt Zsuzsi looked up and smiled.

"Betsy, these are really good. Better than anything I ever did at your age." She placed the sketchbook on the night table "You have a gift, *honicam*. You're an artist."

She picked up the cigarette and cupped her hand under it to catch the long ash as it fell. With her other hand she touched Betsy's cheek, then she bent down and kissed her goodnight.

Betsy turned out the lamp and leaned back. She could hear the sounds of laughter and music downstairs, and through the open window, passing cars. It was so different from home, where insects would be buzzing outside, and the air would smell like honeysuckle instead of car exhaust. There probably wasn't a honeysuckle blossom anywhere in this city.

But Betsy was here. And she was an artist. Aunt Zsuzsi said so.

Chapter 33
September 1953

One of the best things about having her period, Betsy decided, was that in spite of the discomfort of cramps, pads, and belts, she and Ronnie had grown much closer. Ever since that magical week last summer, the highlight of Betsy's life so far (eighth grade graduation, after all, was still a long school year away), Ronnie had begun to initiate Betsy into the principle of suffering for beauty's sake. Thanks to Ronnie, by the time school started, Betsy had stopped wearing her hair in braids and instead had it cut it shoulder length. Each night became a running battle, with hair curlers as a primary weapon, forcing her natural waves into a fairly smooth pageboy. Results were mixed, depending on each morning's relative humidity, but Betsy felt more grown up, which made the uncomfortable night's sleep worthwhile.

She'd gotten used to waking up during the night anyway. Her bedtime was still hours earlier than Ronnie's, but Betsy was a light sleeper, and no matter how quiet Ronnie tried to be, Betsy always woke when her sister opened the door to their bedroom. Their mother had tried to get Betsy to move into Del's room now that he was gone, but even though it was Betsy's favorite place to sit with her sketch pad, moving in never felt right to either Betsy or Ronnie, so they stayed in the same room they had shared for as long as Betsy could remember. Now she was especially glad, because at night Ronnie would sit on the side of the bed, kick off her shoes, and roll down her stockings, all the while chatting to Betsy about the movie she'd just seen, or the date she'd had.

Betsy was thrilled to have become Ronnie's confidante. She was learning something about the art of kissing, for one, and she now understood what people meant by "getting to first base." Even better, she knew before their parents did when Ronnie had a new beau. Ronnie had gone out with several new boys since being promoted out of the steno pool and into the accounting department at Van Dyke & Son. Two weeks ago she had been promoted once again, and now Ronnie was secretary for the chief accountant, Mr. McLaughlin. A steady parade of young accountants and clerks passed her desk every day, and she sat in on all the department meetings, taking minutes and passing out reports. That was how she met Ted.

Something was up, Betsy could tell right away, when Ronnie tiptoed into the bedroom that night. Ronnie usually climbed into bed before she remembered to brush her teeth, or she would forget her water glass and have to get up again, or she'd lie down without first taking off her earrings. Betsy thought it was just a way to get attention. After all, she worked as a secretary, for gosh sakes, and didn't secretaries have to be organized? How did she ever get promoted if she was as scatterbrained at work as she was at home?

But this night she was exceptionally quiet. She remembered to remove her earrings, to brush her teeth, and even to put a full glass of water on the nightstand between the beds. It was a cool evening, so Betsy had closed all the windows, muffling the racket of crickets and katydids. Ronnie lay down in bed and pulled the covers to her chin.

"Well?" Betsy whispered.

Ronnie's bed jerked. "Oh, Bets, you startled me. I didn't realize you were awake."

"I'm always awake when you come in."

"You are, aren't you? Well, goodnight." Ronnie rolled onto her side, away from Betsy.

Betsy leaned up on one elbow. "That's it? You aren't going to tell me how it went?"

"It went fine."

"Come on, Ronnie, give. You dated a new guy tonight. Did he have bad breath or something?"

Ronnie rolled onto her back again and sighed. "No, actually, he was very nice. Really. Really nice."

"What's his name?"

"Ted Bialkowski."

Betsy sat up straight. "He's Polish?"

"Yes, in fact, he is. So what?"

"So didn't Pop have a canary when you told him?"

Ronnie was silent.

Betsy gasped. "You didn't tell him?"

"He was grading compositions. I just said I was going out with friends from work."

"You told me you had a double date." Wow. Ronnie hadn't exactly lied to their father, but she sure had committed a sin of omission. Was that a venial sin or a mortal sin? Betsy couldn't remember, even though she'd had a quiz about it in religion class just last week.

Ronnie fussed with the bedcovers, folding the end of the sheet over the comforter and smoothing it down. "I didn't see any point in making a big deal about it. First dates don't always work out, you know. Besides, there just aren't any Hungarian boys in the office. And I'm sure Daddy wouldn't want me to go out with a factory worker just because he had the right last name."

"When are you going to tell him?"

"Soon enough. We're going out again tomorrow night, just the two of us."

"That's moving fast."

In the sliver of moonlight that edged past the venetian blinds, she could just see Ronnie smiling in the glow of the nightlight, moving her fingertip lightly over her lips.

"Ronnie Nemeth—did you let him kiss you on the first date? You weren't necking, were you?"

"Shh!"

"Holy smoke!"

Ronnie threw a pillow at her.

"Shush, for heaven's sake. They're coming upstairs."

Betsy lay down just before the door opened. She was practiced at taking slow, deep breaths, especially on a school night when she was supposed to have been asleep hours ago. In two three four, hold two, out two three four. In two three four, hold two, out two—and the door shut.

She waited until she heard the bedsprings creak once, twice, in her parents' room. But when she sat up again, she could see that Ronnie was already asleep, and not faking, either. She'd have to get the details in the morning.

Ronnie wasn't very forthcoming, though, at least not about her first few dates with Ted. In a couple of weeks they were seeing one another exclusively, though, and by that time Ronnie was so forthcoming Betsy was sick of hearing how wonderful Mr. Bialkowski was.

"He has only a six handicap at golf. Imagine that!" Ronnie boasted. Betsy didn't know what a golf handicap was, nor did she care. She already knew that Ted was practically Phi Beta Kappa at Seton Hall; that he was so thrifty he drove a ten-year-old Buick; that he was going places, because he was already a senior accountant only three years out of college; that he was clever, because he played bridge; and Betsy had no doubt he loved children and small animals equally well, because he was already an uncle, and his mother had a toy poodle.

By the end of September, when Ted was old news, and Betsy's parents officially approved of the paragon despite his ancestry, even Betsy had to admit that she liked him. He had the deepest blue eyes she had ever seen, so that was a point in his favor. Also, he treated her decently whenever he waited for Ronnie to finish dressing for a night on the town, never giving her the brush off, and offering to teach her to jitterbug. Betsy wanted to find something wrong with him, because things were moving so fast, but she was forced to give up and admit that her sister might just have found mister right after all.

Now that was an interesting thought. Ronnie was bound to get married. She wanted to, desperately. She talked about it with her girlfriends on the telephone. She clipped newspaper articles about weddings out of the women's section of the newspaper. And she couldn't pass a baby carriage without stopping to admire and coo at the occupant.

Betsy didn't understand this burning desire to get married and have babies. Of course, Ronnie didn't have a real career, she was just marking time until marriage. Betsy wasn't going to do that. She wanted to be just like Aunt Zsuzsi—a successful career woman, living in a big city, with lots of eccentric friends. That's what Ronnie had called them, anyway, the people they'd met at Aunt Zsuzsi's party. "They're artists and writers, Betsy, they're supposed to be eccentric."

Eccentric was neater than ordinary. Ordinary was okay for Ronnie, who seemed happy enough working in a boring office and planning her wedding, even though she wasn't even engaged yet. Betsy wanted something else, like Uncle Frank had with his restaurant, like Del seemed to have found in the army. She couldn't cook and she certainly didn't want to join the army, but she had plenty of time to figure out how she was going to seize her opportunities, when they came. Look at Aunt Zsuzsi. Why, she was nineteen before she even went to art school.

They had talked about it in New York, while Ronnie was getting her hair done in a fancy salon. Aunt Zsuzsi treated Betsy to ice cream at Schraft's, and while they ate hot fudge sundaes, Betsy asked Aunt Zsuzsi about how she knew what she wanted to do when she grew up. So Aunt

Zsuzsi told her about going to art school, and how hard she worked to make a name for herself in the fashion industry.

"And you never wanted to get married and have children?" asked Betsy.

"I think it would be wonderful to have children, if they were all as fine as you and Ronnie and Del. But it just wasn't meant to be."

"Because you're a career woman."

Aunt Zsuzsi winced as though the ice cream hurt her tooth. "That's one name for it. Certainly my career played a big role in my life. A woman has to make difficult choices, Betsy, especially if she wants to succeed in business. I put all my energy into my work."

"And are you happy?"

"As happy as anyone can be, I suppose. Very happy, in fact. I live my life the way I want to."

"But what about—never mind." Betsy spooned up the last of the chocolate syrup from her sundae.

"What about what?"

Betsy shook her head. "It's none of my business."

"Betsy, you're experiencing a lot of new things this week. If I can help you sort it all out, then by all means, ask. You won't hurt my feelings."

"Well, it's just that, you know what we were talking about the other day, after the Statue of Liberty, and Ronnie said that only married people did...but you're not married, so, I was wondering if that meant you never, you know...." She looked down and smoothed the pleats of her skirt.

Aunt Zsuzsi wiped her mouth and folded her napkin before answering. She leaned toward Betsy across the table, and when she spoke, her voice was so quiet Betsy had to lean forward, too.

"Betsy, I am sure the nuns, if they ever discuss the subject at all, will tell you that it's a sin for someone to make love without being married. They think it's a sin to French kiss, for heaven's sake, which is ridiculous. But for women like me, 'career women,' as your mother says, who aren't going to get married, well, it's unnatural to expect us to—to live like nuns ourselves. The act of love, however you experience it, is a beautiful thing, and I personally don't understand how showing someone you love her—or him—can possibly be wrong. But you have to understand that most of our society agrees with the nuns, or at least that's what they say, and so this isn't something you should talk about to just anybody. And I expect your parents would be very unhappy to know that I said any of this to you. But I want to be honest with you, at least as honest as I can be. So promise to keep this just between us, okay?"

Betsy nodded. Aunt Zsuzsi smiled and reached for Betsy's hand.

"You know, I once had a conversation like this with your mother. Please don't worry that I'm missing out on anything. And don't think I'm going to hell because of it. Life is a lot more complicated than they teach you in school, *honicam*."

But Betsy was worried, or at least confused. What if the nuns were right? Would Aunt Zsuzsi go to hell? How could such a nice lady end up in hell? But if Aunt Zsuzsi were right, then the nuns were wrong, so why did they teach all that stuff? She wished she could ask Ronnie what she thought, but she couldn't break her promise to Aunt Zsuzsi. She talked to Mary Alice, at least in general terms, not naming any names, but Mary Alice was convinced that anyone who even French kissed was committing a mortal sin, just like the nuns said. That seemed awfully severe to Betsy, who knew that Ronnie French kissed all the time. Personally, Betsy didn't know any boy she'd let put his tongue in her mouth, but she'd seen Ronnie and Ted doing it, and they sure seemed to like it. So it must be something you enjoyed when you got older. And wasn't that always the case? Everything important in life was always just out of reach. She was always too young to understand it or appreciate it. Would she never be caught up with everyone else?

She wished Del were home. Not that she could actually talk to him about this specific issue—you couldn't talk to any boy about it, especially your own brother—but she sensed that he would have a different perspective on everything. There was more to life than Hardenbergh, he had told her before he left, and his letters home had been filled with wonderful detail about weekends spent in Paris and Rome and different parts of Germany. He was a world traveler now, a soldier, experienced.

Any day she expected to hear that he was coming home for good. Even though Del wrote home every two weeks, like clockwork, she still pedaled home from school eagerly every afternoon, hoping for word. His tour of duty would be over in exactly twenty-two days, she thought, as she swerved the bike to avoid a wooly bear. Just three more weeks, and then he'd be home.

She put the kickstand down and ran up the porch steps.

"I'm home, Mama," she called. Her mother looked up from ironing a shirt.

"Hi, honey. You got a letter from Del," she said. "It's on the table."

"I got a letter? Addressed to me? All right!" Sometimes Del included a separate note to Betsy in the envelope with the letter to the whole family, and he sometimes sent her a postcard, but this was the first time he ever addressed a whole letter to her. She took the letter upstairs and reached under the bed for the cigar box that held his other notes and cards. There were a few German coins in there as well, and a candy wrapper from a chocolate bar he'd sent her. The doll dressed in Bavarian costume, which he sent for her birthday two years ago, was too big for the cigar box, so she stood on top of Betsy's dresser, next to the statue of the Blessed Mother.

Betsy sat down cross-legged on the bed and tore the envelope carefully, to preserve the postmark and the stamp.

"Dear Peanut,

"It was great to read your last letter. I am glad you are in Sister Dénes' class this year. She was a lot nicer to me than Sister Ignác ever was. And I am real proud that you got 100% on your last spelling quiz. You are a smart cookie! It's hard for me to believe you are in the 8th grade already, and will be in high school this time next year. Time flies, huh?

"You probably are wondering why I am writing to you specially this time. Well, I have something important to tell you, and I wanted to tell you before I told anyone else.

"I think you remember what we talked about before I joined the army—how I didn't want to go to college, and how much I wanted to see what was out there in the world. I sure have met some amazing people, and been to lots more places, than if I'd stayed home. And I think you can tell from my letters that the army has been pretty good to me these past two years. So, I decided to re-enlist. Now, don't get excited—it doesn't mean I can't come home. I can, and I will, just not in October. I get a whole month's leave because I re-upped, so I'll be home for the whole month of December. I'll be home for Christmas this year! I figure that will make up for coming home a little later than we had planned.

"See, it just makes so much sense for me to stay in the army right now. The war is over, thank God, so even if I got sent to Korea now nothing would happen to me. But they already told me they're keeping me here. And that's great. It's great being an MP. It isn't hard duty—mostly just rounding up guys who get drunk on weekends—and I get to travel on 48-hour passes. Europe is so much smaller than the USA, I can get to a lot of places easy. How many guys from Hardenbergh got to see the Grand Prix in person? I did! But it's not just seeing the sights. The army has given me good training—a few more years as an MP, I may not only get to be a sergeant, but when I leave I can use what I learned, and join the police force, maybe even the state police. Then I'll have a good job at home, and I won't be in any damn—sorry—darn factory.

"So I hope you understand. This is just too good to pass up. I'm sorry it means I won't be home for two more months. I miss you, all of you, and that's the only bad thing about being here.

"Well, that's the story. Tell Mom and Pop, or show them this letter if you want. I'll write to them soon. December is just around the corner. I'll be home soon. Love, Del."

Betsy's hands shook as she held the letter. Her first impulse was to crush it into a ball and flush it down the toilet. It wasn't fair. The war was over, the army didn't need Del anymore, but she did. She did!

She ran down the steps and out the door, ignoring her mother's call. Through the yard, across the street, under the tangle of honeysuckle and brambles, she ran, dodging tree roots and hanging branches, until she came to their rock. She sat down just as the tears she'd been fighting overflowed.

He liked the army more than he liked her! He didn't miss her as much as she missed him! He didn't need her the way she needed him!

She picked up a rock and hurled it into the underbrush. There was a whirring noise and a rustle of leaves as a flock of mourning doves burst up from where they'd been roosting. Something rustled on the ground, and then the woods were silent again. She walked over to the roost, stepped over a tangle of raspberry canes, and saw the dove, wings outspread, blood on the leaves beneath its small head.

"Oh, jeez!"

She felt the anger leave her body in a rush, leaving her shaking and weak. Why couldn't she do anything right? Anyone else would have hit a tree, or the rock would have landed on the ground and not hit anything worse than some fallen twigs. She'd been mad at Del, not this dove. She knelt down, and stroked the soft breast of the bird.

"I'm sorry!" she murmured, as tears overflowed again. "I didn't mean it." Maybe that made it worse—if she'd meant to hit the bird, at least it would have been an honest act of cruelty. Was this new guilt she felt her punishment for getting angry, or was something more yet to come?

It was hard to imagine feeling any worse than this, with Del lost to the army and the world, and now a dead bird, its black, blank eyes staring up at her.

She pulled newly fallen leaves off the forest floor to cover the bloody bird and its impartial eyes. She recited a Hail Mary, then stood up and began to walk home, wondering how big a penance she would get when she confessed to killing one of God's least offensive creations. She was suddenly tired, and not terribly comforted by knowing that God would forgive her.

What was forgiveness, when you didn't have love?

Chapter 34
March 1955

Snow began falling around midnight, a steady mist of tiny flakes, the kind that promised to go on for hours. By morning a good four inches covered the ground, burying Jolan's crocuses that only a day ago had seemed ready to burst into bud. Jolan filled a thermos with hot cocoa while Tibor shoveled the porch steps and cleared the car's windshield. Betsy tarried, listening to the radio, hoping to hear a school closing report, but when her father honked the horn she had to go with him.

They drove slowly along the street that hadn't been plowed yet, the tires almost silent, the whole neighborhood hushed by the snowfall. Betsy hated going to school on days like this. When the weather was clear, and she could ride her bike, it was easier to pretend she wasn't the Latin teacher's daughter. But when it rained or snowed, her father insisted on driving, and there was nothing to be done except slouch down on the seat and hope none of her friends could see her.

"Betsy, sit up straight," her father said. She inched up as little as she could get away with. St. Brendan's required her to take at least one year of Latin. Betsy hadn't realized how difficult this would be. Not the study itself; she'd grown up with Latin books and papers in the house, and could already translate "Omnia Gallia in tres partes divisa est" by the time she was twelve. But being called on by her own father was mortifying, and she more often than not stumbled over words she knew inside out when she did her homework. She knew her father sensed how difficult it was for her. She thought that was why he insisted that all the students call him "Magister," instead of Mr. Nemeth, which would have sounded absurd from Betsy's mouth. She also knew, from conversations overheard in the girls' room, that many classmates suspected she got extra help from her father, or that she was given A's and B's as a matter of course. So Betsy deliberately flunked her midterm test.

He had called her into the study the day he graded those tests. "I know why you did this, Betsy," he had said. "Your sister tried it, too, when she was in my class. Del, unfortunately, didn't have to pretend to flunk. But you and I know that you know Latin better than this. I want you to take this again."

"No, Daddy," she had said, and it was probably the first time in her life she ever openly defied him. "I won't take it."

"Betsy, you'll ruin your average, and for what? Next year no one will even think of you as my daughter." She could hear the hurt in his voice. "And I have no doubt you won't be taking Latin II."

"I'm sorry, Daddy, I know how much you love Latin. And you're right about next year. But that's a long way away, and I have the rest of the school year to get through. High school is hard enough as it is. Please don't make it any harder for me." She had burst into tears at that point, a sure tactic for getting her way, and it worked, but she didn't have to force the tears this time.

Maybe her father realized that. Because he let the grade stand, and now Betsy had a respectable C-plus average in Latin, which, combined with B-minus grades in history, religion, French, and English literature, nicely offset her straight A's in math. Now she had only two-and-a-half more months to endure not only Latin, but also the nightmare called gym. Once a week, in the two periods before lunch, she faced the horror of changing into her gym suit in a locker room full of girls who were more slender and better built than she was. Although no one could possibly look good in white bloomers and the white, short-sleeved, short-skirted abomination that must have been designed by prison inmates, Betsy knew she looked worse than most. Her natural tendency toward plumpness wasn't helped by the way her mother baked cookies as though Del were still home to eat half of them. It wouldn't be so bad if there were only her mother's cookies to deal with, but she also had to contend with Grandma's strudel and Aunt Margit's pies and Aunt Eva's lemon squares. Even Uncle Frank always came over with food, like a pint of pistachio or slices of chocolate cake.

Gym period itself wouldn't be half bad, despite the ordeal of changing, if Betsy could only keep up with the other girls, but the only exercise she ever got was biking the mile-and-a-half to school on fair-weather days. There were true athletes in her class, too, girls with unerring aim in dodge ball, girls who could throw a softball hard, girls who could tumble and vault, girls who never got out of breath doing jumping jacks.

When the humiliation was finally over for another week, they all changed back into uniforms without benefit of showers, because St. Brendan's couldn't afford showers in the girls' locker room. Betsy had to go through the afternoon with a sticky blouse, unwilling to raise her hand lest her sweaty armpits offend, and with her carefully constructed pageboy deteriorating into frizz.

But today was Friday, the day of her salvation, when she had neither gym nor Latin but could take refuge in art class. Here she could finally do something better than the dodge ball sadists. Art was taught by Sister Thomas, an ancient and diminutive nun who had spent her entire career at St. Brendan's. Although her hand had a slight tremor, her eye was still sharp and her memory vivid.

"I can't get over how much your work is like Zsuzsanna's," she told Betsy before class, while Betsy erased the blackboard. She enjoyed leaving lunch early to help Sister Thomas prepare for class, and to hear her stories about Aunt Zsuzsi. It was fun to think of this tiny old nun in her prime, teaching here thirty years ago, when her aunt was Betsy's age.

"Thank you, Sister. Aunt Zsuzsi still talks about how you helped her get into art school."

"Oh, that wasn't any doing of mine," said Sister Thomas. "That was pure talent, and hard work on her part. I hope you will work as hard over the next few years."

"I will, Sister. I want to go to college, and study art. I want to be a painter."

"Well, that's a very lofty goal. If God is willing, I'm sure you'll succeed. But you should think about a more practical vocation as well. Being an art teacher has been very rewarding for me."

"I'm sure it has, Sister. And you're a very good teacher. But I'm going to be an artist."

The bell rang before Sister Thomas could answer, and students began to file into the classroom, where they leaned back in their chairs in an after-lunch stupor. Fifty minutes of art, followed by fifty minutes of religion, and then assembly before they could go home and begin the important fun of the weekend.

"Today we shall work on complementary colors," said Sister Thomas, picking up two pieces of chalk, one blue and one yellow. But before she could say anything further, the PA system crackled.

"Attention, all teachers. Because of the continued inclement weather, school will be dismissed after this period." The cheers made Sister Thomas lift her hands. "Shush, shush."

"The pep rally scheduled for assembly today has been canceled, and school buses will be at the usual exits in one hour. Students will walk to their buses in an orderly fashion and no deviation from the line will be tolerated. There will be no throwing of snowballs on the school grounds or while boarding the buses. Any boys who normally walk to school are requested to stay to help shovel the walks. Many hands will make light work. Thank you."

"All right, ladies and gentleman, let us settle down and get back to work," Sister Thomas said in as loud a voice as she could muster. "We have a full class period to go. As I was saying, today we shall learn about complementary colors."

Betsy had been waiting for this lesson all semester. Sister Thomas insisted they spend most of their time working in black and white, drilling them on the fundamentals of drawing. Though Betsy enjoyed working with charcoal and pencils, she had been eager to explore the beautiful colors in this box of German pastels that Del had given her for Christmas. Leave it to Del to give her the perfect present. How could he still know her so well, when he was a whole ocean away?

She already understood the principles Sister Thomas was explaining to the class, so she began to sketch a blue and yellow vase filled with roses and ferns. She worked, absorbed with problems of shape and color, ignoring the restless stirrings around her until the bell rang, then continued drawing until Sister Thomas tapped her hand on the desk.

"Time to go home, Betsy," she said. "You can finish the drawing there—you don't want to keep your father waiting."

"Yes, Sister," she said, closing the box of pastels and folding up her sketchpad. She did want to keep her father waiting, at least until most of the students were on the bus, but she could picture him clearing the windshield off by himself, and she felt guilty enough to pick up her pace. She had to push against the wind to open the door.

"Ouch!" Blowing snow stung her face and she pulled her coat collar up. The steps, which had been cleared repeatedly during the day, were already whitening over. She descended carefully and walked toward the car, bending her head to avoid the worst of the wind. Her father had the engine running and was clearing off the rear window when she got to him.

"Hi, Daddy," she said. She brushed snow off the windows on the passenger side and got in the car. The heater was on full blast but she knew they would be almost home before it produced any truly warm air.

Her father got in the driver's side and rubbed his gloved hands together. "What an afternoon," he said. "How was art class?"

"It was okay."

Her father pressed the accelerator and the rear tires spun. He shifted into first gear and then back into reverse, rocking the car until the tires bit into the snow. "It's going to be a slow ride home." He pulled out of the parking lot carefully, rolling down his window to see because the interior of the car had fogged up. Betsy took a tissue out of her pocket and wiped the windshield as well as she could.

They drove home at ten miles an hour. Even though it was midafternoon, Tibor put the headlights on, illuminating swirls of snow. There were very few cars on the road, which was fortunate when Tibor skidded right through a stop sign.

"Are you all right?" he asked Betsy once they finally stopped, clear across the intersection.

"I'm fine," she said, unclenching her hand from the door handle.

"They never should have held school today," he said as he rolled forward again. "The roads are downright dangerous. I shouldn't have taken the chains off so soon."

"But Daddy, who knew it would snow so hard at this time of year? Mama's crocuses have been up for a week. It's almost spring."

"It was almost spring. It may as well be January out there today."

He slowed almost to a stop before pulling into the driveway. Jolan held the door open for them against the wind.

"Hi, Mama," Betsy said as she pulled off her mittens. "Guess what happened to us on the way home?"

But Jolan seemed not to hear her. She held a letter out to Tibor, and Betsy could see that her mother's hand was trembling.

"What's this?" Tibor asked. He hung his coat on the coat rack and reached in his jacket pocket for reading glasses.

"It has a Swiss postmark. It says it's from Del, but that's not his handwriting."

Her father slowly unfolded his glasses and set them on his nose with a precision that made Betsy want to scream.

"Look at the return address," said Jolan.

"It says 'Sgt. Wendel Nemeth' but you're right, this isn't Del's hand," Betsy's father said. "Still, it can't be anything serious—if it were bad news they'd come to tell us in person." But his voice was too unsteady for Betsy to believe him. Suddenly, their wild skid through the intersection was trivial. Nothing mattered but Del. She held her breath.

He tore open the envelope and spread the page, looking first at the signature. "It's signed 'Corporal Augustus Reed'." He frowned and began to read from the beginning:

"Dear Mr. and Mrs. Nemeth,

"Sarge is okay—" Jolan made an odd noise, like a small chirp, and Tibor looked up and smiled. Betsy felt her legs go slack with relief. She flopped to the floor and sat Indian style. Her father cleared his throat and continued:

"Sarge is okay but he asked me to write to you because he had a small mishap and he's still feeling a little woozy. We are on 48-hour pass, and this morning we arrived in Grenoble, Switzerland, to do some skiing—"

"Del doesn't ski," said Jolan.

"Apparently he does," said Tibor.

"Daddy, what happened?"

"Well, if you and your mother stop interrupting I will do my best to find out." He cleared his throat again and read on:

"This afternoon we were skiing down a pretty steep slope, and the Sarge must of hit a patch of ice, and he fell. Unfortunately, where he fell was near a small outcropping of rock, which stopped him from going over the edge, which was good, but it also sort of broke his leg.

"Sweet mother of God!" Jolan whispered. Betsy rubbed her hand along her shin, feeling the strong bone, wondering that anything so hard could break at all.

"Now, Sarge is waving at me because he wants me to be sure to tell you he's going to be fine, it's just a broken leg, and it was a real clean break, not compound or anything, but the Swiss nurses are real pretty so he's going to stay here for a little while, maybe a week or two.

"They gave him some stuff for the pain—not that it hurts real bad but it is broken and all—so Sarge can't write this himself, and he kind of wrenched his shoulder trying not to slam into the rock so his arm is in a sling—it's his right arm and left leg, by the way—but the docs have fixed him up real good and he's going to be fine.

"The brass may let him come home to recuperate once he can travel so maybe this is a blessing in disguise, Sarge says, and he says to say he loves you all and really it doesn't hurt much so Ma, don't worry. He'll write more in a couple days when he's feeling a little more perky.

"Yours truly,

"Corporal Augustus Reed."

Tibor put his glasses on the end table and folded the letter. "Well, It's not the most grammatical piece of writing I've ever seen but I'm glad he wrote it."

Jolan snatched the letter, read it herself, and then waved it across her face like a fan.

"I don't understand how you can criticize the grammar when our son is lying in a foreign hospital, in agony, I have no doubt. Why he has to be so far away..."

Tibor pulled out his handkerchief and handed it to Jolan. "He's going to be fine, dearest."

"He could just as easily have broken his neck!" she wailed. "Skiing! Of all the stupid..."

Tibor put his arms around her, saying "Shh...shh.." as though she were a child. Betsy took the letter from her mother's hand and read it herself. Then she went upstairs to Del's room, opened his closet, and leaned into the shirts that still smelled, ever so faintly, of Old Spice. She closed her eyes, inhaled deeply, and murmured, "Poor Del."

The next letter was from Del himself, out of the sling and recuperating well, but it contained no news of his coming home. The third letter did, arriving on a fine Saturday after the snow had melted for good and the whole yard smelled of sweet mud. Betsy was in the driveway, pumping air into the front tire of her Schwinn, when she heard her mother's angry voice through the bedroom window. Betsy stopped pumping, wiped the sweat off her forehead, and listened. She couldn't make out the words, but the tone was unmistakable. Her easy-going mother was furious.

Betsy tiptoed onto the porch and opened the door, leaning into it so the hinges wouldn't squeak. She stepped into the kitchen as though she were feeling for a land mine, holding the door open so she could pretend to be just walking in if her parents came into the kitchen suddenly.

"Don't you dare take his side!" Jolan hissed.

"I am not taking his side, but I am trying to understand his motives," said her father in a tight voice.

"His motives are perfectly clear! Why should he come home for his recuperation leave when he can shack up with some—some Prussian *kurva!*"

Betsy didn't know exactly what a *kurva* was, but from the context, she could guess.

"She's Bavarian, Jolan. And a nurse. And he's in love."

"Oh, so that makes it acceptable to do what they're doing when they aren't even married?"

"We came pretty close to it a few times ourselves, my love."

"But we didn't. Besides, we were engaged."

"Maybe they have an understanding."

"Blessed Mother, Tibor, how can you be so naïve? There's only one thing Del wants from this girl. The army has coarsened him. And if she's the kind of girl who'll live with him openly without a wedding ring then she's the wrong kind of girl for him."

"Then you would be happier if they got married?"

"Over my dead body!"

Betsy stepped backwards and closed the door. She doubted her parents heard the latch close. She finished pumping up the bicycle tire and then pushed off down the driveway, ignoring mud puddles and the thumping of her own heart. She pedaled faster and faster, not thinking, just concentrating on the sound of the bicycle chain and the swish of puddles as the tires sliced through them. Finally, miles later, she was out of breath and forced to stop. Only then, as she let the bike fall with the back wheel still spinning, did she let herself think about Del, who would rather stay in Germany with some fraulein of dubious repute than come home to his family for a few weeks. And when she did think of it, she wanted to spit in his face.

She pedaled home again, ready to take her mother's side in the argument, but when she got home her father was gone and her mother was in the garden, hoeing the muddy ground with short, violent strokes. Betsy went to her room instead, pacing back and forth, wishing Ronnie were home instead of out with Ted. It was so unfair! First the army took Del away, then he re-enlisted, and now, his first chance to come home in months and months, and he actually chooses to stay in Europe with some girl instead of letting Betsy and her mother take care of him.

She stumbled against the box of pastels that lay half under the bed. She gave the box a kick that sent it out from under the bedspread and against the wall, where it cracked open, scattering color across the carpet. Betsy stomped on the piece that flew toward her, grinding the crimson chalk with her heel.

The crocuses dropped their yellow and violet petals as daffodils and hyacinths took up the slack. Complementary colors: yellow for spring, purple for Lent. Mary Alice asked her what she had given up for Lent. "Are you kidding?" Betsy answered. Her friend was hurt by bitter tone behind the words. Was she excited about the school play? No. Wasn't it great to be practically sophomores? No. Jeepers, was she on the rag? NO.

What she wanted was to have Del come home. No, that wasn't entirely true. She also wanted Del to *want* to come home, and because he didn't, she started carrying a chip on her shoulder. It didn't make any sense, not even to Betsy, so how could she ever explain it to Mary Alice, who after a few tries just left Betsy alone because she seemed to want it that way. And maybe she did.

Most days she lingered after school, sometimes hiding in a stall in the girls' room, because there was no one to go home for. Her parents were speaking again, but it seemed to Betsy that they were just accommodating Ronnie, now officially engaged to Ted and making the most of it. Ronnie seemed oblivious to the tense undercurrent between their parents, and she didn't even seem to mind that Del never came home. She just chattered on about flowers and dresses, or stared at her engagement ring. Betsy never felt so alone.

One day, as she tarried after school, she walked past two girls who were leaning against the school fence. They wore mascara and lipstick they'd put on as soon as school was over, and she recognized them as girls who had been suspended for smoking in the lavatory. They were sophomores who went out with seniors from the public school, boys who drove hot rods and wore leather jackets. She had always been a little afraid of them, but when they offered her a smoke, she walked up to them and took the cigarette. One of the girls, a peroxide blond whose dark roots were showing, held a match to it. Betsy inhaled too deeply and coughed. The other girls laughed, but not too unkindly, and she tried again with more success.

"Not bad for a virgin," said the girl who'd held out the Luckies. She had dark hair combed over one side of her face, like Veronica Lake.

"You haven't been hanging around with the goody-goody crowd lately," said the bleached blond.

Betsy took another drag on the cigarette and shrugged. "So?"

"So nothing. We just noticed," said the dark-haired one. Betsy looked at her for a moment and then nodded. She was becoming an outsider, and that gave her something in common with these girls.

"That's okay," she said. The three of them stood there, smoking. No one said anything more, though the blond girl hummed a tune Betsy didn't recognize. The dark-haired girl nodded, snapped her fingers. "No one does it like Bird," she said. Betsy had no idea what she was talking about. She considered the possibilities of joining up with these girls. And she considered the possibilities if her father saw her smoking with them as he left the building. She finished the cigarette, and ground it out with her shoe.

"Gotta go. Thanks."

The blond lifted her hand in a desultory wave. "Be cool," the dark-haired one said.

Betsy nodded, trying to be cool, whatever that meant, as she walked over to the bike rack, savoring the taste of tobacco, the sense of companionship she'd had with the older girls. It was tempting to think of going along with them, of sneaking out to smoke and maybe even to get drunk, of letting her grades slip even further than they'd begun to.

She pulled her bike out of the stand and pushed off. Who was she kidding? She was still a goody-goody who rode a bicycle to school. If a boy in a hot rod asked her out, she'd probably have a heart attack. And if she let her grades slide anymore, not only would her parents want to know why, but she might also jeopardize her chances of getting into college. That was something she would never let happen—it was the first step toward becoming an artist. No, she was stuck being the Latin teacher's pudgy kid, at least for the next three years.

She sniffed her sweater, and smelled the cigarette smoke on it. She pedaled faster, hoping the breeze would pull the smoke out of the fibers.

Saturday morning she woke with a start. She'd been dreaming about him again, something about running and khaki and snow and cigar boxes. She closed her eyes again, but it was gone, and so was Del. She couldn't

424

picture his face anymore, not clearly. She couldn't even remember the shape of his cheekbones, the depth of the dimple in his chin.

She dressed quickly and quietly and went into his room. The air smelled stale and the room looked exactly the same, but it felt wrong. He had no presence here anymore. She reached for the photos of him on the dresser, one taken after he'd won all-state, and one of him in uniform. One showed a boy, the other a man. It was the boy she wanted back, though she'd settle for the man.

She took both pictures, her sketchbook and pastels, and tiptoed out the front door. Rising sun made a mist of the dew. It would be chilly in the woods, so she went back inside and pulled the crocheted blanket off the couch. Kettimama would be horrified to have her handiwork taken outdoors, but she would never know.

Betsy crossed the street and walked down to the gap in the honeysuckle. Bright new leaflets contrasted with the leathery dark green of last season's leaves. Birdsong stopped suddenly as she ducked through, but overhead she heard robins trilling their aubade, the lovely word she'd recently learned in English class. Small creatures scurried through the leaf litter as she made her way to the rock. She could almost, but not quite, picture him sitting here, and that was wrong. She folded the blanket, sat, down, and opened her sketchbook.

She looked at the photographs one more time and then closed her eyes. Her hand hesitated over the sketchpad for a moment, and then she opened her eyes and began to move the chalk. A line became a curve, became the shape of his brow. This, the proper depth of his eyes, and this, the angle of his cheek. This was the firm jaw, and this the honest mouth. She nodded to herself. Art would give back what time and distance had taken away. She would draw him into her memory, forever.

Chapter 35
October 1956

"This wedding is going to be a disaster," Betsy thought for the umpteenth time. By some awful trick of nature, she'd grown five inches in the past year. At five feet seven, she was now one of the tallest girls in her class. In the high heels she was about to wear she stood nearly five ten, taller than the usher who was going to escort her down the aisle during the recessional and who would be her partner for at least one dance at the reception. Not only had she gotten taller, but no matter how much she avoided chocolate malts she remained undeniably plump. In this orange organza dress, Betsy looked and felt like a pumpkin. It was Aunt Zsuzsi's only mistake in her whole career. The color was perfectly suitable for the time of year, but the drape of organza over the breast and around the otherwise sleeveless upper arm made her shoulders look twice as wide, and the waves of chiffon over the full petticoat made her feel like a gigantic pair of hips. The more she looked at herself the rounder she felt.

"We're going to look like a row of jack o'lanterns," she muttered. She pinned the short veil on top of her head, which felt and looked like a helmet of frizz, thanks to the permanent wave her mother allowed to set for too long before rinsing. Then she slipped on the pumps, dyed to match the dress, wincing as the pointed shoes crunched her toes. She wasn't used to high heels, either, not this high at least, and she had visions of tripping on the white runner that would line the center aisle of St. Elizabeth's. Orange shoes. When would she ever have occasion to wear orange shoes again?

With nothing left to do except pull on the matching elbow-length gloves, she opened the bedroom door and walked downstairs, where her sister stood in the center of the living room like the figurine from the top of a wedding cake. Ronnie's hair was a soft cap of brunette under the white circlet that held her waist-length veil. Her dress, a plume of white chiffon that cascaded from the nipped-in waistline, succeeded everywhere that Betsy's dress failed. The bodice was made of beaded satin, with a low-cut sweetheart neckline that showed a demure hint of cleavage, accentuated by the gold heart Kettimama had lent her yesterday. To Betsy, she looked like Elizabeth Taylor.

Though Betsy felt more like Ethel Merman, she couldn't be jealous of Ronnie today. Her sister had waited a long time for this wedding. And Ronnie seemed happy enough, but Betsy often wondered if one could feel a second love as deeply as she imagined one felt the first. Not that she had any personal experience with first loves; most of the boys she knew in high school were immature, sports crazy and given to practical jokes. There was no college in town, so the only older men she had met at the Hungarian-American Social and Athletic Club worked at the plant, and she was determined not to fall for a Van Dyke man, or any man, just yet. Maybe when she was a famous painter she'd want to settle down, and even have children as Ronnie longed to do, but she was more determined than ever to emulate Aunt Zsuzsi, whose glamorous life as a New York fashion designer was still the epitome of Betsy's ambitions.

Their mother stopped fussing with the hem of Ronnie's dress just as Betsy stepped into the room.

"Oh, honey, you look so pretty," said Jolan, but Betsy didn't believe that for a minute. In comparison to Ronnie she had always felt like the Ugly Duckling. It didn't help that Ronnie was ten years older, and always more sophisticated. When Betsy was five, Ronnie already wore makeup and hose. When Betsy put on her high-school uniform in the morning, Ronnie walked out the door in a business suit, on her way to the Van Dyke office where she still worked as a secretary. Now Ronnie looked like a movie star, and Betsy looked like a pumpkin.

Ronnie's bags were already packed for the honeymoon. She and Ted were driving all the way to Miami Beach for two weeks. Tonight they would make the first leg of the trip, to Washington, D.C. How empty the house was going to feel. Worse even than when Del left.

Their father took Ronnie's arm, to escort her to the car, and Jolan steered Betsy out the door. There was no turning back now.

Betsy thought she would be in church before going on display, but the neighbors were waiting for them, crowded onto the porch and arranged like a gauntlet down either side of the steps. Old Mrs. Haring, who was too frail to come to the church, became teary eyed as the bride stepped through the door, "She looks like an angel," Mrs. Haring said, "and how handsome Betsy looks!" Betsy winced, hoping Mrs. Haring would think she smiled. Mercifully, Mrs. Laputka merely beamed and waved before rushing to her car so she could arrive at church before Ronnie did, and no doubt tell everyone present that the bride was on her way.

Betsy wished she could duck into the woods across the street, but that was the stuff of childhood. The present was for grownup women in high heels and veils, something she had always ached to be when she was younger. So why did she feel like an imposter, a kid playing dress up in a woman's clothes?

At least she didn't trip walking up the aisle, as she had feared. She tried to put a ladylike smile on her face but felt like she was grimacing instead. Ahead, on the left, stood Aunt Zsuzsi and Kettimama, really Great-Aunt Margit, but as a baby Betsy had been unable to pronounce the endearment *kedves mama*, and so the pet name Kettimama stood. In the front pew were her parents and her grandmother, who wore an old-fashioned babushka on her head, with a narrow fringe of black wool that framed her wrinkled face. Betsy gave her a genuine smile as she walked by.

The wedding itself was a blur of music and incense, murmured vows and an embarrassing sermon about procreation. Soon there was nothing to do but stand in the receiving line at the church door, collecting lipstick smudges on her cheek—until her mysterious cousin stood before her. He was, it was whispered, a refugee who had escaped from Hungary only a few months before. He was not much taller than Betsy, but assuredly thinner, with dark gypsy eyes and hair slicked straight back from his forehead, like Bela Lugosi. They had never spoken before, and he didn't say a word now. He just looked at her—from her eyes down to the bodice of her dress, and then back up again. She felt herself blush, which made him smile. Then he walked away, lighting a cigarette. The smell of the smoke made her mouth water.

Now she knew firsthand what people meant by the phrase "undressing her with his eyes." The nerve. And yet...she fussed with her bouquet, looking down not at the yellow chrysanthemums and orange carnations, but at the bodice of her dress, where the gold cross on its thin chain lay just at the top of a dark line of cleavage. Granted, she was wearing a push-up bra, but still, there was enough of her there to be attractive, maybe even desirable. Suddenly, this dress and this day weren't such a disaster after all.

As they posed for photographs on the church steps, she looked at the crowd on the sidewalk, but she couldn't find him in the mass of faces. She wasn't sure whether to be relieved or disappointed.

Ronnie and Ted descended the steps in a hailstorm of rice. Betsy climbed into the front seat of the best man's car, a blue Chevrolet decorated with crepe paper streamers attached to a small doll, in a fluffy white dress, acting as hood ornament. Betsy sat down awkwardly, stuffing her dress in as well as she could. Andy Golembeski, the best man, pulled two bottles of beer from beneath the seat.

"Here," he said, passing them back to Ted. "Betsy, there's a churchkey in the glove compartment."

Betsy retrieved the bottle opener and passed it back to Ted.

"Thanks, Sis," he said. He opened each bottle and passed one to Ronnie. "Here you go, Mrs. Bialkowski." He leaned over and kissed her. Andy shifted into first gear, leaned on the horn, and pulled away from the church. He surprised Betsy by turning toward the lake.

"This isn't the way to the restaurant," she said.

"We have to kill some time, to let the guests arrive first," said Andy. "We're just going to the park for a few minutes."

They took a roundabout route, with horns blaring, so that people stopped on the street to wave and cheer. When they got to the park, one of the ushers turned on a small portable phonograph and played a Chuck Berry record. Andy took Betsy's hand and whirled her into a jitterbug.

"Hey, you dance all right," he said. Betsy beamed at him.

The next record was a Nat King Cole's "Mona Lisa."

"Come on," Andy said.

"I don't know how to slow dance," said Betsy.

"Then you need to practice before the reception." Andy put his arm around her waist and took her hand. "Just follow what I do," he said.

She stepped on his foot. "Relax," he told her. "All we do is move back and forth, in a slow circle. Watch my feet."

She looked down, and began to match his steps.

"Not bad, for a beginner," he said. "Now look up at me instead of my feet."

Betsy smiled. Andy was a nice guy, far too old to take her seriously, but he was gracious enough not to make her feel awkward for being so tall, and he didn't treat her like a kid. All she knew about him was that he worked in the same office as Ted, doing something mysterious with money that sounded pretty boring to her. Now she also knew he was a good dancer.

As she relaxed, she followed him more easily, and grew confident enough to look over his shoulder at the others. Each couple in the bridal party danced smoothly, and smiled as they glanced over at Ronnie and Ted, who had forsaken dancing for a lingering and passionate kiss.

Andy kissed her on the cheek when they stopped dancing to get back in the cars. Betsy wished he had kissed her on the mouth instead. She needed to break the ice sometime. This was the most grownup she had ever felt, and she didn't want any more reminders about her youth.

Like being allowed only one sip of champagne during the toast to the bride and groom.

"If Uncle Frank were caught allowing a minor to drink in his restaurant, he'd lose his liquor license," explained Tibor. "I'm sure you wouldn't want that to happen."

Betsy sighed as Tibor took her full glass back to the table where he and Jolan sat with Ted's parents, Kettimama, Grandma, and Ted's grandfather. He sat down, and drank from what had been her glass.

What was the use of sitting at the bride and groom's table when she was the only one drinking a Shirley Temple? She sighed. She was seated between Ted's friend, Johnny Krauszer, and Ted. Ted was understandably preoccupied with his bride, and Johnny wasn't much of a talker, especially now that the prime rib—Uncle Frank's specialty—had been served.

When she and her family came to Uncle Franks's for dinner, he usually went into the kitchen to cook for them himself. Today, dressed like a maitre d' in dinner jacket and black tie, he caught her eye and winked as he walked around the room, making sure every guest was taken care of. He was being a good host for Ronnie's sake, but Betsy knew election day was only a couple of weeks away. Uncle Frank, who was running for city council, was no doubt campaigning a little as dinner was served.

She watched as he worked the room, then she spotted her mysterious cousin, holding his fork differently from anyone else. She cut into her own prime rib, but the knife slipped and the meat landed in her lap. Quickly she brushed it to the floor, but too late. A small grease stain was already soaking through the organdy fabric. Typical. She wiped at her skirt, then leaned back to get Ronnie's attention.

"Hey Ronnie!"

"What is it, Sweetie?" Ronnie turned to her with a broad smile.

"Who is that weird guy at the table with the Laputkas and Dr. Biro? Isn't he a cousin or something?"

Ronnie looked at the far end of the room.

"No, not a cousin exactly. He's Uncle Dezso's wife's brother's son." It took Betsy a moment to work out the genealogy.

"So he's not even related? What's he doing here?"

"I think Mama felt sorry for him. He doesn't know a soul, and we're the closest thing to family he has. After all, he's only been here six months."

Betsy remembered the hushed conversations of a year ago between her parents and Aunt Zsuzsi. It was all very secretive, and she wasn't even supposed to know about it, but money had changed hands, cloak and dagger stuff, and this cousin—or so they had referred to him—had been smuggled out of Hungary and into the United States. He'd been granted some sort of asylum, and Zsuzsi found him a job in the garment district. Today was the first time he had come to Hardenbergh, and the first time Betsy had seen him.

The waitress removed her plate, and the band—a jazz quartet that played at Frank's every Saturday night—began to play a tune that sounded like "The Farmer in the Dell." It was Ted and Ronnie's cue to walk over to the wedding cake, four white tiers that Betsy had been eyeing ever since the wedding party marched in.

"And the bride cuts the cake, the bride cuts the cake," sang the bandleader. "Hi ho, the derry-oh, the bride cuts the cake." Betsy rolled her eyes as Ronnie shoved a huge slice into Ted's mouth. He grinned and spluttered and took the knife for his turn, cutting an even bigger slice. The guests applauded as he plastered the cake into Ronnie's face, and then the cake was wheeled into the kitchen to be sliced. The quartet began to play "Daddy's Little Girl."

Tibor stood and walked over to Ronnie, who wiped the last of the frosting from her chin. He took her hand and led her to the center of the room, where they danced a slow foxtrot. Sentimental as it was, even Betsy felt sad to think of Ronnie leaving their house for good. Halfway through the song, Tibor brought Ronnie back to Ted, and then held his hand out to Betsy. She had no idea her father was such a wonderful dancer. When he led her around the floor, she felt like Ginger Rogers, and she never once stepped on his foot.

Tibor kissed her on the forehead. "I am so proud to dance with my two girls," he said. "My oldest and my youngest." He twirled her around the dance floor. "If only your brother could have been here to see it."

She wished he wouldn't spoil the afternoon by talking about Del. How could the army take back his leave just because "tensions" were high in a part of Europe where he wasn't even stationed?

"Why are you scowling?" asked Tibor. "Aren't you having a good time?"

"Of course I am, Daddy. Are you going to dance with Mama next?"

Her father grinned. It was good to see him smiling like that. "You bet."

The next dance was a cha-cha. Betsy would have sat this one out but Aunt Zsuzsi grabbed her and led her to the dance floor. Then the band played a polka, and Mrs. Laputka scooped her up. Then came a *czardas*, the alley cat, the hokey pokey, and the throwing of the bouquet, for which Betsy stood as far to the rear as she could, with her hands firmly clasped behind her back.

She finally got to eat her wedding cake, and then felt so full she needed fresh air. She stepped outside, where the Indian Summer warmth still radiated from the sidewalk. She leaned against the restaurant and slipped one foot from its shoe, rubbing the arch against the opposite foot's instep.

"Cigarette?"

Betsy jumped.

"Holy smoke! You startled me," she said. Her ersatz cousin stepped out from the shadow of the awning, holding a pack of Luckies. "Cigarette?" he repeated. Betsy wondered if that was all the English he knew. She looked to the left and right, put her foot back in its shoe, and took one of the cigarettes.

"Not here," she said, as he held out a lighter. She began to walk up the street. "My parents don't know that I smoke."

Halfway up the block she stopped and held the cigarette to her lips. Her cousin lit the end, and she took a deep breath. Ah, much better.

"I'm Betsy," she said. "What's your name?"

"Gellért," he said. "In English, Gerard. You call me Gerry, yes?"

"Sure, Gerry."

"*Beszel Magyarol?*"

"What?"

"You speak Magyar?" He rolled the "r" as he said it.

"*Nem*," said Betsy. "And *igen*. Oh, and *Hol Vagy*." She shrugged. "No, yes, how ya doing. That's it."

"Too bad."

"You speak English well enough, Gerry" she said.

"Accent too thick," he said, pronouncing it "teek." "But I learn." He looked at her. "You bride sister."

She nodded and took another satisfying puff.

"How old?"

"Me? I'm sixteen. Why?"

He shrugged. "Young."

Darn it. Not from him, too. "How old are you?"

"Two and twenty."

That was older than Betsy had thought. She stood up a little straighter. "There's the school I go to," she pointed. "Next year I'll be a senior, and then I'll go to college."

"What is 'college'?"

"College, the university."

He shook his head. "What for, university? You grow up, get married, have babies."

Betsy stopped walking. "Look here, buster, don't start that barefoot and pregnant stuff with me. This is 1956, not 1856. I'm going to have a career." He looked at her, clearly amused. She suspected her tone came across even if the individual words didn't. "A career. A job. You have a job?"

He grimaced. "Job. Yes. In New York. Put clothes on truck. Take clothes off truck. On truck, off truck. All day long."

"It's a paycheck," said Betsy, who had never held a job in her life.

"A paycheck. Yes." He sighed.

"What did you do in Hungary, Gerry?"

He stubbed out his cigarette and immediately lit another. "I was *terveso*"—how you say—I draw things. Machines. Parts. Things."

Betsy puzzled it out. "A draftsman?"

He nodded. "Drahfussman. Yes."

"I draw, too, but I draw people and landscapes. You know, fine arts." He nodded.

"Why don't you work as a draftsman now?" she asked.

He looked at her sideways. "You kidding? I refugee. No read English. No write English. Put clothes on truck."

They reached the entrance to Lenape Park. Betsy sighed. "I suppose we should go back."

"For hokey pokey?" he asked. He moved his foot to the side and back again. "Putted right foot in, putted right foot out, putted right foot in—then what?" He grinned and wiggled his hips. Betsy laughed.

"Well, it's a custom, I guess, or a tradition, or something." They walked toward a bench, shaded by a maple tree. Betsy sat down and took her shoes off. "My feet hurt. New shoes." Gerry sat down next to her. He smelled of cigarettes and too much cheap cologne.

"Let me," he said. He took her left foot in his hand and rubbed the instep. Betsy was too surprised to pull her foot away. Besides, it felt wonderful.

"Do you miss Hungary?" she asked.

He threw his cigarette down and ground it out with his heel before answering. "Yes. No. Is—how you say—not easy, not one thing, but many, mixed up."

She thought a moment, trying to translate. "You mean complicated?"

He nodded. "Com-plee-cated."

"How so?"

"Communists kill my father. In war, like Uncle Deszo—your uncle, too?"

"Yes. My mother's younger brother."

He spit on the ground. "Deszo communist. Communists no good. No good for me. I no commie. They no like. I get out." He began to massage her other foot. She leaned back against the park bench and sighed with pleasure.

"But your aunt was married to Uncle Deszo. Couldn't she help you?"

He shook his head. "She killed, too."

"I'm sorry. You must be glad you're not there now."

"No. Give me gun. I go back. I shoot commie son-of-a-beech. You listen Radio Free Europe? Is bad in Hungaria now. Very bad."

Across the wide expanse of lawn, a family tossed a football, and a boy ran with his dog. The sounds of laughter and happy shouting drifted to them in the clear air. Lake Lenape sparkled. The scene couldn't be more peaceful. Even though Betsy had seen the newspapers, Hungary seemed unreal and very far away. Gerry brought it much closer.

He lit another cigarette and held out the pack. Betsy took another cigarette, which he lit. He took a long puff on his cigarette and blew the smoke out of his nostrils. His nose was straight and when his nostrils flared he looked patrician, like a nobleman, a nobleman in a leather jacket.

"I'd like to draw your picture sometime," Betsy said. Gerry laughed.

"I'm serious. I meant it when I said I'm going to be an artist. Like Aunt Zsuzsi."

He raised one eyebrow. "Zsuzsanna? She make clothes."

"Oh yes! She's a wonderful designer. Better than Dior. And she knows so many famous people. She even met Grace Kelly, did you know that? I want to live in New York and paint. I want to be just like Aunt Zsuzs."

Gerry laughed again. "Just like Zsuzsanna? You no like boys?"

"What do you mean? Of course I like boys."

"Well," he said. "Zsuzsanna no like boys."

"Because she never married? Don't be silly. Marriage is so bourgeois. Aunt Zsuzsi is a career woman."

"Aunt Zsuzsi is *sebész*—how you say? Like man. Tough? No. Butch."

"Butch?" Betsy thought for a moment, and then felt color rising to her cheeks. "Do you mean—Are you trying to say—You think she's a—" she lowered her voice to a whisper— "a lesbian? How dare you!" Her face grew even redder. "And to imply that I—oh!" She stood up and looked for her shoes. "Well, I never!"

"Hey! Take it easy. Maybe I wrong. I don' think so, but maybe I wrong."

"You certainly are, buster!" Betsy sat back down and put her shoes on. "Aunt Zsuzsi is a wonderful, kind, generous person. Don't ever say that about her! To anyone, you understand?"

"Sure, sure."

Betsy sat back and puffed her cigarette so hard she inhaled a sliver of tobacco. Gerry clapped her on the back until her coughing subsided, then took the cigarette from her fingers and ground it out. They sat in awkward silence for a moment.

"So. You like boys, huh?"

She was beginning to dislike that amused undercurrent in his voice. It made her feel like a hick.

"Yes, I like boys."

"Let's see," he said, and leaned over to kiss her.

She opened her mouth to say no but his lips were on hers before she could speak. He moved his lips slowly and softly at first, and then pressed harder, putting his tongue inside her mouth. Betsy's tongue touched his and began, almost against her will, to move in slow, deep circles. He tasted of cigarettes and beer, and she began to feel lightheaded. But he pulled back first.

"First time?" he asked. "Pretty good."

Betsy was too flustered to lie. She thought about Andy's polite kiss on the check this morning, and how she had wanted him to kiss her on the mouth. Somehow, she didn't think he would have kissed her quite like this. She wanted Gerry to kiss her again. And he did.

He put his arms around her and they kissed for a long time on the bench. She wasn't sure why she let him do it. She didn't think she liked him, for one thing. Sure, he was good looking in an exotic kind of way, and he was foreign, and older, and certainly experienced, at least when it came to kisses. She'd never done anything like this, necking in a public place. She'd never even had a date. But while her mind raced with half-formed questions, her body unconsciously pressed close to him, and she knew he could feel her breasts against his chest. The motion of his lips and tongue made it hard for her to think of anything but his kiss. Why? Why him? Why now?

He pulled away again, stood up, and held out his hand. "Come," he said, his tone half invitation, half command. Betsy stood up, out of breath, her lips tingling, almost numb, and walked with him toward the lake edge, where the bandstand stood like a sentinel. They walked around it to the lakeside, where no one could see them from the rest of the park. Gerry took off his leather jacket, and spread it on the ground for her. They sat down, leaning against the latticed base of the bandstand, and this time, when he kissed her, he also reached for her breast.

It was wrong. Betsy knew it was, and this wasn't any venial sin that a quick Hail Mary would take care of next Saturday. Her mind said it was wrong but her body said it was right and her heart was totally confused. Gerry's hand caressed the curve of her breast, his fingers reached into the bodice of her dress and pushed into the cup of her bra. His middle finger circled her nipple, and she felt it harden in response. How was this happening? How could she have so little control over her own body? He squeezed her breast hard and the feeling that shuddered through her at his touch went straight down to that unmentionable place between her legs. She felt her panties getting wet. And all the time, those incredible, long, deep kisses, that moving tongue, those velvet lips!

Still, she could stop it. She just had to push his hand away, to say no, to sit up and brush the autumn leaves out of her hair. Even though she hardly knew this stranger she sensed he would stop if she asked. He'd be greatly amused, she had no doubt, he'd think she was a child, and she'd feel humiliated at letting it go this far, but she would probably never see him again, and that would be that. She'd go to confession next Saturday, admit to committing an "impure act," that handy, catch-all phrase, say her penance and still be a good girl.

The problem was, she didn't want him to stop. She wasn't even so sure she wanted to be a good girl. Maybe it was just curiosity, when you came right down to it, more than the need to prove to him and to herself she was not a lesbian, more than the need to protect her reputation, that sacred virginity so many martyrs died defending. Maybe it was the overpowering intimacy, knowing she was not alone, not ignored, but wholly present to someone as she hadn't been to her family or friends in a long time. Then maybe it was just his hand, moving down the bodice of her dress now, past her stomach, rubbing her through the voluminous folds of her skirt and sending electric shudders through her whole body.

Like fire. It was like fire.

Maybe it was just time, time to show that it takes more than a first pair of high heels to be called a woman.

So she didn't say no, not when he moved his lips to her breasts, not when his hands lifted her skirt and pulled down her underpants and unzipped his black slacks, and not when he moved on top of her, pressing the organza and tulle up toward her face, so that more than ever she felt like a gross and bloated pumpkin about to become a jack o' lantern. As though he were a knife slicing through the very heart of her, an eager hand reaching inside over and over and over again to pull out the moist pulp, and the wet seeds.

Epilogue
November 1956

Margit pulled up her coat collar as a cold gust sent a whirlwind of leaves spinning among the headstones. She put the trowel and empty flowerpots in her tote bag and brushed the dirt from her hands before standing up. The white and yellow mums looked pretty in front of Emil's grave. Margit knew that frost would take them soon; still, she needed to make the gesture. In front of the yellow mum she set a small American flag into the ground; in front of the white mum, a flag of Hungary.

If Emil were still alive, the past twelve days would have been the high point of his career. She could picture him in the *Hirlap* office, proofreading each special edition. There would have been twelve of them, and once again the *Hirlap* would have been a daily paper. Each edition would reflect either joy or despair, depending on the wire service news, and the reports from Radio Free Europe.

Margit picked up her tote bag and turned toward home. As a human being, her husband would have hated the deaths of so many people, but as a publisher and patriot he would have done all he could to help. He probably would have emptied their small savings account for the cause of the freedom fighters. It had taken money enough to get Deszo's wife's nephew out of the country.

The wind was at her back now, so the walk home wasn't too bad, and the fresh air would drive the lingering scent of mothballs from the woolen fabric of her good coat. The weather had changed abruptly from the lingering Indian Summer and she had only retrieved her coat from the attic a few days ago. Now it was time to wash the lightweight curtains and put them in the attic, and hang the winter drapes. She and Piros would move the sofa and chairs to give the living room floor a thorough vacuuming and she would wash the windows to complete the fall cleaning.

She turned the corner onto Kossuth Street and saw Betsy walk down the steps of her house.

"Hello, Kettimama," Betsy said. She kissed Margit on the cheek.

"I was visiting Grandma after church," she said. "I'm just on my way home. Shall I carry that for you?"

"I've carried it this far. I can manage the next few feet," said Margit. "Don't you feel well? You look pale."

"Actually, that's why I'm going home," said Betsy. "Cramps." She kissed her great-aunt goodbye. "I guess that's why they call it the curse. See you tomorrow."

Margit shook her head as she walked through the alley between the houses. Young women were much too bold these days. When Margit was Betsy's age she would never admit to having cramps, not even to her mother. She'd be under the weather or call it a headache, or at the very most might hint it could be a "female" problem. Children today had no sense of decorum. Playing nasty *fekete* music, dancing like wild Indians. Why Jolan and Tibor allowed such behavior she couldn't imagine.

Margit put her gardening things on the back porch and stepped into the kitchen, where Piros sat the kitchen table, looking at the pictures in the Sunday paper.

"I'll make you some coffee," she said. She rose stiffly and lit the flame under the percolator. "Betsy just left."

"I saw her." Margit walked into the bedroom to hang up her coat.

"She had cramps, she said," called Piros. In a much quieter voice she added, "She seemed quite happy about it," and she smiled.

"What was that?" asked Margit as she came back into the kitchen.

"I said she seems very happy today."

"Well, why shouldn't she be? She's sixteen. She's been spoiled by her parents. She hasn't a care in the world. It would be a different story if she were in Budapest. Is there news?"

"It's so exciting," said Piros. "Nagy is premier and named his cabinet. Cardinal Mindszenty has given a speech. But the Soviet tanks are in Pecs. I don't know what's going to happen."

Margit poured two cups of coffee and went to the refrigerator for milk. She poured a generous amount in each cup and handed one to Piros before sitting down.

"I wish we knew what's happening there now," she said. "It's so hard to wait for the evening news on the radio."

"Are you hungry?" asked Piros. Margit shook her head. "Let's go sit in the parlor."

They sat down on the couch. Margit picked up her crocheting; she was just using up odd scraps of cotton. Her fingers were beginning to grow stiff with arthritis, but she could still turn out a pretty doily in an afternoon's work.

Piros turned on the radio and sat back with a sigh as violin music filled the room. Her back ached so with the change in weather. She couldn't even go to the cemetery with Margit today. She would like to have paid her respects to Emil. Such a courteous young man he was, last time she saw him so many years ago, almost as handsome as her beloved Laci. What a good husband he had been to Margit. A shame he passed on before she could see him again, God rest his soul.

She watched Margit crochet. Piros used to crochet, too, when she was first married and her babies were small. Then the Great War came, and no one had time or energy for fancy work anymore. Years of farm labor left her hands too callused for such things now. She folded her hands in her lap and closed her eyes, letting the violin transport her back home.

Margit, too, was lost in the rhythm of the music and her stitches. The thin crochet hook caught the light as she worked it under and around the cotton thread, creating the petals of the rose that patterned this doily. How many doilies had she made in her lifetime! She must have drawers stuffed with them. So did Jolan, and Zsuzsi, though Margit doubted Zsuzsi ever used them. Zsuzsi had grown too far away from her roots. Calling herself Mlle. Suzanne, going to Paris every year. Sure, she had more money than Margit or Tibor and Jolan would ever have, a fancy car, a big apartment. But was she any happier than the rest of them? Margit compressed her lips, suspecting the answer was a resounding yes.

Jolan, now, Jolan was so much like her mother. Domestic to the core, and still crazy in love with Tibor after all these years. What a hard time they'd had, though, losing two of their boys, three, if you counted that wayward Del, gallivanting around the world as though he didn't even have a family. Sometimes Margit wondered how Jolan managed to live with it. There, too, she supposed, Jolan took after her mother, who also lost her sons.

How very odd to have Piros sitting right next to her, after all these years. Poor Piros hadn't a thing to her name, was even wearing borrowed clothes when the Red Cross finally found her in the DP camp after the war. She'd lost everything, every photograph, every memento. Letters, linens, locks of her babies' hair.

So here they sat at last: elderly sisters with bad backs and aching joints, together again, now that both were widows. Maybe because they were widows, and there was no chance for Piros to steal again what Margit once thought she'd had.

"What was that?" asked Margit. The violin music stopped, and the announcer was speaking. "Turn up the volume." They listened intently.

"They've attacked Budapest!" said Piros. "*Yoy, Istanem!*"

Margit set aside her crocheting and moved closer to Piros.

"...Soviet forces have taken airfields, bridges, railways," she heard. "Their tanks have entered Budapest, where heavy fighting is reported. Gyor and Sopron have fallen. Just a moment, ladies and gentlemen...this just in. Janos Kadar has been named premier. I repeat. The Communist Kadar has been named premier. We have no information about Imre Nagy and whether he is still in Budapest, whether he is under arrest or even if he is still alive. Radio stations are broadcasting calls for help from Western nations....Here is...a recording from a broadcast received just a few minutes ago, a call from the Hungarian Writers' Union: 'To every writer in the world, to all scientists, to all writers' federations, to all science academies and associations, to the intelligentsia of the world: Help Hungary!' The transmission ends there."

"Our poor people!" whispered Piros. She reached for Margit's hand. "God help them!"

God help them indeed, thought Margit. The broadcast continued, stories of desperate freedom fighters lobbing hand grenades and fifteen-year-old girls firing submachine guns as tanks swarmed across the beautiful city of Budapest, which Piros had never been to and which Margit had seen only once, briefly, on her honeymoon fifty-two years ago.

The light faded, but neither one got up to turn on a lamp. They merely sat, side by side on the couch, listening and praying. Two sisters, holding hands.

About the Author

Patricia Valdata writes novels, poems and nonfiction. Her publications include the novel *Crosswind* (Wind Canyon Publishing) and the poetry chapbook *Looking for Bivalve* (Pecan Grove Press). Pat received an MFA in writing from Goddard College. She is an adjunct associate professor for the University of Maryland University College (UMUC) and writes occasional articles for *Chesapeake Bay* magazine in addition to her day job as a business writing consultant. Pat and her husband Bob live in Elkton, Maryland, with a standard poodle named Chunks.

CPSIA information can be obtained at www.ICGtesting.com
Printed in the USA
LVOW09s1416160614

390255LV00003B/32/P